Also by David Levien
and featuring Frank Behr

CITY OF THE SUN
WHERE THE DEAD LAY
THE CONTRACT
(published in the United States as
THIRTEEN MILLION DOLLAR POP)

signature
KILL

DAVID LEVIEN

CORGI BOOKS

TRANSWORLD PUBLISHERS
61–63 Uxbridge Road, London W5 5SA
www.transworldbooks.co.uk

Transworld is part of the Penguin Random House group of companies
whose addresses can be found at global.penguinrandomhouse.com

Penguin
Random House
UK

First published in Great Britain in 2015 by Bantam Press
an imprint of Transworld Publishers
Corgi edition published 2016

A CIP catalogue record for this book
is available from the British Library.

ISBN
9780552162258

Typeset in 12/15pt Caslon 540 by Falcon Oast Graphic Art Ltd.
Printed and bound by Clays Ltd, Bungay, Suffolk.

Penguin Random House is committed to a sustainable
future for our business, our readers and our planet. This book is made from
Forest Stewardship Council® certified paper.

MIX
Paper from
responsible sources
FSC® C018179

1 3 5 7 9 10 8 6 4 2

signature
KILL

Indianapolis Police officer Denny Hawkins rolled his cruiser through Northwestway Park shining his prowl light past the dormant playground swings when the beam caught a shape, white and confusing, on the ground just before the tree line. Hawkins tapped the brake, refocused the light, and sat and stared for a long moment. There was *something* familiar about what he saw, but he couldn't properly make out the featureless pile. He took his foot off the brake and rolled closer.

Flesh.

The lone word came to Officer Hawkins's mind. He thumped the cruiser into park and stepped out, one hand wrapped around his six-battery Maglite, the other resting on the butt of his Glock .40 duty weapon. He walked closer, his feet making a slight crunching sound on the grass, crisp with frost. He passed his light over the pile, and what he saw made his mouth go dry. There was a racing in his chest and a sickening drop in his stomach. Sweat popped along his back and crotch as adrenaline hit him hard. It was

9

a woman's body, or parts of her body, naked in the night. He almost retched, then shined the flashlight around the vicinity. He stood and listened. All was quiet and still. He was alone. Finally his hand came off his weapon and reached for the radio mic on his shoulder and he found his voice.

'Fifty-two thirteen, I'm mobile at Northwestway Park, request assistance at my location. I've got a ten-zero . . .'

'Say again,' dispatch came back.

'I've got a body – I think it's all here. Victim is unidentified white female. Request Homicide Unit and coroner.'

ONE

MOVEMENT IN THE pin oak on the hillside caught Frank Behr's eye. He stood hidden in thick trees on a low rise two hundred fifty yards away, scanning the underbrush above the shallow bowl of a meadow. Gray and stealthy, the whitetails picked their way down toward the good feed, and the horizontal lines of their backs broke the vertical pattern of the trees. Behr felt the nerves along the still-healing left side of his collarbone call out in protest as he slowly raised his Remington 870 Express and used the four-by scope to get a better look. The deer were all doe. Even the controlled movement of his lifting the gun was enough to give them pause. They stopped, three of them, their heads perfectly still, save for their ears, the insides twitching white as they rotated around to capture a telltale sound. Behr stood there, gun steady, watching. After a long moment the deer continued, in

11

serpentine fashion, down toward the edge of the meadow. When his arm started to throb, he lowered the gun.

Over the next half hour several more doe and a pair of forkies came out of the trees and began their evening graze. Behr waited. He'd been doing this a long time, and he was familiar with the habits of whitetail. The cagey big bucks often let the young ones, and the doe, go first. There was no change for several long minutes until, like a gray ghost of the forest, the senior buck of the herd became visible far up the hill. He was out of range and in the shadows of deep cover.

Behr carefully slung his Remington and pulled a pair of old antlers from his belt and began clacking them together. The rut was on, and he hoped to rattle the old boy out into the open looking for a fight. Behr slid a plastic tube up out of his coat and blew a breath into it, causing it to emit a low grunt. He saw the buck look in his direction, but felt the silhouette of his six-and-a-half-foot, two-hundred-forty-plus-pound frame was broken up enough that the buck couldn't see him. As long as the wind didn't change, Behr had a chance.

The buck picked his way down to the edge of the meadow, stopping behind a brake of prickly ash. Behr gave a final knock and scrape of the antlers, then tucked them into his belt and raised his Remington again, snugging the butt onto his shoulder. The last rattle had caused the buck to lift his head and scent the wind, and Behr finally got a clear look at the old boy's rack. He was a ten-pointer with thick beams and a wide spread. Bramble slightly obscured the shot, but Behr was able to put his crosshairs square on the deer's chest. He held. If the buck continued into the open and quartered broadside it'd be ideal, but this was a good shot, and one Behr had made before. He clicked the safety off and let out a slow breath, closing the valve on the anticipation and the pity and all other emotion in his chest. When hunting, a cold, clean killing edge is best. He was ready. The ideal time came and went. He should have squeezed. But something made him wait. He watched the deer for a long moment. The moment continued as the buck ticked forward a dozen more steps. Behr felt his mind drift.

Trevor. Six months old now, but one day I'll be standing on a hillside like this with my boy, teaching him the ways of the woods, how to shoot, how to hunt.

Behr refocused his eye and the reticle. Then he saw the buck flinch, and a millisecond later the boom of another slug gun echoed off the hillside. The deer in the field scattered, and the old boy's head whipped to the side and he disappeared into the foliage.

The crack of breaking branches and the thick chunking sound of hooves knocking against downed trunks reached Behr in his spot as the buck, hit and hurt, careened heedlessly into the deep timber. Behr waited a few minutes, until he saw the blaze orange of Lester's cap, atop a suit of Mossy Oak Break-Up pattern, make its way like a bobbing cork above the bramble, then he started down the hill and across the meadow to where he'd seen the buck plunge into the trees.

Behr reached the deer first and found him in a clearing, rolled up on his left side, face plowed into a carpet of dead leaves. There was a small hole just behind the shoulder that oozed only a trickle of blood. It was a near-perfect shot. Lester made the clearing seconds later, breathing hard.

'Hot damn,' he said over a lip full of Copenhagen when he saw what he'd collected.

'Well done, Les,' Behr said and gave him a whack on the shoulder. In his late sixties, Lester Dollaway was the father of one of Behr's old college football teammates, Des, a reservist who'd died in Afghanistan five years back. The hunting trips had been a long-standing tradition between the three of them, and Behr hadn't considered ending them just because his friend was gone. That first year when it was just him and Les pulling permits had been difficult. The pain in the older man's darting black eyes was almost unbearable. Things had gotten easier with each passing year. A native Iowan, Les lived only an hour away from where they were now, and he knew all the landowners and got permission to scout in the spring and hunt in the early winter season.

'It's the last day,' Lester said, taking off his cap and rubbing up his steel wool hair. 'I can do this if you want to get on over the hill and look for them forkies or something.'

Behr gave some thought to his $400 nonresident antlered deer license that would go unfilled.

'Nah, I'll help you and we can drag him down together.'

'It'll be dark before long,' Les said. 'You won't get a shot.'

'Probably not.'

'I thank you.'

'Want me to dress him?' Behr offered and pulled the drop point skinner off his belt.

'If it's no trouble,' Lester said. 'These damn eyes . . .'

Behr nodded and removed his coat, then pushed up his shirtsleeves. 'Seemed fine when you squeezed off on this old boy.'

He rolled the deer onto his back and made the first cut from sternum to crotch, his blade parting the white belly fur and whiter layer of fat beneath it before the red of muscle and blood leapt forth. Once the buck was opened up, Behr reached up into the warmth and wetness of the cavity and removed the organs. After splitting the pelvis, Behr cut the heart free. It came out thick and heavy and purplish in his hand, and he set it off to the side before he tilted the carcass downhill to drain. As the garnet fluid soaked into the dry ground, Behr looked at the battered forehead and broken brow tine on the old buck.

'See the Roman nose on this one? He was a fighter,' Lester said.

Behr absently rubbed his own nose with his upper arm. Had he not liked his shot? he wondered. He'd made many as difficult and some much more so. Maybe he'd seen too much gunfire recently, or perhaps an awareness of the damage a gun like the one he had brought could do was still just too fresh. He wasn't sure and it didn't matter. He hadn't fired and hadn't filled his tag after four days of hunting.

'Couldn't believe you didn't take him before he came on down toward me,' Lester said. 'You're in for some meat after I get him to the butcher.'

'Thanks, Les,' Behr said.

'Hell, you rattled him right in.'

Behr used the remainder of his water bottle to rinse the blood and gore from his hands and forearms. Lots of guys wore rubber gloves when field dressing these days, to prevent picking up infection, but not Behr. It wasn't how he was taught. And he'd yet to catch a disease from a deer. He couldn't say the same for people.

The sun throbbed crimson and dropped down over the hill, flattening out the light in the meadow to a pale purple as they each took a hind leg and dragged the deer a half mile to Lester's truck.

TWO

*I*T'S HAPPENING AGAIN . . .
    The words come from a place deep within him.
He feels that stuff down there, bubbling and-
stirring, as the thing inside him that is other looks to
push up and outward. He has to take it for a ride.

*It's happening again and before long the red curtain will
come down once more . . . Soon.*

So soon it is almost confusing.

He should be at work by now, but he finds himself
turning toward Irvington instead. He'll have to make up
the time on his own. His bosses just want results, they
care less about his coming and going and being punctual
as long as the work gets done. And he has seniority.
Besides, he doesn't know this neighborhood. Yet.

The streets are filled with cars this morning as people
go to their jobs, the sidewalks populated with mothers
and their children on the way to school, along with the
occasional jogger bundled in a sweatshirt moving down

the road, blowing cold clouds of breath. He rolls along, as slowly as he can without getting in the way, without becoming noticeable.

He turns the corner onto East Lowell, and sees a lone woman walking. In her late twenties or early thirties, she has blond hair streaked with light reddish brown the color of ground cinnamon. She isn't out for a healthful stroll, he can see by the cigarette in her hand and the black leather jacket and jeans that look like they were worn to a bar the night before.

Dirty girl, dirty girl . . .

He slows, trolling behind her for a bit. She is petite, with a light stride. Young.

Go to work. Now. A voice inside tries to instruct him. But it is weak. Certainly not strong enough to win out, and it will soon fall mute.

He no longer feels the car around him. All is silent. He is flying, floating along next to her. He is near her, with her, *of* her . . .

Finally, his senses return. The steering wheel is in his hands, the seat beneath him, and the pedals under his feet once again. He speeds up and pulls abreast of her for just a moment before continuing on, her presence and her location filed away automatically in his mind. A certain fluttering sensation arrives in his gut – the one that comes along when he's found a new project.

Hello, Cinnamon . . .

THREE

BEHR CRACKED THE window and allowed some winter air to blow into the car as he drove home along I-74.

The trip back from bluff country was six hours plus. He'd planned on leaving before sunup so he could get home comfortably during daylight, but the bottle of single-barrel bourbon Les had pulled out to celebrate his successful hunt had slowed Behr down by an hour that morning and the light was starting to fade by the time he neared Indianapolis and home.

He and Les had passed a pleasant final evening. They'd hung the buck on a gambrel to drain at the landowner's barn until morning, when Les would take it to the butcher. Then they'd cleaned up and had gone for dinner at the good local restaurant they'd saved for the last night and talked about their lives over T-bones.

'I love them,' Behr said of Susan, his girlfriend

and the mother of his son, Trevor, 'that's a fact. But it became clear pretty quick that that's not enough to make things go smooth between her and me.'

'Well . . .' Les said.

'She moved out with Trevor after three months, when I'd healed up and my wing was working again,' Behr continued. He moved the arm and tested the clavicle that had been pulverized by buckshot half a year back.

After surgery, Behr had spent countless agonizing hours on 'The Rack,' which was what he called the continuous passive-motion chair he'd rented, painfully regaining the mobility in his shoulder joint, as well as doing isometric exercises for strength. He was about ready to graduate to real weight training again and looked forward to it despite knowing how much fresh pain was coming his way.

'My place was never intended to be a home. We were all supposed to move to the new place together. But I . . . my job . . . if you can call it that – hell, I've only caught two cases in the past few months – doesn't particularly lend itself to a happy family.'

'Well . . .' Les said again, tilting back his bourbon.

'So there's the money thing on top of the rest.'

'Sure don't help.'

'It never mattered before, but now . . . a little

breathing room would be nice. To be able to provide all the things for 'em that they should have,' Behr said. 'But I've tried the kind of jobs that make that happen, and you know . . .' Behr didn't really have to go on. Les had been in the service as a young man and had then spent his life running a construction company, and his knowing, darting eyes had seen it all.

'Frank, if there's one thing I've learned,' Les said, 'it's that pleasing everyone is pretty damn near impossible, but pissing everyone off is a piece of cake.'

Behr could only raise his glass to that. They laughed and pushed their plates away and accelerated the bourbon.

Behr clicked on his blinker and exited onto 465 to skirt Indianapolis and head toward his place when a woman's face on a large billboard filled his windshield. She was a bit younger than Susan, also a blonde, though the woman on the billboard had more dark roots in her hair. The sign wasn't an advertisement. There were words in block print along the bottom that read:

Do you know what happened to Kendra Gibbons? Reward for information leading to answers, arrest, conviction: $100,000.

Good luck with that flashed through Behr's mind. The woman's eyes were sparkling and alive. There was the hint of someone's arm wrapped around her shoulder. Perhaps the picture was taken at a party and cropped. The billboard was visible in the passenger window for a moment, and then it was gone from Behr's peripheral vision and thoughts, his concentration fixed in front of him. He decided not to head home, but to go see Trevor instead.

Behr knocked on Susan's door and entered to find her preparing dinner.

'Hey! You're back,' she said, turning her face toward his for a kiss before resuming the chopping of red peppers. Even though they were living separately, they were doing their best to try to make it work. A wok was on low sizzle on the stove and smelled delicious.

'There he is,' Behr said, crossing to the Pack 'N Play where his son, Trevor, sat, banging away with a block on a shape-sorter toy. The boy smiled up at him. 'That's a triangle, son. It goes in this slot.' Behr helped him and the wooden piece dropped away, then he picked the boy up and turned toward Susan. 'Trying to fit the wrong peg into the round hole – just like his old man.'

'He's six months old, what's your excuse?' Susan asked.

23

Behr didn't answer and instead lifted Trevor, tossing him aloft, pretending to miss the catch, before grabbing him up. The boy squealed in delight. Behr stared into his eyes and thought of Tim, his first son, long gone now, as he did every time he saw Trevor. Surging joy and piercing pain mixed inside him. It was something he'd been unable to escape in the past six months and doubted he ever would.

'So how'd it go?' she asked.

'Good,' Behr said, turning toward her. 'Weather was perfect. Les got a big one. I didn't fill. But it was good.'

'All right, a long walk in the woods then,' she said.

'Pretty much,' Behr said, his attention pulled to the television, which was tuned to the news. There were a slew of official vehicles behind Sandra Chapman, the reporter from WTHR, who was doing a stand-up from a familiar-looking park playground.

'Is that . . . that looks like Northwestway. What happened?'

Susan glanced over. 'They found a body out there in the park. A woman. It's been all over the news while you've been away.'

'Murder?' Behr asked.

'Yeah. Cut up in pieces. Awful.'

'Christ,' Behr said, turning away when the news switched back to the anchors and the next story,

24

about a local high school basketball all-star team.

'I'm making stir-fry. You want to stay?'

'Sure.'

Behr sat at the table and bounced Trevor and watched Susan move about the kitchen as she finished preparing the meal. She was nearly back to her pre-baby weight, just a bit of extra fullness remained around her hips and breasts. Behr saw her wrestle with the cork on a bottle of Pinot Grigio.

'Trade you,' he said, handing her Trevor and opening the wine.

She poured and served, after putting the baby in a little bucket seat that rested on the table. Behr drank the white wine to keep her company even though he didn't like it much. As they ate, they talked almost solely of Trevor and his activities and accomplishments, like rolling over and commando crawling, which were limited but endlessly fascinating to them. They finished eating and cleared the dishes, and then gave the boy a bath together. She fixed the milk while Behr read him *Show Me Your Toes*. Then Behr fed the boy the bottle, passing him back to Susan so she could burp him and put him down.

When all was quiet and they'd closed the door to his room, Susan bumped up against Behr in the hall with intent. He put his hand behind her head and pulled her in for a kiss. He tasted the wine on her lips and felt her respond. Soon they found their

25

way to her bedroom and their clothes came off.

Afterward, once they'd dozed for a while, Behr's mind returned to a state of restlessness. It was the crossroads moment of whether to head home or to stay where he was and try to go to sleep for the night. None of this was unexpected. A cycle of domestic bliss that came to its ultimate, restive end was their routine of late. Another moment passed and Behr extricated his arm from beneath her and swung his feet to the floor.

'You have an early morning?' Susan asked from half slumber as he dressed.

'They're all early,' he said. It was true. Even though he wasn't currently working cases, his nights often dragged on late before he managed to get in bed, and he was up long before the sun.

'Lock the door on the way out,' she said.

'Yep,' Behr said, bending and kissing her on top of the head. He stopped in Trevor's room. It smelled of baby lotion and diaper ointment. He stood over the boy and watched his tiny chest rise and fall rhythmically. Behr reached in and touched his son's hair, which was smooth as corn silk, and then he left.

FOUR

IRVINGTON IS QUIET in the light of the moon. The streets that had been so busy in the morning now sleep. But he drives the grid, letting the layout of the neighborhood sink deep into his cortex: the houses and small apartment buildings, the alleys and cul-de-sacs, the fences, the garbage cans and detached garages. He turns onto East Lowell and thinks of her, his little Cinnamon, walking along with her cigarette. As he passes by the homes, only a few with lights on, a few others with televisions glowing behind window shades, he wonders in which one she lives. He'll find out. It will take days or weeks, but it will happen eventually. It's a question of luck and timing, of schedules and effort invested.

He's seen enough for now. It is time to clear out, but he can't go home. Not yet. Instead he steers north toward the airfield and parks in the near-empty lot of Lover's Lane. The adult bookstore's red neon sign shines down on the hood of his car. He gets out and whiffs the jet fuel on the cold night air, and then he goes inside, where the chemical smell of bleached filth takes its place.

There are only a few people shopping at this hour – two other men around his age, and one much older. The clerk strokes his ponytail, a worn paperback copy of *Game of Thrones* facedown on the counter, as he speaks to the only other customers, a young couple who already have their cylindrical purchase in a black plastic bag.

He moves past them into the store, beyond the expensive lingerie and high-heel shoes, down the rows of DVDs and sex toys. The shop is a little high-end for his taste, but there aren't many like it left anymore. The Internet has replaced them and threatens to render them obsolete altogether, just like it will do to people one day. But he's grown up with magazines, and they are still what he prefers, and this is where to get them. He thinks of the hundreds he has in his garage, maybe a thousand. The frozen images and the slick feel of the paper in his hands bring him back to his childhood. He still remembers the day when he was eight years old and discovered the cache of blue magazines at Grandfather's house. His young body and mind had exploded in excitement at the sight of the pages.

All the pretty women, with their cone-shaped

breasts and tight-fitting girdles, standing with a leg up on the bed, or bent over chairs, as they looked back at the camera. His heart had pounded at the images. He understood then, deeply and immediately, that it would always be the images for him. What he didn't understand was what the magazines were doing there in Grandfather's study in the first place. Did *Grandfather* look at them? The question didn't stay in his mind long, because soon, mixed in with the others, he'd discovered some old-school crime journals. *Startling Detective*, *True Crime*, *Police Tales*. They were even better than the porno books.

While he didn't dare take the nudie magazines, he had cadged two issues of *Detective Dragnet*. Leather-gloved hands were wrapped around the neck of a startled-looking young blonde in her underwear on the cover of one issue. He had to have it, and another with a similar scene. He was shocked and relieved that Grandfather had never discovered them missing or at least hadn't pursued where they'd gone.

But then, weeks later, Mother had. She thought he'd stolen them from a newsstand, and he'd kept Grandfather's secret.

You little thief . . .

Then came the smack and thump of her open hand.

You little thief . . .

29

His head hit the wall.

You little thief . . .

It went on. Oh, how it had gone on.

He didn't cry at the beating, he never did, even though that made Mother go after him worse, and he hadn't been able to get out of bed and go to school for a week afterward. But it was worth it.

There is a jingle as the young couple exits the shop. He reaches the 'literature' section, passes by what he doesn't want, *Hustler*, *Genesis*, *Club*, and the like – fluffy crap – and then rounds the aisle and finds what he is looking for: the vintage stuff. *Stalked*, *Captured*, and *Fettered*. He waits for the familiar flutter in his stomach, the tingle in his limbs, at the sight of the buxom young women on the covers, shackled, gagged, staring pleadingly out at the reader. The colors are supersaturated, the lighting stark and procedural. The images pop in a highly detailed way. His reaction to the covers has hardly waned over the years. He gathers up a few issues he doesn't already own and goes to the register to pay.

While the clerk makes change of his fifty-dollar bill, his hand goes into his pocket and his fingers slide around the smooth souvenir there. It was white once, years ago, but has aged down from exposure to air and his touch. He used to carry the piece every day, though now he takes it out only when he's feeling a certain way. It is a length of bone, the first proximal phalange from someone very special that he'd known briefly long ago. It is both a reminder of the past and a promise of the future.

'Have a good night,' the clerk says, perhaps recognizing him from his other visits, perhaps not. At some point he needs to stop coming to places like this. There are cameras and it isn't wise to continue. Of course, he's thought that for years and years and nothing has happened, nothing has changed. The fact is: he's invisible.

'Thank you,' he says to the clerk.

He leaves the store and heads for home.

31

FIVE

BEHR GOT HOME and carried his hunting gear inside. His clothes went straight into the washing machine, his boots back in the closet. The slug gun got a wipe-down with a chamois, but since it had gone unfired, it did not require a full cleaning before it was placed in the gun cabinet. It was late and he was nearly ready for sleep, but something kept him from his bed and steered him toward his computer.

Kendra Gibbons, Indianapolis

He typed the name from the billboard into a Google search. He didn't know what caused him to do it. Four articles about her came up: three within days of each other dating back eighteen months, and then a more recent one, from the beginning of the month. Behr read them in chronological order.

The first piece was a brief posting about a twenty-three-year-old woman who'd gone out for the night and hadn't come home or called, which was highly unusual.

Her mother, Kerry Gibbons, age fifty, of the Millersville Boulevard area, had called police. 'I know something bad happened to her, because I was watching my daughter's baby girl, and she always comes for her first thing in the morning, or at least calls. She always calls. Always. Even from jail.'

Jail? Behr thought.

The second bit talked about police efforts to locate the woman and intimated that she was a prostitute who had gone out to work for the night. A shoe had been found, a lavender-colored pump. Kerry Gibbons was trying to positively ID it as one of her daughter's but wasn't sure. The third article linked the Gibbons disappearance to a few others that had occurred over the past three or four years. 'Women get into cars with these men around here or out at the Dr. Gas truck stop on 70, or the one on 465, and a lot of them don't come back and we don't see 'em again,' a neighbor commented.

Behr felt the familiar cold weight of parental grief as he read the last, most recent piece. It was about the unveiling of the billboard he had seen and the reward fund that Kerry Gibbons had established.

'I appreciate all those who've sent in their money.

I *will* find out what happened to my daughter so my granddaughter doesn't have to wonder, if it takes my whole life and every cent I can spare.'

Doing something for the money usually ends up costing plenty.

Behr had risen early, and this was the thought in his head as he tied his running shoes and slipped on a heavy pack. He hit the street, his breath clouding in the cold morning darkness. The pack strap cut into his recovering collarbone and reminded him of what had happened six months ago. How the shotgun blast had come out of nowhere and leveled him in falling rain. He set out for Saddle Hill, hoping to outrun the memory.

If there was one positive by-product that came along with the paucity of work lately, Behr thought, it was his cardio. His empty plate and inability to lift heavy weights allowed him to run more regularly, and for longer than usual. While ten sprints up and down the long steep of the Hill used to constitute his morning run, he'd lately built to thirteen, then fourteen. He didn't time himself, but he was pretty sure his pace had picked up. His strength at the finish surely had. He'd gone to swim with Susan a few times at the I.U. Purdue pool too. They took turns, each watching the baby on the side while the other swam laps. She put him to shame, though. She sliced through the water like a game fish, while he just wasn't buoyant. He was made of lead apparently. She'd be done and toweling off while he churned up a lane, his thrashing dissuading other swimmers from sharing with him, mostly ignoring her pointers, until his heart was chugging like a steam engine and he'd finally call it a day. No, the asphalt was where he belonged. One foot in front of the other, just like his life. He hammered up the incline, road salt shifting and shaking in the pack like a seventy-pound maraca.

It's a stupid idea, he thought about the Gibbons case, on the way down.

How could it hurt to just take a look? he wondered his next time up.

If the police have nothing, how can you do better? Up he went.

Because I have time. He huffed his way down.

Why bother?

A hundred grand. Trev and Susan.

The thought repeated itself on the way up. The same thought stayed in his head on the way back down.

By the time he was finished, he'd decided.

SIX

IRVINGTON IN THE morning again. The streets are becoming familiar now. Some of the same joggers jog. The mothers with the strollers stroll. He is starting to recognize coats, scarves, faces. Several passes by Lowell and Ritter and Arlington. No soaring feeling. No luck. No Cinnamon. Time to go to work.

SEVEN

BEHR'S TORONADO ROLLED to a stop on a patch of pea gravel outside a modest but well-kept brick bungalow in Millersville. There was a Ford Taurus parked in front, and a pink tricycle tipped over against the side of the house next to a small plastic Playmobil jungle gym and slide set. He also noticed a once-yellow ribbon that had been tied around the trunk of a maple tree. It had faded to a pale buff color and was frayed along the ends. Behr continued toward the door and knocked.

'Mrs. Gibbons?' he said when a petite woman, around fifty years old, with cropped platinum hair opened the door.

'You're that detective? Call me Kerry, and come on in.'

'If you're here to get hired, you can forget it,' Kerry

Gibbons said, handing him a cup of Vanilla Bean Taster's Choice.

'Ma'am?'

'It's not that I won't spend the money, it's that I been down that road. A couple three-thousand-dollar rides to nowhere. So there's no retainer or hourly or anything on this one.'

'I understand,' Behr said.

'She's dead, my little girl. I know it in my bones,' the woman said without excess emotion. 'I know there's no finding her alive. I just want to know how. Who . . .' It was only then that her anger rose up beneath her words. 'I want the son of a bitch who did it sent to Terre Haute and shot full of juice.'

'Well . . .' Behr said after her words had settled. 'This kind of thing isn't easy.'

'How'd you end up coming to me?' Kerry Gibbons asked, lighting a slender brown More 120 from a red pack.

'The billboard,' Behr said. He'd already mentioned it on the phone, but he supposed she had a lot on her mind.

'Of course,' she said. 'I figured I'd get a lot more phone traffic after it went up. Even cranks and such.'

'And?'

'Not as much as you'd think,' she said. He couldn't tell if she was disappointed about it.

'Ma'am, if you don't mind my asking, where did you come up with this reward money?'

'Raised it,' she said, tapping her ash into a coffee cup with no handle. 'First six months I offered ten grand – that's all I had. Posted flyers everywhere. But that didn't stir the pot. So I upped it. Had a series of community benefits and drives. People knew Kendra around the neighborhood. They cared about her.'

'I'm sure they did,' Behr said.

'Kendra's friends and me out at intersections with buckets.' Then she smiled. 'And those friends of hers, those little girlies, had a couple carwashes last summer in their short-shorts and halter tops, splashing around. Ten dollars a car. Twenty dollars a car. Plus tips. I was there too, but just organizing. No one's paying to see these old things get soapy anymore.' She juggled her breasts and barked out a nicotine laugh that Behr couldn't help joining.

'Well, it is a lot of money,' Behr said, 'but still . . .'

'I know, I know, it's impossible,' she said, stubbing out the cigarette in the cup and waving away the smoke. 'But I've learned in my time that you can do damn near anything if you put your mind to it.'

Behr nodded. It was something he'd learned too. After spending a moment in thought over her Taster's Choice, she put it down and the photos came out. They were snaps of Kendra. One was of her smiling brightly in her high school graduation gown, another with a bunch of friends in jean shorts on the hood of a Dodge. Party shots. She seemed to be a vibrant, beautiful young woman. Then came picture after picture of the girl with an infant. There was the full version of the photo that had been cropped for the billboard. This one featured a swarthy, muscular young man with a proprietary arm around Kendra's shoulder.

'Who's this?' Behr asked, holding it up.

'Kendra's dirtbag of an ex-boyfriend, Pete,' Kerry said.

'Pete what?' Behr asked.

'Lambrinakos. He's a Greek.'

The last picture was also from graduation day, the mortarboard and tassel atop her head, blond hair pushed back, diploma displayed proudly.

'That was a great day. Kendra was in the top quartile of her class.'

Behr looked up.

'Yeah, quartile. We're not just a bunch of dummies in this part of town,' Kerry said. 'Wish she could've hung in at community college, things would've been different.' Then the woman picked up a folder from the coffee table, which was cluttered with knick-knacks and television remotes and *TV Guide*s.

He took the folder from her and felt right away from its weight and thinness that there wasn't going to be much of use inside. He flipped it open to find a copy of the police report from eighteen months prior.

Gibbons, Kendra, White Female, age 23, resident of Millersville, reported missing. Subject's mother notified IMPD her daughter had gone to East Washington Street corridor. (Subject's purpose of visit appears to have been prostitution.) Two witnesses (statements attached) saw Gibbons that evening before 9:00 P.M. No other witnesses saw Gibbons talking with anyone/getting in vehicle. Recovered in the vicinity: One female high-heel shoe, lavender color, Nine West brand, size 7. Mother unsure if shoe was her daughter's. Confirmed she was a size 7½, but could wear a 7 depending on the make/style of shoe. No DNA recovered from shoe. No further information at this time.

Behr flipped to the witness statements. One was from a Village Pantry clerk. Kendra Gibbons had bought a pack of More 120s and Tropical Fruit Trident from the convenience store that evening around 8:00. Store security camera footage confirmed it. No other customers were in the store at the time. An acquaintance, a woman named Samantha Williams, with the notation 'also known prostitute,' gave a statement that she'd seen Kendra across the street and waved to her, but had then 'met a friend' and 'gotten a ride from him.' Behr made a mental note to himself to talk to her.

The police report was dust – even finer than dust – it was motes of pollen on the wind. He'd read many of them in his day, enough to know that when they started off this flimsy they never did get closed. Never. Behr finished reading and looked up at Kerry Gibbons, pretty certain that his being there was one of the poorest ideas he'd had in quite some time. As if sensing his lack of will Kerry Gibbons started talking.

'Just so you know, that money's currently residing in escrow in an interest-bearing account. It goes to whoever provides information leading to arrest or conviction. No funny business.'

Behr nodded.

She dug around on the table and came up with a statement from PNC Bank and handed it to him. The statement showed $97,500.

'I'll find a way to make up the difference and get it all the way up to a hundred if anything comes of it.'

Behr was thinking about how to extricate himself from the house and this stone loser of a scenario, and was contemplating whether or not he should try some direct marketing by calling his past clients to see if they needed his services. He tipped back his cup and drained it, placed the folder on the table, and stood to say his good-byes when a little girl came out of a back room. She was perhaps two and a half years old, her blond hair in pigtails, overalls printed with a pattern of strawberries, and her right Mary Jane unbuckled.

'Hey there, baby girl,' Kerry Gibbons called out to her granddaughter. 'This little mermaid is Katie.'

'Gamma.' The girl's bright blue eyes shone as she ran over to them. She glanced at Behr and stopped, but apparently had no great fear of strangers because she didn't shrink back at his presence.

'It's okay, sweetie, I'm talking to the man about your dear mother,' Kerry Gibbons said.

'Mommy,' the little girl said, her voice a song. Gears started churning around in Behr's guts.

'She doesn't know who that means anymore, I'm afraid. She was so small when Kendra went missing.'

'And her father?' Behr asked. He wondered instinctively if it was a custody dispute gone bad.

' "Father" is just a word, you know. There were a lot of men it could've been who made my little sweetie, but none of 'em were anything close to a real daddy to her.'

'So it wasn't Lambrinakos?'

'Hell no. Whoever it was isn't in the picture – that's the way we seem to do it 'round here – so I'm all she's got now.'

Behr felt himself slide back into his chair.

'Do you have children, Mr. Behr?' Kerry asked.

It was a question that pained him, one he'd once hated but now withstood. 'Two. Two boys. I'm raising the one I have left,' he said.

'Oh, I see,' Kerry Gibbons said, a sense of warm knowing rising up from her own reservoir of pain. He watched her get up and swing the girl around by the arms, causing the child to erupt in delighted giggles.

'So, you think I could get a copy of that billboard photo and the names of those friends of your daughter's?' Behr asked.

'Sure, but I don't think they know nothing. I've spoken to 'em a million times about it.'

'It'll be different when I talk to them,' he said.

EIGHT

H E'S BLAZING THROUGH his work when his mind stops. All of a sudden the cost projections sitting in front of him swim away, the figures and notations just inkblots on paper and marks on a screen. The stark fluorescent light spilling down from above him becomes intense, like a crossbow bolt through the temple. The lines and numbers roll and wave before his eyes. His mind is in Irvington. He is thinking of Cinnamon. She is a shade darker than his usual type, but there is something about her . . . He wipes his palms on his trousers and stands. It's near lunchtime, a perfect opportunity to see if she is out on the streets. He closes the documents on his desktop and grabs his keys.

NINE

'WHAT'S IT ABOUT?'
      The tall, thin, dark-complexioned
      woman blocked the door with her body.
The smell of nutmeg and baking apples reached
Behr from inside.

'Kendra Gibbons,' he answered.

When she heard the name, the woman's face fell.

Behr was at the home of Elisa Brook, a woman
Kerry Gibbons had said was her daughter's best
friend. He'd come armed with her address, a copy of
the thin police file, which was no more than a waste
of paper, and the name 'Jonesy,' apparently a local
protector or pimp of girls in the profession according
to Gibbons. Besides that, Behr didn't have much
else with him besides a mild sense of futility.

Elisa Brook may have been close to Kendra, but
missing her friend wasn't the sole cause of her dismay
at the moment. She pushed a strand of dark hair

away from her face and cast a half glance back over her shoulder into the house. A baby stroller was visible in the entryway next to her.

'I heard that you used to work together. That you shared some contacts in that world,' Behr said.

'Look, can we do this some other time? My husband's at home. I'm recently married and he's not a hundred percent clear on my . . . past employment history.'

'Well . . .' Behr began. He didn't like rescheduling an interview with someone who was looking to avoid him. It generally turned into more canceled appointments, and his trying to catch up with the subject. The pattern was often repeated until it became a test of wills. He usually won the battle, but he preferred to avoid it in the first place if he could.

'You have any information on where she might've gone?' Behr asked. Even though Kerry Gibbons thought her daughter was dead, Behr had the odds as being much better that the girl had just taken off in search of the mythical 'better life.'

'Oh, I don't think she went anywhere,' Elisa said.

'No?'

'Nope.'

'Why's that?'

'Her daughter, obviously.'

'Uh-huh,' Behr said. 'Plenty of young women have run away, leaving a child in the care of their mother.'

47

'Not Kendra,' the woman said.

'I see. Who's Samantha Williams? You know her?' Behr asked in reference to one of the witnesses in the police report – the remaining one, the Village Pantry clerk, had recently returned to his native Bangladesh. So far Behr had been unable to locate the woman. All the Samantha Williamses listed in the vicinity were either too old or too young to be the likely candidate.

'Don't have a clue,' the woman said.

'You know if Kendra had a boyfriend? Maybe one from out of town?' Behr had of course started his efforts by researching Pete Lambrinakos, the Greek ex-boyfriend Kerry Gibbons had mentioned. He and Kendra had broken up two years back, before she went missing, and he'd been jailed in Toledo on car theft, evading arrest, and past warrants at the time of the disappearance. But that didn't mean there wasn't a new boyfriend in the mix. 'Or a client from out of town who something romantic had developed with?' he continued. 'Did she talk about wanting to get away to someplace?'

'She didn't have a boyfriend,' the woman said, crossing her arms. She really wanted Behr to leave, but he wasn't going anywhere.

'I'd like to learn a little bit about Jonesy.'

Elisa grew even more agitated at mention of the name.

'Ooh, he is *not* someone I've kept up with,' she said.

'Maybe you can give me some background on him then, and an address where I can find him.'

'He lives with his girlfriend – girlfriend of the moment slash wife type or common-law something or other, but you did *not* hear it from me.'

Behind her, inside the house, a toddler walked by behind a toy lawn mower that popped colored balls inside a clear dome as she pushed it.

'My daughter. She plays with Kendra's daughter sometimes. Used to anyway. My husband isn't her father.'

'I see,' Behr said. If she turned out like her mother the little girl would have heavy eyebrows and a light mustache by the time she was thirteen, but she was as cute as a gingerbread cookie right now. And then the twice-mentioned husband appeared in the doorway beside his wife. He was stocky and powerful looking, with the first few buttons of his starched dress shirt open and a gold chain around his neck.

'The pie is browning,' he said to his wife, and then turned to Behr and asked: 'What's up?'

Behr said nothing.

'The pie is fine. He's a salesman,' Elisa Brook said.

'What do you sell?' the husband wondered.

There was a quiet desperation in the woman's

eyes that found Behr. The modest rambler on the quiet street must've been a huge step up from nights spent climbing in and out of truck cabs on Pendleton Pike.

'Encyclopedias,' Behr said.

'Yeah? People still use them?'

Behr shrugged.

'Where are your samples?'

'Not printed books that take up your shelf space. Online. We sell an access code to the website,' Behr said.

'Don't you guys usually just do e-mail blasts?' the husband continued.

Behr didn't want to jam the woman up but wasn't sure how long he was going to continue with the pretense.

'We don't like to spam potential customers,' he answered, patience near an end.

'Well, that's good to hear. Kid's only three. Doesn't even read yet, so thanks anyway.'

'I'm gonna slide him a couple of referrals,' Elisa Brook joined in. 'He said I get a free access code if I give him five names.' When it came to lying, there was nothing like a hustler who'd perfected her craft on the stroll. Her delivery was as smooth as polished glass.

'Whatever,' the husband said and walked away.

Elisa Brook nodded her thanks but didn't speak it.

Instead she quickly got into what Behr had come for.

'I'm out of the life. Have been for over a year. It's apple pies and bullshit now, but it's better for my daughter and me. Kendra was my homegirl. We were *down*. We had so much fun together – she could be a real wild child. But what happened to her – what happened to some of the other girls – it freaked the crap out of me.'

'What happened to Kendra? What other girls?' Behr asked.

'I don't know. She just went gone. Others too, over the years. Plenty of 'em come and go. Lots of the time they tell you they're leaving to try L.A. or Miami. Vegas. Other times they just pack up and go. This is different. The feeling started spreading around that girls were getting into cars and never coming back. Jonesy, and guys like Jonesy, were supposed to prevent that kind of thing, but they weren't a broke-dick bit of good. What was I supposed to do?' She lifted her palms. 'So I bailed.'

'Where can I find him – Jonesy?' Behr asked. 'I have a number and I texted him but got no response. And what's his real name?'

'He rolls a new number every few weeks. He won't text you back if he doesn't recognize your number anyway. His first name is Adam. Adam Jones. He's got a place on Rural and Sixteenth.'

'Rural Sherman?' Behr asked. It was one of the worst parts of the city.

'Yeah, that's right,' she said, and gave him the house number.

'Thanks,' Behr said. 'Good luck with that pie.'

She just nodded and closed the door on him.

DAVID LEVIAN

Eventually he points the car back toward his office,
but he knows he isn't going to let him rest now. He
knows it, because he's felt it like this before.
He knows where it will end up. Once the building
starts, it's just a question of where he points it,
because it is going to blow . . .

TEN

THE STREETS OF Irvington are ghost-town
quiet during the middle of the day, save for
delivery trucks. UPS, Coca-Cola, U.S. Mail,
Frito-Lay, Brown's Fuel Oil, FedEx. The drivers are
the only people he sees. They park in front of stores
– small markets, gas stations, Mail Boxes Etc., a
Beverage Barn – but there aren't any people out.
Only the Kroger shows signs of life as some house-
wives push their carts from the store to their cars.

He rolls along the streets, feeling it start to bubble
down there inside of him, the thermal geyser. The
thin crust that keeps things in place breaks away
inside of him under the force of the building pressure,
and the hot lava starts sliding around. *Other* is up and
about. He feels his breath coming shallow. An hour
passes, and then another.

Where are you, Cinnamon, where are you?

Eventually he points the car back toward his office, but he knows it isn't going to let him rest now. He knows it because he's felt it like this before. He knows where it will end up. Once the bubbling starts, it's just a question of where he points it, because it is going to blow . . .

ELEVEN

JONES, ADAM, A.K.A. 'Jonesy.'
White male, age 32.
Height: 6'2".
Weight: 290.
Eyes: black.
Hair: bald.
Tattoos: multiple. See attachment.
Arrests: Assault. Extortion. Resisting arrest. Attempted murder (charge dropped, insufficient evidence). Assault. Larceny. Promoting prostitution. Public intoxication. Possession. Parole violation. Assault.
Time served: Four years, eight months, three separate terms. Released–overcrowding. Suspended sentence. (No credits for good behavior during time served.)

There was a booking photo of the man: flat black

eyes that radiated hate above a black goatee and mustache ringed around sneering lips. A face a mother had probably slapped.

Elisa Brook had given Behr the full name, and with it he'd been able to run a full P-check on him. The portrait that had come back was one of what his former brother officers in the Indianapolis Police Department would call a 'Radar Delta Bravo,' or Regulation Douche Bag. That was the style in which the man lived as well.

Behr sat across from a decrepit ranch-type house on Rural and 16th. An ancient Corvair was up on blocks in the stripe of driveway next to it. An oxidizing jungle gym was where the grass should have been. The swing on the jungle gym dangled by a single chain, just yards away from a toppled death-trap refrigerator, its door still on. A hyena-like dog beset by an advanced case of mange paced the area inside the rusted chain-link fence. There was a brand-new DirecTV dish mounted on the south side of the buckling roof, of course. People are the same the world over; they'll live in squalor as long as they have a flat screen and channels.

The place was a survival course for the children living inside, of which there were two, as far as Behr could tell from his surveillance, both young boys, poorly dressed for the weather. He hadn't seen any sign of Jonesy over the past two days. The guy had either been inside the whole time or away. Behr wasn't sure exactly what to look for besides the face either. Six foot two and 290 was certainly large, but it could be flab or it could be jacked, and there was a big difference.

Behr had door-knocked the dump on day one, and a massive mocha-skinned woman had answered, a hearty baby clad only in a diaper cocked on her hip. Before he could even run a pretext on the woman, who was Samoan or Hawaiian or Fijian as far as he could tell, she started right in.

'He don' do nothing.'

'Ma'am—'

'He not here and he don' do nothing.'

'Okay, look—'

'He don' violate his parole and he don' do a damn-damn thing.'

The woman was practically violent in her assertions. Behr tried to peek into the house and learn something of value while she ranted, which was difficult for two reasons: the first was her size – she filled almost every inch of the doorframe – and the second was the mess inside. The living room was like an interior version of the yard.

Behr didn't even bother with his 'assessor with a potential reduction in property tax' gambit. Instead he retreated and found an inconspicuous vantage point down the block from which to monitor the house. Proper discipline on a stakeout required engine off, windows closed, no music. It wasn't pleasant, but it was a protocol that was best followed. Cops and Treasury agents with windows down and radios on had been rewarded with bullets in the back of the head. A closed window didn't offer much protection, maybe bullet deflection at best, but it was better than a muzzle pressed against the temple. It got bitter cold in the car before long, but it beat extreme heat.

After he'd spent the bulk of forty-eight hours on the sit, less three thirty-minute breaks to say hello to Susan and Trevor, use the bathroom, and reload on sandwiches and water, Behr had to admit Jones wasn't home. He'd also had ample opportunity to feel foolish about the case itself and did his best to push these thoughts from his head.

At one point the woman went out, piloting a beat-to-shit Honda Odyssey from the cluttered one-car detached garage, apparently on a shopping trip with the kids. Behr considered making entry to the house but decided against it. He had nothing concrete to look for, and he didn't feel like getting arrested or contending with the dog. The woman and kids returned an hour later with a bunch of bags from Target. Sometimes patience was the only thing that worked, and every time Behr lost his he pictured his son, and that kept him rooted to his spot.

It was almost dark on the second day when he was rewarded. A matte black F350 rolled up, and getting out of the passenger seat was a tree trunk dressed in work pants, boots, and a Dickies jacket. Behr checked the mug shot he'd sat with for two days. It was Jonesy. And unfortunately Jonesy had not been sloughing off when it came to the gym time. He moved around the truck to the driver's side with surprising dexterity and slapped five with the driver, who took off in a spray of loose gravel as Jonesy headed for his house. Behr watched him go in and waited five minutes. Cutting off a man before he'd seen his wife and kids, causing him to wonder if they were okay or had been hassled, didn't seem like a good idea. The mangy dog followed him inside too, and that was a plus.

After the requisite time had passed, Behr got out of his car, though he left his key in the ignition and the door leaning closed but not shut. He'd knocked on enough strange doors to know it was wise to be prepared for a hasty retreat. He also grabbed a can of pepper spray out of the glove box, not sure if he was thinking of the dog or Jonesy, then passed through the rusty gate and up the two steps to the house's battered front door.

'Yeah?' Jonesy said, the word loaded with distrust, when he opened the front door, leaving only a heavy screen door between them.

Before Behr had a chance to answer, the common-law wife spoke from inside the house. 'I already told him you don' do nothing.'

He's not a parole officer,' Jonesy said to his woman. 'Who are you and what do you want?'

Behr took in the man's thick neck. A white-collar geek who made the bad choice of not paying a certain hooker in some hot-sheets hotel room would soon be quaking in his loafers upon this man's arrival.

'I'm here about Kendra Gibbons,' Behr said, omitting an answer to the question of his name.

'Goddamn slut!' the wife spoke from behind Jonesy.

'Shut the fuck up,' the man said to her. 'What about Kendra?'

'I'd like to know what you know about her disappearance,' Behr said.

'I don't know a damn thing 'bout what happened to that slut,' Jonesy said. Behr had to admit that sympathy for a prostitute he'd never met was pretty pathetic, but he didn't care much for the way Jonesy referred to Kendra Gibbons. He supposed it was either a testament to the mother, Kerry, whom he'd liked a great deal, or a sure sign he was going soft in his middle age.

'It was a long time ago,' Jonesy continued. 'Now get the fuck off my front door.' A sense of dismay settled on Behr. He was losing his appetite for dealing with pricks. He ought to have been immune to it by now. It was one of the only parts of being a cop he didn't miss, but he still had plenty of opportunity for it as an investigator.

'Did you see her the night she went missing?' Behr asked, trying to stay on point.

Jonesy said nothing, but Behr clocked a shrewd spark in the man's eyes that he couldn't ignore, and beyond that he was surprised to see some actual, if well-hidden, concern.

'Did she have a problem with anybody? A customer that you got involved with?'

'If she had a problem with a customer and *I* got involved, there wouldn't be no problem anymore,' Jonesy said, despite himself and his desire to blank Behr completely.

'I can see that,' Behr said, trying to flatter the man's ego. There was something here worth digging for, he believed. 'So no customer messed with her that you know of? What about your other girls, any of them know anything?'

'What "other girls," douche bag?' Jonesy said, a ridge of flesh on the top of his bald head puckering in anger. 'What do you think I do? Who the fuck do you think you're talking to?'

'A guy who keeps his girls safe—' Behr began.

'Don't try and stroke me,' Jonesy said, his voice flat. 'Plenty of other motherfuckers better than you have tried that con. And it was a fail.'

'Can you just tell me—'

'Only thing I'll tell you is what I already told you: get the fuck off my front door.' Jonesy bent his knees slightly and leaned to the right, and when he straightened back up he was holding an aluminum baseball bat.

They stared at each other for a long moment before Behr spoke. He was thinking of Gene Sasso, his old training officer on the Indianapolis Police. There were few things about being a cop, and a man, that Gene didn't know. He spouted long sets of rules pertaining to various situations on the street. He did so with such authority it was hard to tell whether they were written on tablets by the finger of God and handed down, or if he made them up himself. But for a moment like this he'd say: 'When a fight's inevitable, you can't be too violent too soon.'

'I'll get off your front door when I'm good and fucking ready,' Behr said. His voice was flat now too. The dismay was gone. They were now having an entirely different conversation.

'Oh shit,' the wife said from inside the house and Jonesy stepped forward, blasting the screen door open as he came.

Behr had to jump back to let the screen door miss him, and he was off to the side when Jonesy reached the porch. The big man had stepped right past Behr and into the wrong spot. He had no chance of swinging the bat and connecting from this angle. Behr seized the moment before Jonesy turned and readjusted, grabbed him by the shoulder and collar of his canvas jacket, and drove him toward the steps, sweeping the man's feet as he did so. Jonesy flew through the air and down the two stairs to ground level, where he landed face-first and hard, the air squeezing out of him in a grunt. Behr was right behind him, jamming a knee into his back.

'You had to go and be an asshole,' Behr said.

Jonesy squirmed a bit, but he had no real chance to move as Behr dropped all of his weight on the knee. That's when things turned into a full-on reality show.

The sound of crying children in the background was issuing from the house, so Behr hadn't heard the screen door open and shut, or the footsteps, he just felt a mass of soft flesh hurtle into his back and knock him off Jonesy. It was the wife, and the two of them tumbled to the cold dirt of the yard in a heap. This was the concern that police and investigators had when walking into any domestic setting – families stuck together. Countless cops had been shot or stabbed by the very same abused wives and girl-friends they'd been called to protect once they began taking down the husband or boyfriend who had been doing the abusing. As Behr and the wife landed, the woman commenced hitting at him around the face with inconsequential openhanded blows. She began shouting incoherent epithets in a foreign tongue too. Behr swam out from under all that flesh and onto his back to face her, doing a hip escape and sweeping her over easily. He'd gained top position and was preparing to disengage from the woman and stand when he caught movement out of the corner of his eye. Jonesy was up with his bat. He rotated into a backswing, raising the bat, and at the last moment, Behr rolled, bringing the wife around on top of him just as Jonesy took a vicious cut.

The blow landed hard across the woman's upper back, and she let out a moan and went limp. Behr scrambled out from under her, trying to create distance between himself and Jonesy, but Jonesy was less concerned with him than with leaning down and checking on his wife.

'Honeyknees! You okay?' he asked.

That's when Behr heard a growl and realized the mangy dog had gotten out of the house when the wife opened the door. He turned just in time to see the feral-looking creature coming at him for a piece of the action. Behr swung his leg and connected with a hard, low kick to the dog's jaw. He reached for the pepper spray in his back pocket, but there was no need. The dog was whimpering, and limped away across the lawn, dragging his head low. Behr turned quickly to see Jonesy standing up and raising the bat.

'You motherfucker,' Jonesy said, coiling and flexing what appeared to be every muscle in his body. Behr rushed him before Jonesy could swing, leaving his feet and closing the distance with a lunging punch. It landed just below Jonesy's ear, causing the big man to sag, but not go down. Behr dropped the pepper spray, grabbed the jacket collar again, and raised his leg for a stomp-sidekick to the back of Jonesy's knee. This crumpled the man to the ground, and Behr followed up with a stomp to Jonesy's floating rib. Behr rolled him over, yanking the felled man's arm straight, and landed a final stomp to the inside of Jonesy's shoulder as he ripped the bat free.

Jonesy rolled and writhed, spittle flecking his mouth. Behr straightened, grabbing a breath of air, and tried to decide if he'd wandered into a rerun of *Dog the Bounty Hunter*.

'Now it's time to talk, *motherfucker*,' Behr said, leaning down and jamming the business end of the baseball bat into Jonesy's sternum. 'Send your woman inside and tell her to bring the dog with her.'

'Honeyknees . . .' Jonesy said, still curled up in a ball. The common-law wife had risen to her knees and was pawing at her back.

'She'll be fine,' Behr said.

'Go on in,' Jonesy told her. 'Take Banzai with you.'

The woman hobbled over, gathered the dispirited dog by the collar, and went toward the house, pausing only to ask: 'Should I call the police?'

'Shut up, and get inside,' Jonesy told her. He tried to sit, but Behr kept him pinned with the bat in his chest.

'Please don't violate me,' the downed man pleaded.

'I'm not here to violate you,' Behr said. 'Now what's the story with Kendra?'

'Kendra was my good girl, man,' Jonesy said.

'What, were you with her?' Behr asked.

'I'm with all my girls, man, that's how it works,' Jonesy said, and Behr understood why it was a problem for him to discuss it in front of the common-law wife. 'She was a sweet thing. Lots of fucking fun. Called her my little rabbit. She gave it her all. Man, she had a great ten years ahead of her.'

Ten years as a prostitute, Behr thought, that was the loss the man was lamenting.

'And what happened when she went missing?'

'That I don't know.'

'Nothing? Did a client rough her up? Did she O.D. and you had to get rid of her body?' Behr pressed the bat along with the inquiry. 'Or was it you?' He thought of the hundred grand at the end of it. He thought of an answer for Kerry Gibbons.

'None of that. No. Okay, here's all I know: A girl

– someone else's girl – this janky-ass bitch thinks she saw Kendra get into a car up on East Tenth Street. She don't remember if that was the last time she saw Kendra or not, but she thinks it was.'

'What kind of car?' Behr asked.

'She don't know. A blue one.'

'Two-door? Four? Foreign or American made?'

'She don't know.'

'What about the driver?'

'White.'

'White? That's it? Male or female?'

'A dude.'

'A white dude,' Behr said. 'How old? Tall or short? Bearded or clean-shaven? Bald?'

'A white dude. She thinks. That's it. Believe me, I looked into this thing. I spent a month searching for Kendra. I opened whup-ass on every bitch on the walk and every broke-ass pimp that ran 'em, trying to get some info. I looked for this blue-car-white-dude every night, man. Figured I'd find the cocksucker and get my girl back. Or find out where she went if she left, or whatever happened to her. Police didn't do a damn thing. *I* dogged this bitch through and through and through, because that's how much it mattered to me. But I came up dry.'

'If she had run off and you'd found her, what would you have done?' Behr asked. He was more curious than anything on this point.

'I'da gone and dragged her ass back. No girl of mine has the right to leave 'less I tell her to go,' Jonesy said, as if it were obvious.

Behr appraised the man on the ground. He was no humanitarian, but he seemed genuine in recounting his efforts to find Kendra, and more so about the warped kernel of feeling he clearly had for her.

'Who's the girl – the janky-ass one? Is she Samantha Williams?'

'Her name's Shantae. *Shantae* Williams.'

If she'd given the police her real name, Samantha, but lived as Shantae for a long time, that would explain why Behr hadn't been able to locate her.

'You seen her lately?' Behr demanded.

'No.'

'You think you can find her again?'

'Think so,' Jonesy said.

'Good.' Behr flung the bat across the yard, where it landed with a clunk in a pile of refuse. He put a knee on Jonesy's belly and dropped a business card down on him.

'If Shantae sees this guy and this car again, I want her to call you and then I want you to call me,' Behr told him.

Jonesy nodded slowly.

'And if I *ever* have occasion to come talk to you again and you welcome me with a baseball bat, I will break every fucking limb off your body.'

Jonesy just lay there frozen as Behr stood and, to prove his point, went to the refrigerator, opened the door, and ripped it backward off its hinges. Then he picked up his pepper spray and walked away.

Jonesy just saw there is ven as their stood and to prove his point went to the refrigerator, opened the door, and tipped it backward off its hinges. Then he picked up his pepper spray and walked away.

TWELVE

I T IS AFTERNOON, after the school buses have left the streets, in the pale before winter's early dark, when he finally sees her again. Cinnamon. He is sitting at a traffic light, and the door to a package store swings open and she emerges carrying a small sack. Time goes liquid. The light changes. She starts walking south, toward Lowell Avenue. He watches her go until he becomes aware of a horn honking from what seems a far-off distance. He takes his foot off the brake and makes a right turn. He isn't anxious. In fact, he is totally relaxed. He knew this moment would come. He creates a box, making the next right, and the next, turning the corner back onto Lowell. He doesn't see her, not at first. He wonders if she's gone into another store. Then a couple of pedestrians clear as they enter a fried-chicken stand and she becomes visible, walking away from him at her own smooth pace. Her head bounces slightly as she walks, and he perceives she is listening to music through small in-ear headphones, though he can't see them. He remains where he is, allowing her to walk away from him. He will stay where he is until she's almost drawn out of sight or she turns. He is good at this.

After a few long moments she does turn: a left, onto Hawthorne. It is only then that he puts the car back into gear and drives slowly after her. He reaches Hawthorne as she nears midblock, and she is in his sight when she turns onto Marquette. He repeats the move of reaching the new street after she's had a chance to go about halfway down it. He noses the car around the corner in time to see her walk up three stairs and into a small brick house. She doesn't use a key – the door must be unlocked. She didn't knock, though. Her manner is proprietary. She is home.

He puts the car in park and watches and waits. He considers making entry. Going right in. The idea is always there. There is plenty of pressure for it inside of him. But not so much that not going in is out of the question. He is able to wait, so he does. No one else comes or goes as he sits and watches, but that is no guarantee she lives alone. Besides, his kit isn't in the car. It is of no matter. He knows where to find her now. There will come a time when he can't wait any longer, and when it does, he will be ready. Until then, his mind races off through the dark places and he waits. After three hours he has grown hungry, but not for food. He puts the car in gear once more and drives away from her house – one he will be back at again soon.

THIRTEEN

BEATING UP PIMPS didn't come cheap, and Behr waited for any one of the countless potential injuries that went along with that kind of activity to announce itself. At his age even winning a fight could result in a blown shoulder, a torn calf, a dislocated wrist or ankle, at best. But this time there seemed to be none. He'd come through his tussle with Jonesy clean. Of course he had tweaked his neck when the woman tackled him, and his foot was sore – bruised but not broken – due to his kick, because fighting a pimp's wife and dog didn't come cheap either.

Behr had gone on and spent the rest of the day trying to find a known address for Shantae Williams. Now that he had her street name along with her real one, Behr had thought he'd be able to find her quickly. He'd thought wrong. Live long enough on cash with no credit cards, no mortgage, someone else on the rent and utility bills, don't register to vote, and move after a last arrest, and a person can disappear in plain sight. Behr figured he'd find her eventually, but for now he was dead tired, and headed for Susan's place.

'There he is, the Chairman of the Board!' rang out in greeting when Behr walked into her living room.

Chad Quell, Susan's coworker and friend, was sitting there with Trevor near his feet. Chad was wearing socks, a pair of trendy pointy-toed lace-up shoes sitting nearby. Susan was in the kitchen making a salad. Behr and Chad hadn't gotten off to a great start and hadn't been particularly fond of each other for a while. But after Behr had prevented Chad from getting a life-altering beating, things turned around pretty quickly. The young man used to be flippant at best, but now whenever he saw Behr, instead of Frank, it was 'Francis Albert' or 'Chairman of the Board,' as in Sinatra, as a sign of respect.

'Slick,' Behr said back, with perhaps slightly less respect. They slapped hands, and Chad jumped up and pulled Behr into a bro hug with a back slap for good measure. For his part, Behr used to consider Chad akin to a device used to clean a certain part of a woman's anatomy, but he'd actually grown fond of the kid's wise-ass ways.

'Hi, Frank,' Susan called out.

'Hi,' Behr said, picking up the baby, amazed as always at how light and compact he was. It felt like there was hardly more to him than the cotton clothing he was wrapped in, yet Trevor was the magical source of joy for him and Susan.

'You find that guy you were looking for?' she wondered.

'I did,' Behr said.

'What's the case?' Chad asked.

'A windmill I'm wasting my time with,' Behr said. 'What about you?'

'I was just telling Susan about "The Two,"' Chad said.

'The two?' Behr asked.

'More Chad war stories,' Susan said, arriving at the table with the salad she'd made.

'I see,' Behr said.

'Yeah, "The Two" are this pair of dime pieces I know.'

'Dime pieces are hot girls,' Susan volunteered.

'Thank you. I've been on the street, so I know.'

'They're friends with my ex, actually, but you know, not *good* friends,' Chad went on. 'We were out at Average Joe's, and the shots were really flowing and then this sort of Truth or Dare game got started. Soon I'm wearing two pair of panties around my wrists like bracelets . . .'

Behr felt himself tune out and vaguely follow as the conversation seamlessly moved off of Chad's exploits and on to office gossip down at the *Indianapolis Star*, where he and Susan both worked. At some point Trevor was buckled into his seat and put at the end of the table, where he could oversee the dinner proceedings. Then Chad launched back into more tales of the girls he was dating and sleeping with – which were not mutually exclusive categories. The subtext that bled through to Behr was that none of the women involved were the true focus of his desire, which was Susan.

But Behr's mind was mostly cluttered with Kendra Gibbons, and what to do next. Then, when he turned his head toward the television and saw a news report saying that the body found at Northwestway Park had not yet been identified, Behr had an idea. He stood and kissed first Trevor, and then Susan, good-bye.

'Where are you off to?' she asked.

'Something I've got to go do,' he said. 'Take care.'

'See ya in the wee hours, Chairman,' Chad said.

As he reached the door, Behr glanced back for just a moment at Susan and Chad on opposite sides of the table, with Trevor in his seat between them, and in that flash took in the perfect portrait of a family. One that he was not in.

FOURTEEN

*O*THER NEEDS A TASTE.

The night surrounds him, fluid and deep. He moves through it, the camouflage it provides him complete. The lights of the city bounce off his windshield like star points. He cruises the strip off Pendleton Pike between Shadeland and N. County Line Road over and over, his car engine a rhythmic hum, watching as the filthy working girls show up to find their spots, then catch their customers, and then, finally, disappear one after another into strange cars to do what they did for money. There are black girls and Latinas mostly, but whites too, and after about an hour he sees her. The one he wants. *His.* She is almost six feet tall, though a lot of it is the shoes. Spiked towers of black patent leather that reflect the night. She can barely walk on them, so she totters and twirls more than strolls. She wears a faded black denim skirt punched with rhinestones

77

and no stockings, her bare legs as thin, white, and shapeless as PVC pipe. A short, tight leather jacket is her only concession to the cold. She has on hardly any makeup, he sees during his first pass, just red lips. But her hair is blond, piled on top of her head, held up by a large plastic clip.

After a second pass he feels a gnawing sensation inside that someone else will stop and get her, so he pulls over quickly and lowers his window. She points her way over to him, like a newborn horse.

'Hi there,' she says, leaning down.

'Hello,' he answers.

He smells the mint of her gum over crushed cigarettes when she speaks, and the manufactured fruit essence of her hairspray.

'You looking to party?' she asks.

'Yes,' he answers. Stupid words he's heard many times, though he supposes it is a party, of sorts.

'A shorty or all night long?'

'I don't know yet,' he says.

'A hundred for the hour, or three hundred for the whole shebang.'

'I want to go to the Always Inn.'

'Oh, baby!' she says, moving around and getting in the passenger side. 'That's good news. It's way too cold for this car bullshit. Besides, I can't do my *thang* good in a car. It's a little far, will you drive me back afterward? You're gonna be so happy you stopped . . .'

He isn't really listening to her, because the humming in his head is rising louder and louder. He drives to the motel and parks away from the office. She has the heat cranked and is playing with the radio when he leaves her. He buys the room with cash. The clerk makes him leave a credit card imprint for security. He has one specifically for this purpose, and it doesn't bear his real name. It wasn't difficult at all to get. He's had it for years and never actually charges anything on it. He takes the key card, goes back to the car, and pulls around to the room.

They get out near the door.

'You got any stuff?' she asks.

He shakes his head. It does feel odd walking into the room without his kit, but he is empty-handed tonight.

'Okay, so no toys,' she goes on. 'Lots of guys like toys, you know?'

He doesn't answer. Just flicks on the light.

'You want to get drinks, or . . . ?' she asks.

He sits down on the foot of the bed, his hands in his lap. The sense of calm he feels is overwhelming. He has an image behind his eyes of a glacial mountain lake, with no current, no wind, no people, no boats, no fish, no birds upon it, nothing at all to ripple the surface. He is the lake.

'You're a quiet one, aren't you?' she says. She drops her purse on the small round table by the window and takes off her jacket. She has large breasts, pressed together and upward by a tight tube top.

'So, player, what'll it be?' she goes on. The cold has made the top of her chest pink, the color of processed ham in a supermarket case. 'Something specific, or should we just, you know, take 'em off and try it?' She sits down next to him on the bed.

'How much,' he asks, 'to punch you in the face?' His voice sounds level and distant to him.

'What?' she says, a laugh in her throat.

'How much,' he asks again, 'to punch you in the face?'

'Ha-ha,' she says, 'two hundred bucks.' She shakes her head. 'Seriously, what would you like to . . . ?'

But his hand has gone to his wallet and has taken it out.

'What are you doing?' she asks, the first tremor of worry arriving in her.

'Two hundred dollars it is,' he says.

'Two hundred bucks to what?'

'To punch you in the face.'

'No, no. Hold on—'

'Shhh,' he says. He pinches two hundred-dollar bills between his fingers and slides them free from his remaining money.

'What the fuck are you doing?' she says, alarm now in her voice as he puts the money on the bed.

'Shhh,' he says again, a finger pressed to his lips. Then he touches her cheek and pats her hair, which has a stiff texture thanks to the spray. 'Shhh.' He can't allow anything to ripple the lake.

'Oh God,' she says quietly in the moment of calm before he draws back his fist and hits her in the face with a crushing blow. There is an audible crack as his knuckles meet her eye socket. She gasps. A youth and young adulthood spent in manual labor running punch presses, welding and fabricating metal, operating heavy machinery, sinking fence posts, pouring concrete, and pounding framing nails provide the power behind the punch. A pure jolt of pleasure runs through him. He isn't completely sure, but thinks he's fractured her orbital bone. She doesn't go out. Good for her. But her face drops into both her hands for a moment as she scream-sobs, then she stumbles back, grabbing the money and her purse and jacket, and runs for the door.

His breathing comes ragged and excited as the door slams shut behind her and he quickly undoes his pants. The room seems to vibrate in the silence that remains in her wake and he is able to finish himself off.

A short time later, cleaning himself in the bathroom, he feels light and free. A spill gate has been thrown open to release built-up pressure. But then he looks

at himself in the mirror and takes in the appalling
visage that is still sometimes strange to him: his
moonlike face, his physique like that of a Belgian
blue bull, muscles rippling, their smoothness broken
only by spidery veins under skin so pale it almost
glows. And in that moment he wonders how long the
release will last.

82

FIFTEEN

FRANK BEHR SAT over his second pint of Bass ale and stared out the window at wisps of fake smoke floating from the lid of a massive kettle barbecue that was suspended over the front door. He had a corner stool at the bar of the Weber Grill and was probably the only silent one in the place. The Pacers game had just ended, and a bunch of rowdy Maverick fans were celebrating their win. Behr had been waiting close to an hour, but as he had asked a big favor, he was in no position to be impatient.

Finally, Behr saw the broad-shouldered, overcoat-clad figure of Gary Breslau enter the place. Breslau, a lieutenant on the IMPD, worked a piece of gum in his mouth as he scanned the room, then spotted Behr and sliced through the crowd toward him. Behr was pleased to see he carried a large yellow-padded envelope under his arm, but when Breslau got close,

Behr noticed with disappointment the bunched-up sleeves of some dress shirts puffing out of it.

'Behr.'

'Breslau.'

The lieutenant took a seat next to him and put the envelope down in front of them, and Behr supposed he was in for a lecture on staying out of police business instead of getting what he'd asked for, which was IMPD's file on the Northwestway Park killing.

'Why do these assholes think they can come in here and whoop it up like this?' Breslau began as he settled in, pointing out over the crowd. 'It's a regular-season game, not the finals.'

'Ought to call in a sweep and take them all down,' Behr suggested.

'Yeah, try out those new Tasers. Send 'em back to Dallas with sore asses,' Breslau said, signaling the bartender. 'Give me a Stella,' he ordered, and then turned back to Behr. 'I'm fancy like that.'

'So it's a no-go on the file then?' Behr asked, pointing at the envelope on the bar top.

'Huh?' Breslau said, taking a drink of his beer. Maybe asking for the file on an open murder case, especially one that was getting so much media attention, was an overreach. He and Breslau certainly weren't friends. In fact, they'd gone through some choppy waters thanks to Behr and a matter he was involved with when they'd met not long ago.

'Just some old shirts going to my cleaners nearby. They're open late,' Breslau said. 'What are you on that you need that file?' Breslau wondered.

'Well, you still don't have an ID on your Northwestway Park body, right?' Behr asked.

'You mean our *parts*,' Breslau corrected.

'It wasn't all there?' Behr asked.

'It basically was. A few things were missing. But to me a *body* is intact, and parts is parts.'

Behr nodded. Breslau took another drink.

'We sent out DNA. We're checking it against missing persons and hoping for a match off the national computer, but for now she's a Jane Doe. So what are you working?'

Though he wasn't proud of his case, which wasn't even a case but a pathetic reward chase, Breslau had asked twice now, so Behr told him. 'Kendra Gibbons. A pross who went MIA a year and a half back.'

'Oh yeah, the billboard girl,' Breslau said.

'The billboard girl.' Behr expected some mockery from Breslau, but all he got was a slight sigh and another sip of beer.

'Shit,' Breslau said, shaking his head. 'Why the hell would I give you that?'

Behr was ready for the question. 'Well, I imagine the family has been up the department's ass. You don't put up a billboard without having been by the station a few hundred dozen times, right?'

'Uh-huh . . .' Breslau allowed.

'If I had something like cooperation I *could* intimate to the Gibbons family I'm working their case as an unofficial liaison to the department. Keep 'em away from you.'

'You want to play make-believe?' Breslau said, but he sounded interested. 'Gibbons isn't mine . . . but it's in my office and the supervisor would probably appreciate being left alone. The mother is difficult and the case is a mule – stubborn and smelly and not going anywhere.'

Behr let Breslau weigh the merits of his offer for a minute.

'Look, let's say I personally don't have a problem with you seeing the file . . .' Breslau said. 'I also can't be in a position, if asked, where I have to answer that I gave it to *you*. You understand what I'm saying?'

'I do,' Behr said. He thought for a moment about where this left him, and if there was another way he could get a look at it. But Breslau provided it.

'You know Ken Bannon?' Breslau asked. 'He's a former, like you.'

Behr knew the name. Bannon had been a detective years back. But he didn't know him personally.

'No,' Behr said.

'What about Don Fallon?' Breslau asked. Behr

thought he recognized the name of a former lieutenant who'd gone into private work. And he got where Breslau was going.

'Nope,' Behr said. 'What about Gene Sasso? He was my old training officer.' It was the second time he'd thought of him within a few days.

'Oh, so *he's* the one we all have to thank . . .'

'Right.'

'Well, him I know,' Breslau said. 'Now, see, he's an ex-cop – a friend of the department – who I wouldn't have any trouble giving a file to for a consult. For help. What he does with it, within reason, is up to him.'

Behr nodded. He had a conduit to the information now.

'So I'll give you Northwestway Park, and we get a gold star with the Gibbons family.'

Behr nodded. 'Am I going to find anything useful in the file?'

Breslau shrugged. 'She was taken apart with bladed instruments—'

'Medical grade?'

'Not quite. And power tools,' Breslau said.

Behr took a drink and allowed that to settle for a moment.

'Any perp DNA recovered?' Behr wondered.

'Nada,' Breslau said.

'Any chance I can check my girl's DNA against the victim's?'

Breslau looked at him. 'Sure, just have the next of kin sign a release.'

'Thanks.'

'Man, we're so at sea on this Northwestway deal, even *you* can't fuck it up any worse for us.' Behr knew there was some derision coming his way, and there it was. It was just the way cops spoke to each other.

'Am I supposed to say "thank you" to that?' Behr asked.

'If you do, I'll say "you're welcome,"' Breslau said. 'Anything else you think you need?' He sounded like he was joking, but Behr wasn't.

'Matter of fact—'

'Oh, Jesus—'

'How about related cases? Missing persons, similar settings, similar MOs.'

Breslau turned directly toward Behr before he spoke. 'Are you fucking kidding me?'

'Do I look like a comedian?'

'Not a funny one,' Breslau said. 'What do you want with ancillary cases?'

'A slay like Northwestway may not be an isolated type of deal,' Behr said. 'Maybe there's something in another case that relates to mine. C'mon, man, I need it, and I'll feed you anything real that I find.'

The IMPD lieutenant sat there and swilled his beer and looked miserable. 'Christmas is coming,

Breslau. I'll put a bottle of Johnnie Walker Blue Label in your stocking.'

'I don't drink Scotch. Why did I even come here tonight?' Breslau blew out a long, weary breath and Behr knew he had him. 'Check with Sasso tomorrow and knock yourself out.'

'I'll do my best,' Behr said.

'Please do,' Breslau said. 'When *you* get in the way shit happens.'

Breslau raised his bottle and Behr touched it with his pint glass. They drained their beers. A highlight played on the flat screens above the bar – a Mavs power forward dunked hard over his counterpart on the Pacers. The partisan crowd roared.

'I'm getting out of here before I start shooting people,' Breslau said, standing and gathering his envelope.

'I'm walking out right next to you,' Behr said, getting up. 'I got this.' He put money on the bar and they left.

As they split off in different directions, Behr called after Breslau.

'What was missing?'

'Huh?' Breslau paused.

'In Northwestway. You said most of her was there. What was missing?'

'Some parts that made her a woman,' Breslau said, and continued on into the night.

SIXTEEN

'**M**R. BEHR,' Kerry Gibbons said as she exited her house and saw him. 'Didn't expect to see you for a while.'

'Frank, please,' he said,

It was a cold morning, and the ground he'd walked across was as hard underfoot as the grim mission he was on.

'Frank. Do you have some information?'

'No, ma'am. Like I said, it'll be quite some time, most likely, before I do. That's *if* I do,' Behr said.

'Then what do you need? Think I told you everything already and I got to get Katie to her program,' she said. The young girl appeared next to her grandmother, all bundled up in a coat and scarf.

'Something I should have asked for the first time I was here: I could use a DNA sample on your daughter, and permission to check it against unidentified bodies.'

'Oh dear,' Kerry Gibbons said.

'Or barring that, one on you and the little girl to crossmatch. It could be an old toothbrush, a pillow-case that we could recover some hairs off of, a sports mouthpiece, a razor, a whistle – anything with saliva on it. I don't suppose her doctor might have an old blood sample?' Behr wondered.

'Okay,' she said, 'wait here for a minute.' Kerry Gibbons disappeared back inside the house for a moment, leaving Behr alone with the little girl. She ran over to her jungle gym and stood at the base of the slide.

'Lift up,' Katie said, looking at Behr. He took it to mean she wanted to go down the slide, and he picked her up and set her at the top for a quick trip down.

'Whee,' the girl said, as if by rote, without much joy in her voice. 'Again.'

Behr obliged. He looked at the girl's pale white skin, her raisin eyes, her runny nose. Losing her mother was a tough deal, but having her grandmother was a break in her favor. She was starting out some-where close to even, and Behr wondered where she'd end up.

It was the fourth or fifth time down the slide when Kerry Gibbons emerged from the house. 'Here you go,' she said, extending a Ziploc bag that held a blue plastic Goody hairbrush pretty well covered with blond strands. 'That's my daughter's. Probably some of mine and Katie's in there too. But like you said . . .'

'It should work,' Behr said. Then he had her sign the standard release he'd printed out.

'Any way I can get that back after the test?' Kerry Gibbons asked. 'It was hers after all.'

'Sure,' Behr said.

'Did you end up finding that Jonesy?' the woman wondered.

'Yes, Jonesy's been found,' Behr said. Her eyebrows rose in interest at this, but his tone discouraged further questions, and she didn't ask any.

'Well . . .' she said.

'Oh, one other thing.'

'Yeah?'

'I'm getting some pretty good courtesy extended from the police, so it'd be good if you ran any further inquiries into the case through me,' Behr said.

Kerry Gibbons took his measure with eyes that seemed to know all the angles, and when she was done she must've arrived at an acceptable sum. 'Okay, Frank,' she said. 'Will do. You're my investigator.'

SEVENTEEN

'SHOULD I DROP you right fucking now and save the run up?' asked Gene Sasso, the stocky and now bald owner and bartender of the Trough.

Sasso was not happy to see him. In case Behr missed the scowl on his face, Sasso reached under the bar and came up with a sawed-off baseball bat to make the point doubly clear.

Behr hadn't been to the bar, in fact hadn't seen Sasso, in close to seven years. He'd last been there in the middle of a period of heavy drinking, self-disgust, and all-around antisocial behavior. Behr had gone from rowdy-patron status, beyond old-friend-in-a-bad-way dispensation, and had even careened past oh-no-it's-him-again standing.

'Not here for any trouble, Gene,' Behr assured him. He didn't think Sasso really meant to hit him, but he wasn't completely sure. Somewhere in the

93

no-man's-land of his mid-fifties, Sasso was still strong-looking and had a beard going that helped cover the ravages of countless late nights, first as a cop, then as a tavern owner.

'You never come for any, but the shit manages to show up just the same when you're around,' Sasso said. 'All six of my pool cues ended up broken last time you were in. Same for a bunch of my customers.'

'That was a long time ago. And *I* didn't break 'em all,' Behr said.

'I'm counting the last three that got busted over your back. And then there's that . . .' Sasso pointed at a badly patched piece of drywall between the doors to the men's and ladies' rooms.

'Some of your clientele are real assholes, what can I tell you. Didn't I pay for the damage?' Behr wondered.

Sasso just looked at him, and Behr supposed the answer was no. Not that anyone would notice. At the time the Trough had opened, it looked like the interior wasn't quite finished, and it hadn't made any progress since, although that had been nearly ten years ago. The place currently sported a thin crowd of day drinkers seated along the dozen mismatched stools that lined the bar. The assortment of battered tables and chairs was unoccupied, as was a pool table that almost shined because the felt was worn to the slate.

After a moment, Sasso stowed the bat and reached into his shirt pocket for a flash drive, which he held up.

'How you got a world-beater like Breslau to give you this, I'll never know,' Sasso said.

'My charm is underrated,' Behr answered.

'Charm? Fuckin' please,' Sasso said, and almost smiled despite himself. He'd always had a soft spot for Behr, even back when Behr was a complete newbie and they'd first been paired up. They'd spent countless nights cruising the streets of what used to be referred to as the 'Spaghetti Bowl' – the place where a bunch of interstates and main thoroughfares twisted together. They mopped up blood and hauled in DWIs, barroom brawlers, and wannabe gangsters. And while they rode, Sasso kept up that steady patter of 'rules to live by.' Like *'The faster you finish the fight, the less shot you will get,' and 'Be polite, be professional, but have a plan to kill everyone you meet.'*

'What do you want with it anyway?' Sasso asked, putting the drive on the bar top. 'Shouldn't you stick to the neck brace and rusty zipper cases?'

'Probably.'

'Department wouldn't give you the files directly?' Behr shook his head.

'So you figured "use your old T.O."?'

'Yeah,' Behr said, 'I know you keep good ties.'

'Yes, *I* do. Because people – regular people – keep up friendships, relationships, warm human contact.'

'Uh-huh,' Behr said.

'Like I tried to do with you, long after you gave it up.'

'I didn't give it up,' Behr said. 'It just . . . went.'

Back after his first son had just died, Behr seemed to systematically burn down everything around him. He hoped that time was past.

'I wouldn't wish what happened to you on my worst enemy. But it's been a while now, Frank. I gave you all the space you asked for, and then some. And you had plenty of chances to come find me, buy me a drink, and make things right. Instead you did what you did, you let a quarter of a lifetime go by, and now you show up for this.' Sasso put a finger on the flash drive and slid it across the bar.

'Thank you,' Behr said, taking it. 'And I get it, Gene. I'll come buy you that drink one day.'

Sasso nodded, and Behr, not knowing what else to say, left.

EIGHTEEN

NOTHING LIKE THE smell of formaldehyde in the morning, Frank Behr thought to himself as he entered the brown brick building that housed the coroner's office, though the place didn't smell *only* like formaldehyde. Truth was it smelled like overcooked ground beef.

'How are you? Frank Behr to see Jean Gannon,' Behr said to the middle-aged woman sitting at the reception desk. He hadn't been in touch with his friend Jean, a forensic pathologist for the city, in a while and it'd be good to catch up in person before he asked for her help. Behr had a small sack of chocolate truffles and a few airplane-size bottles of Grand Marnier in one coat pocket, the bag holding the hairbrush in the other. It was his custom to bring Jean gifts when she was doing him off-the-books favors. The fact that he had clearance on this one didn't stop him from keeping up the tradition.

'Jean's not here,' the receptionist told him.

'Not here as in out getting a coffee, or not at work today?' Behr wondered, glancing at the trophy case across the lobby that held macabre souvenirs of past deaths – a piece of plastic a child had choked on, a length of rebar that had impaled a construction worker, a paper-like hood of dried facial skin, including the nose, of a burn victim. Morgue workers had a specialized sense of humor.

'Not here at all anymore,' she answered. 'Jean took early retirement a few months ago and left the office.'

'What?' Behr uttered. He wasn't surprised often, but this got him. Jean had loved her work. The sense of time moving by was a blow to him. Then there was the fact he no longer had a connection in the coroner's office.

'I know,' the receptionist said, then rolled her chair to a bulletin board and took down a business card. 'Here,' she said, passing it to him. 'This is where she's working now.'

The card read: Scanlon Brothers, Mortuary and Funeral Home.

'Here,' Behr said, placing the chocolates and Grand Marnier on the desk.

'What's that for?' the receptionist asked.

'That's for you,' Behr said.

'Thanks!' She smiled. 'What'd you say your name was?'

'Frank Behr . . .' he said, and leaned in for some small talk. The receptionist was a long way from a forensic pathologist he had history with, but he had to start somewhere.

Next stop was the Indianapolis–Marion County Forensic Services Agency – otherwise known as the place that did DNA testing. It shared a building down on South Alabama with the jail. He was there to drop the hairbrush, which he produced along with his license and the release form when he got to the buttoned-down-looking young clerk.

'I need you guys to run DNA on these hairs against the Northwestway Park victim. I've got clearance from Lieutenant Breslau, IMPD, and the family,' he told the young man.

'All right,' the clerk said, and took the information from Behr, which he attached to the bag that held the hairbrush. 'Just so you know, DNA can only be recovered from hairs with the bulb still attached. There might be some here, but it'd be better if you plucked the hairs.'

Thanks, CSI, Behr almost said. Instead he opted for: 'That's not an option. How long will it take?'

'Things are kind of backed up,' the clerk said. 'It's going to be a couple of weeks at least.'

'Anything you can do to help it through the system would be much appreciated,' Behr said. 'I know

Lieutenant Breslau feels the same way.'

Truth was, he didn't know how Breslau felt, but it wasn't the first time a little bullshit had been spread around this particular building, and it wouldn't be the last.

'We're on it,' the clerk said to Behr's departing back.

NINETEEN

THE DAY HAS been bright yet cold, the sun promising but failing to warm the air. He sits outside Cinnamon's house in his car. He's spent a good part of the afternoon there when he should've been at work, but the project has taken him over now. He's tracked her enough over the past few weeks to know her routine: She takes a walk in the morning and comes back from the White Hen Pantry with a big coffee and a fresh pack of cigarettes. She smokes one along the way home. In the afternoon it's down to the Prime Time Package store and a walk back with a brown paper bag that looks about the size of a quart bottle of beer. She doesn't appear to have a car. He can't be sure if she lives alone or if others are in the house, though he hasn't seen anyone. He doesn't know what else she does during the day. He supposes she goes out occasionally. He can't sit there all day long though. He has to appear at his office at some point. He considers knocking, or going in the back door, but he develops a slightly different idea. He doesn't know from where it has come, only that it arrives fully blown and seems like it will work. He feels his heart surge with the joy of creation when he thinks of it. Her front door swings open and she emerges, zipping her tight leather jacket, her breath a cloud around her, and it has begun.

She walks up the block and he turns on his ignition and drives past her. He keeps the car at a normal speed, perhaps even slower than the limit. He has time. He drives to Prime Time Package and parks in the lot along the far side of the building. He's circled the store many times and learned there are no cameras back there. Dusk has usually fallen by the time she reaches the store, and today is no exception. The blazing orange orb of the sun drops behind the trees, and within moments the day goes from brilliant to bruised. He parks, but leaves the car unlocked and enters the store.

Cases of beer are stacked all along the entrance, and since the brand doesn't matter, he doesn't bother going any deeper into the store. He picks up a case of Stroh's in cans and puts it down at the register, then gathers two twelve-packs of Labatt Blue in bottles. The clerk, a Pakistani, comes around and rings up the purchase. He pays cash, and he spots her through the window between the specials signs, coming toward the store. He pockets his change and stacks the twelve-packs on top of the case.

'Do you want bags for the bottles?' the clerk asks.

'No,' he answers.

He heads for the door. He needs to be outside before she arrives, everything hinges on that. He puts his back into the bar and eases the glass door open, then turns toward her. He feels his heart thumping lightly in his chest as he faces her, in person at last. She is even smaller than he'd thought, height-wise. Her frame is compact and well formed. Her eyes sparkle above rings of black eyeliner along her bottom lids. A cloud of cigarette smoke hovers around her. Her hair catches the day's remaining light. Then he speaks.

'I got too much,' he says. 'It was on sale. Help me carry it to my car and I'll give you a six-pack?'

She looks at him for a moment, as he strains against the armful of beer, and shrugs.

'Sure, noodle arms,' she says, and the corner of her mouth rises in a quarter smile. She puts the cigarette between her lips, reaches out and takes the twelve-packs off the top, and he begins walking around the corner toward the parking lot. She follows.

'I'm just over here,' he says, mild and unimpressive, as he heads to his car. Loose gravel and old broken glass crunch under their feet as they cross the lot. He walks along with her, his exterior calm, but inside his true self is savage as a meat ax.

'Not too sure about your taste in beer. Stroh's? Can I get a six of the Labatt at least?' she asks.

'Sure,' he says.

There are no other cars in the lot. He fishes in his pocket for his keys and pops the trunk. He puts the case of cans inside and steps back, giving her room to deposit the twelve-packs.

'So, should I just take—' she begins speaking but stops. She stiffens as she sees the lengths of duct tape and nylon cord, precut and tied, in the trunk. She can't know what they are for, only that it feels wrong. But that is all she has time to consider. He punches her in the back of the head, a short, sharp blow just at the base of her skull, and she sags as she goes out. Her cigarette hits the ground, and he pushes her right in on top of the beer and swings her legs into the roomy trunk. He secures her hands and feet with the lengths of cord, puts a strip of tape across her mouth, and closes the trunk. From the street, a passing motorist would merely glimpse a man placing packages in his car. He gets behind the wheel and drives away, euphoric, into the falling darkness.

TWENTY

TREVOR WAS ON the floor on a play mat that was festooned with boinging, buzzing, and clicking gadgets that had probably been scientifically engineered by a team in a lab to stimulate a child's senses. The boy was ignoring most of that, however, and was instead engaged in what looked like a wrestling sit-out drill. From time to time Behr would glance over to see one of Trevor's limbs give out and plant him on his face upon the padded cotton mat. It didn't seem to faze his son though.

Behr surveyed his place, which had turned into a command post for his task force of one. The idea that his missing woman had gotten into the car of someone hunting women was a long shot, but Behr woke up thinking about the reward most days now. The idea of the money played in his head, while the actuality of his bills piled up and his savings dropped, and it was causing him to work long and hard. After he'd gotten the flash drive from Sasso, he'd run his laser printer like a coal engine for two days straight, stopping only to go to Staples for another box of paper and a new printer cartridge. He'd then set about reading and organizing what he'd printed. He'd put up a large city map so he could pushpin the locations of bodies and murders, as well as a bulletin board for other important facts. The case files themselves went into stacks by year. An index card timeline of all the cases stretched around the walls at eye level. There was another box for witness statements from the other cases. Breslau hadn't been particularly judicious but had been generous with what he'd sent. Behr had fifty-seven unsolved cases going back roughly eighteen years to sift through.

So he concentrated his focus on the cases resembling his. Young women, known prostitutes, those who may have been prostitutes, and those who were at-risk types and could've been in similar situations to the prostitutes. Those most like Kendra Gibbons. Over the first few days of reading, he tossed a dozen of the cases – the drug-related killings, women who were older than fifty, women killed in office settings. He booted the domestic violence cases that hadn't been successfully prosecuted. Then there were the shooting victims, the African

American, Asian, and Latina victims, blunt trauma cases, vehicular homicide, and an apparent poisoning. That pared the number down to thirty-seven dead Caucasian women, between the ages of eighteen and forty-six, who'd been killed by stabbing or strangulation by currently unknown assailants and had been found either intact or partially or fully dismembered over the past sixteen and a half years.

It was a lot to contend with, a formless sea of information. But out of that formlessness, a shape had begun to emerge. Behr couldn't recognize it with his conscious mind, but he felt it floating at the edges of his perception like a ghostly figure. There was a term for what he was looking at, but not one he was yet prepared to utter . . .

That's when he realized the sun had gone down. And that he hadn't fed Trevor for a while and Susan would be home from work soon, so he put the pages he was reading back into a file folder and got Trevor's jacket. The boy was his little mascot these past few weeks, staying with him during the day while he worked instead of going off to day care. It could be distracting once in a while, but it was money saved and good time spent.

'All right, buddy, time to go home,' Behr said, rubbing his face in an attempt to wipe off what he'd been reading. 'Let's go see Mommy.'

* * *

Susan was just taking off her coat when Behr walked in, Trevor in one arm, a bag of takeout food in the other.

'Hey, babe,' he said.

'My men,' she said, smiling and taking Trevor for hugs and kisses.

'I got Boston Market,' he said.

'Who's better than you?' she asked.

'Hell if I know.'

Later, they lay in bed, the sheets bunched up between their feet, she in her pajamas, and he in his clothes. They had begun fooling around, but she'd pulled away.

'There's something about the routine of this that's starting to make me feel cheap, Frank,' she said.

'That's not the intention,' he told her.

'Yeah, but it's getting to be the result.'

'You know that's not the way I see you. Not the way I feel about us,' he said.

'Okay.'

He was moments away from that inner alarm binging and causing him to get up and return to his endless cases of gore and pain when she spoke.

'What are we doing, Frank?'

'You mean why do you two live here and I don't?'

'Yeah.'

The silence between them was his only answer. Then she spoke.

'I don't know much, beyond the obvious, about why your marriage failed. But from what you've told me, your ex said it was because you just couldn't get out from under the sadness. The grief. The misery.'

Behr had too much to say about all that she'd just brought up, so he simply nodded in the dark.

'And has that changed yet?'

'Hold on. You don't think my life is different? With you? And him?'

'Your life is different, but you still haven't gotten out from under.'

She was right. He wasn't out from under. Somehow solving this case and claiming the reward represented a new start. But for now he was still caught in a riptide of crap, and like an experienced ocean swimmer he was swimming parallel to shore until it let go. But he didn't say any of that to her. He couldn't. Instead he swung his feet to the floor and started getting dressed.

TWENTY-ONE

THE AIR INSIDE the garage already has the close, shrine-like feel he yearns for. Everything out in the world is too clean now. That's the problem with this age. It is all plastic and sterile. *But not in here.* In this space the air smells of sacred fluids: urine, blood, and semen. They will run together onto the floor. Some of them already do, darkening the concrete. It is elemental.

When they arrived, he had pulled his car in, unloaded Cinnamon, and moved the car back out. Now it is dark and quiet inside, a moment of calm. He goes to the sofa, which is covered by an old blanket, and stands over her. Her hands and feet are bound. Her jacket, shirt, and brassiere lie on the floor along with her shoes, socks, and jeans. He'd cut those off immediately. She wears only panties, pale and pink colored. Outside, the world carries on, people walking around clinging to the myth of escape, desperately seeking the safe, the happy, the normal. But reality is inside, here, between them.

It is time . . .

escape, desperately seeking the safe, the happy, the
normal. But realities made her... between them.
Big time.

TWENTY-TWO

*B*ODIES, AND PARTS *of bodies, intact and taken apart,
naked and partially clothed and bound and tied
and posed, some identified, some unidentified,
going back years and years and years surrounded him.*

Picture time for Behr. He'd pinned police department victim photos, both in stark black and white
and in lurid color, on bulletin boards and along the
walls of his office, and they were quickly becoming
plastered across the surfaces of his brain. Motel
rooms, wooded areas, roadsides, Dumpsters, a warehouse, a fifty-five-gallon drum, parks, including the
most recent find along the tree line of Northwestway.
That one was the most bizarre tableau and seemed
to have been staged with great care.

Behr had run through the half dozen sets of photo
printer ink cartridges he'd picked up for the project.
He was aware that now, along with his time, he was

spending his own money combing cold cases, but so far none of the unidentified bodies announced themselves as Kendra Gibbons. He was also aware, painfully so, that he had nothing substantive that connected her to any of these past cases.

'Huh,' Behr said aloud, as he stood back and appraised the shots in total. He'd hung them in chronological order, and he had begun to recognize a very clear difference in them, a progression, starting about six years back. The difference was in the quality and in the impact of the photos. At first he ascribed it to the advent of digital photography and the new, sharper lenses that came along with it. But he soon realized the distinctions went beyond that. There was a skill level at play, lighting-wise and compositionally, even in the overall density of image, in the more recent photos that far outstripped the prior ones. Behr moved closer and noticed a tiny photo credit in most of the recent batch that read 'D. Quinn.' He stepped back again and understood what made the difference.

When looking at crime scenes, Behr had been trained to concentrate on the edges. The investigator can't ignore the central piece – the body, or the blown safe, or the looted car – but too many investigators got sucked into that element. It was only natural. It was, after all, the reason for the investigation. But the mind tended to become overwhelmed by it. It caused a type of tunnel vision that shut out other pertinent information. So one was advised to instead focus on the periphery, where a pen might've been touched or a drinking glass used, or a bottle or a footprint or a tool might've been left by the criminal. Behr realized that the pictures of the more recent scenes seemed to be shot with this aesthetic. The bodies were in the photos, of course, and they were central, but they weren't dead center in the frame, and the surrounding spaces were included in a highly detailed manner. Behr stared and studied the more recent batch for hours. He pulled up a chair and continued. He didn't see anything that helped. He knew he might not for a long time, if ever. But at least he knew there was a chance.

TWENTY-THREE

*S*ERIAL KILLER.

Behr woke with the words in his head, the ones he had been unable to utter to himself the day before.

A serial killer of women.

He'd done his early-morning running and rehab – exercises with a thick band of rubber that caused the tissue and joint of his damaged shoulder to burn like napalm – and now stood in front of the grisly photo tableau that, along with the case files he'd been reading, told him that it was so. Whether or not Kendra Gibbons had met a similar fate, he had no idea. And he felt plenty foolish about it, because though he'd worked murders, he was no dedicated homicide cop. Then there was the fact that no one else, neither police nor journalists, had made the claim. He was alone on this. But it was in his head now and he couldn't ignore it. That's when the phone rang. It was the county forensics lab.

'I'm calling about the DNA sample that was submitted on the Northwestway Park body,' a technician said.

'Yes,' Behr said, feeling a jolt of anticipation about the result.

'It came back nonpositive.'

'Not a match,' Behr said. Disappointment at the lack of an answer mixed with relief that Kendra wasn't officially dead.

'No match,' the technician repeated.

'Thanks,' Behr said and hung up. He gathered up the case files into a tall stack and began looking for a cardboard box.

'Welcome to the land of the dead,' Jean Gannon said, pulling off a pair of blue elbow-length rubber gloves with a snap. The basement mortuary area of Scanlon Brothers Funeral Home was bright white tile, stainless-steel sinks, yellow tubing, and shining oversized refrigerators. The space was cool and immaculate, with the sharp tang of preservative chemicals in the air.

'How's it going, Jean?' Behr said.

'You know what they say . . . .'

'Business just keeps rolling in?' he said.

She nodded and draped a sheet over the body of an elderly woman that she'd been working on and turned back toward him. Jean looked five years younger than she had the last time Behr had seen her and he told her so.

'Thanks. For me?' she said, lifting a supermarket poinsettia plant off the top of the cardboard box in Behr's arms.

'Office warming,' he said.

'Everything changes, huh – none of the usual treats?' she asked, thinking of the customary liquor and chocolates.

'Someone down at coroner's is the beneficiary of those. Real surprise to find you gone.'

'It was time,' she said. 'Even though I hadn't been there forever, it was starting to feel like it. I was surprised that's what happened on account of getting into it so late in life, but it did.' Jean had only gone to med school and begun her career after a life as a mother and a wife and a marriage that had crashed and burned.

'So the new job agrees with you.'

'It's still wall-to-wall stiffs. But the good part, besides playing with makeup half the day, is that most of 'em get to me when they should. You know? Occasionally there's a young mom or dad, or you know, a kid.' She winced. 'But it's mostly old folks whose time has come. Not at all like working at the other place. Down there it just smelled like . . .'

'Hamburger?'

She nodded. 'I just couldn't seem to wash it off of me.'

Behr had a momentary pang of guilt over what he was there for as he put the box down on her desk.

'Well, I'm sorry for what I brought then,' he said. 'I tried to lay off you when I heard you'd quit, but I couldn't.'

'It's not the same when it's on paper.' She shrugged, pointing to a chair. 'Sit. Wait.'

An hour and fifteen minutes and two cups of coffee passed with some nods and murmurs of recognition from her as she reviewed the case files. Behr figured she'd worked some of the bodies over the years when she was with the coroner's. Finally, Jean closed up the folders and removed her reading glasses. She leaned back and stretched in her desk chair.

'You are a messenger of delight, aren't you?' she said.

'Nothing but,' Behr said. 'What does it say to you?'

'My opinion? If these are random kills, the world has officially gone to shit, and if this was done by one person, you're dealing with some kind of fucking monster.'

'Is that the clinical assessment then?' Behr said. 'Glad to see all that higher education put to use.'

'Hey, I calls 'em as I sees 'em,' she said. 'Seriously, what's your interest with all this?'

He told Jean about the billboard and Kendra Gibbons and how he'd come to this point.

'Bit of a "Hail Mary," isn't it, Frankie?' she asked. 'But I guess that's you in a nutshell.'

He let that one pass before he said, 'Even though a lot of the details are different case to case, you see certain related factors like I do?'

She nodded. 'You know it wasn't exactly my bag, but there's at least a few, if not more, common elements to these.' She patted the stack of files.

'Is there any direction you can point me in?' he wondered.

She twirled a pen around her fingers and thought for a minute.

'Not me. But I know someone who may be able to help you,' Jean said, taking out her cell phone and scrolling her contacts. 'You may like her too. Most people are scared shitless of her, but you won't be. She's a criminal psychologist. From New York, relocated here a few years back. She's got experience with this stuff. Worked with the FBI and NYPD.'

'A profiler?' Behr asked.

'You could call her that.'

Jean dialed a phone number. 'Hi, Lisa? Jean Gannon here,' she began. 'Yeah. No, you heard correct. No longer with the office . . .' There was a pause and Jean laughed and said, 'I'm over at Scanlon Brothers, making 'em look pretty before they get planted.'

Jean listened for a moment, and then spoke. 'Look, I'm calling because my friend – he's an investigator on a case – could use your type of help. It's kind of a fun one.'

Jean listened again, pulling the phone away from her ear and covering the receiver. 'She's saying she's busy and doesn't really do this type of thing anymore.'

'So it's a no-go?' Behr asked.

Jean shook her head and whispered, 'Blah, blah, blah. It's the same shit every time. She'll do it.'

'Yeah, no, listen, I hear you. But this is a really good guy, my friend. You'll like him. Just give it a look. For me, all right?'

Gannon nodded, then handed Behr the phone.

'Frank Behr here,' he said.

'Lisa Mistretta, nice to meet you over the phone,' a forthright voice with a hint of an East Coast accent said back. 'What do you got?'

'A bunch of murders that I think are related.'

'We'll see about that. You got case files?'

'A mess of 'em,' Behr said.

'If the files are too big to e-mail, send me hard copies along with a CD-ROM.'

'I'll compress 'em and send 'em,' Behr said.

'Fine. Send the hard copies anyway, please. I don't like fucking with my printer if I can avoid it. The thing has it out for me.'

'Sure,' Behr said. 'How long before we have a follow-up meet or whatever?' Considering the volume of material he was sending, he imagined it'd be at least a week.

'Well, I won't know that until I see what you send,' she said.

'Of course,' Behr said. 'And – ' He looked to Jean, handing her back the phone. 'She hung up. You want to give me her info?'

Jean scribbled down an address and an e-mail and handed it to him.

'Really appreciate it, and owe you one, Jean,' he said, standing.

'Yeah, yeah.'

'Why are people scared of her?' Behr wondered on his way to the door.

'You'll see.'

TWENTY-FOUR

I'LL NEVER DIE.

The idea flashes in his mind.

No one who experiences this ever can.

A power surges through him like high-voltage electricity.

He's spent the special time with Cinnamon, three hours' worth, right after her end. There is something magical in the silence, in the utter void of her being. As always, when it is done, he is totally used up. A deep sense of exhaustion and peace creeps up through the soles of his feet and spreads through him. He covers her, there on the floor, and it is time to leave the garage. Cinnamon has to go through this next part alone.

He knows too much about it. The Latin words: *rigor, algor, livor mortis.* Her tissue will stiffen until her body is like a board, literally like stacked cordwood. She will cool, until she is as chill as the air, as cold as the concrete floor, but somehow feeling even colder to the touch. And her blood will pool in the lower planes of her body until the skin of her back is a beautiful speckled reddish purple. This is a time he prefers to be away, inside, eating a good meal, drinking tea, regathering his energies, poring over his books and planning for the work ahead. By the next night or so, when he goes back to her, she'll be soft and supple once again. Then he will have his hours, perhaps a few days because it is winter, to finish the project before it is time to move her. He's waited too long in the past, before he'd known better, only to see black flies and seething larvae boil over a ruined piece. He won't make a mistake like that again. By now he knows exactly what he's doing.

TWENTY-FIVE

'YOU READY FOR me? 'Cause if you're ready, I'm ready.' It was Lisa Mistretta on his voice mail.

'That was quick,' Behr said when he called her back. It had been a day and a half.

'It was only a review, how fucking long should it take?' she asked, some amusement in her voice.

'Okay, where and when?' Behr asked.

She actually answered this time before hanging up.

'My place, at eleven, same address you sent the stuff.'

The house was a tidy brick job in Broad Ripple off East 61st, behind the bars and restaurants. Behr parked in the driveway in back of an amber-colored Infiniti SUV and could see Mission-style furniture in the living room beyond the house's picture window.

But standing in the doorway of the detached garage, an aluminum coffee cup in one hand, the other cocked on a curvaceous hip, was a woman with a mane of black hair. She wore tight jeans and a black turtleneck.

'This way, buddy,' she said. She only went about five foot five, but her attitude was much bigger. 'So you're Behr?' she said, sticking out her hand.

'And you're Ms. Mistretta,' he said. Her grip was firm, her palm cool and smooth.

'Call me Lisa or you'll remind me of my old lacrosse coach. The guy was half a fucking perv.'

'Frank.'

'Okay. Come on in, Behr.'

The car evidently lived outside, because the garage had been converted into a comfortable office. The concrete floor was covered with a plush white rug. A gray sofa and black leather chair offset a long brushed-steel desk topped by a high-tech computer. The shelves along the walls were lined with books, mostly clinical texts and medical journals. The only bright spots in the room were an orange beanbag that sat next to a low coffee table piled with the case files Behr had sent her, and Mistretta herself.

'Sit,' she said, pointing to the couch, and then curled up on the beanbag.

'So, thanks for this,' Behr said.

She shrugged. ''S no problem. I'm glad to. My feet were going to sleep and I didn't even realize it,' she said.

'How'd you end up out here?' Behr asked.

'Indy?' she said. 'New York – my New York anyway – became a fucking nightmare.'

'Because of the work?'

'Because of the work, and other things. Then about four years back, my husband got a chance to relocate here. So we came.'

'How's that working for you?' Behr asked.

'Working pretty good. Winters aren't bad. Nice house. Not much traffic. The boys are a little boring. No offense,' she said.

'None taken.'

'Though you look like *you* might have possibilities with a few drinks in you.' She pointed a thumb at a trio of bottles – high-end Scotch, vodka, and tequila – that rested on a silver tray atop a credenza.

'Not sure you want to go there,' Behr said. 'And you said "husband."'

'I think we still had stuff in the moving boxes when that was done. You know they say some marriages are made in heaven?'

'Yours made in hell?'

'On Earth, anyway,' she said. 'He got a girlfriend, I kept the house. Fuck him. And how do you know where I'm willing to go?'

'Okay,' Behr said, smiling despite himself. 'Can we talk about my case, such as it is, and save the rest of it for later?'

'All right, stick-in-the-mud. Your *case*, sure,' she said. 'You know I charge a buttload of money for this ordinarily.'

'I'm aware,' Behr said, wondering if he'd success-fully kept the twinge of pain he felt off his face.

'But I haven't had a juicy one in a while. And I've missed it more than I thought. So I'll go pro bono.'

'Thanks,' he said. 'How about this: if I score at the end of this, I'll take care of you?'

'What score?' she asked. Behr told her about Kendra Gibbons, that he wasn't out to catch some killer, that he didn't have definitive proof that she hadn't just run off, but had started to wonder if she'd met a gruesome fate similar to those of some other victims, and that there was a reward in the case of an arrest and conviction.

'Who's that patron saint of lost causes, Saint What's-his-face?' she wondered out loud as she cocked her head with a look that seemed to calculate the odds of his endeavor succeeding. 'Anyway, it's a deal,' she said, and put her hand on a thin folder at the top of the stack. 'Two of these are bogeys.'

'Really?'

'Yeah.' She nodded and flung the offending folder into a wire trash basket. 'One, even though it was a knifing, lacks the control element.'

127

'But I thought—'

'Yeah, yeah, it's an easy assumption to make. The other – do you even care or do you want to trust me? It's not related.'

'Okay,' Behr said, feeling he *could* trust her. His eyes tracked across to the low table holding the remaining files.

'The other twenty-four, however, are, in my clinical opinion, related,' she said, a more serious and professional tone in her voice now.

'Twenty-four?' Behr asked. He'd handed over the files on all thirty-seven unsolved murders of Caucasian female victims who had died by cutting or stabbing or had been dismembered.

'I separated by one more distinguishing factor,' Mistretta said. 'Eleven weren't blondes. The rest were. You'd need to know to look for diaminotoluene in the chemical report.'

'What's that, a chemical in—'

'Yeah, in hair dye. It means some of the victims would have appeared blond even though driver's licenses and other records might suggest they weren't. So two bogeys, and eleven brunettes. That brings it to twenty-four blondes.'

'Really? Shit . . .' Behr said, trying to formally accept what he'd previously just entertained.

'I don't know how many cases you were pulling from, but you did a hell of a job with the knitting here.'

The compliment was diminished by the reality of it. *Twenty-four women. Sixteen years.*

'So,' Behr began, 'a serial killer . . .'

Lisa nodded. Her rigid shell softened for a moment.

'Yeah. Well, a signature killer, more accurately, engaged in serial predation. A serial killer is two or more, by any means. But we use the term 'signature' because even though the MO can change from crime to crime, due to the specific and random circumstances of each act, the key element of the crime that gives the killer the satisfaction is the same even when the little details present slightly differently. There can also be an evolution with these guys – a slowly changing style. But that signature element stays the same. That's what you intuited in these cases.' She took a sip of coffee while Behr absorbed it.

'You learn your stuff at Quantico, Professor?' Behr asked.

'BSU? I've *taught* those pussies,' she said.

'So the element is the control,' Behr said, almost thinking out loud. 'The evidence of binding . . .'

Mistretta nodded.

'And the way the bodies are being found, the dismemberment?' Behr asked. 'Even though they're different every time—'

'Right. The presentation changes, but not the fact that there *is* a presentation. Even though the early kills seemed like they were discovered, he didn't fail at hiding them. What you figured out is that they were just less brashly placed.'

'He's becoming more direct.'

'Yeah.'

'I read the FBI *Crime Classification Manual*, trying to determine whether he was an organized or disorganized personality. I keep going back and forth,' Behr said.

'Right,' she said. 'He's organized, but moving into a disorganized state,' she said.

'Didn't know that was a possibility,' Behr said.

'It is.'

'And at first I had him as an anger-excitation killer,' Behr said. 'But then I started to consider—'

'Sadistic-lust.'

'Right. But there wasn't real evidence of sexual activity. No semen, no DNA at all in fact.'

'Well, it's always anger. And it's always sexual with these bastards, even if the act isn't ... standard,' she went on. 'You familiar with the Psychopathy Checklist– Revised?'

'Yeah,' Behr said. The PCL-R was a twenty-question test devised by a social scientist that gauged narcissism, pathological lying, lack of remorse, absence of empathy, all the delightful qualities that predicted sociopaths and their proclivity to reoffend to such a degree of accuracy that prisons and law enforcement had been using it for the past decade and a half.

'High score of forty, and anything over what – twenty-something? – indicates a psychopath,' Behr said.

'Twenty-nine,' she said. 'And shit, I'd go a lot lower than that. But applying the scale is more of an art than a science. Most of the time.'

'But in this case?'

'In this case our guy' – Mistretta pointed to the files – 'he'll have checked off every damn box. Doesn't matter what test you use – the Minnesota Multiphasic, the MCMI-III, fucking Rorschach – he'll be an over-achiever. And honor rollers like him, it's like they're emotionally deaf. The part of the brain where we create compassion or sorrow – his will be a flatline. Just shut off or missing. Show this guy a picture of a dead kid and then one of a Christmas ham, there will be no differ-ence in his physiological response, his heart rate, his breathing. It takes extreme stimulation to even register with them, and that's what allows them to do what they do. And sexually . . . well, it's a big fucking problem. For instance, this guy? He's a picquerist. You familiar with that term?'

'Using a knife or blade as a . . .' Behr began.

'Yeah, as a stand-in for the penis,' she continued. 'And he could be climaxing from the stabbing.'

'Which is why there's no DNA?'

'Could be *a* reason,' she said. 'But the way the bodies are being found is obscuring that. See, all this psycho shit can make crime scenes misleading, especially for an overworked police force.'

'It's why the press hasn't picked it up,' Behr said.

'Maybe,' she said. 'The crimes are pretty spread out, time-wise.'

'And location-wise,' Behr added.

'Right,' she said. 'Some of the bodies weren't found for a long, long time afterward. Some were found right away. It obscures the pattern. Some haven't been found at all, I'd guess.'

'You think there are more,' Behr said.

'Well, I don't know, of course. But we have to assume.'

'Right . . .' Behr said, and then silence fell at the possibility, the probability. After a while they went on talking about various other aspects of the killings, but Behr had temporarily run out of questions until he processed what she'd told him.

Finally, she pushed herself up off the beanbag and went to the corner of her desk where a pile of books rested. 'These are for you to borrow.' Behr got up and took a look at the spines and saw words and phrases like *slay, kill, understanding murder, landscape of evil*, and *killer's mind*.

'Some light reading,' he said.

'Right.' She smiled.

'If I showed you suspects, could you help me determine if they looked good for this?' Behr asked.

'I've been known to. I could try,' she said. 'Do you have suspects?'

'No,' Behr said.

'You got police access to a suspect pool?'

'We'll see,' Behr said, taking out his phone and sending a text to Breslau: '*I need to meet.*'

'I wish you luck, buddy, because these guys don't stop until they're locked up or dead. And it's not the threat of being locked up that ever slows 'em down either. In fact, these dreamboats do real well in prison. They're front-page celebrities inside and they spend their sentence reliving every moment of every single crime. They relish the memories, *luxuriate* in them. Replaying it all is almost as much fun for them as the doing.'

Behr absorbed this, picked up the books, and turned to her. 'Going back to his signature. It's not just the dismemberment, it's this . . . reassembly. He needs them to come apart so he can put them back together, his way, according to his vision.'

'Yeah, I'd say it's the source of his feelings of power,' she said, nodding.

'So I'll follow up with you on this.'

'You fucking better!' she said, and hit him with a smile that he felt in his knees.

TWENTY-SIX

FINALLY, THE THROBBING is too much to bear. He's been lying awake for hours, staring at the ceiling in the dark. There will be a full sleepless night of it ahead of him if he doesn't do something about it. In a controlled rush of motion he swings his feet and gets out of bed. He puts on a sweatshirt over his pajamas, and slippers. That's when Margaret rolls over.

'What's wrong, dear?' she asks.

'Nothing.'

'Where are you going?'

'Think I might've left my soldering iron plugged in out in the workshop,' he lies. 'Gonna go check.'

'You and your projects.'

His wife rolls back over and goes to sleep. He looks at her sleeping form. *What does she know?* She's not a bright woman. *Or is she, but keeping it to herself?*

He moves off through the darkened house and

134

makes his way downstairs. He is in a hurry now, as he exits out the kitchen door, steps briefly through the cold night air, and lets himself into the garage. He closes the door behind him and stands there in the dark, sensing her, his mind traveling back to the moment a day before . . .

He'd clicked on the light on his workbench, then slapped Cinnamon lightly on the cheek. She'd been crying and had passed out, but she roused, looking up at him through wet eyes. The tears had caused her makeup to run into black smudges on the tops of her cheeks. He was naked, and her eyes took in his body. He interpreted what he saw in them, and it was horror.

'I'll take the tape off if you don't make any noise, Danielle,' he offered. Danielle Crawley. That was Cinnamon's name. Her driver's license said so. He savored this basic piece of information.

After a moment she nodded. He took a few steps toward the radio on the back corner of the utility table and turned it on. It was tuned to a classic rock station, and 'Magic Carpet Ride' played loudly. He'd used egg-crate foam, insulation, and other baffling materials when he'd fitted out the garage, so it wasn't really necessary, but he didn't mind the music when he worked and he'd been through it enough times to know how likely it was that she'd scream when he removed the tape.

Danielle Crawley didn't though. She just looked at him, breathing panicky breaths through lips that were reddened from the adhesive. He kneeled near her, the concrete floor cold, hard, and rough against his skin.

'How are we doing, Danielle?' he asked.

She didn't answer.

'I said, "How are we doing?"' he repeated.

'Please let me go,' she said.

'Ahh,' he said in response. He put his hand on her flank, and felt her shudder and inch away as much as she could despite the binding. His eyes roved over her body, pallid, white, and unmarked except for a cluster of moles at her abdomen, and a tiny faded shamrock tattoo on her right calf.

'The ropes are hurting my wrists and ankles,' she said.

'No one is exempt from pain and suffering. Nothing is,' he explained.

How had he come to know this?

He thought back to when he was young. All he'd wanted then was to know God, to touch His existence. The desire had pulsed inside him. But he'd sit in the church between Grandfather and Mother and nothing would happen. He'd listen and speak and kneel and sing, but he knew he was being ignored, for he was alone. He knew that He existed, because everyone else around him seemed to be able to touch Him or at least believe. As a boy he would try it in his room too, kneeling and praying, but He who had caused everything to be wasn't there either.

So he'd gone out on his own and tried to master life, in the woods behind his house. He had set snares and caught things. Squirrels, chipmunks, birds, stray cats. But he had failed miserably in his labors, and only succeeded in bringing death. Whitening bones, and skins tacked to pieces of bark and drying under rock salt, were all that remained. He was being mocked for his efforts. A jealousy rose inside him over His power and it consumed him. Day by day he learned the eternal truth: that everything had a miserable end.

The final form of the lesson was a robin chick that had fallen from its nest. Seized of an idea, he'd bolted to the shed and retrieved a yellow can of Ronsonol. The little bird burned in a glowing ball of blue. He'd hardly call them flames. The tiny creature's beak triangled open, calling out with barely any sound, not so much in pain but indignation. That won him over. He had a momentary pang and wondered about extinguishing the fire, seeing if the chick survived, or at least ending its pain with his heel or a rock. But instead he stood there and watched for another two or three minutes, transfixed, while the fire advanced and the bird's downy feathers and delicate skin, then bones and organs broke down, until the thing was just a loose gelatinous ball. Eventually he'd kicked it off the trail under some low brush and never went back to look at it again and came away knowing he did have a power, the power to govern that end, to administer it and to feel the clarity that came along with it.

That's when the song on the radio had changed to a British band from the eighties, and it brought him back from his reverie. He looked at Cinnamon again.

'Tell me about this,' he said, touching the tattoo of the shamrock.

'Just something stupid I did when I was in school,' she said. He thought about that for a while, as she looked at him. It seemed they were both considering all of the moments and events in her life that had brought her here.

'You must mean everything to someone,' he said, with appreciation.

'No,' she said, some pleading in her voice.

'To your family. Someone . . .'

'Not really.' The calm they could show was admirable.

'Well, you mean everything to me. Now.'

'Thank you.'

He took off his glasses and set them aside.

'You're nervous. Are you wet?'

'I don't know,' she said.

He reached out and pulled the panties away and felt between her legs as her body shook and recoiled.

'Ah, you are.'

'Let me go, motherfucker,' she said, low. There was strength in her voice, but it was thwarted and futile.

His gaze came to rest on her nakedness. He took in the light hair at her crotch that just touched the place of opening, of confusion and mystery, that tabernacle of life. When he was no longer a boy, he knew he was capable of bringing life, together with a woman. But to what end? It wouldn't get him any closer to God. He felt the love and hate surge inside him.

'What are those?' she asked, looking up at the hooks, connected to an iron bar, suspended from the ceiling.

'It's called a gambrel. You don't need to worry about that,' he assured her.

'Why are you doing this?' she asked, her ability to control herself diminishing. 'Why did you take me?'

'It's not something to cry about, it's just something that happened,' he said.

He picked up a wooden-handled steel awl and ran it down her sternum to the soft skin of her belly and began pressing.

'You're hurting me,' she said.

'I know.'

Then he put his mouth on hers. She didn't resist, but merely submitted. It wasn't remotely satisfactory.

'That kiss wasn't sincere.'

'Please,' she said.

He put his mouth back on hers, cutting off her words, but this time he bit down and yanked his face away without letting go. He spit out pulpy chunks of her flesh. She was screaming now, but the sound was wet and indistinct, on account of her lips being gone . . .

He can't wait anymore and flicks on the lights and sees it there, resting on a plate on the corner of his workbench: Cinnamon's head. Her eyes, lids hanging open, eyeballs beginning to go soft, mouth fleshy, the remainders of her torn lips pursed, and that streaked blond hair still shining, though it is starting to fall out.

He feels the urgency in his pajama pants anew and loosens the drawstring, letting them slide down to his thighs, and then he moves toward her head in order to relieve it.

Later, he slips back into bed. Margaret is sleeping heavily and doesn't move. He stares up into the darkness and knows he'll be looking for a new project in no time.

TWENTY-SEVEN

I T WAS A MISTY morning in the fields near Elwood, home of the Cross Creek Conservation and Gun Club, the location where Gary Breslau had texted Behr to meet. The thermometer said forty degrees, but a moist, bone-chilling breeze made it feel at least twenty degrees colder than that as Behr stepped out of his car. Barks of 'Pull!' and the popping of skeet guns filled the air.

Behr asked for Breslau in the small clubhouse and was told what field he was on and given a set of earplugs. Rolling the bits of foam into cylinders, Behr stuffed them into his ears as he walked past a man holding the leashes on a pair of young springer spaniels getting trained to the gun. He continued on toward the end of the skeet range, where he arrived in time to see Breslau, dressed like something out of the Upland Hunting page in a Cabela's catalog, finish off a clean double.

'Nice,' Behr said, as Breslau turned and broke his gun, sending the spent shell casings flying over his shoulder in a curling cloud of gun smoke. An old-timer in a blaze orange hat and vest who was holding the skeet release switch drifted off a ways for a cigarette.

'Seventeen for twenty. I'm pulling off my follow-through,' Breslau said and shrugged, not particularly pleased or displeased with the effort. 'What do you want?'

'A password.'

'To what?'

'Your bank account,' Behr said. 'To the Department's criminal index, what do you think?'

'Why?' Breslau asked.

'For my Gibbons case.'

'We don't give civilians access to that. Liability reasons.'

'C'mon, I need it.'

'Yeah? I need things too. Like back rubs and blow jobs. Should we get out our lists?'

'How about I'll shoot you for it?'

Breslau gave Behr a look. 'One time around?'

'That's right. I top your last round, you give me a password.'

Breslau weighed the offer for a moment, an amused half smile on his lips. 'You don't top it, you get out of my face,' Breslau said.

'Fair enough,' Behr answered. 'Do I go rent a gun?'

'Use mine,' Breslau said, passing over the still-warm Browning Citori 20-gauge over-and-under with perfectly polished stock and gleaming barrels. Behr recognized it as a $2,500 firearm. It practically floated in his hands.

He dug in his coat for a pair of sunglasses, and Breslau handed him a box of shells, which he dumped in his pocket before stepping to the line. The old-timer drifted back, ready to operate the thrower.

'Pull,' Behr said, after sighting up on the high house, and commenced shooting at a pair of clay pigeons that flew by at crossed angles. He promptly missed the first, but corrected and picked up the second, eliciting an intrigued snort from Breslau. Behr rotated counterclockwise through the stations, powdering some of the disks, while others he just nicked and cracked. He finished his round, having missed numbers one and twelve, broke the smoking Browning, and handed it back to a sour-faced Breslau.

'Eighteen for twenty,' Breslau said. 'Goddamnit, Behr, don't you know it's bad form to outshoot your host?'

Behr shrugged. 'Blame it on the well-balanced gun.'

'All right,' Breslau said and indicated a picnic table behind them where his gun case rested. They went

143

and sat down. 'What have you found out that you need this?' Breslau asked.

'That it involves a signature killer,' Behr said. His words sounded stark and half ridiculous in the bucolic sporting environment. But Breslau didn't react to what Behr had said like it was crazy. In fact, he didn't seem surprised at all, he just sat there, and that told Behr plenty.

'You already know,' Behr uttered. The 'you' implied the department, not just Breslau.

'Know that it's a bad time to be a Northeastside prostie? Yeah, well *we're* not gonna take out a billboard announcing it,' Breslau said.

'That's why you're helping me on this . . .' Behr said, the realization settling on him. He'd been used by the department before, at times without his knowledge, other times more willingly. At least this time there might be something tangible in it for him.

'Tell me what you have,' Breslau said.

'Looking at everything you gave me, it goes back years, and based on the dates, the killer's cycle is accelerating.'

'Crap.' Breslau spat on the cold ground. 'You sound like you've been studying up.'

'I *have* been studying up.'

'What else do you know?'

'This killer would be classified as organized, with

elements of a disorganized profile. And the combination of the two is the most difficult to recognize, much less apprehend. I'm guessing it's why this hasn't been picked up in the press.'

'Right,' Breslau said.

'He's in the sadistic-lust category. And the guy is what's known as a picquerist. He uses knives and bladed instruments as a stand-in for his cock. Killing is sexual for him.'

'Like Jack the Ripper,' Breslau said.

'Yeah. In some ways. The only reason these guys stop is if they're caught or die. Once in a while they just burn out and cease their activities, and then they get away with it.'

'You're ruining my Saturday, Behr,' Breslau said.

'Believe me, it's ruined more than that for me,' Behr said.

'Use *my* ID and password,' Breslau said, writing it down on the cardboard flap of a shell box. 'That way I can keep track of where you've been in the system. Don't do anything over the line or you'll be on the other side of a firewall – and I'm not just talking about the database.'

'Got it,' Behr said.

'And don't *you* go to the press with this,' Breslau cautioned.

'I won't,' Behr answered, 'and I think you know

that.' Behr got up and dusted off his pants. 'But, Breslau, whether I say anything or not, you know it's only a matter of time until this story comes out.'

'I know.' Breslau sighed. After a moment he put his earphones back on, took his spot at the first station, and loaded the Browning.

Behr heard 'Pull!' and then the double pop of Breslau's gun as he walked back toward his car.

TWENTY-EIGHT

*H*E'S FINALLY FOUND *the spot*.

The long drives have paid off. The last few nights have passed in a state of calm anticipation. He's driven the city in the early evening on the way home from work, as the end-of-day traffic dissipated, looking for just the right location to finish it. And then he'd seen it. Or did it call to him? Long, low, black, and hulking. He's passed it hundreds of times – the corporate campus of a drug company that has gone under. It stands darkened and abandoned now, waiting to be used. He douses his headlights and noses his car down the lane leading into and around the complex, through parking lots that are empty save for white lines marking the stalls no longer filled by workers' vehicles.

He goes all the way around to the back of the main building. It too is darkened. He parks and makes his way to the rear doors on foot. He doesn't expect anyone to be inside for any legitimate purpose, but it is the kind of location that groups of kids find their way into to drink and smoke, for all kinds of foul reasons. But he tries the doors and they are locked tight, the windows unbroken. He sees no security cameras either, just empty mounts. Back in his car, he pauses by the man-made lagoon in the front of the complex, its fountain sitting dormant. The place looks like a stage, a pedestal, and he knows exactly how he is going to use it. The spot is going to work. It is going to be beautiful.

TWENTY-NINE

NAMES. A SWIRLING sea of them. Hundreds. Aliases. Criminal records. Warrants. Not a sea, a bottomless pool. A suspect pool, and Behr deep-dove it. Using Breslau's password, he had worked all through the weekend and into the following week and was able to search and cross-reference offenders with assaults against women, attacks on prostitutes, rapists, murderers, and all types of other delights. Toward the end of the week, Susan had gone out of town with Trevor for a long weekend to visit her folks in the suburbs of Chicago, something they did every month or so. She'd floated a halfhearted invitation to him. Behr had been up there a few times. It was one thing sitting in a La-Z-Boy next to her father, not much to say, during the summer while a Sox game was on every afternoon and her mother was cooing at the baby. But it wasn't baseball season and he was busy, so he stayed home printing reams of information and combing over name after name. He didn't let anything rule out a suspect other than death or lengthy incarceration during the period of the crimes. By the time he was done with his initial pass, the pile of paper stacked next to his desk reached from the floor to his thigh. He didn't wait. He jumped in. He pounded coffee and started making two piles: a 'who knows?' and a 'no way.' The 'no ways' got taller, but there were still a ton of candidates in the 'maybe' stack. He worked through Thursday night, Friday, slept three hours Friday night, and kept pounding until Saturday afternoon, plagued by the thought that maybe this killer wasn't among the records he was searching, or maybe had no arrest record at all, when he finally passed out again.

Waking up in the dark, Behr didn't know what time, or even day, it was for a moment. He shook his head and looked at the clock and saw it was 8:30 Saturday night. He brewed himself a double-strength pot of coffee that smacked him in the face and sat down to his desk, where his 'suspects' now awaited him. There were several dozen of them – representing days, if not weeks, of background checks and other investigative work to winnow them down – but one name jumped out from all the rest: Jerold Allen Prilo. It wasn't by some advanced investigative technique or intuitive genius that Behr got to this idea. It was much simpler. Jerold Allen Prilo was already a convicted murderer.

Behr remembered the case. Five years earlier a twenty-one-year-old girl named Mary Beth Watney, who was not retarded but was borderline incompetent based on her low IQ, had become a fixture in her local bar – a place called the Wishing Well that had a pool table along with some old video game machines and a dartboard in the back. Behr had been there, and besides being on the other side of town, it wasn't very different from the Trough, Gene Sasso's place.

One spring afternoon a long-haul trucker who lived in the area stopped in and was seen playing a game of pool with young Mary Beth Watney. He left first but stayed in the parking lot, according to surveillance cams that showed her leave the bar next, to converse with, and walk out of frame with a waiting Prilo.

Apparently the two had gone back to the house where Prilo was living with his girlfriend, who was also a long-haul driver, away on a run at the time. They had drunk whiskey and had sex and that's where the story broke down. Prilo had said it was consensual and rough by request, and that though it had gotten out of hand and she might have been injured, the girl had left on foot afterward and it was the last he'd seen of her. Watney's body, cut to pieces, wasn't found until weeks later, down south, in an escarpment below Weed Patch Hill in the Knobs. By then Prilo was in Arizona dropping off a load of pipe before picking up a consignment of sheet metal, which he hauled to Washington State and dropped off, before picking up a load of lumber, which he drove back to Indiana. The police were waiting for him when he arrived.

The prosecutor's version of events included plying a mentally disabled girl with alcohol, rape, and a vicious beating with fists and foreign objects that left the walls and ceiling in need of repainting, which Prilo had done, before the calm disposal of the body. The problem was there was no *proof* that Prilo's version wasn't true. The body was found among large rocks. A fall amidst them could have caused some of the initial damage. There was further degradation of the corpse due to weather and animal activity. As for the dismemberment, the specifics of that came to light only later. The prosecutor was concerned about putting the case in front of a jury that might acquit the man outright.

Authorities scrambled to match assaults and murders along Prilo's trucking routes with the dates he'd driven them. There were missing-persons reports and concerned eyewitness accounts of young truck-stop hookers seen in Prilo's company and then never seen again. But once more, there was no concrete proof. The only thing law enforcement could agree on was that Prilo should be off the streets and locked away for the good of everyone.

Finally, with the help of a savvy defense lawyer, Prilo pleaded to sexual assault and no contest on manslaughter, not murder, and cut a deal. He fleshed out his version of consensual bondage and rough sex with the details that something had gone wrong with a 'choking game' they'd been playing and that he had panicked when the girl stopped breathing. He said he'd cut her up and tried to dispose of her body out of simple fear. When it came to suspicions over other seemingly related murders, authorities were unable to bring charges. Due to the condition of the body, prosecutors were frightened of a successful insanity defense with a short stay at a mental facility. So they made a deal under which Prilo instead got a seven- to nine-year term in maximum security, with consideration for the time and expense saved on a trial. The sex charge bought law enforcement the bonus of Prilo having to register as a sex offender for life. It was cold comfort to the family of the victim, and the general public. But the outcry simmered down after a few weeks had passed. There was nothing for the prosecutor to do about it, and by the time Prilo served three and a half years of his sentence and was kicked to a halfway house on the Near Westside of Indianapolis due to prison overcrowding, the case had been largely forgotten.

Until now, Behr thought.

Behr noticed, though, that there were a few vexing aspects in regard to Prilo as a suspect. Namely, two of the murders had occurred while Prilo was in jail. But they happened to be murders that were on the far edges of the pattern. Perhaps those killings were unrelated. He wasn't sure, but he knew someone who might be. He saw it was already 10:15, but he picked up his phone anyway.

'Hi, it's Frank Behr, not too late to call, I hope,' he said.

'Behr. What the fuck is up?' Lisa Mistretta said back.

THIRTY

'IT'S THE FERTILIZER,' he says. 'The smell will dissipate once I spread it.' Though he's sitting at the kitchen table across from Margaret his thoughts are elsewhere, out in his work space, where he'd just gotten started before she knocked to tell him that dinner was getting cold and to come inside.

'Fertilizer in the winter?' she asks, spooning the last of the green beans onto his plate. She's been complaining about the smell around the outside of the house.

'Yes, in the winter. The nutrients go down into the soil. You want to do it before the spring,' he says.

'I don't remember you doing it in the winter before—'

'Well, I have,' he says, and that is the end of it. He spent time on farms growing up, so she won't debate with him about things like that.

155

'Maybe I do remember, come to think of it,' she says.

They'd eaten the last of the flank steak, which was a little tough, stringy and flavorful, just the way he likes it. He doesn't care for filet or other soft cuts of meat. If he is eating flesh, he wants to know it.

Margaret turns from the sink and takes a folded piece of paper from the bulletin board. He recognizes it.

'What's this?' she asks as she unfolds it, crossing over to him. 'I found it in your jacket pocket.'

It is a preliminary sketch of his installation in Northwestway Park.

'Nothing, just a doodle,' he says.

'Are those supposed to be limbs?' she asks, concerned. 'And these resemble breasts . . .'

'No, no. I told you, it's nothing.'

'It looks familiar somehow . . .' she muses.

'Maybe I saw it on TV, on the news,' he says. 'That's why I drew it.' Then he snatches the page away from her and crumples it up.

Margaret shrugs and clears the last of the plates. Her back is to him as she bends over the sink.

What does she know? he wonders for the second time in the last little while. *Has she been in the garage?* he asks himself.

He stands up from the table, a wooden-handled

steak knife in his palm, and considers her back as he walks toward her. He stands there for a long time, feeling the knife's grip under his fingers, looking at her. Nothing could be easier, or clearer. But he isn't really moved to it. Finally, he sighs and drops the knife into the sink to be washed with the remaining utensils, and then he moves off to the closet and finds what he is looking for.

'Where are you going with your camera?' Margaret asks, the dish towel over her shoulder.

'Out to shoot a project I'm working on.'

'I want to see one of your projects one of these days,' she says.

'We've done that, haven't we?' he says, recalling a time many years ago, before they'd moved to this house, when she'd entered his darkroom unbidden, letting light in and exposing a batch of film he was processing. The utterly berserk way in which he'd reacted to that, the terror he'd seen in her, reminds him that going into his work space is not something she'll ever do again. She wouldn't dare. Even now he sees her gaze fall to her feet.

He pauses to straighten a portrait of the house that he's taken, a gelatin silver print matted directly onto a block of wood. Occasionally he shoots buildings or landscapes to give credibility to his claim of being a shutterbug and provide the ostensible reason he needs all his equipment and supplies.

'They're not very good anyway, just something I do,' he says. He is lying. His real projects are very good. They are amazing, unlike anything ever created by man.

'Wood or metal this time?' she asks.

'Well . . .' he says, when the phone rings.

'I'll get that,' she says.

'Thanks,' he says, and continues out to the garage.

He works with total concentration, and skill built upon thousands of hours of contemplation and hundreds of hours of experience. He can't stop and he can't bring himself to go to bed. He loses all track of time. He works in a coat, the heater in the garage turned off, the winter cold outside chilling the air. He moves his hands over her velvet flesh, her still-pliant viscera. He has his saws and sharp knives. The textures and aromas are almost overwhelming. He positions the elements into the perfect composition and he shoots the whole thing with his camera placed in just the right position. It will soon be time to go out.

THIRTY-ONE

'UH-OH, YOU'RE getting the *look*,' Mistretta said, as Behr walked inside. This time he entered her house, not her office.

'What look is that?' Behr wondered.

'The zombified look of a zombie hunter,' she said, and raised a rocks glass full of clear liquid over ice. 'Patrón Silver and a lime squeeze. Want one?'

'Sure,' he said.

She led him in across the small foyer, through the living room with the Mission furniture, and into a good-sized kitchen that had been recently renovated. Music was playing through both rooms.

'Is this . . . ?' he asked and pointed to the ceiling speakers.

'Wilco,' she said.

He took a seat on a stool at the center island while she went to a stainless-steel fridge-freezer and started putting his drink together.

'Glad I wasn't interrupting any important plans when I called,' he said.

'A whole lotta nothing on a Saturday night,' she said, turning around and sliding him his glass.

'Well, I'm outed on that front too,' Behr said.

'When's the last time you slept?'

'A whole night? It's been a while,' he allowed.

''S what happens,' she said and raised her glass. 'Why do you think I bailed?'

He raised his glass and they touched rims. They drank and the tequila hit him with a burn. She was wearing a sweater dress over tight leggings and those shearling boots that had caught on a few years back and never really went away. Her black hair had a bit more curl to it than it had the last time he'd seen her, and only her eyes and lips were touched with makeup. He caught a mini-cyclone of perfume and liquor off of her as she sat on the stool next to him. It was said the only subjects that mattered were sex and death, and she seemed to have them both well covered.

'So what do you got for me?' she asked.

He opened a yellow envelope and brought out the papers. It was background on two suspects – a violent man named Jose Aldes, with a history of assaults on women, and a man thought to be a serial rapist named Cowen, who had supposedly moved away to Wyoming nine months back. Neither man had apparently bound, killed, or mutilated. Prilo's records were also there beneath the rest. Behr wasn't testing her as much as trying to reclaim some objectivity.

They finished their drinks as she read through the Aldes file and tapped the edge of her glass, sending him for refills. Halfway through the next round she was coming to the end of the Cowen report when she murmured to herself, 'What is this shit?'

Behr waited as she moved on to the Prilo documents, and murmured, 'Oh . . . okay . . .'

She kept reading for a few more minutes, until their glasses were empty, and then got up. This time she did the refills, throwing the Aldes and Cowen paperwork in the garbage on her way. 'You don't mind, do you?' she asked.

Behr just shrugged. She leaned across the center island countertop so their heads were close together, bent over the Prilo history.

'This guy is a full-on beast,' she said.

'I know,' Behr said.

'What was with those others?'

'A selection of one is no selection,' he said.

'Right,' she said, smiling. 'But I saw your timeline notes on the Prilo pages. What about the kills when he was locked up? I don't like it.'

'I didn't like it either. But here . . .' He went back into the yellow envelope for the case files on the two

161

murders in question. 'Don't you think there are enough elements outside the pattern that those two could've been committed by someone else? Then Prilo resumed his activities once he got released?'

She read silently for a moment. Both of the victims were white females in the early half of their twenties. One of them had been discovered in a sealed fifty-five-gallon drum. She had been a grad student from Ohio. The other was found buried in a shallow depression near an access road in Wayne County. That one had been missing a leg and had not been positively identified.

'Well,' Mistretta said. 'Could be. They weren't showcased as much as the others. The evidence of binding and torture is there. But why have the other bodies been so easily found and these hidden?' she wondered aloud.

'Hell if I know. Maybe he was trying some new form of presentation,' Behr posited. 'Oh, and by the way, Mary Beth Watney was as blond as a wheat field.'

'Look, Farmer Brown, I like them for the same guy as the others. And the guy you're going with was in jail at the time, so I give him a loud buzzer.'

'Yeah, on paper,' Behr said. 'But with Prilo we've got a restraint-rage sex killer. Admitted and convicted. We've got mutilation. Operating in the same location. I mean, how many of these guys could there be in any given area?'

A dark look came to Mistretta's eyes. 'You'd be surprised. Also, you have to consider that maybe the guy isn't from the area and travels in, or worse, he's got no record.'

'Let's not go down those roads for now—'

'Besides, where's the DNA? Not a speck on these bodies. Prilo left DNA on Mary Beth Watney, which is why he confessed. Or vice versa.'

'There was no one else's DNA on these two vics that would rule Prilo out. None at all. I'm just saying, I'm gonna like him until I don't like him—' Behr stated.

This time she cut him off with the actual buzzer sound as she moved around the island next to him.

'No, no. Like him. A little,' Behr insisted.

She gave him the buzzer again. Louder.

'All right—'

Buzzer.

'You want to make a night of it, going back and forth like this?' Behr said, nearly laughing.

She shrugged. 'Wouldn't be the worst I'd spent in my life,' she said, and gave him a bit of a body check with her shoulder. 'Whoa, didn't move you an inch.'

'Little thing like you can't move me,' he said.

'Okay, big man . . .' she said in a mocking voice.

Their shoulders remained touching. Behr felt the

air in the room change and grow charged. Their faces met in the space between them, and they kissed. Her full lips pressed against his, and he tasted tequila on her aggressive, seeking tongue. He turned toward her, still seated on the tall stool, and she pressed into him. He felt her warm, full body in his arms. He wanted her, but even as he did he felt self-disgust at breaking promises that he had not spoken, but had made nonetheless. Stirring passion mixed with deep feelings of dread and guilt within him. After a moment he broke off and pulled back.

'Yeah, I've gotta stop. I'm in a thing,' he said.

'Ah, fuck me!' she said, her dark eyes sparkling like glitter. 'That kiss said maybe you're not so sure.'

'I'm sure. Sure I'm in it, maybe not so sure what it is. But I can't do this now.' Even as he said it, he felt regret, both for being there and at the idea of leaving. He'd put himself in a situation where remorse was behind every door, including the one to her bedroom.

'All right, Behr,' she said after a moment. 'I'll give you a free pass this time – even though you did get me revved up.'

'That's two of us who are revved,' he said.

Their breath returned to them, and the atmosphere in her kitchen lightened like that of a surfacing submarine.

'Can we still work this thing together?' Behr asked, gathering up his papers.

'Of course we can work it,' she said with a smile, 'we're not freshman lab partners, for fuck's sake!'

'Good,' he said.

'Leave this with me,' she said, putting her hand on the Prilo pages. 'I'm going to go back to the cases and next time we meet you're gonna really see what I can do.'

THIRTY-TWO

*I*T IS DONE.

Cinnamon is out of his life. She's been given back. He has released her to the world, and it is beautiful.

The silence was complete that night. There wasn't a frozen cricket chirping. He'd worked quickly and then he'd left the office park, stopping between pools of streetlights to pull strips of black tape off his license plate. Then he drove away into the darkness. There was nothing left in the space she had filled but relief. Everything inside him was like a well that had been pumped off, leaving a void, a soothing, relaxing void.

Drive straight home, he tells himself.

But he can already feel new pressure seeping in. It will rise and get more turbulent with each passing day and it will soon be roiling again.

Drive straight home, he tells himself again.

But he doesn't. Other won't allow it. Instead he drives to the wrong part of town, where the girls work late. He sees them out there on the corners as he passes by.

Are we already considering the next one?

He wonders at himself, and the thing that is inside him that seems to be pushing up and taking over. He thinks about that stupid hooker, and how that punch wasn't nearly enough. He drives around for over half an hour looking for her. But he doesn't see her. He only sees black girls out tonight and that isn't going to work. So he finally drives home.

THIRTY-THREE

'We've got another one, a real meat puzzle.'

It was Breslau calling at 6:45 A.M. Monday. Behr was awake. He'd already been out in the dark for his early-morning roadwork, in fact, trying to outrun the lingering memory of Mistretta's tequila kiss.

'Like Northwestway. Even worse. We're down at Donovan-Grant. It's a complete fun house.'

'Can I come down?' Behr asked.

'Consider this your engraved invitation.' Breslau hung up. Behr dressed quickly and was almost out the door four minutes later when he remembered.

'Suze?' he said into his phone. 'Did I wake you?'

'No, what's up?'

'I was supposed to take Trev today, but I can't. Something came up.'

'You're really jamming me here, Frank, I told day care he wasn't coming.'

'You think you can get him in?' he asked. There was a strained pause in which Behr saw his shot at the crime scene vanishing before his eyes.

'Yeah, I guess. They'll probably be able to take him . . .'

'Great, Suze, I'm sorry—' but she'd hung up, so he headed for the door.

Behr was at the scene within twenty minutes, and 'fun house' was an apt description, if not an understatement, of what he found there. A line of police vehicles, ambulances, and coroner's vans were parked along the winding two-lane drive that led to the campus of Donovan-Grant, a large pharmaceutical corporation that had gone out of business two years earlier on the west side of town. Uniformed officers kept a perimeter more than twice the normal distance, and a few arriving news vans were being held at bay. Behr showed his identification and waited while an officer radioed for clearance, which was quickly granted. He was shown where to park at the end of a string of cruisers, and then he walked toward the cluster of uniforms and windbreakers bunched around ground zero.

The smell of death and vomit hit him as he reached the edge of the crowd. A few less-seasoned officers had lost their breakfasts. A couple of them had gone down to their knees and were being treated by EMTs and then walked away from the scene, probably for immediate counseling. Behr took a step closer and nudged his way inside a ring of vets and caught a whiff of menthol in the air, as the experienced cops smeared Vicks VapoRub under their noses and passed the tub along.

Behr cleared the row of onlookers and finally saw it. He felt his eyes zoom and spin trying to take in the unnatural sight before him at the edge of the parking lot. The body of a female victim, her skin alabaster against the black asphalt, had been cut apart and twisted and then reassembled, into a strange, squat pyramid. Her head was pointed in the opposite direction it was meant to. Facing away from him, it sat on top of the pile. The base of her skull, covered by lank blond hair with dark ginger streaks, rested directly on the shoulders of the torso, while the neck was missing altogether. Then after another instant Behr located it, a cylinder, removed from its points of attachment, the severed spinal column a white ring centered by pink marrow, like a round steak, tucked between a pair of crossed and amputated feet. Behr saw that her breasts had been hacked off, and if they were on-site, he couldn't see them.

He circled counterclockwise around the remains, passing between more officers who looked on in shocked silence, until he saw her face. Beyond life-less, what remained of her eyes stared off into infinity. Her mouth hung open and was torn apart – as if small animals had gotten to it. Her hands were pressed to her colorless cheeks. Behr was no patron of the arts, but even he recognized the resemblance to the famous painting *The Scream*, by Edvard Munch. Except this version was real, and the subject's hands were no longer connected to her arms.

Bobbing somewhere between horrified and mesmerized as he stared, Behr had to force himself to catalog his next impression, which was the lack of blood. There wasn't as much as he expected. There was little, actually. What there was of it appeared to be seepage, as if the body had been vivisected and bled out elsewhere, before being placed.

Makes sense. The blunt sentence came to Behr's mind, as he tried to think rationally. It would be impossible to do this kind of butchery out in the open. But the coherent thought was pushed away by panicked impulses of mortality, of death foretold, and the inevitable end of all living creatures that flashed through the core of his being at what he saw.

Then Behr noticed the quiet. It was as near silent a crime scene as he'd ever stood on. There was a man-made pond in the near distance, with a fountain that had been dormant since the company shuttered its offices, so there was no sound from it. There were occasional footsteps, some radio crackle, and a muffled sob or two, but no loud instructions were being barked, nor were there any of the caustic jokes one could count on being tossed around a crime scene, no matter how gruesome, as a defense mechanism.

Then a smooth burst of concerted movement at the edge of the site and a series of clicks and flashes caught Behr's attention. A lithe, medium-sized man with longish hair clad in an army field jacket crouched down on the ground with a big-bodied Nikon digital. Speed lights on low stands cut the flat, slate gray of the sky. The man kneeled and kept on, lining up shot after shot, seemingly unaffected by his subject.

'Still life of death,' Breslau said, appearing at Behr's elbow, chewing gum, a whiff of menthol about him, and a shine of Vicks above his upper lip.

'Huh?' Behr said.

'That's what Quinn called it,' Breslau said, jutting his chin toward the photographer. 'A still life of death.'

'Are those GSWs to the upper torso?' Behr asked of a pair of angry red holes on each side of the chest.

'No. First thought, based on the wounds, is that she was pierced and potentially suspended by rods or hooks through the skin.'

172

'Je-sus,' a cop next to them who'd overheard said.

'Has she been identified?' Behr asked.

'Nah. Is she yours?'

'Doesn't look like it. Ninety-nine percent sure she's not Kendra Gibbons.'

'That's good, I guess.'

'Yeah. I'd like to do a DNA check though.'

'Sure.'

Behr's eyes stayed on Quinn as the photographer moved in for a series of close-ups.

'You have anything?' Behr asked.

'We're checking if security cams caught any footage, but it doesn't look good. They seem to have been turned off and pulled out a while back when the company shut down the location.'

'Any security guards?' Behr knew that even defunct office buildings often employed night watchmen to keep trespassers out and reduce liability.

'Just doing twice-daily pass-bys. That's who found this. He didn't see anything, and he doesn't know whether to shit or go blind right now. We're talking to him anyway.'

Quinn was up from the ground now, dusting off his knees and drawing back several dozen yards, where he set the Nikon on a tripod.

'Lieutenant?' an officer said to Breslau.

'Yeah, Tommy?' Breslau drifted away to his conversation, and Behr headed for Quinn.

* * *

Behr waited a distance away while Quinn composed his shot, clicked the shutter, paused for a long beat, and clicked it again. He adjusted the aperture and took another few frames. The photographer reminded Behr of a hunter on a range sighting a rifle scope, such was his precision. Finally, he removed the camera from the tripod and began snapping what seemed to be final shots.

'Quinn?' Behr asked.

'Yeah,' the photographer said.

'Name's Frank Behr. I'm an investigator here on a potentially related case.'

'Think I've heard of you. You used to be on the job?' Quinn said.

'Yep.'

'Call me Django.'

'Okay,' Behr said, wondering if it was his nickname or given one. 'So, you ever see anything like this?'

'Well, they're all a bit different, but I've seen plenty of shit.'

'You don't mess with the Vicks?'

'Nah.'

'You're used to it.'

'I save the crying and the puking for later,' he said, 'but on the scene, I owe them . . .' Quinn waved his camera at the remains. 'The least I can do for them is keep it together while I'm working.' The sentiment echoed Behr's own feeling of duty at a murder scene and he nodded his agreement. 'Ahh, the truth is: there's not so much crying or puking. Not anymore. Fifteen years is a long time to be doing this shit.'

'Right,' Behr said. 'I see you've got a real thorough approach to it.'

'I generally try to shoot from the same level the viewer would see the scene. No going up ladders or lying on my back, or other bullshit I've seen guys try.' Quinn lowered the camera, reached into a pocket, and changed his camera's memory chip. 'Some shooters try to reinvent the wheel. I like to limit the scope, so the viewer's eyes don't have to move much. I frame so the viewer's field of vision approximates my own while on the scene. That way they can experience being here. I hope. I just got it in my head this would be the most helpful to the detectives going over the photos later. I've been told it is.'

'I've noticed your work's in a different league than the guys before you,' Behr said.

'Ah,' Quinn brushed it off, 'they were good.' He held up his camera. 'I've got this thing. Digital. I can outshoot my predecessors ten to one at no cost to get my shots. Imagine Tiger Woods with a wooden driver versus Ben Hogan with a Burner.'

'I see.'

'Anyway, you know Locard's principle?' Quinn began, focusing for his next shot.

'Yeah,' Behr began. He'd read about the pioneering French criminologist from the early 1900s back in college. 'Said anyone who enters a crime scene takes something of it with him and leaves something of himself behind. Especially the criminal.'

'Right,' Quinn said. Locard was referring to physical evidence – fingerprints, hair fibers, blood, soil – and beyond physical evidence, his theory included the methodology and psychological imprint of the killer. Behr believed the exchange went even further. Investigators on scenes like this one took horrible memories away with them, and left a small piece of their well-being behind each time too.

'That's what I'm trying to do with my camera,' Quinn said, flashing a few frames. 'I know I'm not actually going to capture a carpet fiber or DNA in my shots. But it's metaphor, you know? If I do my job well enough, there'll be something in the pics that helps solve it.'

'I appreciate the ambition,' Behr said.

Quinn finished, slung his camera, and began breaking down his other equipment, as the coroner's crew who'd be handling the body parts, dressed in paper biohazard jumpsuits, hoods, and rubber gloves, moved in.

'That's a hell of a shot there,' Behr remarked. The team looked like Roswell scientists huddled over alien remains.

Quinn gave it a glance. 'Yeah. Can't shoot it though. If I did, it could be subpoenaed in cases of alleged mishandling of evidence or whatever. Better not to even take it.'

'You photographed Northwestway?' Behr asked.

'I did indeed.'

'Related?'

'Look, that's not my field . . .'

'But?'

'But I'd have to say so.'

'Because of the mutilation.'

'Yeah. I mean, you've got the low probability that there's more than one of these animals out there dumping bodies in this condition. It's not my area of expertise. I leave that to the detectives and number crunchers. But beyond that, there's the visual impression. It hit me the exact same way there as it did here.'

'How would you describe it?'

'Like one of those fancy restaurants that serves everything stacked up in a tower on the plate. You've got to knock it all down before you can even eat that shit. They're trying to create a big impression. That's what this guy's trying to do,' Quinn said. 'But what the fuck do I know, right?' he added.

Maybe plenty, Behr thought. Then he asked: 'You mind if I get in touch? Maybe talk to you more about Northwestway, and some of your other scenes?'

'Yeah, thing is, I'm kind of busy,' Quinn said, covering his face with his camera.

Behr realized that despite the friendly chatter, he was just some donkey investigator bothering a guy at work.

'Got ya,' he said and turned toward the body, where Breslau now stood, his legs spread and planted, arms crossed at his chest, like some sentry of the dead. Breslau looked up and waved Behr and Quinn over.

When they got there they found a coroner's assistant kneeling next to the body, holding the victim's left leg in his gloved hands.

'Show 'em,' Breslau said. The assistant turned the leg and revealed a chunk of missing flesh the size of a quarter that was as deep as it was round.

'What do you think, trophy?' Breslau wondered aloud.

'Hmm,' Quinn said, as he focused and shot it. 'Do a bite impression?'

'It's not a bite,' the coroner's assistant said.

Behr looked at the spot and tried to imagine the woman, alive, intact, and whole.

'You think?' Behr said. 'I'd check Missing Persons for alerts on women with identifying marks.'

'Birthmarks, scars, tats.' Breslau nodded.

'Yeah, maybe he cut something off, to keep or to mask her identity. Give it a shot,' Behr said, and noticed Quinn's eye come up from his camera's screen and fix on him for a moment.

Soon the body parts were marked and bagged and loaded in a coroner's vehicle, and then there was nothing left on the scene besides yellow 'Do Not Cross' tape, and it was time for Behr to go after his suspect. He was just turning to leave when Quinn spoke.

'Bro,' he said, as his fingers went into his field jacket pocket and came out with a business card. 'E-mail me if you want to talk, we'll set it up.'

THIRTY-FOUR

'H EY...'
He stops and turns and sees that it is
Bob, his neighbor, calling out.

'How's it going?' Bob says.

'Hello, Bob.' He grips his briefcase in his hand. This was no way to start a Monday morning.

'Man, the smell . . .' he says.

'Sorry, Bob, raccoons got into the garbage again, and I've been lazy about picking it up. I'll do it now.'

'It smells like something died, man.' Bob speaks politely, but he is angry, the veins in his neck say so.

Maybe something did. He isn't sure if he's said it aloud. They stand there staring at each other for a long moment.

He knows how to stop the complaints. And he might one day. Until then Bob should count himself among the lucky. He doesn't even know how lucky.

'Get some bungee cords for your damned cans or something.'

'Will do, Bob. I'll take care of it right away.'

He stands there watching as Bob nods his thanks, walks back to his driveway, climbs in his car, and drives away.

THIRTY-FIVE

URDERER JEROLD ALLEN PRILO drove up to his home in an old silver Toyota Camry. Prilo lived in half of a divided two-family house. He parked in a little cutout along a rusted chain-link fence and got out. Prilo was big and strapping, without excess flesh on his frame, and had thinning hair wrapped around his pale crown. He wore Carhartt work clothes and heavy Red Wing boots. He crossed to his house carrying a canvas tool bag in one hand. He wore canvas gloves as well, which Behr found interesting.

Behr was parked across the street watching through binoculars. When he had arrived at the address, Behr had figured Prilo wasn't in. There were no lights on in the house, no car in the driveway, so Behr had waited. With his cooler packed with sandwiches and drinks, he had sat for three hours. The day before, he'd called Center City Rapid, the local trucking company for which Prilo had worked since his release and since he couldn't drive long haul anymore due to parole restrictions. A helpful routing manager had e-mailed Behr Prilo's routes, so Behr checked them against murder sites while he sat. Neither the body-dump locations nor the places where victims were last seen mirrored the delivery routes exactly, but they were certainly close enough for a motivated individual to have diverted off course and visited. It could have all taken place during nonworking hours too. And Prilo didn't have such a busy driving schedule that he didn't also have a lot of free time. His schedule was part-time, patchy at best.

After about an hour and fifteen minutes inside, Prilo reemerged from his place, this time without the canvas tool bag, but still wearing the gloves.

What are those for, huh, buddy? Behr said aloud, starting his car and taking up a loose tail. Behr followed as Prilo drove around seemingly aimlessly for about half an hour. Finally, Prilo pulled into a Marsh's parking lot and went inside. Behr considered following him in, but thought it was a bit aggressive, not to mention pointless. He didn't need to surveil the guy browsing produce. Twenty minutes later Prilo emerged with several plastic grocery bags and Behr followed him home. It was dark by then, and Behr did a gut check before digging in to sit for the night. The idea that on night one Prilo would emerge and Behr would follow him on a body dump was beyond a long shot, but he had never succeeded at anything without adding a few layers of leather to his ass. So Behr sat and froze and reflected and grew bored and cramped and sat some more. He thought about the victims, and Mary Beth Watney, and Susan, and Trevor, and money, and Kendra Gibbons, and Lisa Mistretta. He thought about her too much. And while Behr went through three Red Bulls, Prilo didn't go anywhere.

At 7:20 in the clear morning, Prilo broke the monotony by exiting his house with his tool bag. Behr followed as Prilo drove to the Center City Rapid lot and picked up a Mitsubishi Fuso light-duty box truck. Then Behr trailed along as his subject made a pickup of cardboard boxes at a computer company and drove them to a long-range trucking firm's yard before off-loading them. There were a few more pickups and drops, but by then Behr was so tired he was ready to drive into a telephone pole, so he called it.

Years back Behr could sit surveillance for three days straight before breaking, but right now he needed to sleep and piss and not in that order. That was getting old, all boiled down. Behr got home and regrouped and slept and he was back on Prilo's house by 5:30 that evening, in time to see the man moving about his kitchen. It was another night in for Prilo, another sitting outside for Behr, and the next day passed in the same way as well.

Behr was home the next morning, hurrying to get himself organized and go back to work on Prilo after a quick shower, when his phone rang. It was Susan.

'Day care's got an infestation of bedbugs.'

'Really? That's nasty,' Behr said. 'Where'd they come from?'

'Funny, they didn't say,' Susan said, 'but I've got work. Can you take Trevor? You haven't seen him in days.'

It was the truth. He hadn't seen Trevor since the boy had gone to his grandparents' for the weekend. He hadn't seen Susan since their conversation in bed, and his subsequent moment with Lisa Mistretta. He knew himself better than to pretend it was a coincidence.

He had to get back on Prilo, but he had no choice.

'I'll be over to get him,' Behr said and hung up.

Even though it wasn't by the book, Behr ran the heater on stakeout now. Because while it was one thing to leave an infant strapped into a car seat with toys and an iPod playing 'Baby Einstein,' it was going a little far to freeze him too.

After collecting Trevor, Behr had managed to get

back to Prilo's place in time to pick him up going to work. He'd followed him on his routes for a while, before Prilo returned his truck and got in his personal car. He then returned home for several hours.

Along with a wave of happiness, Behr felt like an asshole every time he glanced back in the rearview, or turned around to give Trevor a bottle, but he just couldn't bring himself to break off the sit. Trevor was a trouper too: he hardly complained while in his seat, or lying on the backseat while Behr changed his diaper. The kid had sitting surveillance in his blood. Maybe it really was hereditary.

Trevor was napping in his car seat and Behr was calculating the cost of things like orthodontia and college when Prilo hurried out of his house, got in his car, and screeched away.

Interesting development, Behr thought, and tailed him out east to some warehouses on 30th Street. The buildings were abandoned low-slung brick jobs that stretched for several hundreds of yards. There were no lights showing through from inside rows of casement windows that were broken in a pattern resembling a jack-o'-lantern's smile. The parking lot was deserted, too, when Prilo pulled in. Behr slowed to a stop out on the road on the other side of the fence and used his binoculars to see Prilo park, root around in his trunk for something, and then head inside the partially open loading bay of one of the buildings.

Something's going down inside that building.

Behr felt it. And he needed to know what. He sat there for a long moment considering what he should do. He could wait for Prilo to come out and resume the tail. Or he could peel off and take Trevor to Susan now, but that would be twenty-five or thirty minutes round-trip without counting time for explanations. He could call the cops and have them come down and enter the building and see what they found. The problem was: he didn't even know what to call in.

Man with a dark past inside a building? Behr glanced back in the rearview mirror and saw that Trevor had nodded off to sleep. He put the car in gear, took his foot off the brake, and eased into the lot.

Behr drove down near the loading bays and saw the door Prilo had entered through was suspended partially open by some tangled chain. He couldn't see very far inside due to the darkness, but all looked quiet. He took another look in the rearview. Trevor was still asleep. Behr turned up the heater, reached into the glove box for a Mini Maglite, and eased the car door open. He stepped out into the cold afternoon air and gentled the door shut. He moved away from his car, over the cracked asphalt toward the chest-high landing by the open mouth of the loading bay.

Clicking on the flashlight, Behr swept the beam around the loading bay. He saw nothing inside but some old, broken wooden pallets littering the floor. He put the flashlight between his teeth and vaulted himself up to the level of the bay, then crouched and went inside. Daylight behind him, Behr found himself in the half darkness of the defunct company's shipping department. Abandoned racks and box chutes and more pallets were scattered about. He saw a set of stairs leading to a door that was slightly ajar, one that seemed to give entry into the main part of the building's interior.

Behr looked back. He could still hear the hum of his running car engine, and if he bent his knees he could just see the hood. He felt a sense of dread in his next steps as his car went out of sight, but felt powerless to check the urge to advance. He walked a dozen more paces, then paused and listened. The engine was very faint, nearly inaudible now. The space smelled like bird shit, and he saw scores of pigeons lining the window ledges above him. He could no longer hear the car as he progressed into growing darkness. But his eyes adjusted to the low light and he continued. He cleared a towering set of storage racks and felt the first blow. Deep and numbing, a bolt of pain exploded in his upper back.

He stumbled forward, turning, and saw what it

was: Jerold Allen Prilo, mouth clamped shut, coming at him with a claw hammer in one hand, a hook-bladed carpet knife in the other, and cold murder in his eyes. Most of the puffed-up pains in the ass that Behr dealt with in the course of his work were merely antisocial. They wanted to posture, bluff, and threaten on their way to working themselves up to actual violence. This was different. This encounter was *asocial*. Prilo came at him without a word, without a sound, his arms pinwheeling. He wasn't trying to prove himself, or impress anything upon Behr. No, Prilo was trying to kill him.

Prilo advanced another few strides and Behr retreated. He knew this backing away would only result in failure, in his maiming or death, but he picked up a valuable piece of information as he did: Prilo was not light on his feet. The man's work-boot-shod feet stomped straight forward with inchoate fury. Behr flashed desperately on Trevor, alone in the car, and what would happen to the boy should he be incapacitated, and should Prilo be the one to walk out of the warehouse. He lunged away at an angle, forcing Prilo to turn. Behr cut toward him and threw a looping overhand right, clipping Prilo below the ear. Prilo straightened and renewed his attack, swinging the claw hammer at Behr's head. Behr tucked his chin behind his shoulder, taking the blow along his upper triceps, then wrapped Prilo's hammer arm under his and stood up, straightening it and popping the capsule of the elbow.

Prilo grunted in pain, and Behr heard the pleasing sound of the hammer coming loose and hitting the floor with a steel-on-concrete clang.

He won't be chopping anybody up with that arm for a while, Behr thought.

But before he could react further, Prilo took the opportunity to slash at Behr's face with the knife in his remaining good hand. Behr managed to get his arm up to block it, but took the blade along the outside of his forearm. The cut was long and somewhat deep and Behr sucked in breath between clenched teeth. Only the sleeve of his thick canvas coat saved it from being disastrous. Behr had kept Prilo's arm wrapped under his and used it to jerk the man into two punches, and was happy to discover his slashed arm was still functioning. He used it to neutralize Prilo's knife hand by gripping the wrist, and drove a knee to the body that doubled Prilo over. Behr quickly enclosed Prilo's neck in an arm-in guillotine choke. It was solid and deep and Prilo was able to fight on for only another moment before dropping to his knees. This allowed Behr to increase his leverage and sink the choke in deeper. He felt his surgically repaired collarbone grind and strain, but hold. Then Behr took a risk and released the choke and Prilo's arm, shifting to a straight guillotine.

He regripped and cranked the choke hold. The pain in his sliced arm was intense, but he tried to ignore it as a distressed gurgling noise emitted from Prilo, and within seconds the man went limp and was facedown on the concrete and out.

Behr released him and stood, sucking in air. He kicked away the carpet knife and picked up the hammer, then found blood soaking down his pant leg, but on the opposite side from the arm that had been cut. He rolled Prilo over and saw the source: Prilo's tongue had been caught out and stuck between his teeth. The tremendous pressure the choke put on his jaw had taken a chunk out of it. Blood poured from his mouth. Behr slapped him, and Prilo came back to consciousness sputtering and gagging.

Behr got him by the front of his shirt and jacket with his left hand, holding the hammer in his right.

'What the fuck?' Behr said.

'You broke my arm,' Prilo said, drooling and spitting blood. Even with the lacerated tongue Behr could pick up a bit of southern Indiana or even Missouri twang in Prilo's speech.

'Dislocated the elbow. May not be broke,' Behr said, trying to gather his faculties and ask a reasonable question.

'What you want?' Prilo asked,

'What are you doing in here?'

'Who are you? You not a cop,' Prilo said, more blood falling out of his mouth.

'No, I'm not,' Behr said.

'You a relative?'

'Of who?'

'Of hers,' Prilo said, and suddenly Behr knew whom he was talking about: Mary Beth Watney, Prilo's victim.

'No.'

'You been following me.'

'You set me up for an ambush,' Behr said. 'What do you use this place for?'

'Nothing. I just 'membered it from delivering here before it closed. You been following me,' Prilo said again.

'I want to know about you and Kendra Gibbons,' Behr demanded.

'Who?' Prilo asked.

'Kendra Gibbons. Young blond girl. Prostitute. Disappeared eighteen months ago. Don't give me the dumb act.'

'I don't know nothing about her,' Prilo said. 'What do you think I am?'

'I know what you are,' Behr said into Prilo's face. 'You're a goddamned murderer of women. And I think you murdered Kendra Gibbons.'

'It wasn't me,' Prilo said.

A moment passed with only the sound of their

breathing. Behr felt blood running down his arm as he stared into the eyes of a killer. But he'd killed too, and he wondered for an instant what Prilo saw staring back.

'Telling you: it wasn't me.'

Prilo's denial sounded truthful. But there was something else behind his words that resembled knowledge. Ordinarily Behr could take his time. He could strap the guy to a chair and interrogate him. He could hold him or call the cops. Or throw him in the trunk and drive him into the woods and make him think he was going to be executed. But Behr had no time for that. His body and soul were split in half – one side needing to go to Trevor, in the car alone, but the other desperate to know what Prilo knew. He wanted to go check on his son, but he wasn't about to leave Prilo, and he wasn't going to bring him along and show him he had the boy there either. He had to hurry, and he considered crushing the bones of Prilo's face in order to get him talking, and raised the hammer.

'Don't give me that bullshit. Tell me what you know about the dead women turning up in this town or you'll never leave this fucking warehouse.' Behr smacked him across the head with the side of the hammer. There was a dull thud as unyielding steel met skull. Prilo lurched over to the side, gulping air through his bloody mouth. Behr straightened him up. 'What do you know?' he demanded.

'Okay . . .' Prilo said, panting. 'Someone's working the Near Northside of town. Other parts too.'

'Someone's working?' Behr said. 'You mean a signature killer?'

Prilo nodded.

'How do you know? You know who he is?' Behr asked. He considered whether there was some kind of club made up of these sick bastards.

'No,' Prilo said. 'I just know it. I seen the news. Other reports over time. It's obvious: he's hardcore. A binder and a chopper who been in mid-cycle for quite a while and now he going "nova."'

'That's all obvious?'

'To me it is,' Prilo said

Gene Sasso used to say: 'A good cop sees what's happening. A great cop understands what it means.' Behr supposed it was no different when it came to one sociopath recognizing another's handiwork.

'Keep going,' Behr said.

'Why? You think you want to find him? You don't want to find this boy, believe me,' Prilo said, almost smiling, showing bloody teeth.

Behr raised the hammer. 'You want to be eating through a fucking straw?'

'Okay. Okay,' Prilo said. 'What you want to know?'

'Who am I looking for? Black, white, Asian? Old or

young? Criminal past? Employed? Manual laborer?'

'Oh, I don' know. Could be a brother who hate white women. But probably a white man.'

'Why's that?'

'Just more righteous white men out there. Gotta play the odds,' Prilo said, his twisted mind working now. 'I wouldn't say he's young. Young boys maybe want to kill their mama. But this boy been at it for a while and working with control. Maybe he want to kill himself but as a young woman. Or kill his mama young, like when he was a boy. Maybe he just likes blondes. Either way, he gotta be thirty-five, forty, forty-five.'

'What else?' Behr demanded.

'I don't know, man.' Prilo shrugged.

'Sexual element?'

'Shit, you thinking like a grade schooler. Course there is,' Prilo said.

'There hasn't been any DNA found,' Behr said.

'None?' Prilo said, seeming surprised for the first time, then impressed.

'Not a trace.'

'Well, there's ways . . .' Prilo said. It chilled Behr, and made him certain that Prilo had killed multiple times and had gotten away with it.

'Give me more,' Behr said. The side of him that needed to go to his son was gaining strength and he had to leave.

'Well . . .' Prilo considered. 'He got something about being public.'

'Public?'

'Yeah. He putting 'em out there now. Some he has, some he hasn't over time, I'm sure. But now he showing himself. He making a relationship with the world. He needing the attention.'

'You're saying he's looking to get caught?' Behr asked.

Prilo shook his head. 'No, no, no, no, no. *You* said that. I'm not saying that. When you fools catch a man it ain't ever for all he done. You don't ever know what a man's really done . . .'

Behr didn't have any more questions that made sense. He felt his arm throbbing now.

'What you gonna do, call the cops, get me sent down?' Prilo asked.

What could Behr call the cops with? No proof of attempted murder. It'd be called a simple assault that would be knocked down to self-defense after Prilo's lawyers made a case that Behr had followed and surprised him. Breslau wouldn't like that, and Behr didn't need it. But he knew in his bones that the man at his feet had done unspeakable things to numerous women. He considered beating him to death with the claw hammer and leaving him there, a rotting pile of pulp to be discovered or not. He tried to close the valve inside him. The same one he did when deer hunting and a downed animal required finishing, or when he was wing shooting and a wounded bird needed its neck wrung to end its misery.

Finally, after a long moment, Behr released Prilo's jacket and flung the hammer into the darkness of the warehouse, where it landed with a faint chiming sound.

'I won't call the cops. On one condition: you talk to me again if I need to.'

After a long moment Prilo nodded.

'How do I reach you?' he asked.

'Nah. I'll reach you.' Behr turned to go when he heard Prilo's voice behind him.

'I know what you was thinking about just now. I know . . .' Behr still heard Prilo thumping his chest as he walked quickly from the warehouse. 'Look in there. You may not find your man, but you'll find what you looking for in there. You'll find what you need . . .'

Behr ducked under the loading bay door and into sunlight and broke into a run. He leapt off the bay platform and hit the ground in a sprint for his car, where he found Trevor screaming in terror at being left alone, but otherwise unharmed. As soon as he saw him, and his real life came flooding back over him, Behr understood what he'd almost allowed to happen. He'd been caught in that undertow and it had slowly and inexorably dragged him away from shore.

A current of panic unlike that he'd felt even when facing a murderer's knife and hammer began rising in his chest and he tried to force it down.

'It's okay, baby boy,' Behr said, stroking his son's head. He kept trying to hush and reassure the boy as he got in the front seat. Behr wanted to take his son out of his car seat and cradle him. But he needed to be gone before Prilo emerged. He chunked the car into gear and pulled out in a spray of gravel. He sped along 30th until he saw a strip mall and pulled into the parking lot. He held Trevor there, trying not to bleed on him, until the boy quieted. Behr's heart pounded at what he'd done.

THIRTY-SIX

*Y*OU *SHOULD BE in the office, you dumb son of a buck, get back there.*

But he isn't in the office, and he isn't going back. Not yet. He knows that much about himself. The reason is: it just doesn't last anymore. Not at all. It used to keep him for months. After a work, he was good for a season. Then it had reduced to months, then weeks. And it was down to days now and he didn't know where it would go from here. He was getting like one of those science experiment chickens in a cage, heedlessly pecking the button for cocaine instead of corn and starving itself to death.

He is trolling for a new project now, as he has been for the last few days. Thus far he's seen nothing. But sometimes you went out with your rod and your bait and came back with just your rod and your bait. And sometimes you came back with no bait at all and nothing to show for it.

He keeps driving the streets of Fall Creek Place. He just has a feeling. The red light changes to green and he makes a left onto 24th, and that is when his luck changes. He sees her running along the side of the road, a jogger in her early thirties, tall and strong, in a purple long-sleeve top, black tights, and white sneakers, her blond ponytail bouncing like a sunbeam, and he knows he has to have her. He will have her.

He follows along at a respectful distance, watching her run for a long time, a good three-quarters of a mile, cataloging her route and mentally predicting her weight, her scent, the coarseness of her pubic hair, the density of her flesh. She could go to a café, to a store, or her car or office, or to meet a friend, but that's when he knows powerful forces are smiling upon him, because instead, he is right there when she slows to a cool-down walk for a last block and enters a small house on North Talbot.

He sits there in his car a few doors down and lets some relief settle on him. He can go back to work, for the time being, because Sunbeam is in his life now, he has her address, and he has a new center to his universe.

THIRTY-SEVEN

BEHR NEEDED STITCHES, but there was no way he was bringing Trevor with him to the emergency room. He'd texted Susan to come pick up their son so he could go on his own, and he'd ignored a half dozen calls from her while she was on her way. Nothing credible beyond outright lies had come to his mind about why he needed her to come get the boy, so he was hoping to avoid the conversation altogether. When he heard her keys in the door, he realized that was unlikely.

'Where have you been? I was worried,' Susan said as soon as she entered.

'Out ... doing a few errands,' Behr answered lamely.

'Errands.'

'Yeah.' *Fuck*. He felt her eyes find the peroxide and bloody dish towels on the kitchen counter behind him.

'Did you go to the bank?'

'No.'

'The car wash?'

'No.'

'Did you buy formula and diapers?'

'No.'

'Where were you, Frank? What *errands*?'

He didn't answer.

'Damnit, Frank! Where is he?'

'Taking a nap.' She moved past Behr, grabbing Trevor's snowsuit, and saw the blood on it.

'Whose blood is this? Did something happen to him?' She raced into the living room and pulled the sleeping baby from the Pack 'N Play. Her hands began picking at his clothes, trying to uncover him.

'No. He's fine. It's mine.'

As she turned she glanced through the open door to the second bedroom and saw the photos of body mutilations all over the walls in there.

'You've got to be kidding me,' she said, turning Trevor away and covering his eyes, even though they were closed and he was still asleep. 'You think this is a suitable environment for our son?' she asked.

'He doesn't go in there, and they're covered up when I know he's gonna be over here, Suze,' Behr said, knowing how foolish it sounded. 'It's not like he's reading the reports.'

'Still, Frank ... What happened today? What

happened to you?' she asked. 'Did you take our son on your case?'

'Susan, don't get yourself all hyped up. Do you think I'd put him in—'

'I don't know what the fuck you'd do,' she said with force. She didn't go in for that kind of language ordinarily. It was a big deal to her. She was that mad, and he knew she had a right to be. She stared him down. 'All I know is that this little being is my whole life. And I thought you were a part of it. But now I just don't know . . .'

'Don't you think he's that to me too?'

'Well, apparently chasing missing hookers and God knows what else is part of your life too,' she said.

Behr said nothing.

'Tell me what happened right now.' He'd tried to cover the rag wrapped around his arm with a long-sleeved shirt, but it had soaked through with seeping blood. The shirt was dark colored, so he didn't know if she could actually see it, but the time for obfuscation was over. He gave her a brief recounting of the day's events. Her mouth hung partially open, her eyes blinking rapidly as she assimilated the facts.

When she finally spoke her voice was so flat and free of emotion it chilled him to his core. 'Something's really wrong with you,' she said. 'I thought you were struggling to get out from under, but now I know what's really going on: you're not even trying, you're just bored and hungry for action.'

The accusation hit him like an artillery round. He almost felt his mouth gaping, like a fish out of water, as he tried to answer, but she spoke first.

'Do me a favor: don't come by for a while.'

'Suze, no way—'

'Just a little while. Get your thinking straight.'

'Come on—'

'Jesus H., Frank. I'm thinking about getting a lawyer involved here.'

'Don't do that,' he said, more volume and anger to his voice than he intended. 'Please don't,' he modulated.

'You exposed our son to a killer. A goddamned murderer.'

He had nothing he could say in response.

An interminable silence followed, and they stared at each other before he finally nodded. With Trevor in her arms, his snowsuit wrapped around him, she left. When the door had slammed, the quiet and emptiness that remained were absolute.

THIRTY-EIGHT

BEHR LEFT THE ER with twenty-two stitches in his arm, instructions not to work out for five days, a prescription for Vicodin, and a blister pack of samples. Besides that, he felt like he had nothing else in his life but his case. The medical resident who had sewn him up had been curious about the nature of the injury, and he'd kept asking even after Behr had told him, truthfully, that a carpet knife had caused it. Behr had expected this, so while he was waiting he'd placed his wallet, open to reveal his retired police tin and P.I. license, on the bedside table next to his phone and keys. The doctor's eyes finally found the small badge, and he stopped asking and finished with the sutures.

Behr wasn't prone to carrying his gun regularly. The places he generally went weren't that dangerous, and he was big and trained and willing and able to defend himself physically. But there was a moment he reached on certain cases when the time came to start carrying a weapon. That's where he found himself now. In some ways he wished he'd made the decision before the moment with Prilo in the warehouse. He wouldn't have any stitches in his arm. But then Prilo would be dead, and Trevor would have been with him and in the middle of all that, so perhaps it had worked out as well as it could have.

With the Vicodin sample in his bloodstream, and the exchange with Prilo rattling around in his head, Behr found himself in his car texting Lisa Mistretta, and then he found himself in front of her door with a bottle of Patrón Silver under his good arm.

'You must be starting to get the impression that I don't have *anything* to do with my nights,' she said. 'And you might not be wrong.'

'The way I keep showing up, you must be pretty sure I'm in the same boat.'

She was dressed in jeans and a sweatshirt with her hair pulled back. She let him in and didn't say anything when he took off his coat, revealing his bandaged arm. They were in the kitchen with drinks before either spoke again.

'You were right, I was wrong,' Behr said.

'You're gonna find that's a trend.' She smiled. 'About what?'

'About Prilo,' Behr said. 'He's no good for this.'

'How do you know?' she asked.

Behr shrugged.

'Get the fuck out!' she said. 'You talked to him?'

'Oh, it was some kind of talk,' Behr said, as he saw her eyes go to his injury.

'He did that to you?' she asked. Behr nodded.

'Stabbed you?'

'Cut me.'

'Tell me everything.'

She poured fresh drinks, and Behr relayed the details of the fight, her eyes flickering with excitement that she barely tried to hide. She poured refills, and they moved to the living room couch and got to the start of the 'interview.'

'What'd he know?' she asked.

'Everything,' Behr said. 'Nothing, as far as hard facts, nothing about Kendra Gibbons, but everything about our guy and what he's doing.'

'Fuck me . . .' she said, for the first time of the evening, and shook her head and sipped her drink as her mind ran.

'He confirmed a repeat signature killer at work, and your assessment about the type.'

'He used the same language?'

'Not as academic as yours, but he's got a PhD too, you know?'

'Yeah.'

'He said whoever's doing this is putting the bodies out there, but also putting *himself* out there,' Behr said.

'He craves the attention.'

'That's what Prilo said. He's making a relationship with the world.'

She nodded, deep in thought, and they both fell silent.

'Hey, Behr,' she said, looking up. 'How did you get him talking? After you fought and you choked him out. You kind of glossed over that part. I don't imagine he was real willing.'

'No, he was pretty reluctant . . .'

'So?'

'Well, I had his hammer in my hand,' Behr said. 'And he got convinced.'

That's when he saw a desire in her eyes that matched the hunger he felt deep inside him. Their bodies came together. She was electric, her body supple and charged. She tasted like tequila and lime squeeze. Their mouths and hands were all over each other, and they started on the couch but weren't finished until they'd moved to her room and destroyed her bed too. Afterward, Behr lay there in a tangle of sheets, her hair and her smell, drunk and happy and miserable all at once.

Sometime later, it could have been hours, neither of them sleeping, he heard her voice in the darkness and felt her fingers on the mottled buckshot scars along his collarbone.

'Would you have done it? You know, with his hammer . . .'

The question floated there in the air for a moment. He knew better than to answer it.

'I should go,' he said and started to move.

THIRTY-NINE

TIRED AND HUNGOVER from more than the tequila and pills, Behr stepped out of the shower and leaned on the sink. He peeled the plastic garbage bag from his stitched arm, used a hand to wipe the condensation from the mirror, and stared into his own eyes for a long moment. Animal and abject with pain and emptiness, he was glad when the steam reclaimed the spot he'd cleared. Thoughts of Trevor and Susan filled his head, as they often did, especially in the morning, and he pushed them away with an effort that was almost physical. Facing the loss of his family could make a person crazy. Behr had heard stories about his friend Eddie Decker, who'd lost his in a horrible manner. The ex-cop was on the West Coast now, and he had taken to going into biker bars wearing a Hells Angels patch even though he wasn't a member, and fighting all comers who took exception. Behr understood it was his method of purging the pain, or his penitence, or practice. He had been there before himself. He stood in the bathroom for another moment and steered his attention back to his case, and Prilo's words rang in his head: *he's making a relationship with the world.*

Behr walked out of the bathroom in his towel and began to get dressed. It was a little after 7:00, still too early, but he knew where he needed to go.

'I just need to retrace my steps, that's all I need to do ... And tell myself: this is a good job for me ... Slow down ...'

The middle-aged librarian, a small mentally challenged man who'd steered Behr to the art section, was now talking to himself as he wheeled away a cart of books to be reshelved.

'Just very anxious about getting it all done ... It's just the way my mind is ... Just need to retrace my steps ...'

Maybe he's speaking for the both of us, Behr thought.

Behr had spent the morning in the stacks of the university library sifting through books and magazines, looking at the works of painters and sculptors. If the body found at the pharmaceutical plant evoked *The Scream*, perhaps it was an insight into the killer's mind. So Behr was going over extreme images, by Lucian Freud and Francis Bacon, Damien Hirst and

Patricia Piccinini, and others, to see if the way the bodies were being presented actually mimicked their famous works. If he found that, Behr hoped it would lead to further information. As he flipped through pages of their portraits he noted how visceral and violent their depictions of their subjects could be. They trafficked in intense emotion, even madness, but nothing he was seeing resembled any of the bodies that had been found.

After a few hours his hope had begun to die as he recognized that what he was doing was ludicrous. He'd set out to learn what had happened to a young quasi-prostitute. That had evolved into the search for a murderous butcher, and now he had ended up in a library. It was not a progression that Gene Sasso would have put much stock in.

Behr felt a warm flood of humiliation, even though no one knew what he was doing. The idea that these bodies had been staged as copies of classic works of art, and that they would lead to a killer's identity, was a silly fantasy. But as he continued to thumb through the texts that accompanied the paintings, Behr read about the condition of the artist, and the artist in relation to mankind. It was all suffering and alienation, desperation and lack of human connection, and that *did* evoke the interior state of killers in his estimation, so he continued. While Behr's initial supposition began to crumble into rubble, the foundation that remained was an actual idea: that this man, this murderer, wasn't a copycat or appreciator, but saw himself as some kind of an artist and his kills were his works.

Before long, Behr found himself reading some of van Gogh's letters, because he knew the man had worked in obscurity and had apparently died by his own hand. He hoped to discover something illuminating in such a tortured soul but was surprised to find writings that were filled with positivity and appreciation for people, for life, and the belief in the search for a higher power that if not God was something akin to grace, so Behr moved down the row until he pulled a book on a Swedish artist who had lived in England in the 1800s named Oscar Rejlander. He flipped through the images and then read the biographical section on the flap and felt his mind stop.

'I'm in the wrong section,' Behr said aloud, realizing how quickly the library environment could get you talking to yourself.

He took out his phone right there in the stacks and made a call.

'Quinn? It's Frank Behr, I need to see you.'

FORTY

'COFFEE?' DJANGO QUINN offered.

'Only if you have any ready,' Behr answered.

'It will be in three minutes.'

Quinn lived in the Block, a large building that had once been the W. H. Block Department Store but had been converted into residential lofts. If Behr expected a dwelling featuring more gore than his own thanks to a profusion of Quinn's crime scene photos, he was very wrong. Instead there were countless framed photos, shot by Quinn, hanging and stacked against the walls of the stylish space, but all were of living subjects. Most were striking black-and-white studio shots of a beautiful son and daughter who bore Quinn a strong resemblance. As they played on jungle gyms, skipped rope, and ran in the park, Behr felt what a charmed life the photographer was leading. There were also portraits of musicians,

214

not to mention landscapes, and shots by other photographers, and no pictures of victims whatsoever.

'So, Django – is that your real name? Not one you hear every day,' Behr asked.

'My dad played jazz trumpet, still does. But he loves the guitar and hoped I'd take it up, so he named me after Django Reinhardt. I picked up a camera instead. It was just an old Pentax ME, but once I made my first picture, that was all she wrote.'

'What was it?'

'A shot of my dog. I still have it somewhere.'

Quinn's wife Sheri, a pretty, petite brunette, emerged from the kitchen with a tray bearing cups and a pair of steeping French presses.

'You want me to push these, or can you able-bodied men handle it?' she asked, revealing a bit of Michigan in her accent.

'You do it, honey. You know how I always botch it up,' Quinn said.

Sheri shot Behr a look. 'He can break down and reassemble a camera body in the dark, but he can't push a cup of coffee,' she said as she pressed down the plunger and then poured.

'I just like your touch,' Quinn said.

'Oh, my ass,' Sheri said.

'That too.'

'Enough out of you,' she said to Quinn. 'If *you*

need anything else, Mr. Behr, let me know.' With that Sheri Quinn left them. Full-bodied and robust, the coffee was one of the best cups Behr had ever tasted, and it made his own life seem the poorer for the crap he served himself.

'I'm glad you called,' Quinn said. 'I was thinking about you this morning. Did you see it?'

'See what?' Behr asked. 'I've been in the library all day.'

'Papers and website announced it – the body got identified. Name was Danielle Crawley. The DNA was getting run on a rush, but there was a missing-persons report out that fit the description and mentioned a tattoo on the right calf – a small sham-rock. They called in the girl's sister who had filed it, and she made the ID.' Quinn put down his coffee. 'The girl was a bartender, DJ, and played in a rock band. She still drank a little, but she was recently out of rehab, clean after getting caught up in hard drugs.'

'Really,' Behr said. 'Police checking known associates from that world?'

'They are,' Quinn said, 'but she'd only recently got here to stay with the sister. She'd been living up in Milwaukee, and no one has reason to believe any trouble like this would follow her. Since we got the other cases with similar circumstances they figure it's related to that. Point is: that tattoo – you identified that body.'

'It was just an idea. Someone else would've had it,' Behr said.

'Yeah, but *you* did,' Quinn said.

'Do the articles tie it to Northwestway?'

'Yep, you know it.'

Behr winced, knowing what a pain in the ass this would be for Breslau. 'What about any other murders?' he asked.

'Official line: "Police are looking into connections to past cases,"' Quinn said. 'So what can I help you with?'

Now Behr put down his coffee and took out his notebook.

'*A still life of death*. That's what you called it out at the crime scene. It's an art term.'

'Right.'

'And that, along with some other elements, got me thinking: this guy we're dealing with is a killer, but he sees himself as an artist. He feels cut off and at odds from society in many of the ways artists do.'

'Yeah,' Quinn said, interested. 'Misunderstood, misanthropic.'

'It hit me: his medium is killing, and mutilation. But there's also a visual component that's supposed to last afterward. So I thought: what if the bodies are just the *subjects* of what he considers his real work?'

'I see where you're going.'

'At first I thought he's keeping souvenirs, certain

217

parts and pieces, but that's not really enough. So then I thought: painter or a sculptor? But that seemed like it was coming up dry, and right when I started to doubt myself, I found a book on this guy Oscar Rejlander, who'd—'

'He started out a painter and became a photographer.'

'Yeah.'

'He was considered pretty damn good with the brush, but he abandoned it for photography when he saw how well a photograph captured the folds of a sleeve. He made some haunting images, especially for his time . . .'

Behr nodded and saw Quinn hit by a bolt of understanding, just as he had been.

'He photographs them. He's making pictures before he puts them out . . .' Quinn said aloud.

Behr shrugged. 'I think he might be. I started looking up well-known photographers after I called you, figuring I could find one he was imitating, and it would lead somewhere. But the books in the library were mostly portraits, famous actors, buildings and mountains. Fashion. Henri Cartier-Bresson, Ansel Adams, Man Ray, Diane Arbus – no one on the library shelves is even close. Man, I don't know where else to look.'

'No, no, no. Those aren't the right references,' Quinn said, excited now. He motioned Behr over to his bookshelves. 'These are more along the lines ...'

Quinn started pulling large, worn coffee-table-sized books of black-and-white prints from the shelves and handing them to Behr. 'E. J. Bellocq. He shot New Orleans prostitutes ...' Behr took a look at the grim, evocative portraiture of the fallen women of Storyville until Quinn handed him the next volume.

'Weegee – his real name was Arthur Fellig. The guy is my personal North Star, he's like the godfather of crime scene photography.' Behr took the book and began flipping through pages of stark, graphic imagery of downed bodies on flashbulb-lit pavement, and denizens of the streets of New York City in raw couplings back in the 1940s, long before such things were considered acceptable. The shots created a visceral reaction in Behr, the mark of good art, he supposed. 'There's something hypnotic in a photo of a body,' Quinn said, almost to himself, as he looked over Behr's shoulder, offering a window into his profession. 'The way light hits a dead eye. It reflects total ...'

'Nothingness,' Behr said.

'This is a Danish guy named Asger Carlsen.'

Behr looked over black-and-white photos of headless bodies with extra arms and legs jutting out in various directions. The images were odd, but there was a certain smoothness to the presentation that made it all slightly comfortable.

'Ah, here it is . . .' Quinn said, pulling a book from the shelf. 'Witkin.'

Behr opened the heavy book and froze. Nothing he'd seen in the crime scene photos was specifically re-created in its pages, but the distressed black-and-white images there were gruesome, gothic, and sickening, almost like high-level torture porn. There were genitals punctured and stretched, nipples with nails through them, people in black masks hanging from hooks plunged through the skin of their chests and backs, cut-off heads. The photos communicated a deep pain and sadness of existence, not just in the subjects but in the photographer as well.

'My God,' Behr said quietly as he continued flipping. Beings from beyond the edges of regular society – hermaphrodites and dwarves, massively fat women wearing crow-like masks, emaciated and wrinkled ancient men – all passed before Behr's eyes. He wasn't sure how the images had been created, what special effects were at play in capturing the decapitations and amputations. Perhaps he used lifelike mannequins or corpses he'd acquired somewhere.

'I haven't looked at these for a long time,' Quinn said. 'The feeling is similar to seeing our killer's *displays*. Shit, I should've thought of this. You're getting inside his head.'

'That's where I need to be,' Behr said. 'Can I borrow this?' He raised the book.

'Sure, give it back whenever.'

'I need to find a way to smoke this bastard out,' Behr said.

'How?'

'I don't know.'

'Well, I doubt he's gonna invite you to his gallery show.' Quinn laughed over the rim of his coffee cup.

Behr looked up with an idea. 'No, he's not, but I can invite him to yours.'

FORTY-ONE

WHAT DOES HE know, and what is there yet to learn before he acts?

There is no man in Sunbeam's life. No husband or boyfriend who lives with her, he is fairly sure. He's been watching her for the better part of the last several days and hasn't seen one come or go, and she sleeps at home each night. So no husband or boyfriend, or even one of those popularly, and disgustingly, referred to as 'friends with benefits.' He could be wrong, the significant other could be out of town, or merely a much more infrequent visitor, but he just has a feeling: she's alone.

He's learned she works at Crossroads Hospitality Group, which oversees a group of mid-level restaurants, according to their website, in a free-standing building off Rangeline. He knows she parks next to the building and that the lot is too well lit. And that her daily jogging is limited to daylight hours, with plenty of traffic on the streets, and that the sidewalks and paths she uses have too many people on them for his taste. On an inclement day he saw her drive her Honda Accord to a fitness center that has a row of treadmills and stationary exercise bicycles displayed behind a plate-glass window, where she and her brethren worked themselves into a repetitive sweat in the name of health. He admires it as much as he doesn't understand it. The only strength building and fitness he is familiar with is the kind that comes with hard labor. Muscles built by and for utility, and not for vanity or as a mere hobby.

Still, he just can't seem to get her good and alone outside the house. Darkness has fallen while he's been sitting outside, waiting and watching. She doesn't lead an external life. She doesn't bebop down to local bars, or to liquor stores like Cinnamon did, so her home will have to do. In fact, she is home now. He clicks open his car door and feels the cold night air flood in, washing over him like river water. He closes the door behind him and walks deliberately across the street. He doesn't belong, but nothing announces that more than creeping about, lurking and hoping not to be spotted.

He nears her front door. It is solid and well fitted with shiny, new-looking locks. The windows appear almost new as well, weather-tight and strong. He can test them and see if any are unlocked, but there is risk to it – if neighbors catch sight of him doing that, they'll call Sunbeam or the police right away. Instead, he steps out of the throw of the streetlights and melts into the shadows along the side of her house, then heads toward her backyard.

The yard itself is more of a patch of grass, bordered by her neighbors' chain-link fences on two sides and on the other her detached garage – which she doesn't seem to use since she parks her car in front. There are a few skinny young trees, red maples maybe, without leaves, and he stays near them in order to break up his silhouette, although he isn't much worried about being seen now. The lights are on inside, which makes her visible to him and prevents the opposite. From where he stands, he sees her emerge from the depths of the house and enter the kitchen. She pours herself a glass of red wine. She opens the refrigerator and cabinets repeatedly as she prepares some kind of food. She shakes and moves as she works, and he realizes music must be playing because she is dancing.

He glances at the glass sliders – which wouldn't be difficult to bypass unless she was smart enough to place a bar or wooden dowel in the track. Then he looks past them and stares for a long moment and drinks in her life force. It is beautiful. It is why he is here. He wonders if she takes that energy for granted, if she recognizes how important her life is right now. Then he wonders how long she's lived in the house, wonders from where she's moved, where she grew up . . .

Suddenly he knows how he'll get inside and be with her, and he won't need to break any locks or climb through any windows to do it. No, she'll invite him in. He doesn't have his hit kit with him right now, so it won't be tonight. But it will be very, very soon. It is practically done already.

FORTY-TWO

'I DON'T WANT TO do it,' Breslau said.

'Yeah, but *will* you?' Behr asked.

'A police-backed community outreach meeting . . .' Breslau mused aloud. 'Shit.'

They were at Floral Crown Cemetery, a run-down place on the west side, standing inside a vestibule in the memorial chapel, holding but not drinking foam cups of burnt, overly hot coffee. The occasion was Danielle Crawley's funeral. Behr was there on the hoary theory that killers attend their victim's funeral, Breslau on behalf of the department.

'I don't need captain-level brass and a detective squad,' Behr said. 'Give me one body. *You* come.'

'Oh, I don't think I'm gonna be there,' Breslau said. 'No way in hell that's happening . . .'

There had been a bleak, sparsely attended grave-side ceremony. The cemetery spread big and flat around them, with its winter-brown grass broken by low headstones, and just enough bare trees to remind everyone that there should've been more trees. And more mourners. It was only Crawley's sister and her husband, an aunt, and an aged female family friend. The sister, dry-eyed in her sorrow, read a message from a recovery sponsor from Milwaukee who couldn't attend, but who commended Danielle on her efforts at getting clean and her hopes for the future, and expressed his fondness for her. The event was completely devoid of suspects in Behr's opinion. Breslau agreed. Out of respect they had followed along as the funeral moved inside for a last prayer.

'Shit,' Breslau said again.

'The department rep, whoever you send, tells people to lock their doors and take care when alone at night. We show a couple of the more palatable crime scene photos, we advertise that in advance, in the hopes of drawing this animal in. In the meantime I'm getting license plate numbers, video. I run 'em and cross 'em against any parking tickets or violations or eyewits' sightings at the times and locations where the snatches or drops have taken place.'

'That's a lot of ball sweat,' Breslau said.

'My sweat, my balls,' Behr said. 'The thing's in the news already. Have you seen the comment section on the websites? People are freaking out over it.'

'Don't I know it. And doesn't your girlfriend work

over at the *Star*? Couldn't you have had her spike the story for us?'

'First of all, she sells ads these days, she isn't in Editorial. And at the moment my favor account with her is seriously overdrawn.'

'Oh, you do have a way with the people, don't you?'

'Come on, Gary, what's the harm that can come from what I'm asking?'

'The harm is that we look like a bunch of dipshits with no leads,' Breslau said.

'As opposed to what you look like if I do it on my own without Department backing,' Behr suggested. 'A concerned private citizen, in the security field, with a law enforcement background taking action where the department won't.'

Breslau slowly looked at Behr. 'You're not doing that,' he said.

'Oh no?'

'Listen, you go there, it's the deep freeze for you. Every time you get out of your car it'll be ticketed and towed. And that's just for starters.'

'I don't mind walking—'

'Don't play hardball with me, fuckstick,' Breslau said.

'Settle down. We both want the same thing here. Help me out.'

The funeral service in the main room had ended, and the family was ready to leave. Behr and Breslau jettisoned their coffee cups and turned to give their final condolences.

'I'll have to check it with my superiors . . . but it'll probably fly. Just don't make jerks out of us.'

Behr raised his palms in innocence. 'Who, me?'

FORTY-THREE

A THOUSAND THINGS CAN *go wrong when you work quickly. But they won't. They didn't. Not for him.*

He is alone and alive in the night, every nerve ending firing, perceiving, sending him information as he gets out of his car, dusk just falling, an unthreatening canvas shoulder bag dangling in his left hand, and knocks on her door with his right. This is the moment. The door swings open and Sunbeam faces him. Her eyes are blue and clear, her teeth are white, her skin pale, and her hair the color of Acacia honey. It shines like liquid glass. There can be fleeting disappointment when he is finally up close and personal with a subject. But not this time. No, this time perfection is close at hand.

'Hold on,' she says into the cell phone she is talking on, and then addresses him. 'Can I help you?'

'Oh, maybe. It's no big deal,' he says. 'I used to

live here. In this house. I can come back some other time . . .'

He sees her eyes light with curiosity, then she speaks into the phone again. 'I'll call you back, sweetie, someone's here.' She hangs up.

'Like I said, I used to live here.'

'When was this?'

'It was a while back. A long time ago. When I was in high school. Did you guys buy the house from the Halls? We sold it to them.'

'No. It's just me, and I bought it from the Putnams – with a little help from my dad. The Putnams bought it from the Halls. I think.' She is right, they had. He's researched the chain of buyers and sellers on the place going back thirty years. It is all in the library and on the Internet – tax payments, real estate listings, sales announcements. He is pretty sure he knows it all better than she does.

'Right, we sold when my dad got transferred. We moved away right when I was supposed to finish high school. Then they held on to it for quite some time,' he says.

'They did.'

'It sure looks different now.'

'The Halls did a lot of work on it, I did the rest. I'm doing it anyway, as fast as I can.'

'You're doing good, the place looks great.' He

smiles. 'I carved my initials on the wall down in the basement. You see that?'

'Basement? You mean the little furnace room?'

'Yep, that.' He feels a momentary sense of concern surge in his chest. He didn't anticipate there not being a basement.

'I never saw any initials down there,' she says.

'I could show you where.'

She hesitates for the first time then.

'I know, I know,' he says. 'Just feeling nostalgic, I guess.' Then he looks at his watch. 'Well, I have to go meet my wife in five minutes.'

The idea that he has someplace to be, and a wife, puts her at ease. Then he reaches for his back pocket.

'This is me by the way . . .' He extends his driver's license. It doesn't provide her any protection, of course, but he's learned that a willingness to show who he is creates some kind of instant, misguided trust in his target, and this time is no different. The fact that she can identify him makes her feel safe. As if she'll get the chance.

'Oh, I see you don't live too far away,' she says.

'No, just moved back kind of recently.'

'Well, okay, come on and take a quick look,' she says, and steps away from the door to allow him in.

FORTY-FOUR

*Y*OU DON'T DESERVE *them. You're an asshole who doesn't deserve them and that's why they're there and you're sitting here . . .*

Behr was in his car across the street from Susan's place, watching her get Trevor out of his car seat. He didn't care much about being spotted, so he didn't bother parking out of sight, and when Susan turned she saw him. Her hands full with the baby and plastic shopping bags, she kicked the car door shut and marched right toward him.

'What are you doing?' she said when he'd lowered the window.

'Just wanted to see him. You. But wanted to respect your wishes—'

'You're weirding me out, Frank,' she said. Then she pointed Trevor toward him. 'Okay, say hi, Trev, say hi to Daddy.'

Behr smiled despite himself when he saw his boy.

'How you doing, buddy?' he asked.

'He's doing fine now,' Susan said, 'just going to day care and being with me. Not chasing murderers.'

'I said it before and I'll say it again: I'm sorry,' Behr said.

'Good,' she said. 'And now you've seen him, so you can go.' Susan turned and walked away, leaving him sitting there.

FORTY-FIVE

SUNBEAM LIES ON her bed, trembling and sweating, as tears squeeze out of her eyes and slide down the sides of her face. It is very quiet. She hasn't had a chance to scream. She'd followed him down into the tiny space that houses the boiler and hot-water heater. He walked over to the corner in the dim light of the weak, bare bulb hanging overhead and pointed.

'There it is,' he said.

He stepped aside so she could take a look, and that's when he leapt on her and choked her unconscious. It was really quite easy, like a game the kids played at school growing up, before they'd even learned how to sniff glue. When she came to, she saw she was hog-tied and bound to her bed, most of her clothing having been disposed of via a sharp knife that had left several nicks on her previously pristine skin, and that's when the shaking set in. He's gagged her with rags. All of it has been precut, knotted, and arranged in his shoulder bag, his little hit kit. But he isn't sure he even needs the gag, she's so docile when her eyes open. Then she starts to try to say something. He edges the wad of cloth to the side of her mouth so she can speak.

'I'm ... I'm going to be sick.' He pulls the gag further aside and she turns her head and vomits softly. Things can get messy.

'You're okay,' he says. He takes another hank of rag from the shoulder bag and wipes beads of perspiration from her forehead. There is a glass of water on her bedside table, and he holds her head and gives her a small sip.

'My husband will be home any minute,' she says.

'No, Pam,' he answers. The knowing in his voice seems to devastate her. She begins hyperventilating. He considers putting a plastic bag over her head and strangling her now, but he waits. Her name is Pam Cupersmith. She is five foot seven, one hundred and twenty pounds. Hair: blond. She is an organ donor. He smiles at that. He is looking at her driver's license, which was on her dresser, and though he'll forget all the particulars soon enough, he'll never forget Sunbeam. That's what she'll always be to him. Just like all the others, he'll have to rack his brain or study news archives to recall their real names, but it is easy for him to call forth who they are to him. Besides

Sunbeam and Cinnamon there are Kit Kat and Sweetie, Muffin, Plummy, Bean and Malibu – not the place – Starbuck, Nova, Coco, Baby, Tawny, Stork, Misty, Lonely and Pearl ... All the pretty women, how he cut them up.

He stops thinking about his list when her breathing calms and the room grows quiet. That's when he hears footsteps somewhere across the house, the sound of a door closing, and the faint splash of someone urinating while seated.

'Who the fuck is that?' he says quietly.

'My niece. My sister's daughter. She's staying with me. She's feeling ill and took a nap. She's only eleven years old please don't hurt—' He shoves the gag back in her mouth and flies from the room, his shoulder bag clutched in his hand.

By the time he reaches the bathroom door there is water running and then the sink shuts off. The door opens in toward the bathroom, and he holds the knob pulled firmly closed with one hand and digs in his bag for a length of paracord with the other. He feels the knob jiggle, and then a girl's voice calls out.

'Auntie Pam? I'm stuck.'

'You're going to need to stay in there,' he says firmly.

'Who's there? Let me out,' the girl says.

'I'm a friend of your aunt's. Is there a window in there?' he asks.

237

'No. Let me out.' He hears fear in the girl's voice.

'I'm locking you in—'

'No . . .'

The girl lets out a scream.

'Be quiet or I'll have to hurt you,' he says.

The scream stops and some gulping and gasping replace the sound.

'Get away from the door now,' he commands. He loops the paracord around the knob, ties it tightly, and secures the other end to the leg of a heavy metal shelving unit. He sees the cord straining and the knob working against it. It holds, but the girl is trying to get out. 'Get away from the door, I said. If you try and come out I'm going to kill your aunt and you.'

'Oh my God!' the girl screams again.

'Shut up,' he says, 'or I'll come in there and do it now.' The action on the cord stops, and he hears feet on the floor as the girl scrabbles away from the door. 'Are there towels or a bathrobe in there?' he asks.

'Yes,' comes the reply.

'Wrap yourself up in 'em then, and get comfortable,' he says. He hears some movement, then waits for a moment until he hears nothing, not even sobbing, and returns to Sunbeam.

When he moves the gag again she speaks quickly.

'She's my sister's daughter, please don't hurt her.'

'That's none of your concern right now,' he says.

'No, no, no, no, no, no, no . . .' she cries softly, squeezing her eyes shut.

'Look the monster in the eye,' he says. But her eyes remain shut. 'Come on now, do it,' he says. He wonders if when she does she'll be able to see what's really deep inside him, and if he'll be able to tell she has by looking at her. Finally, her eyes open and she stares into his face. 'See? I'm just a man.'

He learned long ago that everyone compartmentalizes, but what is inside of him isn't something inhuman. *It's the most human part of me*, he thinks.

'I can't take this,' she says, real desperation in her voice, which rises in volume to a near scream. 'Let me go.'

'You have to take it. The other girls did, so you have to take it too. It's just what you have to face. Call it your punishment if you want, or just your lot,' he tells her. He tries to wipe down her face with the rag again, but she tosses from side to side and refuses to be comforted. She begins bucking and straining against the ropes and he sees how it is going to be, so even though it isn't exactly how he wants it, he puts the plastic bag over her head and starts in suffocating her right there and then.

FORTY-SIX

'**Y**OU'RE BATSHIT CRAZY, Behr,' Lisa Mistretta said, 'and I love it.'

Behr was sitting somewhere he hadn't expected to be again anytime soon – certainly not this soon – and that was at the island of Mistretta's kitchen. He'd told her about his community outreach meeting scheme and asked for her help.

'I am *so* in,' she said. 'Honestly, the way you ran out the other night, I thought I'd seen the last of you.'

'Sorry about that,' Behr said, 'I'm not in a real clear place.'

'Who is?' she said and turned her back to him and her attention to the sauté pan where she stirred delicious-smelling Asian food. 'Wha-cha!' she said, flinging in a dollop of garlic chili paste that crackled as it hit the heat.

'How good of a cook are you?' Behr asked.

'I suck.'

'That shrimp pad Thai looks pro.'

'Don't check my garbage can, where you'll find the Siam Square containers. I'm just heating it up,' Mistretta said. 'And, as promised . . .' She handed him a thick stack of printed pages held together by a binder clip. 'Good timing. This might give us a better idea of who we're looking for. That is, if you really think the guy will show?'

'I have no idea,' Behr said. 'But I have to try something.'

'You read, I'll cook and drink,' Mistretta said, putting a bottle of Thai beer by his elbow. 'We'll eat once you've gotten through it.'

Behr nodded and started in on the pages, which were an abstract psychological profile written in a straightforward, quasi-clinical style:

Subject in question is male, organized/disorganized sadistic-lust serial predator engaged in restraint, torture, picquerism, and vivisection. Race probably Caucasian. Not possible at this time to predict identity, age with any degree of accuracy, but if suppositions regarding related cases are correct, sixteen-year span indicates subject is likely in middle age.

Subject likely sustained head injuries, among other abuse, as a child. Likely to have engaged/been

241

forced into traditionally masculine activities such as boxing-wrestling-hunting by dominant male figure (likely that father was not present in home) as a child. Signs and symbols of wealth, authority, and greater masculinity in this male role model would likely have diminished subject's sense of self.

Subject's mother was likely overprotective and overbearing. Likely drank or abused pharmaceuticals/narcotics. Physical abuse at her hands likely.

Subject likely a lonely child. No siblings, or poor relationships with siblings. No or few friends or poor relationships.

Subject likely injured or killed family pets/neighborhood animals as a gateway to blood lust.

School records will likely show a poorly adjusted individual, but one within bounds of normalcy at that time.

Subject will have potentially exhibited diminished capacity to experience anxiety or fear as a child. (Note: these qualities are some of the building blocks of developing a conscience.) Likelihood of cortical under-arousal, high testosterone, extra Y-chromosomes. (Extreme physical strength a potential by-product of these conditions.)

By young adulthood subject would recognize that hurting animals was waning in attraction/no longer satisfying. He would have moved on to fantasies of sexual control and violence with humans and then graduated to ideation phase.

Extent of ideation could have included collection of prurient visual materials, weapons and implements of restraint, torture, i.e., 'murder tools.'

Various indeterminate factors will have led to first 'act.' Act could have entailed abuse, restraint, or sexual assault of human, most likely female. First act will have rendered mere fantasy phase no longer sufficient to satisfy. First murder likely disorganized, sloppy, poorly planned, resembling a 'crime of passion.' (Mode will have grown more refined over time, while being affected by likely real-world variables.)

Aftermath of first murder. Once individual has found the key to acting out deepest fantasies, individual likely continued murdering to repeat sensation.

Second murder often deemed the 'most important/ exciting' to individuals thus categorized. Transformative nature of initial murder complete, killer has fully 'become.'

Likely that subject tries unsuccessfully to re-create this 'becoming' with each murder. Results in declining satisfaction, dissipating excitement. However, left with no suitable alternative stimulation, subject carries on.

Souveniring a likely part of activities.

> Subject is likely a religious man, or considers himself one, or at least attends organized religious services.

Behr broke off from the report and looked up with a question on his lips. 'Religious man?'

Mistretta didn't even turn from what she was doing on the kitchen counter. 'What is religion if not a struggle between sanctification and defilement? That's what our man is engaged in. More specifically, the idea of the resurrection. It's at the very core of Christianity. His killings ape or mock the notion of resurrection, or at least show a complex relationship with it.'

Behr chewed that over and went back to reading:

> Subject is extremely intelligent and/or potentially ex-military or ex-law enforcement officer. (This indicated by lack of physical evidence on scenes, i.e., he likely knows protocols.)
>
> Alternate theory: subject is of diminished intelligence/did not finish high school. This view would entail a subject unable to hold regular jobs, relationships, devoid of trappings of 'regular society,' yet possessed of feral abilities.

There was a handwritten note in the margin that read: 'Behr, I don't think this "diminished intelligence" version is our type, but included it to be thorough.' The report continued:

> Subject potentially contracted HIV or STD, perhaps while in the military, potentially from a prostitute, and is potentially 'cleansing' the world of fallen women.

Behr read on, a few more pages filled with countless potential psychological details. If he'd hoped for a clear picture of a man he'd recognize walking down the street toward him, that wasn't the case. But he had a lot of tangible ideas to consider.

On the last page, written in purple ink, was a note:

> Behr: biggest mistake we make in trying to figure out why these people act like they do is that we look at them through a normal prism. But they are not like 'us.' They're just not. – Mistretta

'This is impressive,' Behr said, closing the pages and turning in his chair. 'What's with the note?'

Mistretta had plated the food and moved to her dining room table behind him. She was drinking tequila on the rocks.

'I wrote it when I wasn't sure if I'd be handing that to you or sending it through the U.S. mail. Just trying to make you see something that's hard to see. Want a proper drink or you gonna stick with beer?'

He saw she had a rocks glass full of ice next to his place setting.

'You think it's a good idea to get the tequila flowing?' he asked, moving to the table, beer in one hand, pages in the other.

'You decide.' She shrugged.

'So we set up on the community meeting. I get pictures of all attendees, license plates on all the cars. You sit back watching behavior, checking for red flags against your profile,' he said, then sipped his beer.

'Deal,' she said. 'But, Behr, our guy isn't going to be reading this.' She patted her report. 'He's going to keep on doing what he wants, the way he wants – the way he needs to – according to whatever's broken inside him. We may not recognize him.'

'I get it,' he said.

She seemed far away and miserable for a moment, and he realized the toll her job took. She spent her time mired in human horror, spent her energy becoming utterly expert in it, and once she had, she saw too clearly the worst in people walking all around her. It was unavoidable. And most of the time no good came of it at all.

'It's not easy, is it?' he asked.

'If it was they'd call it "fun," not criminal psychology.'

'Even if you get it all right, you don't get to go catch 'em.'

'That's what I have you for,' she said, coming back from wherever she was. 'Eat.'

Behr dug into his food. 'Damn, that's good. Spicy.'

'That's how I roll,' she said, the smile back in her eyes.

He had a feeling he knew where the night was going to end up.

FORTY-SEVEN

IT IS MUCH LATER when he pulls out of Sunbeam's
detached garage and back into the rest of the
world. He's collected all of his ropes, cords, tape,
rags, and gags. He's cleaned everything he's touched
and has even taken the water glass with him. He's
taken care of all loose ends. Sunbeam has been in
and out of death's grasp. She was fairly limp as he
carried her out and put her in his trunk, and he isn't
sure what will be left of her by the time he gets her
back to his work space, so he has to drive quickly.

He is halfway home, not far from where he works,
actually, when he comes to the stop sign at an intersection near Copper Road. It may be a high-traffic
spot during the day, but there aren't any cars around
and he is a long way from making a full stop as he
taps the brakes and rolls through. A moment later his
rear window is bathed in flashing red and blue. All

goes cold inside him as he pulls over and waits for the policeman to approach. He is a big guy with a brush cut and steel blue eyes.

'Let me see your stuff, please. License and registration,' the cop says, and appraises the car as if he is in the market for one, running his flashlight around the interior. The beam lingers on the canvas shoulder bag, which rests in the foot well on the passenger side.

He hands over his papers and waits while the cop reviews them. The cop's nameplate reads 'Sgt. Morris.' A glance in the rearview mirror reveals that Sgt. Morris has a partner who is hunched over the onboard computer, undoubtedly running his license plate. Fortunately he has no violations.

'Where are you headed so late?' the cop asks.

'Just trying to get home. I work nearby.'

'Do you know why I stopped you?'

'No, sir, I do not,' he says. If Sunbeam stirs in the trunk, if she thumps or bangs around or utters so much as a muffled cry, it will all be over.

'You failed to come to a complete stop at the intersection.'

'I guess I did give the stop sign a bit of the old college roll, Officer,' he says lightly.

'Have you been drinking?'

'No, Officer.'

'A few beers? Anything?'

'Not a sip.'

'Why are you sweating?' the cop asks.

'Am I? I have the heater up kind of high,' he says.

It has all come down to this. He wonders if Sunbeam can hear any of the exchange through the walls of the trunk, if she is unable to scream around the gag, or if she is drifting in and out of consciousness, too addled to know that her only chance is right now.

Sgt. Morris uses the beam of his light to check the hologram on the license a last time. He looks back toward his cruiser. His partner gives a hand signal, perhaps an 'all clear.'

'All right, sir ... you drive safe and have a good night,' Sgt. Morris says, handing back the driver's license, registration, and insurance card. Sgt. Morris returns to his cruiser, gets in, and pulls away.

He waits another few seconds, reveling in the sensation of winning, again, while he situates his papers in the glove box, before he puts his car in gear and drives home to get down to it.

FORTY-EIGHT

BEHR COULDN'T SEEM to stop ending up in Mistretta's bed. She lay next to him, her black hair spread half across the pillow, half across his shoulder.

'You out?' he asked.

'No.'

'I was thinking about the checklist,' he said.

'The PCL-R.'

'Yeah, and other tests like it.'

'What about it?'

'Where do normal people score?'

'Zero.'

'Zero?'

'Zero to five,' she said.

'To five. I see. Because in your note when you said "they're not like us" you put "us" in quotes.'

'I meant a theoretical "us," like everyone, but not really *us*, as in you and me.'

'So, you've taken it?' he asked.

'Yeah, I've taken it.'

There was a long pause in the darkness.

'And where did you—' he asked.

'Higher than that,' she said quickly.

'Double digits?'

'Behr,' she said, 'there're certain things you just don't ask a girl.'

'So where do you think I'd—'

'You would too,' she said, and he suddenly didn't want to get any more specific either.

He felt her shaking in the dark and realized she was silently laughing. 'Yep, just a couple of psychos in this bed . . .'

FORTY-NINE

H E BACKS THE rear of the car inside the darkened garage, the light on the automatic
door disabled, and pulls Sunbeam's tarp-
covered form out of the trunk before pulling the car
out and closing the garage door behind him again. As
quiet settles, he has a moment's thought of the little
girl back at the house and remembers one time, in
the beginning when he was just a boy. He'd caught a
neighborhood cat and was using a wire loop to take it
to death's door and back, over and over again. The
cat's screams had brought some older kids to
the copse of trees where he'd been experimenting.
One of them had been a bossy type of girl. It wasn't
the first time he'd done some experimenting: the
first cat he'd killed was with a large firecracker
shoved up its rectum. Then there were the birds
he'd caught, after that chick, baiting them with grain
and dropping a box over them, and then injecting

them with bleach and sitting back to watch them shake and die.

I was just playing with it, he'd said, removing the wire loop from the cat's neck, hiding it, and then letting the cat go. But that bossy girl had just stood and stared at him. Just like that girl back at the house had.

Word about the incident got out, thanks to her, and he was called in to the middle school guidance counselor's office.

The counselor, a wrinkled woman with large rings on her nubby fingers, smelled of coffee and kept saying things like: *Don't you feel bad for the cat? What about the cat's feelings?*

Well, she didn't get it, that guidance counselor, not at all. Where would he have even started to explain with someone like her? Especially at his young age, when he was so far from true understanding himself. So he'd said yes, he certainly did feel bad, and he would never do anything like that again. And he'd been allowed to walk out of the guidance counselor's office and to get on with the rest of his life. That bossy girl had stayed away from him, and she'd switched schools not long after the incident and he hadn't thought of her for a long time – until earlier that night when he'd been ready to leave Sunbeam's but had to finish up. He'd opened that bathroom door and had come face-to-face with the niece . . . He never did like bossy little girls . . .

Sunbeam is still alive, but only in the technical sense and certainly not in any functional one. Her breathing is shallow, her pulse weak and thready. The part of her brain that controls her involuntary motor functions has been damaged from lack of oxygen. Once he saw a report on television about college-aged binge drinkers who anesthetized themselves into comas with alcohol, and their symptoms were similar to hers.

He walks around her naked body, roped spread-eagle on the floor, and gets ready. She is beyond terror, beyond conscious comprehension, but soon on a deep, cellular level she'll experience full awareness. It would have been nice to talk to her for longer, to watch her fight her situation with more vigor and fire. Even though those are superficial pleasures, and her condition doesn't really matter to him so long as she is alive for this part.

He moves to his workbench and selects some tools, but then pauses. Suddenly he is back at the jumping-off point, at the beginning of his army service, home on family medical leave to tend to Mother, who was suffering, after a series of mini-strokes, and it was time for it to come to a close. Even that shining hair she'd been so proud of had become lank as straw. If she could have talked, she would've asked him to end it. He was sure. But investigators could take an impression of the inside of the lips, and the depressions of her teeth on the soft flesh there would reveal she had been smothered with a pillow, and that just wouldn't do. It was hardly that complicated or difficult though. He merely pinched her nose shut and covered her mouth and waited. She barely thrashed. The end was a mere spasm, as she looked up at him, her eyes wide with shock, fear, and understanding of what she'd birthed and created.

Later, he'd sat naked and cross-legged, like a giant pale baby, in front of the mirror in her room, Mother's corpse reflected behind him, and he'd wept and laughed until he grew hard and then he'd masturbated feverishly. When he'd returned to post after the burial, and no questions were asked, it was with a sense of utter lightness and freedom.

But this memory puts a different idea in his mind. He crosses over to Sunbeam, kneels down, and puts his mouth over hers, pinching her nose, and he breathes for her. He smiles at the irony, at how differently he had handled Mother, and because at some point he will be doing the opposite and taking Sunbeam's breath from her, but not yet . . .

Because it works, like splashing water in the face of someone who has fainted. He sees her blink and look around at where she is. She's not completely lucid, but Sunbeam is back.

FIFTY

*E*VERY DAMN ONE *of them looked guilty, each a monster hiding in plain sight. Every one of them capable of horrific acts . . .*

Behr had just stepped back inside from the parking lot, where he'd used his phone to snap pictures of license plates and now surveyed the group that had assembled.

Then again, every person alive was. And these were just people – concerned, scared people, dressed in their bland blue and beige and tan clothing, sitting in the stale air of the church basement that smelled of coffee, hoping for some information that might protect them and those they loved, none of them likely responsible for any crime beyond speeding or cheating on their taxes.

The competing thoughts were pointless, and Behr tried to shake them and turn his attention to the front of the room and the Indy police officer addressing the group.

257

'There are only so many of us, and there are many, many more of you, which is why we look to you for some help in moments like this,' Sergeant John Odoms said to the group, nearly finished with his remarks. The burly, bald-headed fifteen-year veteran was shift mates with Officer Hawkins, the young patrolman who'd discovered the remains in Northwestway Park. Hawkins had been asked to appear initially, but he'd been on administrative leave since the incident and wasn't up to talking about it publicly yet.

'We're here to protect, but that starts with you as individuals and as a community being aware and looking out for suspicious behavior, men or groups of men lurking in public parks, around bars, around certain types of hotels . . .' Odoms went on.

The event had been previewed in the *Star* – both the print version and online. Behr had e-mailed Susan, letting her know he planned on asking their friend Neil Ratay, the reporter, to place it.

'Do what you want,' had come her terse reply. 'You will anyway.' And so he had. Behr sent along a fairly banal wide shot Quinn had taken of the Donovan-Grant crime scene, which the paper had run, one that featured the police investigating but avoided the gore of the remains. Behr had also put up a temporary website that offered information and a chance to look at more pictures, but one had to register with name and address and obtain a password in order to do so, and the *Star* ran the link. That way if the perpetrator couldn't be drawn out in person but couldn't help taking a look, there would be some cyber trace of him, even if he used a fake address.

As for his friend, Behr hadn't let on to Ratay the true motivation behind the meeting, and whether the reporter had guessed it or not, all he had said was 'I'm sure the paper will be happy to get behind a concerned citizen such as yourself.' Ratay had also given Behr the name of the volunteer in the church office who oversaw the space, which was also where Ratay attended his AA meetings.

Then, when it was time, Behr went ahead and dug into his own pocket and paid for a few large boxes of coffee and six dozen doughnuts. Until a half hour ago he'd had no idea whether he had nearly enough or would be tossing the bulk of it in the trash. More important, he had taken a pair of pan-tilt-zoom wide-angle surveillance cameras he owned, and borrowed two more, and wired the place. He'd rigged one over the spread of food, another at the door, and one near the photo display, with the fourth set to capture the audience while seated. The digital images would download directly to his laptop.

Behr had arrived early that afternoon, made the

preparations, and braced himself for the humiliation of a poor turnout. Quinn showed up a while later and displayed more than a dozen of his photos printed at sixteen by twenty inches. They used a room divider to block off the exhibit from the main seating area, because unlike the one in the *Star*, these shots included graphic images of the victims.

Mistretta got there a bit later, looking too good in a black dress and short leather coat, a laptop case slung over her shoulder. Behr introduced her to Quinn and they'd made small talk until people started to show up. Behr had begun clicking a hand-held counter as the attendees entered, and saw the numbers had stopped at seventy-eight. Thirty-five women, twenty-seven men, young adult to middle-aged. The rest were teenagers and the elderly.

Should I be looking for the strong ones, the smart ones, the sick ones? He didn't know.

Sergeant Odoms had rolled in with only moments to spare before the announced start time, just when Behr thought *he* might need to get up and do the talking. Big and serious in his dark uniform, Odoms didn't seem eager to be a part of the thing.

'Thanks for coming out,' Behr said, introducing himself and shaking his hand.

'Anything for Lieutenant Breslau,' Odoms said, an unnecessary reminder of how much a law enforcement career was built upon contract and favor bartering. Behr couldn't help but remember how poor a job he'd done of that when he'd been on the force.

'You have any questions about the type of remarks?' Behr asked, trying to be helpful. It hardly mattered what Odoms said, Behr just needed something to draw them in with and keep them stationary for long enough to get their plates and picture and for Mistretta to eyeball their behavior for telltale signs.

'I think I've got it, pal,' Odoms said. 'I've done this plenty. Usually at nursing homes and schools.'

'Good,' Behr said.

'I'll talk about the crimes for ten minutes, rattle some stats, then take questions. I'll finish with precautions and send them to the photos.'

And that's just what Odoms had done.

'Do the police have any leads?' asked a man in the front row with the affect of a high school football coach.

'None that we can share with the public right now,' Odoms responded.

'What are you doing to catch the perpetrator?' a middle-aged woman asked.

'We're devoting tremendous departmental resources to this, believe me,' Odoms said.

'Oh, well that's a comfort,' a man in a Craftsman work jacket said. 'Talk about incompetent!' There was a murmur of agreement in the crowd.

'All right, folks, that's not what this is about.'
Odoms scowled. 'Tell it to your councilman.'

'How many more women have to die before you're
gonna do something about it?' a middle-aged woman
with glasses called out. This sentiment got even
more support.

Odoms's face set in a mask of tightly controlled
disgust, and his eyes, hot with anger, found Behr
where he stood.

Half a dozen more questions and comments,
variations of the first, followed before Odoms said
with finality:

'Anyone else? No? Good.'

There was a mass scraping of chairs and shuffling
of feet toward the photo display. Some attendees left
straightaway, but most stayed and started viewing
the pictures. Sergeant Odoms was among the first to
go. Behr tried to catch him on the way, calling out,
'Thanks and I'm sorry, John.'

'Yeah, that's fucking great, Behr,' Odoms said
over his shoulder and disappeared out the door.

Behr, along with Mistretta, had *wanted* to shock
people with the display, and specifically determine
who *wasn't* shocked. Now he watched, as most of
them grew wide-eyed and pale from what they were
seeing. There were murmurs of 'Oh my,' and 'my
God,' and many less polite exclamations.

Behr drifted over and joined Quinn, who was just breaking off a conversation with a Goth-looking college-age girl with spiky blond hair as he leaned against a room divider and watched people react to his photos.

'So, yeah, I like to close off a stop, to get some more contrast from time to time. And I'll use a tripod for wides because the Department requests it, but I prefer to hold the camera, to make it an extension of myself,' he said.

'Well, cool, thanks,' the girl said and moved for the door.

'Closest I'm gonna get to a gallery show, or a fan, in my line of work,' Quinn said, turning to Behr, betraying perhaps a trace of bitterness.

'Glad you're enjoying yourself,' Behr said.

'Watching people shit themselves? Definitely.'

Behr cut across the room toward Mistretta, where she was set up in a corner watching the crowd and currently engaged in conversation with a man with thinning hair in his early forties and dressed in an inexpensive gray business suit.

'. . . dangerous times for women in this city,' Behr heard the man say. 'I live in Broad Ripple too, so if you ever need a ride home, or company when you're out, look me up.' Then he handed Mistretta his card. 'You could consider me your personal Guardian Angel.'

'Thanks, Bill, I'll keep it in mind,' she said with finality, and the man wandered away.

'Who am I following out of here?' Behr said, taking Bill's place.

'Me, when we go to a bar,' she said.

'Could he be our man?' Behr asked of the guy who'd just walked off.

'If I was profiling a lame-o with an orange belt in tae kwon do, maybe. Only thing Bill's guilty of is using weak-ass pickup material,' Mistretta said, tearing the card in two and letting it flutter to the floor. 'Why's everybody so fucking hatty?'

Behr took a glance and saw what she meant: at least two dozen attendees wore baseball hats and Irish Eight Piece caps, and even some fedoras, which had been back in style for two years, which also meant they were just getting to Indianapolis.

'Can't ask them to take 'em off,' Behr said.

'You sure?' she wondered.

'You seeing anything? Would our guy be last to leave or would he get out early?'

'Not sure. This part's interpretive, not frigging exact,' she said.

'I didn't mean it like that.'

'I know.'

For another moment things seemed as natural as could be expected, but then everything changed. A menacing figure under a baseball hat and dressed in a Carhartt coat slid in the door, surveyed the room, and moved toward the display. Behr recognized him right away and fell back behind a pillar in order to not be seen. The man's arm was in a sling. He was Jerold Allen Prilo. Behr's eyes locked onto him as he moved among the other viewers. Behr didn't know if he was imagining it, it was hard to tell at this distance, but he could swear Prilo wore a slight smirk.

'Listen, I know you never liked my Prilo idea . . .' Behr said to Mistretta.

'Thought you gave up on it too,' she said.

'I did. But he's here.'

'Son of a bitch,' she said. 'Where?'

'Big guy over there in the tan coat. The one wearing a sling on his arm.'

They looked and saw him, his broad shoulders rolled forward and looming above other attendees, as he browsed the photographs. Behr felt his heart pounding at the presence. There was a literal wolf in the barnyard. Behr left Mistretta and circled around to get a better look. Prilo seemed like just another citizen in the crowd, but Behr had the distinct impression that he was there to stalk. Perhaps having a premonition he was being watched, Prilo looked up and surveyed the room, a sickly grin on his face now plainly visible, and then his eyes met Behr's. Before he could duck away, Behr felt himself get recognized.

'Shit,' Behr muttered, and moved toward the man.

The smile ran away from Prilo's face and then he turned and headed quickly for the door. He was gone before Behr reached him. Behr saw him from the doorway, lumbering off into the night. The whole thing just felt wrong. In fact, Prilo's presence was as wrong as wrong got. Behr considered chasing him down, but it was a public meeting and Prilo – his past excepted – had done nothing actionable. Besides, Behr knew where he lived and the event was almost over.

Before long the place had emptied, and Behr, Quinn, and Mistretta were the only three left.

'Well, nobody fell down on the floor and confessed,' Quinn said, as he broke down his prints.

'Is that what was supposed to happen?' Mistretta asked while she plugged Behr's phone into his computer and synced the license plate photos. 'I just came for the free doughnuts – which this crowd mowed through.' There were only crumbs left on the table.

'May as well have,' Behr said, in the midst of removing and packing up the PTZ cameras. 'We did have a bona fide murderer in the room.'

'Who?' Quinn asked.

'Name Jerold Allen Prilo sound familiar?'

266

'He was here?' Quinn said. 'You think he's pay dirt?'

'Let's just say Behr's idea about him is a lot less gamey right now,' Mistretta said, as she zipped her computer into its case. 'Is it drunk o'clock yet?'

Quinn and Behr caught eyes and smiled.

'He was here,' Quinn said. 'You think he's pay

'Let's just see Melch's idea about him to a jot less
gamey right now,' Marmore said as she slipped her
computer into case. 'Is it doubt o'clock yet'

Quinn and Melch nodded to each and smiled.

FIFTY-ONE

THE PLACE SMELLS like old incense, lies, and God, as do all churches and their basements and all meetings of men. He sits there in a folding chair, an anger that seems infinite bubbling within him, as some big cop prattles on with words he can't even hear. Now it is time to view someone else's photographs of his work. He gets to his feet and shuffles along in a herd of frightened fools toward the little exhibit – if it can be called that.

He'd gotten there early by forty-five minutes and had waited down the street in his car until he saw people start showing up. He couldn't afford to get too close or to be inside with a sparse turnout, or possibly be asked to show ID or give his information while someone stood over him watching. He counted thirty people – it appeared the meeting would be well attended after all – before he got out and joined the stream of bodies entering. He wears khaki pants, an olive drab canvas coat, and an unmarked tan base-ball cap. He may as well be cloaked in a force field of invisibility. He's had this sensation many times before – that no one can really see him. He finds a seat at the edge of the middle, and before long other people have filled in around him and swallowed him up. He looks on as a dark-haired slutty-looking woman and large man speak to each other off to the side, and then watches the police officer when he arrives. Later on, another man, who is clearly the photographer, since he's been busy tweaking his display along the far wall of the space, joins them. Then the cop finishes warning people about things that don't concern them, with ways to protect themselves that won't work, and it is time to view the pictures.

It is worse than he imagined.

He keeps his coat on and cap pulled low throughout the presentation, and still wears them as he walks past photographs that supposedly depict *his* work, but which actually reduce it, ruin it, turn it all to shit. It is infuriating. The pictures were shot straight on, the digital images too clean and too bright, and the colors stark and unfiltered.

It shouldn't be like that, he thinks. The images bear no relation to what he is really doing. How can this joker call himself a photographer?

D. Quinn. That's the name digitally burned onto the lower left-hand corner of the prints. So it must be Quinn himself who stands there showing off his camera to some girl. The young man, dressed in cargo pants, a fisherman's sweater, and an earring, with a padded bag over his shoulder, disgusts him. He seems more concerned with playing the role of artist than the work itself.

But despite it all – despite the shooter's limitations – just seeing anew what he has done is magnificent. It stops him in his tracks and makes his heart beat powerfully and causes his blood to surge. His works are his prayers, his testament to his own godliness and immortality, and that comes through. He almost doesn't notice how the time has passed and that the crowd has started to break and file out. It is all ending so soon, but it won't do to be caught alone and too interested in the display, so he bends his head, tugs the brim of his cap downward, and walks quickly toward the door along with two couples, seeming, to all outside appearances, one of their group.

He goes back to his car and waits down the street for a long while until the place has cleared out completely. The last to leave is Quinn, who walks out with two other people, the big man and the small, dark-haired woman. They get into separate cars – the woman is parked directly across from him, but seemingly unaware of his presence behind the wheel. He stays with Quinn, following him as he drives off in a silver Toyota Prius. He isn't surprised when the photographer parks in front of a trendy-looking bar and grill he's never heard of called Kilroy's. He is more surprised to see the small, dark-haired woman and the large man from the church meet Quinn in front and see them enter as a group. He adjusts himself in his seat. Finishing the project in his garage can wait, this cannot.

FIFTY-TWO

'**O**H-HO, SAY HELLO to the regular,' Gene
Sasso said, turning around from stacking
glasses.

Frank Behr had just walked into the tail end of a
quiet Wednesday night at the Trough.

'I said I'd come by for a beer,' Behr announced,
taking a seat at the bar, 'and here I am.'

'Well, I'm some lucky guy,' Sasso said. He pulled
a Heineken Light on tap for Behr and slid it over.

'Thanks,' Behr said, taking a sip. He'd spent the
last few days crunching the license plates he'd gotten
at his meeting. He had turned up no connections to
the crime scenes and no known felons, besides Prilo,
in attendance. He'd also gone over the video he'd
shot. Plain faces, strange faces, even one guy who
looked like he had his eyebrows drawn on, but no
one was wearing a sign that said 'Murderer.'

'How are you doing with that case?' Sasso

wondered. Behr had been torn by a desire to resume his surveillance of Prilo, or to confront him, but with reams of data to check, he felt he had to be thorough. Now he wasn't sure what to do next.

'Coming up as empty as my pockets,' Behr said.

'Of course you are. That's why you come crawling back to your old training officer, right?'

'Is that why I'm here?' Behr asked. 'Thought it was for the cold beer and fine ambience.'

'I don't know why the hell you're here,' Sasso said. 'Hope you're not looking to drink on credit.'

'Certainly wouldn't pick this place if I was,' Behr said.

Sasso slung a dishrag over his shoulder and leaned his elbows on the bar top. 'So where are you at?'

Behr walked him through everything, up to the community meeting and Prilo's appearance there.

'I saw something about that in the *Star*, and wondered if it was legit or a bogey,' Sasso said.

'It was as legit as I could make it,' Behr said.

'But it was a bogey all the way,' Sasso said, laughing.

'Pretty much.' Behr laughed too.

'Until a murderer walked in.'

'Right. I've been running all the plates, doing geographic profiling, running a circle hypothesis.' It was a theory that suggested that serial offenders didn't go too far from home and lived within a sphere whose diameter was equal to the distance between the two farthest offenses. Generally ten square miles.

'Right,' Sasso said. 'But I'm not sure that theory holds in a car town like Indianapolis. People drive twenty, forty miles a day here and still feel like they never went anywhere.'

'That's where I've ended up with it,' Behr said. 'I've got body dumps twenty-seven miles apart.'

'Besides, even if the guy was there at your meeting, he could've ridden with a friend. Or walked. Or parked somewhere else. You probably don't even have a plate on him,' Sasso said.

'That's starting to settle in on me. Another few hours of work and I'll be through all of it, including the dozen or so who registered on the website.'

'So you really *don't* have squat,' Sasso said. 'Except Prilo.'

'Except Prilo,' Behr agreed. 'Even my expert, who was plenty skeptical at first, is ready to buy.' After the meeting, Mistretta cautioned him not to lean too far into one theory or to settle, but couldn't disagree that Prilo's presence slanted things heavily in his direction.

'Occam's razor says you shouldn't bother looking much further.'

'I don't know if his showing up makes me like him more for it, but it makes me like him a lot for having *some* connection, for knowing something real.'

Behr drained his glass and fell silent while Sasso refilled it from the tap.

'Did I hear right about you having a kid?' Sasso asked.

'You heard right. A son.'

'Holy shit, great news. How's that all going?'

It was a short dagger to Behr's gut. He tried to hide it. He considered spilling his mistakes and regrets and asking for advice on how to put it all back together. But Sasso was just his old training officer and, at the moment, his bartender, and barely a friend anymore; he wasn't his father confessor.

'Going good,' Behr said.

He felt Sasso read him, almost say something, decide not to, and then reach for the tap and draw himself beer.

'Here's to not knowing jackshit,' Sasso said, raising a glass.

'Yep,' Behr said.

'And to your son.'

They touched glasses and drank.

FIFTY-THREE

'WE NEED THE quarterly numbers on Ramapo Industries,' Kenny, his manager, says, standing in his office doorway.

'Okay. I'll have them before the weekend.' It is Thursday afternoon, so Kenny won't have to wait long.

'And the year-to-date projections based on cash flow for Constantine. How you coming on that?'

'That I have for you now,' he says, digging around on his desk and finding a folder.

'My man, Hardy,' Kenny says.

'Paper copy, and I'll e-mail you the file,' he says, handing over the folder.

'Good deal,' Kenny says, and leaves.

Later, he is heading to the kitchen for a coffee and comes upon a group of five people from his department. Claudia and Beth, Tom and Grant, and Kenny. They shift and get a little quiet when they see him, but he's heard what they are talking about: their plans for the evening. He knows he makes them uncomfortable. He is a bit older than most of them, maybe that is why. Or maybe it's the hair, the eyebrows, the alopecia universalis from which he suffers. All the hair on his body started falling out in clumps in his early twenties right when basic training ended. The doctors couldn't explain it. It was some sort of immune system failure, they said, and suggested it could have been brought on by stress. It was right around the time of Mother's illness and death, and grief, they said, could be a trigger. What they didn't recognize was that it was basic itself, with all the talk of killing and the shooting and bayoneting and hand-to-hand, that had lit a magnesium fire in him, and that checking his urges was the stressor. If he'd only recognized what was happening and started in on his life's work sooner, it would have abated, and his whole body wouldn't have become smooth. But it had happened the way it had happened, as all things did. Regardless, the younger set these days expects everything and everybody to be perfect, and turn away from anyone who isn't.

After a moment Kenny clears his throat. 'Colts game at eight twenty, NFL Thursday-night edition down at Scotty's. Are you in?'

'Thank you, Kenny, guys, for the invite, but I am not in. I've got some stuff to do tonight.'

'All right, Hardy,' Kenny says. If there is relief in Kenny's eyes, he can't see it. 'Next time.'

'Indeed,' he says, and goes to fix his coffee. He watches them break up and go their separate ways. He does have something to do. He has a busy night ahead of him.

FIFTY-FOUR

*R*INGING . . .

 . . . Why the hell is my phone ringing in the middle of the night? Behr wondered.

It wasn't like he didn't need the sleep. It was four in the morning on the third day since the community meeting and it was official now: after running all the plates, parking tickets, and traffic stops in the areas of the body drops, he'd come up bone-dry. His effort had been a complete waste of time, and a third of a bottle of Wild Turkey had been his only solace once he'd finished.

The phone rang again and his mind went to Susan, calling about something wrong with Trevor, and his heart raced as he reached out and grabbed his phone from his nightstand but saw that Gary Breslau, not Susan, was the caller.

'What's up?' Behr asked.

'It's Quinn,' Breslau said.

'What about him?'

'Someone got him. He's at Eskenazi, in Smith Trauma. I'm on my way there now.'

'So am I,' Behr said, putting his feet on the floor.

Behr heard the wailing before he even turned the corner and saw the police officers in the hospital hallway standing guard.

'Frank Behr,' he said, as they squared to him.

'Lieutenant said he's good,' one of them told the other, and they pushed the door open, causing the pained cry to grow louder as he entered.

The room was full of doctors and nurses, with Breslau and a few other cops in street clothes, but was dominated by Sheri Quinn, the source of the sound, her petite figure vibrating with anguish and fear. Behr's eyes met Breslau's, but before they could exchange a word, a doctor cleared from the bedside and Behr got a look at a battered and mutilated Quinn. His head was massively swollen and wrapped in white bandages that were stained through with seeping bright red blood. Quinn's eyes were blackened and closed, his nose looked broken, and his jaw appeared to be wired in place. And that was the good news. Behr's gaze traveled down Quinn's body, where bloody bandaged stumps were all that remained at the end of his forearms. Quinn's hands were gone.

That was when Sheri Quinn seemed to notice Behr's presence. With a half scream she babbled something that sounded like 'You ...' and started swiping feeble blows at his chest. A female nurse and another woman, perhaps a relative, got hold of Sheri Quinn's shoulders and pulled her away.

Breslau signaled, and he and Behr retreated to a far corner of the room.

'Some workmen on a paving crew found him wandering around by the railroad tracks west of the stadium. He was all fucked up, didn't even know his own name, but he still had his wallet in his pocket...' Breslau said, his voice low.

Behr looked at Sheri Quinn, seated now, her small frame racked with sobs.

'Blunt-force trauma to the head. Fractured skull.'

'What the hell happened to his hands?' Behr asked.

'They're gone. Amputated, with a blow torch, is the best guess.'

I had that prick Prilo in the room, Behr thought to himself, looking for someone to lash out at, *and I let him leave before getting something out of him ...*

'Ah fuck,' Behr said. 'Why is he still alive?' he asked about Quinn, as quietly as he could.

'He shouldn't be,' Breslau whispered. 'The theory is he was left for dead. Between the bludgeoning and the hands, he should've bled out and died in a matter of minutes, and he would've, but the torch cauterized as it cut and the bleeding stopped pretty quickly. Somehow the tough bastard came to and got up and started walking.'

'Fuck me,' Behr said again. 'This is my fault. For using him . . .'

'Easy,' Breslau said. 'We're thinking the same thing, that you drew the guy out, that he saw the pictures, but no one knows for sure what happened, and it's not on you.'

'Tell me you recovered some DNA this time at least.'

'They went over his body as best they could. No DNA, no evidence of rape or sodomy . . .'

Thank God for small miracles, Behr thought.

'No hits. They went over his clothes with a fine-tooth comb too and they're still working on it.'

'And?'

'You're not gonna believe this – they recovered hairs.'

'Belonging to the perp?' Behr practically jumped.

'Doubtful. Long. Blond. Female.'

'Are they—'

'They're being crossed against recent victims right now. I called a guy in Special to run it as we speak.'

'If they belong to a victim, then this is our guy,' Behr said. He'd struck a nerve. Despite himself,

Behr felt his adrenaline surge. Prilo *had* been there at the meeting, and it had incited him.

That's when they heard some babbling come from the bed, from between the clenched lips of Quinn, and Behr heard his name.

'Tell Behr . . .' the babbling came again, and the nurses and doctors made room for Behr and Breslau to approach the bedside.

'I'm here, Quinn,' he said, 'it's Behr.' Even Sheri Quinn stopped crying and went quiet.

'I'm sorry, Quinn, for what happened.' Behr moved close and Quinn's eyes flickered. 'Was it him?' Behr asked, but before he could say the name 'Prilo,' Quinn babbled, 'Hydroxyl . . . hydrox . . . benz . . .'

'What?'

'Smells like benz . . . benzy . . .'

'Smells like benzene?' Behr asked.

It wasn't a nod, but some movement in the affirmative came from Quinn.

'What does? Where?'

'Where I was . . . Where he put . . .'

'Hydroxylated benzene,' Sheri Quinn said. 'It's a chemical used in developing film. He's been going on about it since he came to. It's all he'll say. That you were right . . .'

The lead doctor, a man with steel-rimmed spectacles, thin red hair pressed to his temples, and an air of extreme competence, stepped forward and made himself noticed for the first time.

'We've got to do the procedure now,' the doctor said.

Breslau nodded and stepped back. Behr looked to him.

'He might have brain damage,' Breslau said low, pulling Behr away from the bedside. 'They want to induce a coma. They need to try and control the swelling to his brain or he could end up a fucking cauliflower.'

'Shit,' Behr said, sick to his stomach. 'Shit . . . What kind of a fucking asshole am I?'

Behr blasted the door open with a kick and stormed out to the hallway between the surprised police guards. He saw a steel medical rolling cart and picked it up, ready to smash it through a plate-glass window, when he felt hands that possessed real strength gripping his biceps, holding him back.

'What the fuck are you doing? Huh?' It was Breslau.

'I did that, in there,' Behr said, raw emotion in his voice. 'I got that guy mutilated, maybe killed. He's got kids, the wife. She could end up feeding him with a spoon. I—'

'Whoa, man. Come on. Who the fuck are you?' Breslau said. 'Who are you that you think you can control everything?'

It stopped Behr cold.

'Put it down,' Breslau said. And Behr dropped the rolling tray back onto its wheels with a clang. The cops cleared a little way down the hall, giving them some space.

'I learned it by my second year on patrol same as you must've: we're out there in the middle of it, but we're not in charge of anything. You open the chute and try and ride the bull. You might think you can dictate where it's gonna go a little, guide it once in a while. But the truth is: that beast is gonna go and do wherever and whatever the fuck *he* wants to and the best *you* can hope for is to hang on for the ride,' Breslau said.

Behr stood there staring.

'And you did. You got something going. You opened the chute. So now ride this fucker. Wait until we get back the match on those hairs, then chase down whatever it is you got.'

All Behr could do was nod.

FIFTY-FIVE

*T*HE LEAD PIPE *hitting the man's skull felt like the truth ...*

He is in bed, Margaret snoring softly beside him, thinking about it as if recalling a dream. Following the photographer off and on since the meeting only served to build his fury. All he could think of, driving behind Quinn, were those shoddy, garish photos.

That first night would've been the easiest. Quinn had split off from his friends, left the bar, drove home, parked two blocks from his loft building, and strolled casually home through the night. But he hadn't been prepared. He'd had nothing with him. He'd had no plan in place.

Over the next few days, Quinn stopped by the police station several times. He worked there after all. And a crime scene – a carjacking that turned into a fatal motor vehicle accident – that he went to shoot was thick with cops. He didn't know where else Quinn had gone, since he'd had to go to the office himself. But today, after work, once it was dark, he'd found Quinn leaving the station, perhaps for home. His senses lit up. By now he knew when the moment was coming. He made the moment come.

Quinn had pulled over at a dry cleaner not far from his place. The length of pipe felt heavy and good in his hand as he waited. The little strip mall housing the cleaner might have cameras. But Quinn might also find a parking spot right in front of his building when he got home and be inside in an instant, so he had to act. It was a calculated risk. It always was. It all was.

Quinn came out of the shop with his clothes on hangers inside a plastic bag and moved around to the trunk. The car slid like a nosing shark and thumped into Quinn's legs, hurling the photographer into the rear of his own car and then to the ground. If anybody witnessed it, it would surely look like an accident. He was out of his car, and glancing around, no passerby to be seen in the darkness, by the time Quinn was struggling for his feet, uttering sounds of protestation and pain.

The pipe cut the night. Quinn's skull absorbed the energy of the dense metal rod. If there was a noise from the first blow, he wasn't aware of it, only a sigh escaping from Quinn as he buckled back to the ground. He delivered one more blow for good measure. This time the skull yielded and he almost couldn't stop himself. He might've struck a few more times before moving on, because he sensed the arm that held the pipe moving up and down as if detached from his body.

Then it was up and into his trunk with Quinn's unconscious form – the hardest part. But it was no more heavy or ungainly than three slabs of quarter-inch gypsum drywall, or sheet metal, or two-by-fours, or feed sacks or hay bales, things he'd lifted and carried all his life through his youth and even college. Back then he'd tried to work himself into exhaustion, in order to not do what he'd been called to do. Small animals were just a silly distraction by then, but he hadn't yet been ready to become all he eventually would. There had been some uncomfortable moments, with girls he'd dated, that had ended in tears, but he'd always managed to talk his way out, to apologize, and to dive back into the work. It was almost as if it all had prepared him for Quinn.

He knew the spot out by the tracks. He had it all picked out. Not as private as his workshop, but this piece of garbage didn't deserve to be brought there. He belonged outside like refuse.

The tank was waiting, just where he'd hid it. The flint sparked like a friendly greeting, and then the oxy mix howled in the darkness while he adjusted the flame.

Quinn's body writhed as his first hand dropped off like rotten fruit, and then the second. He imagined the gouts of blood soaking into the ground in the darkness that would soon carry the hack to his death.

But then the cough of a diesel engine and backing beeps of a dump truck reached him. Some kind of crew was gearing up to work and he had to go.

The hands went into a bag, and it and the tank went into his trunk. His gloves went in on top of it all and he slipped away. He'd done it again, just what he'd had to.

His bed feels soft and warm around him. This was not like his other projects, but all the same he is ready to sleep the black, formless sleep of *afterward*. Quinn has taken his last picture, and by now, his last breath. Sleep comes and pulls him down.

FIFTY-SIX

BEHR PACED AROUND in the street in front of the crime lab, sucking on a vile, ice-cold cup of gas station coffee and waiting for the results of the DNA test. Finally, after hours that felt like days, the door swung open and Breslau stepped out.

'You do know you can come inside,' he offered.

'I needed the air,' Behr said.

'I can see that. They only ran a rapid screen. Showed that the high probability is it's *not* hair belonging to the Gibbons girl,' Breslau said.

'Okay. Who?'

'Unknown. For now. Only that they're white female. It'll take some time to run the full test and cross it against the database.'

'You'll let me know as soon as you get the full results?'

'Sure,' Breslau said.

'Anything else?'

'Django's wife got a call from their dry cleaner. An Asian guy—'

'Just like the old commercial.'

'Which one is that?'

'Never mind. What'd he say?'

'That Quinn picked up some clothes last night right before closing, and the owner found them in the street outside, the ticket still on them.'

'That's where Quinn got grabbed,' Behr said.

'We're thinking the same,' Breslau said.

'Did the owner see anything? Anything caught on camera?' Behr asked.

'Don't think so. But I've got some guys down there checking it out.'

'Can I head over?'

'Go for it,' Breslau said and gave him the address.

Behr drove too fast and hoped too much on his way to the dry cleaner. He saw an unmarked car in front when he arrived and a pair of detectives was inside the store talking to the owner, a slender man in his sixties.

'My name is Behr,' he announced when he entered.

'Breslau called about you. I'm Kelty,' a tall bald-headed detective said and then pointed to his partner. 'He's Sanchez.'

They were in the process of fingerprinting the dry cleaner, who said nothing.

'What do you have?' Behr asked.

'These are Quinn's things,' Sanchez said, indicating hangers bearing clothes covered by a plastic bag. 'We're hoping to get a fingerprint, so we're printing Mr. Kim to exclude him since he handled the bag.'

'I saw it in the street and brought it back inside,' Mr. Kim said, speaking for the first time, his English unaccented. 'I didn't know anything bad happened, I just thought he dropped it.'

'Don't worry about it, sir,' Kelty said. 'You likely didn't destroy any evidence. If there are prints on there besides yours and Quinn's, we'll find them.' The detectives bagged the bag. 'Same with Quinn's car. It was found out front and it's been transported to the lab to be run for DNA.'

'Cross any results you get with known murderers,' Behr said, thinking of Prilo.

'Thanks,' Sanchez mocked. 'How would we have thought of that?'

'Anything show up on the security cam?' Behr asked, ignoring the jab.

'Come with me,' Kelty said. 'Okay, Mr. Kim?' Kim nodded, and then Kelty, Behr, and Sanchez moved around the counter toward the back. They passed between rows of hanging clothing on rotating racks and reached a small cramped office. There they reviewed security footage on Mr. Kim's desktop computer.

The image was from a four-millimeter lens that provided a seventy-degree viewing angle stretching about thirty-five feet before it fell off into darkness. The face of a housewife registered clearly as she entered with her arms full of clothing at close to 9:00 P.M. the night before. Kelty fast-forwarded through her departure and some dead time and slowed down when Quinn appeared. He showed up empty-handed and left moments later carrying his dry cleaning. That was not something Quinn would be able to do perhaps ever again, Behr considered. Quinn left the spill of light and the range of the lens, and if anybody was in the darkness waiting for him, he was not visible in the footage. Before long the store's lights went out, and Mr. Kim came into frame, locking up.

'Nothing,' Behr said.

'Breslau said you'd want to see for yourself,' Sanchez volunteered.

'So no blood on the dry-cleaning bag?' Behr asked.

'None visible,' Kelty said. 'It'll be screened for DNA. We'll keep you in the loop.'

'Thanks,' Behr said and left.

Walking toward his car, Behr passed the spot on the street where Quinn's car had been parked and the attack had presumably begun. Another few

293

millimeters' length on the security camera lens, and the whole thing would've been viewable in Technicolor. But capturing goings-on in the street wasn't why Mr. Kim had the camera, and the 'subject' had gotten away with it again. Behr climbed into his car and his phone rang. It was Breslau calling with the next level of results from the lab. Behr couldn't believe what he was hearing. But before he acted on it, he realized what he had to do next: warn Susan.

He called her right away, but got her voice mail.

'It's me,' he said. 'It's important. I need to talk to you. Don't go to work and Trev shouldn't be in day care. Grab him up, keep him with you, and go somewhere safe. Get in touch ASAP.'

He started dialing his next call as soon as he hung up.

'Holy fuck,' Mistretta said. They were sitting in his kitchen. She'd come over right after he'd reached her. She wore a long-sleeve T-shirt and sweatpants and was clutching a mug of coffee in both hands. Behr had just told her about Quinn, how he was in the coma, his condition otherwise unchanged. He'd also just given her the results of the preliminary DNA tests that Breslau had called in to him.

'So two of the hairs were from the Crawley girl,' Mistretta said, trying to process what she'd just heard.

'Yeah, Danielle Crawley,' Behr said.

'And the other . . .'

'One strand, broken, three and a half inches long, blond female.'

'Oh boy,' Mistretta said, 'did it belong to your girl?'

'Kendra Gibbons? No. No match. Unknown white female.'

'Oh boy,' Mistretta said again, because she knew what it meant. 'The blond female's hair doesn't match any past victims, so there's a better than decent chance that there's a new, yet-to-be-discovered vic.'

'Yeah,' Behr said. He found it interesting that she hadn't said anything, besides the initial expletive, about Quinn and his hands.

'So what am I answering for you right now?'

'Well, my big question is the contamination. If someone grabbed Quinn up, put Quinn in his vehicle, or took him back to his home or wherever he carries out his kills, then why did victims' hair come up, but none of the subject's? And how come none of his DNA has presented at all? And on a related note: Why the hell was Prilo in that church basement? Can he have something to do with this?'

'A few things come to mind. Door number one: our guy is extremely careful. And lucky. Quinn's clothes and person were analyzed, not the sub's trunk, so it's an incomplete sampling at best. Door number two: it was only Prilo's morbid curiosity that had him in that church basement. Besides, how does a man working with one good arm do that to Quinn?'

'He helps someone else. Advises him, is what I'm thinking,' Behr said.

'But . . .' she began, then tapered off.

'But,' he echoed.

'But that's all investigative, not psychological, so it's not why you got me here,' she said.

Behr did his best not to let an awkward silence grow. He watched as the realization dawned on her.

'Oh, shit, this isn't about information, this is about warning me,' she said. 'You think since our guy took Quinn, now I could be in trouble too.'

Behr nodded slightly.

'You have anywhere you can go?' he asked.

'Not really,' she said. 'Nowhere I want to, anyway.'

'Well . . .' Behr said.

'I should probably be all right, right? I mean, he hasn't gone for any non-blondes.'

'He hadn't gone for any photographers either,' Behr said. It sounded stark and pitiless in the quiet of the kitchen, and he wished he hadn't put it that way.

'What should I do?' she asked, the fear fully upon her. There was something deeply wrong about seeing a spitfire like Mistretta cowed. But she wasn't a superhero, and she'd left New York to get away from this kind of ugliness.

'I'm about to get on Prilo like a tick on a hound's ass to find out what he knows, because I believe it's something. After what happened to Quinn, I'm gonna make sure he or any of his associates don't come after you or anyone else,' Behr said.

'And what if it is door number two?' she asked, sounding small and young. 'What if it has nothing to do with Prilo, and whoever else got baited into that basement is lashing out? Then you'll be sitting on the wrong guy.'

'You need to be vigilant, aware of your surroundings when you go out alone, especially at night. Make sure to set your alarm. Maybe get some motion lights outside.' Behr felt as stilted and useless as Sergeant Odoms.

'Fuck that community meeting crap,' Mistretta said.

'Look,' Behr said, 'even if he *saw* you, I don't see how it's possible he even knows who you are. Quinn's name was all over his photos. He's a known figure with the police department. But you were just another person in the room. Your name was never mentioned. And if the guy started tracking Quinn after the meeting and found out where he lived and all that, then there was no way he could've tracked you too.'

Or me, for that matter, Behr almost said aloud. *Or Susan or Trevor.*

He'd been wrong a few times in his life, though.

'Can I stay here?' she asked meekly.

'I don't want to kick you out, but that's not really gonna work,' Behr said.

'Thanks fuckloads,' she said, making him feel callous.

'I just mean I won't be here, so you'd be alone anyway. And if he's looking for you, he could be looking for me, so it won't be any safer.'

There was no sound in the kitchen as they stared at each other.

'Do you have a gun?' he finally asked.

'No,' she said.

'Do you know how to shoot?'

'Yeah, I just don't do it for fun.'

After a moment's consideration Behr reached for his back, pulled out his holstered Bulldog .44, and put it on the table. 'Something to have in the house just in case,' Behr said.

In case the locks failed and the alarm failed and in case their guy really had clocked them together and was going after them one at a time. But he didn't say any of that.

'Don't carry it around. If you need it, point and pull. Five shots. If whatever's coming at you is still moving, throw it at him and run.'

She nodded soberly. 'Can I stay for a little while, just until I get my bearings?' she asked.

'Sure. Hang out,' he said and left her there sipping her coffee while he went off to shower.

Behr heard the knock on the front door as he crossed from the bathroom to his bedroom in a towel.

'I'll get it,' he said, but it was too late. Mistretta was already standing when the door swung open, and he heard her gasp slightly. Susan was standing there holding Trevor. She'd used her key. Behr considered going for a bathrobe, but wanted to cut this off.

'Who are you?' Susan asked.

'No one. I'm ... helping Behr with a case,' Mistretta uttered.

'Are ya?' Susan said. 'You look helpful.'

That's when Behr got to the door and stepped into the domestic nightmare.

'Shit, I'm sorry,' Mistretta said, miserable, and retreated to the back room.

'Hi,' he said, and to Trevor, 'Hi-ya, buddy.'

'You called and I'm here. Do I need the details?' Susan asked, a scowl on her face.

'You can have them if you want 'em, but the upshot is: this thing I'm on maybe got dangerous.'

'Always seem to.'

'And someone helping me got hurt, badly. I have

299

no reason to believe that there's linkage to me, and certainly not to you, but I just felt I had to warn you.'

'Uh-huh. So now I've been warned,' Susan said. 'What should I do?'

'Maybe go stay with a friend, or your parents, until—'

'Until you and your little girlfriend or the police catch whoever you're looking for,' she said.

'It's not like that, Suze,' he began, but she held up a hand.

'Just don't, okay?'

'So where are you going to go?' he asked.

'I shouldn't tell you, right? That way it's safer,' Susan said, with plenty of edge in her voice.

'Right.' It was true. If Behr didn't know, if no one did, there was no chance of information leakage. Of course, there was very little chance the other way. She was punishing him, and he couldn't blame her.

'I should go. On account of how dangerous it is,' Susan said. 'Why don't you go say good-bye to Trev.'

He did and she left.

FIFTY-SEVEN

H IS BEAUTIFUL SUNBEAM, her meat is rotten, clean cuts impossible. Flesh comes off of bone. He uses every technique he's learned over time, but things are *liquefying*. He's been diverted and now he's waited too long. Timing is everything in life, in work, in death. Now she is a waste, a total goddamned waste. Foreigner is on the radio, the lead singer wailing about how it feels like the first time. It is as if they are singing directly to him. That is the worst part – how amateurish it makes him feel, like it is his first time. It brings him back to memories he hasn't entertained in so long.

She worked on post. That's how it had started. He didn't know, yet, that that was how it would always begin – with chance or fate dropping a project in front of him. As a paymaster for the MPs, at the end of his service, he had access to the personal information of almost everyone on post; he had the run of the installation and not enough to do during his shifts. He'd already met Margaret, a major's daughter but a civilian who worked at a local car dealership, and they'd begun their courtship. They'd been spending a lot of time together, but not enough to keep his mind straight. The inhibitions were still in control then, before they weakened and eventually fell. The thought of what *could be* was always with him.

Then he'd started seeing her, given name Lorie, around post far too much. He'd spot her at the PX, in the mess, in the parking lot, and in the base commander's office, where she was a nonmilitary personnel secretarial assistant. She was as popular as could be, tossing her mane of flaxen hair around, clipping it back off her face, hugging soldiers hello, laughing. He was living in a small apartment off post, and when he ran into her at the King Soopers, he knew it was a sign. She was buying dog food, magazines, and a multipack of Kit Kat candy bars, which is how he always remembers her: Kit Kat.

There had been smiles and hellos exchanged between them. That's the way it was at Fort Carson. She might've known his name. She'd probably seen it stamped on the pocket of his BDUs when he delivered payroll reports. He knew hers. That level of personal connection was not a risk he ever took again, but back then, before the first time, he didn't know better. He'd been running on instinct. Things were so pure then.

There hadn't been any conversation at the supermarket that day, just a nod in passing. He turned the aisle, abandoned his cart, and went right out to his car in the parking lot. He waited and she came out and got in her Jeep Cherokee, and he'd followed her to her home, a narrow town house with a slanted roof bunched together with hundreds of other units on Gold Rush down toward the Springs. He needed to tie her up, to touch her, to taste her, to hear her scream. Other, that bestial force that dwelled within him, had awakened, and he'd never felt anything like it.

And so it began, the following. Every day and night for weeks. When she left her job at the post, he trailed her out. When she was home, he'd be outside. When she went to the store or the mall or the bar, he'd be there. It was safe to say she became his obsession. He wasn't sure if he ever had greater focus on anything in his life than he did on that project. And with each passing moment the ache inside him grew.

Before he knew it, his kit had started coming together – rope, tape, blindfold, tarps, hacksaw, knives – the ingredients assembled from far-flung stores, all purchased separately, all paid for with cash.

He had too much stuff. He didn't know what he truly needed yet, didn't know that he'd find a way to use everything he brought, but that using more wasn't the idea. He had easy access to Tasers and stun batons through his job, but he went to a gun store and bought a commercially made civilian model – a small piece of black plastic with metal electrode teeth that snapped a thirty-thousand-volt bite. He hadn't used a stun gun since then, but that was back before he trusted himself.

He had a friend, a sergeant in the motor pool, who'd helped him unbolt the rear seat of his Corolla. He'd never again ask anyone for help in any manner, but he'd told the sergeant he had to move some things so he needed the space. The real reason was he needed a way to transport Kit Kat without her being seen. It haunted him for years, that loose end, and whether the sergeant would put it together and repeat the request to law enforcement. He even considered killing his friend, but decided that would only magnify the risk.

Finally, one night, just as his service commitment was about up, the need was boiling within him, and he couldn't wait any longer. He followed Kit Kat from her condo to a Laundromat. He waited until she'd done her wash and was carrying the basket back to her car, and then he stepped out behind her with the stun gun. The crack of the voltage in the quiet night sounded like a shot to him, and other was finally loosed.

Kit Kat slumped into his arms, and he dragged her to his car. He tied her wrists and ankles and gagged her. He had no idea how long she'd remain unconscious. He covered her with a blanket and closed the door. Straightening and turning from his car, he breathed hard, vapor clouds fogging the crisp night air. He took her laundry basket, her keys resting on top of the clean, folded clothing, and put it in her car. He was wearing rubber gloves, so fingerprints were not an issue. As he rushed back to his car, he felt he'd been on the street for hours, though it was probably less than two minutes. It seemed it was plenty of time for countless witnesses to come running up screaming for him to stop, or to call police who would converge on him in a wash of strobing blue lights and drawn weapons. But nothing had happened and nobody came. The fluorescents of the Laundromat glowed in the distance. He saw the figures of a few customers moving about within. Besides that, all was quiet. He hadn't been seen. He drove away.

That had been the smooth part. He reached the remote spot he'd chosen. There was nothing but empty wilderness not far from the Fort, and he'd strung a dark tarpaulin against the night sky. He was carrying her there over his shoulder, a quarter mile from where he'd parked off a dirt road, which proved to be exhausting even for the fit soldier he was back then, when she came to and started kicking and screaming. He dropped her too hard because of it, mistake number one. And he'd left the stun gun in the car, mistake number two. He'd started to panic at the noise and her strength, so he'd used a rock to subdue her, mistake number three, and a messy one at that. He left her there on the ground and humped it back to the car, which he'd locked his keys inside. Mistake number four. He broke a rear window and got his kit and the stun gun. He used a plastic bag he had to cover her head so no blood got on his clothes as he carried her the rest of the way. He saw the bag sucking feebly in and out of her nose area, so he knew she was still alive.

Once he had her under the tarp and on top of a ground cloth he'd spread, the wonders of what he'd done cascaded over him and caused him to break down in shuddering pleasure. Pleasure that was punctuated by Kit Kat's eyes flickering open. He tried to wipe her bleeding brow and to soothe her, but he was apparently no good at it. Before long, by virtue of the duct tape going on and coming off dozens of times on account of her wailing, screaming, and general noise, her lips – those lovely pouting lips that she kept pink and shiny with constant applications of lip gloss from a small pot she carried

– became raw and torn. That was mistake number five, and while far from his last, it was the last he bothered counting.

Death games, negotiations, and exploration went on for hours that night, as he found his way into what he instantly recognized as his life's purpose. Morning was breaking pale pink over a distant ridge before it was over and he collapsed next to her in exhaustion. There had been no sound or movement during that next day, save for circling hawks and indifferent squirrels and gophers, and he'd barely stirred until it was close to nightfall. He'd sat up and washed and drank from the jugs of water he'd stored at his make-shift camp.

That's when he began on the next phase. He told himself he would take her apart to make the burying easier, but it quickly became clear that that was just self-deception, and he was now in a place where such things were instantly stripped away. He started taking her apart because he *had* to, because he *wanted* to. He made a horrible mess of it. For a moment he wondered jealously at young novices starting in butcher shops, at how they could watch and learn at the heels of a master before trying their own hand at it. There was no apprenticeship for him. He needed to learn on his own, and the truth was: that was how he wanted it. But none of that changed the fact that clean cuts were far from clean, organs were accidentally pierced, joints that would later be severed with minimal effort were snapped with brute force. Her head came off with a pop he heard over his own grunts. His results would have horrified anyone who'd seen them. It appeared a wild carnivorous animal had done what he'd done, and not a sentient being.

The following morning he'd needed to show up to work, so he'd washed again, returned home, showered, and reported for duty. There was some talk about Kit Kat missing a shift, but so far no real concern and no authorities called in to investigate. He put off Margaret for the next three nights, instead returning to the campsite and visiting with Kit Kat's remains, luxuriating in the viscous fluids and fecund smells. He had no real interest in ever stopping, until things became dried and crusted, then liquefied again and maggots swarmed over her disassembled flesh. It brought him back to his senses and he was sick with himself, but only for a moment. His old self was changing, going away. He realized he'd been thinking about killing a person for as long as he could remember.

He dug that deep hole with his army-issue entrenching tool – a tool he possessed to this day. He stacked up the pieces that had been her and beheld their intricate majesty. He sat on the edge of the hole for a long time, filthy, exhausted, sated, disgusted, exhilarated, and more complete than he'd ever been, a deep sense of self-knowledge glowing within.

Then he buried her, her parts tumbling in, one on top of the other, and then all of the implements he'd used, save the E-tool, and one small special part he needed to remember her by: a bone he later learned was called the first proximal phalange. He smoothed dirt and rocks and pine branches over it, and scattered the extra soil so that no passing hiker would ever suspect what was there. It was only later that he'd regretted covering up what he had done. But at that moment he was new. He had *become other*.

And he'd sworn to himself as he drove back to his apartment and his job and life that he'd get much better at all of it, and he had, until now . . .

Now Sunbeam, who'd been perfect, has gone beyond the workability stage and there is nothing to do but barrel her up. What a sorry shame. And then he sees the news that the photographer, Quinn, has survived. It is a cosmic punch in the face. Sometimes the world just kicks your ass, even when you are a world creator. So now he has to dump, not display, to hide a mistake instead of show a masterpiece.

FIFTY-EIGHT

*T*IME FOR THE *bullshit to end . . .*
    Behr had been sitting outside Prilo's place
    for the better part of this nightmare of a day,
and as of yet there was no sign of the man. As he
shifted in his seat he felt the reassuring hunk of
metal heavy on his ankle, where he was wearing his
backup piece, as he should have the first time he
encountered this killer.

*Time for the bullshit to end. Time to apply the necessary
pressure to get answers. And time to collect his reward.*

After Mistretta left, and he'd finished beating
himself up over the mess he'd made with her and
with Susan and with Quinn, Behr had gone to his
gun cabinet and taken out his .357 Mag Pug, a squat,
stainless-steel revolver with a two-inch barrel and
rubberized grips. He'd picked it up for two hundred
seventy-five bucks at a gun show over the state line
in Missouri five years back, and he'd meant to register

it but never had. The guy running the booth had thrown in the ankle holster, which to Behr's mind was a bit of a silly way to carry a gun, but it was the only holster he had for it. Despite the low price, the Pug was built solidly enough and it bucked like a bronco when he put magnum rounds through it a few times at the range, but it was reliable in its groupings and he wasn't taking any more chances. He had opened a box of Winchester Silvertips and loaded it up, and then grabbed a few sandwiches and drinks and headed for Prilo's.

The exchange with Susan had left him with the distinct impression that the friend she'd be turning to for shelter and support would be her coworker Chad. She'd stopped short of letting him know it, but not by much, and it didn't seem as if she minded either way. There was nothing he could do about it, sitting as he currently was, except add it to his already boiling blood.

Fat clouds trekked across the sky, and they darkened as the sun dropped and the day ended. An older man in a flannel coat came out the front door from inside carrying a small metal toolbox and climbed up on a stepladder to change the bulb on the porch light. Behr got out of the car and approached him. The man was large boned and mostly bald, and Behr wondered if he was possibly Prilo's father.

'Excuse me,' Behr said, and the man looked down.

'I'm trying to catch up with someone who lives here. Jerry Prilo.'

'I'm the super,' the man said. 'He's at the hospital getting some surgery. Said something about staying overnight.'

'What kind of surgery? When did he go in?' Behr asked. If it was the day before it might put a hole in his theory that Prilo did Quinn.

'Went in early this morning. For his arm.'

'What hospital?'

'St. Vincent's,' the super said. 'Say, are you a friend of his?'

'No, I'm not,' Behr said, walking to his car.

FIFTY-NINE

CIRCUMSTANCE INVADES THE world he so carefully creates and controls. The chain of events is maddening. Going back to that abomination in the church basement – those photos, that cop, the dark-haired woman, the big guy. He just wanted to have one special thing. It wasn't his mother. It wasn't God. It was his projects. So he'd been forced to act. He'd *had* to. He couldn't just leave Quinn walking around, to risk having him deface another project with his *pictures*. But in effect, that's exactly what Quinn has done.

He pulls out the pale blue plastic rectangular storage boxes he's just picked up at OfficeMax. They have snap-on lids and fit side by side into the trunk of his car. He has the spot all picked out. While the others were meant to be discovered, to be seen in awe and admiration, this is a place where she'll never be found.

Worst of all, the itch is back, the pressure, that bubbling up of greater forces deep in his belly. It demands he act. And soon. Now.

SIXTY

THE FIRST THING he heard was the weeping.
It seemed every damned hospital room Behr walked into these days was full of it. This time it wasn't quite what he expected, though. This time it was Jerold Allen Prilo, propped up in bed, draped in a hospital gown, his right arm wrapped in a cast and suspended in weightless traction by cables. His face was red and wet with tears and slobber as he cried and muttered to himself. Behr had talked Prilo's room number out of a nurse at the reception desk, and no one had questioned him as he walked the sixth-floor hallway. Visiting hours lasted for another hour or so. Plenty of time.

'What's wrong with you?' Behr asked, arriving at the side of the bed.

For a moment Prilo didn't show any reaction at all. He just continued crying, head hanging down, shoulders shaking from the force of it.

'Hey,' Behr said, 'I asked what's wrong with you.' Behr grabbed him by the chin and looked into Prilo's eyes. The man was barely there. Behr checked his IV drip and saw a small bag of medicine in a locked electronic dispenser port: Demerol.

'It all came back,' Prilo said. His speech was rubbery, slurred. Some of it may have been due to the residual damage to his tongue from their fight, but it was mostly narcotic. 'They all came back . . .'

'There's a limiter on your pain meds. What are you on?' Behr asked. No answer came, so Behr looked in the drawer of the bedside table. There were keys, a wallet and a cell phone, and a few pill bottles – OxyContin and Percocet. Behr popped one bottle open and saw it was nearly empty and that there was fine, white dust in the bottom, a telltale sign that Prilo was grinding up and snorting the drugs in a way that intensified their potency.

'How much of this did you take?' Behr asked.

Prilo just shrugged. 'It's been years since I tasted it. Years.'

'You're not on all this shit for the arm?' This time Prilo shook his head no. 'Did I do that, your elbow?' Behr asked.

Now Prilo nodded yes and drooled a little. He was a full mess. But Behr wasn't there on a mission of mercy, and he certainly wasn't there to apologize or dish out comfort.

'Quinn,' Behr said, grabbing Prilo's chin again and slapping him hard across the face. 'Tell me about Django Quinn.'

Coherence flickered into Prilo's eyes. 'The photographer . . .'

'That's right,' Behr said. 'Did you do him?'

'Do what?' Prilo asked. His mystification seemed genuine. 'Don't hurt me, but I don't know what you wanna know.'

'You messed up Quinn, the photographer. You followed him after the meeting. For days. You picked your spot and you took him.'

'No.'

'Tell me. You hurt him, bad.'

'No. That's not my thing. He don't matter to me.'

It was what Behr figured, so with that out of the way, he moved on.

'Right. But you know who he does matter to. And you helped. You and your sick buddy stalked him, beat him, and mutilated him. Tell me who he is.'

'What the fuck?' Prilo said, his eyes rolling in his head.

'I'm gonna ask you again, and if you don't start getting helpful I'll undo everything they just fixed on you. And then some,' Behr said. 'Where were you last night? Who were you with?'

'I was home. I couldn't eat or drink anything after

seven. I was pilled out and sleeping by six-thirty, I think.'

Fuck, Behr thought and picked up Prilo's chart and saw the date of the operation: it was that morning at 6:00 A.M. Could Prilo have been involved with what had happened to Quinn and reported for surgery hours later? As much of a crafty, murdering psychopath as Behr knew him to be, about this Prilo seemed truthful.

'Here, show me who you're working with,' Behr said, pulling out his phone and starting to scroll photos from the community meeting. 'Point him out to me.'

'I don't know those guys, man,' Prilo protested.

'Let's go back to Kendra Gibbons then,' Behr said, starting to feel the slick slide of desperation.

'Your case.'

'That's right. Did the girl get abducted and murdered a little over eighteen months ago?'

'Coulda been, but that's just me guessing.'

'You know something about it.'

Again, Prilo shook his head no.

'You know who's been chopping up these women – the one in Northwestway and the one that was found over at Donovan-Grant,' Behr said, putting his phone down, as Prilo whipped his head from side to side.

Behr changed gears and went empathetic. He relaxed his posture and sat heavily on the edge of the bed. 'I know you don't want to be a part of this, man. I understand.'

'You do?' Prilo said quietly.

'Yes. Things got away from you. You were trying to walk the line, but it's so hard . . .'

Prilo was almost nodding along as he listened, but then he stopped and looked up.

'So just tell me how it went. You met this guy somewhere, or he approached you, because he knew about what you'd done . . . somehow it all got going again. Look, it's okay. We'll put you somewhere you can get some help. The important thing is you give me the other guy. We don't care about him, we care about you.' Behr laid it on thick, the most comforting tone he could dredge up.

'No, man. No. I tell you I'm through with that. I'm all through. I haven't done anything in a long, long time, and I don't know anyone who did.'

Either the empathy didn't work or Prilo was telling it straight. Running low on options, Behr raised the phone again.

'So you don't know the guy. Look at these photos and pick me some likely candidates. Men you've seen around at the wrong places, one you've just got a feeling about.'

Prilo's eyes flickered as the images scrolled by.

'Those are just a bunch of faces to me. Just leave me alone, please.'

'Fine,' Behr said, hopeless and trying to salvage *something* from the visit. 'I'll go if you help me.'

'What you want?' Prilo asked.

'DNA,' Behr said.

'What about it?'

'You seemed surprised that there was none recovered. Why?'

'On account of the semen – he's got to be using them for *that* – and there's no way you can account for *all* of it.'

'You said *there are ways* to get around leaving DNA,' Behr pressed. 'Condoms?'

'I doubt that.'

'He ... finishes ... somewhere other than in them?'

'Doubt that even more.'

'What then?'

Prilo took a pause, a bit more coherence coming to his eyes, then said: 'Bleach, most likely. Sodium hypochloride or a strong hydrogen peroxide solution. We're talking about a PCR inhibitor, see.'

'PCR?'

'Polymerase chain reaction. That's what the lab rats use to amplify DNA so it can be tested.' Prilo was really coming around now, warming to his subject.

'So, bleach,' Behr repeated. 'Bleach destroys residual DNA.'

'Destroy is a big word. But render it unusable? Yeah. See the techs try and amplify it, like I said. You can't let 'em amplify it . . .' Prilo started to lose focus and drift away. 'If they amplify it, you're fucked . . .'

'Why are you taking this?' Behr asked, shoving the pill bottles into Prilo's face.

'The bodies. Those pictures. Our . . . *talk*. It all got back in my head. Everything and everyone from the old days. The old motherfucking visions came back.' Prilo banged at his temple as if trying to knock something loose. 'I didn't want them back. I was trying, but they're so strong. They don't have meetings for what I got,' he said. 'You don't know what it's like, man. Once you've seen what I seen, felt what I've felt . . . being in the regular world is like living on mute. Doing what I done? You have no idea what it's like, no idea.'

'The guilt, you mean?' Behr asked, feeling that perhaps he understood the man and his sorrow and distress for a moment.

But that small smile, mad and maddening, curled at Prilo's lips. 'No . . . the thrill.'

Behr was stunned into silence for a moment as Prilo went on.

'When you find one, a young one, and you grab her up and she's *yours*, and when you tie her down and touch that skin—'

Behr stood and got a handful of the man's hospital gown and put his face an inch from Prilo's.

'Listen to me, you sick piece of shit. You do not hurt anybody else now. You hear me? Because I've got you and I'm looking at you, and if you hurt anybody ever again I'll know about it and I will fucking hunt you down and kill you.' Behr wanted to do it now. He knew he should. Beat him to death, strangle him, find a way to unlock the Demerol IV and overdose him. But Behr controlled himself and slammed Prilo back against the bed, jarring the bad arm and causing him to emit a moan of pain.

'I know you will . . .' Prilo said, his head sagging back down and the tears starting to return. 'I know . . .'

'Stop taking this crap,' Behr said and flung the pill bottles across the room. 'Get yourself into a detox program or a mental ward or turn yourself in to your parole officer. You hear me?'

Prilo nodded, but succumbed to another paroxysm of sobs. The room suddenly felt airless and rife with evil to Behr, and he had to get out of it.

Stepping off the elevator in the hospital lobby, he texted Breslau: 'Check the body cavities for bleach.'

SIXTY-ONE

*Y*OU ARE JUST *being stupid . . .*

That's what he tells himself as he drives the streets of the Southeast Side.

Plain dumb.

He's already had plenty of night. The drive down south to the Shelby County line to White Rock, where there were plenty of swimmers in the deep, cold quarry water during the summer, but no one and nothing in the winter. Then the tough hike to the cliff's edge over the water, and the drive all the way back. He was tired, but did he head home like he should? Oh, no. He went looking. And what he knew well was this: when counting on fate, you can't go looking, to try to force the issue. No, you have to wait for it to come to you.

He skirts the eastern edge of the city and begins driving the East Washington corridor where the prostitutes work.

Find one, find one.

Back and forth he goes, east and west, and north to south on Sherman too. Fortune won't smile. She is indifferent to him tonight. There is hardly any foot traffic. No one is in the cars parked along the road-sides either. He sees one girl walking – she is a large African American. *Can she do for him in a pinch?* No. She may not have even been working, as far as he knew. *She's just wrong.* He continues past.

Failure clouds the car around him, and he finds himself drifting west on 10th, hardly paying attention, when a little strip mall set in a depression below the grade of the road on the right-hand side catches his eye.

Yes.

A tiny blonde in a short skirt and a puffy coat gets out of a white Kia hatchback, slings the strap of her striped bag over one shoulder, and enters the only business still currently lit and open: Oriental Grand Massage.

He knows what kind of place it is, and he slows. He considers a looping U-turn that will put him back in the parking lot in seconds, but instead pulls over to a metered spot on the right. *Careful now.* He doesn't need anyone leaving the place clocking his license plate.

He sits there for a long time, drumming his fingers on the steering wheel, and considers whether or not to go in. He knows he shouldn't, but the sight of the little blonde bouncing through the winter night in her miniskirt has ahold of him. Fortune always comes through if you give her enough time. The black woman, continuing on her way, walks past the car and on into the darkness. He glances over at the parking lot. There are half a dozen cars there. *Too many.* He decides to wait.

SIXTY-TWO

'YOUR SUSPECT IS DEAD.'

The words stopped Behr in his tracks and caused him to turn. After the hospital he'd needed a drink and to see people, to be among them. He'd considered going to Mistretta's. He figured she could probably use the company, but he didn't have it in him to do much talking. So he'd sent her an e-mail asking if she was okay, and she'd replied that she was, and he'd ended up at Sasso's bar. Sasso was off for the night and Behr had drunk alone, watching humanity interacting around him like he was an alien scientist sent from another planet merely to observe. When he'd had enough he headed for home, just after 11:00. He'd gotten no response to his text to Breslau, but here the man was, stepping out of the darkness near Behr's door.

'What?' Behr asked.

'Prilo. Dead,' Breslau said, while Behr's mind

struggled to put the information in place. 'Took a header out his hospital room window. Last visitor was a 'hulking man' who didn't sign in but got Prilo's room number from a nurse and sounds a fuck of a lot like you. Who am I going to see when I pull the hospital security tapes?' Breslau asked.

'You're gonna see me,' Behr said, resigned.

'Motherfucker!' Breslau said through a clenched jaw. 'I help and help you and you grease me up and cornhole me—'

'Nah, Bres,' Behr began.

'Did you toss this shitheel out his window?'

'Hell no.'

'You liked this guy for Crawley, or your Gibbons girl or Quinn or all of 'em, and you went in and it went bad and you sent him.'

'No,' Behr said, unnerved by how close Breslau actually was to the truth of it. 'I did like him for all of it. You're right about that. But then I didn't, but I thought he might know something. So I went to see him, but it was blanks.'

'And now?'

'I don't know. I don't think so. But go check the tapes. They'll have me exiting well before Prilo took his flight. I guarantee it.'

'Oh, you guarantee it? How the fuck can you guarantee that?' Breslau grabbed the front of Behr's coat and yanked him forward. Behr felt his anger surge and thought they were headed for a fistfight. He'd scrapped with cops before and things had stayed hand-to-hand, but whenever armed men were in a fracas, the possibility of guns being drawn and shots being thrown was always there. Behr got his footing and broke Breslau's grips, he didn't want to strike or take him down. He didn't want to escalate things at all, so he merely shoved Breslau back with a two-handed blast to the chest.

'Because I didn't do it,' Behr said, as evenly as he could. 'I didn't kill him.'

All he saw coming back was molten fury in Breslau's eyes. Behr regretted it, because despite the cop being half a prick to him at various times, he liked him and the man had been trying to help him.

'So I'll see someone else coming into the room after you?' Breslau pressed. 'Is that what you're telling me?'

'Maybe . . .' Behr considered the kind of enemies a guy like Prilo could have collected over his lifetime – relatives of victims, people he'd hurt, perhaps – and whether there was a possibility that one of them came to exact payback. Then Behr considered the condition Prilo was in when he left. 'But maybe not.'

'Suicide?' Breslau said, the anger seeming to boil down a bit as Breslau struggled to regain his sense of procedure. 'Preliminary word from the hospital is

that there were no entries after you left. You think he
did himself?'

'I think he could have,' Behr said. 'They'll find a
hell of a drug cocktail in his system. He was in a state
of extreme distress.'

'You help put him there?' Breslau demanded.

Behr didn't answer this. He and Breslau just stared
at each other. 'Gary, this guy was a murdering piece
of shit. And I'm not just talking about Mary Beth
Watney.'

'The one he served time for?'

'Right.'

'You got other cases against him? Gibbons
maybe?'

'None that I can make, especially now, and not
her,' Behr said, and saw the disappointment in
Breslau's eyes. 'It may be a messy situation at the
moment, but this world's better off.'

'Who are *you* to fucking decide?' Breslau asked.

It was a hell of a question and Behr just gritted his
teeth, unable to find words to answer. Breslau dug
his feet into the concrete, ready to leave.

'Did bleach chemicals come up in the bodies?'
Behr asked.

Breslau looked up. 'Yeah ... it was present in
tissue samples from inside Crawley's mouth, vagina,
and rectum.'

'Jesus,' Behr breathed.

'Same with the Northwestway Park victim. There were even traces inside the body cavity on that one.'

The implications of that, of why the killer would need to douse the *inside* of the body, sickened Behr.

'Any more detail will call for an exhumation.'

'Prilo gave me that piece, you know. Told me just what to look for and where. So even though no one likes him for *these* murders . . . well, like I said.'

'Yeah, like you said . . . I've gotta go. I've got a fresh bag of crap over in a house on North Talbot.' Every day was a fresh bag of crap on a big-city police force. Everyone's problems washed up onto your shoes, and nobody's good news ever did. It was something Behr didn't miss.

'What's today's?'

'A strangled eleven-year-old girl and a missing persons on the aunt she was staying with,' Breslau said, and started walking off.

'Hey, if anyone comes up on that tape going in to see Prilo after me, let me—'

'I'll be fucking sure to,' Breslau said, and crossed to his car without another word.

Behr went inside, feeling beaten and confused, which was about the only way he could remember feeling lately. All the dead women and all the suspects and all the information tacked to his walls were swirling around his brain in a hopeless morass. He took out a bottle of Wild Turkey and got a glass of ice and considered doing some serious damage. There was no more case and no money and no tomorrow. The last thing he remembered after his first big pour was sending a text to Mistretta telling her things looked okay, that with Prilo gone she was probably safe. She invited him over but he didn't respond. He fell asleep on the couch only to be awoken by his phone's angry buzzing on the coffee table.

'Yeah,' Behr said. The screen on the phone said 3:40, and only the 'A.M.' made him sure it wasn't the next afternoon.

'Yo, man,' an unfamiliar voice said. 'You told me to call you.'

'Who's this?'

'Jonesy, man. You remember me?'

'I remember.'

'You told me to tell Shantae to call me if she saw the dude.'

'The dude—'

'That *wrong* dude from the night when Kendra went gone.'

'Shantae saw him? When?' Behr asked.

'A little while ago,' Jonesy.

'How's that possible?' Behr said aloud.

'The fuck does that mean, bro? You told me to put

331

out word, to call if she spotted the motherfucker. That's what she did, now I'm calling you.'

'All right, I was half asleep. I'm up now,' Behr said, standing, his adrenaline obliterating the liquor and fatigue. 'Where can I find her and what does she look like?'

SIXTY-THREE

Happy Wok near Sherman Commons was far from happy at just after 4:00 in the morning, though the all-night Chinese spot did indeed smell like a greasy skillet. Behr walked in to find two wrung-out kitchen workers sitting at a back table playing cards, and no customers besides Jonesy, who was looking like all kinds of bad news, sitting with Shantae Williams, a broad, strong-bodied African American woman in her late twenties or early thirties. She had long, twisted hair that could have been a weave, and when she gazed up at Behr it was with rheumy eyes that said she was on something.

As Behr reached the table, Jonesy blocked the other chair before he could sit, and he saw it wasn't going to be a long or friendly chat.

'Tell him what you told me,' Jonesy commanded Shantae.

'I saw that freaky white dude,' Williams said, a cigarette rasp to her voice.

'Okay,' Behr said, 'why was he freaky?'

'He just is.'

'What's he look like?'

'Plain. Just a face. A hat. But weird, you know?'

Behr didn't know. 'Where?'

'Up on Tenth, east of Sherman, I think. I's walking.'

'What was he doing?'

'Sitting.'

'Sitting?'

'In his car.'

'You talk to him?'

'Hell no.'

'License plate?'

'Nope.'

'What kind of car?'

'Blue one.'

'Color was blue. The kind?'

'Four doors. American style. Kind of nice.'

'Model, make?'

'Don't know, I ain't in the detective squad. I ain't fucking five-oh.'

'When was this?'

'Couple hours ago.'

Behr gritted his teeth. Those hours were most likely very costly.

'What happened in between?' he asked.

'I had things needed doing. I forgot, then I remembered.'

Behr looked to Jonesy.

'Don't eye-drill me,' Jonesy said. 'She called me and I had to track down your number. Now you know what she knows, and I can forget all about your irritating ass, right?'

'I'm gonna miss you too,' Behr said, then turned to Shantae Williams.

'Anything else?'

'Not unless you wanna go somewhere and give it a try.'

'What?'

'Go for a roll, big boy,' she said, and half laughed. 'Fitty-dollar ticket to heaven.'

'Tempting,' Behr said.

She shrugged and Jonesy piped up again.

'Pay for her shrimp-fried rice. Least you can do.'

Behr sighed and reached for his money.

'It was a long time ago, you're sure this was the same guy you saw near Kendra Gibbons that night?'

Shantae's eyes momentarily cleared and her jaw set.

'I'm a hundred percent sure this is the stock-same motherfucker.'

Behr had his window open, cold air slapping his face, as he drove the streets in a grid pattern searching for a kind of nice, American-style, four-door blue car piloted by a freaky white dude. It was fairly hopeless. Oncoming cars were just glaring headlights until they passed. Almost everything was closed for the night. Very little life or activity of any kind was taking place at this hour. Even if this guy *was* the guy and he *had* been out, why wouldn't he be home in bed or just generally gone by now?

He kept up the grid though, wondering what he'd do when he'd exhausted the bordering streets and had nothing else to try. That's when he turned onto 10th just east of Sherman and saw some motion in a strip center. Any type of action was too much at this time of night, so Behr drove toward it. He saw two cars pull out – neither one of them blue or American made. And just as he got there he saw a squat Asian man get out of an SUV and enter a business, which was open, and happened to be a massage parlor. Behr got out of his car and followed him in.

Bells on the door chimed and canned Asian spa music greeted him when he walked in, but that was the only thing soothing about the place. Two young Korean tough guys with rooster-like haircuts and bad skin leapt toward him the minute he was inside. One grabbed him by the arm with one hand, and Behr saw he held a rusty five-iron in the other. The other guy held a putter, though they weren't looking to play eighteen holes. Behr pummeled his arm free from the first guy's grip and shoved him, sending him toppling to the floor.

The guy with the putter raised his weapon, and Behr charged him before he could swing. They crashed into the wall as the first guy got up and rejoined the fray. Behr slammed the putter wielder into his friend and used their momentary imbalance to drop and reach for the Mag Pug on his ankle, when an aged woman behind the counter screamed out in frantic Korean. The guy with the putter lowered the club and stepped back, the one with the five-iron squared up with the club still raised while Behr stood straight and opened his hands at chest level.

'Is that him?' the squat man, in his fifties, asked of Behr.

'No,' came the answer from the older woman.

'No,' echoed another female voice from behind the older pair. Sitting on a stool was a petite Asian girl with dyed blond hair. The hair color wasn't her distinguishing feature at the moment. Rather it was the swollen cheekbone and black eye she sported.

'We closed now,' the squat man said firmly to Behr, 'you get out, come back some other time.'

'I'm not a customer,' Behr said. 'What happened here?'

The old lady spoke in Korean, but the squat man seemed to ignore her.

'You not a cop,' he said. 'We know the cops around here.'

'Not a cop,' Behr said. 'What happened?'

Now the young tough guy with the putter spoke. 'A asshole beat our cousin and we gonna crack some fucking skull.'

'I think I may be looking for the same asshole,' Behr said. 'Can I talk to her?'

None of them answered for a moment, then the girl spoke in Korean and slid off the stool.

'I talk to you,' she said, and crossed to a couch in a sitting room. Behr followed.

'You might want to get some ice on your face,' Behr offered.

'I already did that,' she said in a sad voice that made Behr feel for her.

'What's your name?'

'Jasmine,' she said. He doubted it was her real name, probably the one she worked under.

'How'd it go down, Jasmine?' Behr asked.

'Guy come in right after my shift start. I don't see him come in, I in back. He ask for me.'

'By name?'

'He ask for blonde,' she said. 'I the blonde.'

'You ever have him before?'

She shook her head. 'Most white guys his age okay. Not him.'

'Then?'

'We go in back. He no want to take off clothes. He no want nothing. He say he want to hit me. He say he pay me,' Jasmine said.

Behr suddenly felt the bit in his teeth. The guy had probably spotted Jasmine in an online ad, or on the street or someplace else and followed her, thinking she was his type – which she was, albeit not a natural blonde, and that's when Shantae Williams had seen him.

'What'd you say?'

'I say: you joking. He say: this no joke. I say: fuck no. He say: it gonna happen, I pay. I say no. He say he gonna do it.'

'How'd he expect to get out of here clean?' Behr wondered aloud.

'I don't know. I scream, my cousins kill his ass. But he knock me out,' Jasmine said. 'He a asshole. He a motherfucker.'

'Did you call the police?' Behr asked, doubting it due to the nature of their business.

'No police,' a male voice said.

That's when Behr noticed the two tough guys and the squat man had drifted over. They weren't menacing him now. They were just interested.

'Can you describe him?' Behr asked. 'Was he plain looking, wearing a cap? What color hair?'

'He don't got no hair.'

'No hair,' Behr repeated, feeling an excited stab in

his lungs at a piece of potentially strange information. 'So he was bald, or . . . ?'

'No hair, man. None. He got this weird wig under
the hat. He draw on eyebrows with a pencil.'

Behr didn't speak for a moment, as he felt possible
understanding washing around him like an insistent
tide. There had been no DNA recovered on any of
the scenes, and he had already found a potentially
logical reason for how that could be thanks to Prilo.
But no hair fibers belonging to a perpetrator had
been recovered either, on any of the victims, at any
of the sites, even from Quinn, on whom *victims'* hair
had been found. Now Behr felt he knew why.

'He wear a rug, like he have cancer or some shit,
but he don't seem sick,' Jasmine went on. Behr
wondered if the guy had that medical condition that
caused hair loss – he couldn't recall the term at the
moment – then one of the tough kids spoke up.

'Why you looking for him?'

He turned and considered the kid. Would it do
more good for Behr to pretend he had a girlfriend or
sister who had been beaten up by the guy he was
looking for? Without much thought, Behr abandoned
the idea of a pretext and just told him:

'I'm a private investigator tracking a missing girl. I
think this guy may be killing women. I'm trying to
catch him.'

There was the sound of Jasmine crying out in fear

at what might've been, then it went quiet for a beat, before a burst of a staccato Asian dialect between the men filled the room and a decision seemed to be reached.

The squat man was the one who spoke next. 'You come.'

He crossed the sitting room and disappeared through a door into the back. Behr followed, and the two young guys followed him, and he wondered if he was walking into some kind of ambush. But the door led into a cramped office dominated by a desk that was completely covered in an avalanche of paperwork and a battered computer.

One of the young guys sat down and his fingers flew over the keyboard, bringing up split-screen images of several security cameras.

'These no supposed to be here. Very illegal. For safety of girls, to protect from entrapment,' the squat man said.

Or to blackmail patrons, Behr thought.

'You don't say nothing,' the squat man cautioned. Behr nodded his assent.

The images came from half a dozen small rooms and showed a few massages, of varying states of legitimacy, in progress. Most of them had taken place earlier and had been digitally logged. It was possible one or two were happening live. There were even cameras rigged in the bathrooms, and in one an Asian woman with long black hair was in the shower copiously washing her crotch. As the kid typed, the images from one room were played back with high-speed scrubbing, and Behr recognized Jasmine entering her space, which had Chinese restaurant give-away calendars stuck all over the walls, a burning incense stick and candle, and a single pink vinyl massage table with a pillow on it.

Before long the older woman appeared in the doorway with a man, *the* man, behind her. She sent him in and then left, and the tough kid let the images slow to regular speed. Behr watched as the man stepped inside. He was just beyond medium height, perhaps five foot eleven, squared off and solid looking, but it was hard to tell because of his tan canvas coat and roomy-cut khaki pants. On the monitor, Jasmine smiled at him and closed the door. There was no sound, but it appeared she offered to take his coat. He shook his head and kept his hands jammed in his pockets as he sat on the edge of the massage bed. The camera position was high, prob-ably cut into the ceiling or placed in a light fixture or a vent, so the brim of the man's beige-colored base-ball cap obscured his face. Despite there being no truly identifying factors, Behr found something familiar about the man.

Jasmine stood across from him and gestured for him to lie down. The man shook his head. He said something to her, reached for a back pocket, and pulled out his wallet.

'Freeze it there,' Behr said. The kid stopped the clip. Behr stared at the open wallet, trying to see a driver's license or other identification, but the image was hopelessly small and would lose resolution if it were blown up to any decent size. 'All right, run it,' Behr said.

The man continued with his wallet, taking out two bills, placing them on the massage bed and putting away the wallet.

'So this guy had never been in before?' Behr asked.

'Never,' grunted the squat older Asian man.

'Those are hundred-dollar bills.' It was Jasmine peeking in from the doorway of the office.

'What did he say to you?' Behr asked.

'He say he want to punch me, like I tell you.'

The Jasmine on the computer monitor grew agitated, while the squat man spoke in Korean and the real Jasmine in the office averted her eyes. Behr glanced back to the monitor to see the khaki-clad man rear back and nail the poor girl in the side of the face with his clenched right fist. Her head jerked and her neck whiplashed, then she went stiff and collapsed in the way that knockout victims do – like a felled tree and without her arms extended to help break the fall.

The man loomed over Jasmine's unmoving figure, and his right hand went straight down the front of his pants and he began tugging. After a moment Jasmine's legs started twitching, and the man pulled his hand out. Whether he was finished or not was hard to tell.

'The hundred-dollar bills,' Behr said, feeling a surge of excitement over the possibility of a fingerprint. But almost as if the man on the video heard him, he picked up his bills and pocketed them.

'Shit,' Behr breathed.

Then the man looked around the room, spotted a small folded towel on the edge of the massage table, took off his cap, and swabbed his face with it, and in the moment he moved the towel and replaced the cap, Behr realized he'd found his few frames of a chance. Then the man ran out, wiping the doorknob with the towel on his way.

'Freak motherfucker!' the tough kid who wasn't working the computer said.

'How would you feel about calling the police with this?' Behr asked. Maybe Breslau and his resources could help track the guy down.

'Fuck the cops,' the kid on the computer said. Behr looked to the older squat man. All he saw were dead eyes and the man shaking his head emphatically no.

'You find him, we pay you to bring him to us,' the kid on the computer said.

The squat man nodded gravely in agreement. 'We pay you ten thousand for the chance to fuck him up.'

Not nearly enough, Behr thought.

'I'm going to need some stills from that security footage,' Behr said.

SIXTY-FOUR

QUINN HAS MADE IT. Somehow he's pulled through and is under guard now most likely. But that dark-haired slut from the community meet – how can he find her? Or the big guy. How to find him and track him and discover whether he has a wife, or children? He'd like to make him watch as he tore their skin from their muscle . . .

He doesn't have answers for the 'how' though. For now. But he will. He'll plant the questions deep, and his subconscious will sort it out. It always does. That's the way it works. And then when the answers present themselves, he'll know what to do, and he will do those things to make everything right. He will restore order.

The night was okay. It had its moments – moment anyway. But sleep isn't coming easy. It just won't come.

SIXTY-FIVE

I T WAS AROUND dawn when he heard a faint
tapping and looked up. The sound was actually
Mistretta banging on her plate-glass window to
get his attention. After stopping by home, recognizing how hopeless the idea of sleep was, Behr had
driven over to her place, getting there by around
5:45, and parked in her driveway since he hadn't
wanted to wake her.

He was out of his car, computer bag in hand, by
the time she'd reached her front door.

'You my bodyguard or just some kind of freaking
gargoyle?' she asked.

'Not sleeping much, huh,' he said.

'Just an early riser.' She stepped aside and let him
in. One look at her weary eyes told him the truth.
'What's happening?'

'I got something and wanted you to be a part of it.'

* * *

He set up his laptop at her dining table, and she got him coffee while he spouted wearily about DNA and lack of hair and what he'd learned from Shantae Williams. She sat down next to him as he opened an e-mail from the screen name 'daesoodrift,' one of the tough kids at the Oriental Grand, and quickly downloaded the images.

'Who's this?' she asked, as Behr opened and began scrolling the faces from the community meeting.

'A bad, bad man, I believe,' Behr said. He knew exactly where to look. He'd spotted the guy after five or six minutes of searching the footage before he had driven over. He'd gone ahead and sent the picture to Breslau to cross against the crime computer. The department had better software for this kind of thing, which would save hundreds of hours of combing. If the man had a record, eventually he would come up. Behr set the images next to each other on his desktop – a shot of the man with and without his hat from the massage joint and an image of him in similar hat, clothes, and pose in the church basement.

'Holy shit, Behr,' Mistretta said. 'Lookit that.'

They both stared at the pictures of the man at their staged meeting, and of him as he was captured the previous night: with his hat off, intense slate gray eyes, his shoe-polish-brown toupee and drawn-on eyebrows. Behr told her how he'd stumbled into the massage place, what had happened to Jasmine.

'You manage to get a name on this scumbag?'

'No. Not that lucky,' he said, 'but I have an idea. Just need to wait for the stores to open.'

the massage place, what had happened to Ewenhic.
You may ask to get a name on this triumph.
No. Not that lucky, he said, but I have an idea.
Just need to wait for the stores to open.

SIXTY-SIX

HOPE FOR A break and fear of failure wrestled in Behr's gut as he parked in front of Williams Photographic. And fear was winning. The world had changed. Years ago, before shopping online had become ubiquitous, there would have been two dozen brick-and-mortar photography stores to investigate, to see if anyone recognized the picture Behr held. Now there were four. Five if you counted this place, down toward Franklin, which seemed too far away, but which now represented a last chance. The day had bled away in a spiral of dead-end questions and futility, including a call from Breslau's office around lunchtime informing him that the department's software had come up blank on the face in the picture from the Oriental Grand. So whether it was the software's short-comings, or the man wasn't in the system – either way, it was bad news.

Hope: Behr believed his man was a photographer.

That taking pictures was integral to his obsession.

Fear: He could shoot digitally, download to his computer, and print his pictures at home.

Hope: Something about the man, his age, his methods, felt analog, not digital. And Quinn had said something about recognizing the smell of film-developing chemicals during his encounter.

Fear: That Quinn was brain damaged. And after visiting a few Walgreens and Walmarts with photo sections, Behr had learned they didn't even sell developing supplies and they processed their color film in-store while sending out their black-and-white to a lab in Chicago. There was no way this guy would let his images be handled publicly.

Hope: That if Quinn was right about what he smelled, and if Behr was right about the guy being analog, the man might insist on buying his chemicals in person.

Fear: That the other shops he'd stopped in, Courtland Camera and Winter's Imagery, had tiny chemical sections and none of the salespeople recognized the man in the photos.

Fear: That even the most analog types these days just went ahead and ordered hard-to-find shit online when they had to, and if his man did, Behr was all the way back to nowhere.

Fear: He was down to his final stop.

Fear was kicking hope's ass at the moment.

Behr got out of his car and entered the store. As soon as he walked in he felt the pretension of photo snobbery in the air. He quickly found a clerk, wearing a velvet vest over his T-shirt and a straw porkpie on his head, fiddling around with a tripod. Behr showed him the photo from Oriental Grand and asked if he knew the man in it. Velvet Vest hardly gave it a look.

'Nah, bro, I don't. I'm kinda new. Ask Benj, he's been here forever. He might.' Behr's eye went to where the clerk was pointing, and he saw a lanky salesman with a chin beard who was playing with his iPhone near the back of the store.

Behr glanced around for a moment and spotted a display of the most expensive cameras in the place and went to it.

'Can I help you with something there, chief?' Benj, the lanky salesman, inquired. Behr could see his shoes behind the glass counter: hipster sneakers with the white toe caps.

'Maybe,' Behr said.

'You a photographer?' Benj asked. 'Do you currently own an SLR?'

'Have a Nikon D-90,' Behr said.

The hipster salesman nearly stifled his snort. 'Solid body,' he allowed.

'Yeah. Might be time to upgrade,' Behr said.

'Well, there's plenty of room to move up from there,' the salesman said. 'Plenty.'

'Uh-huh,' Behr said. 'Let me see that one, please,'
Behr said, pointing at a boxy black number that
rested on a velvet-covered pedestal.

'That one?' the salesman said reluctantly.

'Yeah.'

Benj took the camera gingerly from the case and
handed it over.

'That's a Hasselblad H4D-60,' he said reverentially.

'Is that right?' Behr said and ran his hands over it
like a low-rent pimp checking out some new flesh.
'Pricey?'

'A little over forty thousand.'

'Wow.' That's when Behr pretended to almost
drop it. Benj leaned forward, almost keeping his cool.
Behr regained control of the camera and said, 'Must
take a hell of a picture.' Then he drifted down the
counter, camera still in hand, toward the film-
processing section, knowing Benj would follow.

'It's a professional's tool,' Benj said, his pretension
evaporating. 'Regardless of income level, it's more
camera than most people need. You could save plenty
and still come away with a great product if you look
over here.' The suddenly helpful salesman pointed
at a nearby glass case.

'That's a relief,' Behr said and practically tossed
the Hasselblad back to him.

'Look, the truth is I'm old-school. I'm interested
in getting back to shooting film, not digital, and

there's this guy who's supposed to know a lot about this stuff. I was hoping to ask him for some advice. Maybe you know him?' Behr took out the photo and showed it. Behr studied Benj, while Benj studied the picture.

'Well, sorry, can't help you,' the salesman said.

'So you don't know him?' Behr said.

The suggestion that he might not know something seemed to rankle Benj. He cocked his head with an air of superiority before answering. 'Look, man, ours is a shrinking business, and I'm not in the habit of giving out sensitive information on customers.'

'So he *is* a customer?' Behr asked.

Now Benj looked pissed. 'Is there anything *camera related* I can help you with? Otherwise—'

Behr picked up a large bottle of film-cleaning solvent and hefted it in his hand. 'Is this flammable? It says here on the label it's alcohol based, must be pretty flammable. Oh yeah, it is, I see the warning now. You have a lot of it? You keep it stored in back? Man, if this stuff caught fire, this whole place would go up like a Roman candle and burn for days. Hasselblads and all . . .'

Behr craned his neck and glanced around. 'I'm sure there's a shitload of security cameras here, so whoever started something like that would probably cut power to the store and come in with a black mask on in case of battery backup, that way no one would know who did it and he'd never get caught.'

Behr let that hang out there for a minute, then finished. 'Or maybe I'm wrong. Maybe it'd only burn for like five hot minutes and there'd be nothing fucking left, not even helpful employees.'

'Are you threatening . . . are you saying you're gonna come burn down the store?'

Behr fixed him with a flat gaze. 'I'm just a solo P.I. on a case who doesn't give a shit about anything except getting a name. So you can tell whoever you want about this conversation, but I promise you this: if this place ever goes to torch, I'll be sitting across town somewhere in public with lots of people, maybe even a cop or two, and it will never, and I mean *never*, track back to me.'

Benj grew very uncomfortable and looked around as if searching for help, but none was coming and Behr wasn't going anywhere.

'Fine. I know him,' Benj said in a small voice. 'It's not like he's some friend of mine, fuck it. We don't see him much in here, but when he comes in he buys heavy quantities of developer, fixer, and stop bath.'

'Name?'

'It's . . . slipped my mind,' Benj said.

'You have records of your transactions?' Behr asked.

'Yeah . . .' Behr followed as Benj went behind the counter and got on the computer. 'He . . . I don't see any credit card information. I see where we've sold a lot of developer – that goes into the system for automatic restocking – but no purchase info.'

'Meaning?'

'He must've paid cash.'

Shit, Behr thought. He envisioned sitting out in front of the store for weeks, months on end, hoping for the guy to show up to resupply while bodies piled up and the reward went unclaimed.

'Oh, there's an old note in here . . .' Benj said, almost emitting a nervous laugh at what he read off the computer. 'There's a phone number. It says: 'Call Hardy Abler when Kodak D-76 back in stock.''

And just like that Behr finally had a name.

'We're good now, right?' Benj said. 'You're not gonna do what you were saying . . .'

But Behr was already out the door.

SIXTY-SEVEN

SOMETHING IS BOTHERING him, and nothing ever bothers him. Not that he can remember. Last night was a little stupid. As delicious as it had felt to crack that Chink hooker – the bitch hadn't even been a real blonde – it might not have been smart to go into that place and to do what he'd done. And smart is a thing he's always been. But so far, so good. He's seen no news coverage. There's no indication that the police have been called and are looking for anyone. His picture isn't on any news websites, so they must not have had cameras. How could they call the cops for help anyway, he wondered, a filthy joint like that? He should be feeling better now, but he isn't.

It's because the sensation of the punch has worn off too quickly, he realizes. His knuckles aren't even sore. Maybe it's an age thing, a midlife crisis. He's heard about how people lose their taste for their pleasures in life. But that doesn't seem right either. He still has plenty of appetite. Too much. It's that merely hitting some girl isn't enough. He is jumping out of his skin.

The sounds of the break room invade his thoughts. Someone is causing everybody to laugh. He looks up from his coffee and sees it is Kenny. Three women are Kenny's audience, Claudia, Beth, and Stacie, and Kenny is really busting them up. Claudia is an old battle-ax of a secretary who's been with the company for twenty-five years. Beth is a married woman about his age, but Stacie, in her early thirties, is a different story. She's worked here for a bit over a year. He's seen her around, but he hasn't really noticed her. Maybe it's because of his strict policy not to act on ones he knows or works with.

But looking at her now, as she tosses her butter-colored hair back while flirting with Kenny, the swell of her breasts against her blouse, her sheer white pantyhose stretched over her ample thighs and rustling against her dress skirt, he thinks he must've truly blinded himself, because she is incredible. He feels the thrill of need and desire. He suddenly knows it plain and simple: here's a project sitting right in front of him.

Why the hell not? Back to the beginning with one I know. He'll take her right away. *Tonight.*

Three ways to go about it pop into his head. He

can disable her car so it breaks down on the way home and he happens by to help her. But he discounts that one right away. It is too inexact. He can't be sure exactly where she'll stop. It will likely be too public. Option two: he can just wait outside in the parking lot and follow her home. Of course he'll have to find a minute to dart home to get his kit and get back before she leaves. But why work that hard? He has access to the company's personnel records. He'll pull her address and show up at his leisure.

She stands with her coffee, her back to him, rearranging her skirt over her buxom hindquarters. She has what regular guys call a 'heart-shaped ass.' He already has ideas forming as to what she'll look like legless, when she turns to go and sees him sitting there.

'Hi, Hardy,' she says. 'How are you doing today?'

'Top of my game, Stacie, thanks for asking. How are you?' He wonders if she can read the thoughts behind his eyes. Of course she can't, no one can, because she'd run screaming in horror if she could.

'Oh, I can't complain, but sometimes I still do,' she says. He smells her vanilla chewing gum in the air.

'I hear you, Stace,' he says, and gives her a smile.

SIXTY-EIGHT

THE HOUSE WAS as benign as a sugar cookie, sitting there on a tree-lined street that must have been positively leafy during the spring, summer, and fall. There was nothing going on behind the shaded windows as far as Behr could tell in the two hours he'd been sitting there. Every few years or so, it seemed, a nondescript home like this one was revealed in the news to be a house of horrors, a wife kept prisoner by an abusive husband, kidnap victims locked up in the basement. He'd even had his own experience with a place more run-down than this, in a worse part of town, used as a temporary depot for unimaginable crimes, where again, the bland façade of suburbia masked pure malice. But this time it wasn't the house itself that held his attention. No, this time his gaze kept shifting to the oversized detached two-car garage. There were no windows on the garage bay doors, which was a bit odd, and the sliver of window on the side of the structure that he could just glimpse from where he sat appeared to be blacked out.

About halfway through his sit, a somewhat portly middle-aged woman arrived and entered the house. After the camera store, Behr had run a quick background, which he finished on his laptop with a Wi-Fi card on his stakeout. So he had the plate on the Toyota Corolla station wagon she had driven up in. He knew she was Margaret Abler and that she had been married to Reinhard Peter Abler, his subject, for the past eighteen years.

Abler himself had served a five-year stint in the army and had gotten out with the rank of first sergeant via honorable discharge. This was about eighteen years ago as well. He had no criminal record, was listed as a member in good standing of and donor to the Bethel Lutheran Church, and was currently employed by Martin, Miller & Elkin, a firm that provided audits, tax management, and advisory services to corporate clients. Though not as large as PricewaterhouseCoopers or Deloitte & Touche, MM&E was in the same mold, and as a director of accounting services, Abler was firmly middle management. He had a blue 2004 Buick Park Avenue registered to him, and Behr had the plate number on that. He had modest credit card bills, low outstanding balances, and no liens against him. On paper he was a most innocuous individual, a solid citizen. But Behr was interested in what was *off* the paper.

That was when Abler's wife exited the house after fifteen minutes inside, got in her car, and drove off.

His gaze pulled away from the house once again and landed on that garage. That garage. They didn't use it for parking their cars. She didn't anyway. Maybe there was a way inside, so he could take a look. He sat there for a long half hour wondering, thinking, sweeping the neighborhood with his eyes in all directions for witnesses. And then he reached for the door handle.

His feet felt like they were hovering inches above the ground, such was the deftness with which he tried to move as he crossed the street, then the lawn, and slipped between the house and the garage. His big concern was that he'd be spotted, perhaps by a neighbor, who would alert Abler that someone was creeping around, giving him the chance to clear out evidence and cover his tracks. Behr couldn't let that happen. He moved along the wall until he got to the window. He peered inside, or tried to anyway. The window had been treated with a darkened film, and there seemed to be another layer of solid blacking on the inside, so there was no seeing through it, and it wasn't the type that opened. Behr moved on until he reached the rear, where there was a regular door.

He didn't have to try the knob to determine if it was locked, because there was a chunky stainless-steel padlock with a thick hasp securing the portal. It was a security measure, to be sure, but to what end – to safeguard valuables inside, to keep people out, or to keep someone in?

Behr gave a quick glance over to the house. The back door would present less of a challenge than the garage and that padlock, but the house didn't hold the answers. Of that he was sure. Then, as he headed back to his car and got in, a sick feeling descended upon him. He took out his phone and looked at it. It was a miserable call to have to make, but he went ahead and placed it.

'Hey, Breslau, it's—'

'I know who it is. Your number comes up under "asshole." What do you want?'

'I was thinking about that DB you mentioned, the little girl. Did her aunt turn up yet?'

'No,' Breslau said.

'You got a description on her?'

'She's thirty-two, Caucasian, five foot nine, eyes blue, hair blond.'

The facts settled on Behr. He felt his eyes go to the garage.

'Have you looked out by where the other bodies were found?' he asked.

'Of course. And by the tracks where Quinn turned up. We're looking everywhere,' Breslau said.

'If I had an idea—'

'Yeah?'

'A potentially related crime that led to a search warrant on a location . . .' Behr was thinking about the assault at the massage parlor, and how he'd made the ID at the photo store. It was circumstantial, potentially rickety in court. Breslau was ahead of him.

'Did this related crime get reported?' he asked.

'Not exactly.'

'We'd need solid linkage. Will the victim come forward?'

'Doubtful,' Behr said.

Breslau took a breath. 'All I can tell you is: I cannot afford a bad search or any other brand of bullshit right now. And neither can you.'

'Shit . . .' Behr breathed. 'You got a pic on the aunt?'

'E-mailing you now,' Breslau said, and hung up.

A moment later Behr's phone buzzed with the incoming message. He opened the attachment, and the photo scrolled onto his screen. Pam Cupersmith was young, lovely, and blond. As Behr stared at the picture, an urgency to get inside that garage exploded within him. She was right there, across the street and inside that small structure, he suddenly knew, in whatever condition, mere wood and glass and metal all that was separating him from recovering her. Hell, maybe she was even alive, as doubtful as that seemed.

But Breslau and the rest of the cops weren't going to help him. They couldn't. He had to help them. He jerked his car into gear and stepped on the accelerator. He drove for MM&E, where Abler worked, moving like an automaton now, programmed for one function at any cost: entry.

Amber plate-glass windows reflected the late-afternoon sun onto a dozen rows of vehicles. Behr had arrived at the office building that housed MM&E, and he drove slowly up and down the columns of cars until he spotted Abler's Park Avenue. Advertised as a slice of American automotive luxury when it was new, it was more like the baked potato of cars now. Innocuous and forgettable, and in a dark blue color that vaguely connoted authority, the car was getting old. But he imagined Abler's reluctance to sell it considering what Behr imagined it had been used for – the collection and transportation of victims. Behr had dug up a police report on file back from 2003 when Abler's prior car, a Pontiac Grand Prix, had been 'stolen.' The car had been found three days later, burned. Abler had collected the insurance. It read like an effective sterilization of evidence to

Behr, but it wasn't a move that could be repeated often, if ever, and Abler was smart enough to know that.

Behr continued past the car, drove out of the lot, and parked on the street. He took a page out of Abler's book, got a baseball cap from the trunk, and pulled it down low. He had to assume there were security cameras in the lot. That was the assumption he labored under in almost every public place these days. He wasn't stealing anything, so there'd be little reason for the footage to be reviewed before it was recycled, but since he was illegally entering a vehicle, he didn't want to be easily identified. He got organized with a few other items he kept stored in his trunk, slammed it shut, and started walking with bland purpose toward the Park Avenue.

No one who saw him from a distance of more than five feet could see the clear vinyl gloves that covered his hands, nor could they see the slim jim he slid out of his sleeve when he reached the driver's door. He hadn't worked a car lock in a while, but it wasn't a skill that took a lot of maintenance, and the age of the car helped. He fed the slender piece of metal between the window glass and the rubber seal, down into the door panel, and fished around for a moment before he was able to pop the lock. Then he opened the door and got in. He slammed the door behind him and breathed in pine-scented air freshener before he found what he was looking for: the automatic garage door opener, clipped on the passenger-side visor.

Behr took out his Horizon-net, a device the size of a key fob. Technically a backup or replacement remote, for all intents and purposes it was a code grabber. If Abler's opener was part of a high-end modern system, with a rolling combination that created a completely new code each time it was used, Behr would be at a dead end because he'd need access to the main unit in the garage in order to duplicate the frequency. But the more basic brands of garage door openers, especially older ones, created codes with the same basic values, and the Horizon-net was able to run a simple resynchronization protocol that basically cloned the remote. Behr took Abler's from the visor and saw it was a Genie that was a good ten years old. He opened the Horizon-net and set the brand jumper switch to Genie. He pressed Abler's remote and then the Horizon-net. His unit blinked red a few times and then went green.

He was done with his business in the car. He put Abler's remote back on the visor and opened the door. He was ready to walk away, but then couldn't resist doing one more thing: he pressed the trunk release button next to the steering column and heard the latch disengage. He got out, circled around to the back, and took a look. The trunk was completely empty, immaculate. Behr didn't know what he expected – handcuffs, knives, bloodstains, a body? There was nothing inside but factory-installed industrial carpet like the day it rolled off the assembly line. He closed the trunk and walked back across the lot toward his car. A tall blonde, about Susan's height, maybe a few years younger, caught his eye as she exited the building, but she peeled off in the opposite direction.

When Behr got back in his car, the sun was already disappearing from the building's side, and he dialed a call on his cell phone.

'Good afternoon, MM&E,' a bright-voiced receptionist answered.

'Yeah, this is John Daniels from Lucas,' Behr said, naming the biggest petroleum company in town. If MM&E didn't handle them, they wanted to. 'I've got some P&Ls to drop off for an Abler in Accounting. How late are you folks around?'

'Would you like me to connect you?' she asked.

Behr considered chancing it and actually getting the man on the phone, but decided it wasn't worth the risk.

'Nah, that's all right. What time does he usually clear out of there?'

'Usually about quarter to six, six.'

'Great, I oughtta just be able to make it,' Behr said, hanging up. He glanced at the clock on the dash. If he drove fast he'd have just shy of ninety minutes.

I oughtta just be able to make it, he said, this time to himself.

SIXTY-NINE

*W*HAT IN THE *goddamn hell is he doing here?* Abler wonders.

He can't be sure, but he thinks he's just seen the big guy from the community meeting crossing the parking lot, from the direction where his car is parked, no less. He almost missed him, so locked was he onto Stacie and her prancing across the lot and getting into a red Mazda 6. Just like a young filly to drive too much car for her salary. *Fine by me, though*, he thinks. *With a flashy car like that parked out front, there'll be no missing whether she's home or not in a little while.*

'You're not breaking out early on me, are ya, Hardy?' It's Kenny, coat on, computer bag in hand. He's the one breaking out early.

'Nope, just getting some fresh air before I finish up.'

'That's good. We're gonna need all those audits done before the last week of the month.'

'You'll—'

'I'll have 'em. I know. Just reminding you.' Kenny continues on. 'Keep up the good work,' he calls back.

'I will.'

I should do a piece of work on you . . .

He stares after Kenny's departing back, then stands there for another moment scanning the lot, watching Stacie drive away and trying to figure out where the big guy went. That's when he sees a maroon Olds Toronado crossing the other way on the street past the exit. It has to be *him*. He breaks into a run toward the corner of the parking lot and the Olds gets stuck at the light, and he's able to make out a license plate number. There are databases that cross-list owners and addresses with plate numbers. There are ways. He'll soon know who the big guy is and where he lives. The projects are just falling into his lap right now.

SEVENTY

THE STREET WAS quiet and the light was going day's-end flat when Behr arrived. The shadows thrown from the trees and light poles were being swallowed by everything around them. Behr rolled to a stop a good distance down the street from Abler's place and doused his headlights. He saw one window illuminated upstairs in the house, but the wife's car wasn't out front, nor was there any movement inside. A neighbor four houses over walked toward home with a large mixed-breed dog on a leash and disappeared inside. Behr felt his heart hurtling around his chest. His mouth went slightly dry. He had to go in.

At least wait until dark, he bargained with himself, which was mere moments away, the gloam falling all around the car, but there was no deal to be made.

Come on, do it, another interior voice urged.

What if the Horizon-net doesn't work? Behr pushed the doubt from his mind.

Do it now, that other voice demanded. *Do it for Pam Cupersmith*. She was inside, and every moment could mean the difference to her.

That voice won.

He reached for the handle of his car door, and in an instant his feet were on the pavement and he was walking through the quiet twilight toward the garage. Each step he took closer to the property spelled potential disaster for his case. If Abler had returned home before him somehow and was hidden behind those shades or in the garage itself, and he discovered Behr, he would be flushed like a game bird and able to disappear, or at the least dispose of any evidence inside. Or, if he had the nerve, he could even call the cops, and Behr would be the one who ended up in jail for breaking and entering. But Behr continued on, feeling as if his feet belonged to another.

He paused when he reached the big bay door, trying to blend in with the corner of the structure, and then came the moment of truth: he hit the Horizon remote in his pocket. The low grinding of the opener's motor and chain that escaped from underneath the lifting door as it moved upward told him the code grab had worked. No light spilled outside from the customary bulb attached to most automatic garage doors – it had been shut off. Behr dropped to the ground and rolled underneath the rising door and into the blackness of the garage, hitting the remote again and closing the door behind him before it had gone up three feet.

He knew immediately, before he even shined his flashlight around, that he was both right and wrong in his assumptions. He lay there in the dark and quiet once the door settled, and sensed the place was empty, at least of anyone living, and that if Pam Cupersmith were there, he was too late. Yet all the confirmation he needed was in the air, which hung heavy with the scent of oxidized blood and entrails. An undertone of bleach and other chemicals stung his nostrils. He recognized the smell from when he was young and worked in a meat-processing plant. He knew right away he had entered a slaughterhouse.

He sat up and took out his Mini Maglite, which he'd fitted with a red lens, and when he clicked it on, a swath of the garage was bathed in a crimson light. There was no car inside. Instead a long couch covered by an old blanket took up the center of the space. He went and checked, quickly, hopelessly under the blanket, and then below some work-benches, and in the corners, which were the most likely places a person could've been hidden, but he was alone.

There was a low chest along one wall that he supposed could've been used for such storage, but inside it he found multiple stacks of pulpy pornographic magazines. Across the space was a carpenter's table, and above that a pegboard covered with tools, both manual and electric. They were not of the automotive variety though, rather the array was of knives, cleavers, machetes, saws, chisels, awls, and all manner of other pointed and bladed instruments. They were items of torment, of annihilation.

As Behr walked toward the wall to get a better look, he stumbled over a depression and saw that the floor was angled slightly toward a rusted metal drain. A channel was cut into the concrete that led from the drain to a large slop sink against the opposite wall, and then something caused him to look up and shine his light. Above him was a set of iron hooks suspended from the ceiling just like the kind livestock and game animals were hung from to drain before butchering. There was also a block and tackle rigged to it, for hoisting carcasses. Behr's head swam as he tried to process all he saw, and his eyes fell upon a set of shelves and cabinets and a large battered refrigerator along the deep wall of the garage opposite the bay door.

He walked with dread toward the shelves, and as he drew closer to them, the weak beam of his light began to pick up the shapes of cardboard banker's boxes. He went to the nearest one, lifted the lid, and found photo-developing supplies inside – chemicals, trays, tongs. The same with the next one. But inside the third he found something else: prints.

Behr had never seen anything like them. With the Maglite clamped between his teeth, he flipped through eight-by-tens of highly stylized yet gruesome images of women, shot extremely close up for the most part, their faces obscured, and their bodies cut into pieces. The photos were an abomination of the human form and all that was decent in the world, and even still the power and the artistry in them struck him. They were masterful for how they made his soul churn. In a strange way, Quinn would've truly appreciated them. One print bore text that appeared to have been scratched into the negative. The words, covering the image of a woman, her head nearly severed and twisted all the way around her torso so her eyes looked out over her back, were the same, repeated over and over: *I am death. I am death. I am death. I am death. I am death* . . .

Finally, he came upon the last picture in the pile, and it was slightly different from the rest. In it, reflected from a mirror that had been placed on the floor beneath an intact naked female, who was hanging from the hooks by her hands, blood running down her thighs, was Abler himself, wearing only a too-small leather jacket. Hers, he guessed. Erect and drooling, the camera dangling by a strap around his neck. Finally, Behr got a good look at the man with neither cap nor toupee on his head, bald and strange, with his drawn-on eyebrows. Behr couldn't identify the victim because of a black hood over her head, sprigs of blond hair protruding from the bottom.

He finished with the pictures, and felt his breath come heavy with dread as he looked over at a refrigerator and practically staggered toward it. His hands sweating inside his latex gloves, he reached for the handle and peeled the door open. The clean light from the bulb inside glowed with menace, and when he saw what the refrigerator held, it caused his legs to go weak.

SEVENTY-ONE

*B*EING BACK ON *the stalk is rocket fuel in his veins.*
The red Mazda 6 is parked in her driveway across from where he sits. Rushing back inside the office, he'd squared away some of what he'd been working on before grabbing his keys and heading out for the address he'd pulled from her personnel file. He can see Stacie inside now, moving around in the living room, dressed in tight exercise clothes, following along with some workout program on the television.

He wonders for a moment if he is working too quickly. There is always the danger of the work losing its meaning if there are too many projects, if there isn't sufficient contemplation and appreciation in between. But no, he's in a groove. He's born to do this, every nerve fiber in his being firing in concert. It will be refreshing to act right away, without undue contemplation and struggle with his urges. His work space is empty and practically calling for a new subject. He thinks of the blue plastic OfficeMax boxes that he'd strapped with cinder blocks and then lugged out to the quarry's edge down at White Rock, where he'd finally dropped his failed work, one, two, three, into the black depths where it belonged. Nestled inside the last box, something that would confuse the hell out of whoever might find it, as unlikely as that occurrence would ever be – an extra pair of hands. Quinn's. He wondered if they had clapped on the way down. The oxy torch was last to go in, the final piece of an abortive chapter, but now the future is filled with promise.

The night unfolds in his mind: the surprise on Stacie's sweat-shining face as Hardy from the office appears at her door with a folder in his hand and a story about something that needs to be looked over and signed off on.

'Why don't you come on in?' she offers.

And then the knowing in her eyes in the moment before he takes her. The scent of her hair. The feel of her skin. Her cries of terror. The bite of the rope as he secures her. Then, back in his space, the recognizable parts of her personality will come apart as she's reduced to a delirium of pain and suffering. Finally, she'll emit the uncontrollable scream of existence, which he'll capture in his mind and with his camera for all eternity. And afterward, the deep black satisfied sleep will come.

Stacie looks like she's in for the night. Either way it seems the workout will go on for a while, and if she does decide to head out when she's done, she'll likely shower and primp and that will take plenty of time. It is a ten-minute trip home to get his kit. Or he can just go and do it and improvise. It's just a simple question of one trip or two. He can practically feel his hands in her blood . . .

SEVENTY-TWO

CLOSE IT, Behr urged himself, but for the moment he could not. The stark light and cold air from inside the refrigerator spilled out onto him. Upon the shelves were jars and lidded glass containers of all sizes and shape, and inside of them floating in brine or vinegar or some other preservative were indeterminate body parts. On the bottom shelf, in a large glass bowl, suspended in clear liquid, were what appeared to be several vaginas.

Behr's very being shuddered at the horror of what he'd found, at the fact that he had been correct about Abler, and at the quandary in which he'd put himself. He had at once made a case and doomed it, due to the illegal entry. If he called the police now, everything inside the garage, every shred of evidence against this monster, would be inadmissible. A pang of sorrow shot through him for what he still owed

Kerry Gibbons, and her daughter, Kendra, for that matter.

Close it up and get out, he told himself. Fall back and drum up some concrete evidence to justify a search warrant, or find another way to stunt up a reason for the cops to get inside legitimately. Before it was too late and Abler killed again or sniffed out that someone had been inside his place and scrubbed it and vanished into thin air. Of course there was always the chance, supposing Behr managed to get him arrested, that Abler could successfully claim insanity – the pictures and other items in the garage would play convincingly in that vein – and he'd wind up spending his days in a hospital facility. Or perhaps worst of all, he'd somehow end up with a sentence like Prilo's and be out in a handful of years . . .

However Behr went about it, it would take time, a day or two at least, to figure out. He had to hurry now. Just as he was about to close the refrigerator, though, he spotted a small amber jar to the rear of the middle shelf, and he reached for and opened it. He smelled the liquid inside, which was formaldehyde, and he gently shook and swirled the jar. A small chunk of flesh rolled and rotated in the fluid. Then he saw the green-colored design inked on the jagged piece of skin. It was Danielle Crawley's shamrock tattoo. Behr hung his head over the jar for a moment before screwing it shut, putting it back, and closing the refrigerator.

That's when he felt the slight vibration of the rear padlocked door rattling and realized someone was coming in. He had to hide, and moved blindly for a spot by the far wall, behind the slop sink, where a tool bench would obscure him. The door swung open with a creak and whoever was there left the lights off . . .

SEVENTY-THREE

HERE. SOMEONE. INSIDE.

He steps in, pulling the door shut behind him, sealing the world out and the darkness in. Stacie, back at home, safe and unknowing, flies from his mind as his fingers find the lock on the knob and make sure it is secure. His feet move silently across the concrete. He heads right for the pegboard full of his equipment, his weapons. His hand finds the cool steel shaft of his entrenching tool. Not just familiar, but hard, strong, and sharp, it is ideal. He begins on a silent loop around the pitch-black space, past the edge of the couch, prodding at the blanket with the pointed end of the shovel blade to make sure no one is beneath it. He methodically eliminates potential hiding places one by one. Then, as he nears the back corner by the sink, he finds him.

He slams the entrenching tool into the floating ribs of the shadowy figure that is hunched by the slop sink. He hears a gasp and senses the man rolling along the floor in pain. He pulls the entrenching tool away and clangs it off the back of the man's head. It should've stilled him, but instead he feels a searing stab of pain in his own knee, seeing that the man has shot out a kick only once it is on the way back.

Recovering, he leaps onto the figure, which is large and strong. His eyes are like those of a nocturnal animal's now, and he sees who it is: the big man who had been in the parking lot, in the church basement, on his trail. His next target has come to him. He pounds away with fury at the body and head with one fist curled tight, and the other wrapped around the E-tool's handle. He hears blasts of breath and grunts of pain. Any one of his blows can be the last one, stunning the man. Then he will own him and go to town. He is going to open this son of a bitch up.

Somehow the man disappears from beneath him. He feels the thud of the man's feet kicking him in the gut, slamming out and thrusting him back and away. Then his own ankles are grabbed and yanked and he's completely free of gravity. He's falling. His head whips in a downward arc through the blackness. It bounces off the floor. Jagged sights float like carousel horses in front of his eyes. A punch to the head. The big man, face in front of his. Metal rapping him in the skull—

* * *

Behr had him down. In the midst of a barrage of
thunderous blows he'd somehow managed a double
ankle sweep in the desperation and darkness. He
heard the man's head hit the ground, but the man
hadn't gone limp, as nearly anyone would have. Even
now Behr heard him hissing and cursing, and sensed
him whipping his head from side to side to clear the
cobwebs. Behr rolled up, put a knee into the man's
chest, and punched him in the face several times. The
back of the man's skull bounced off the floor once,
then twice, and Behr fumbled for his ankle, hoping to
draw the Mag Pug. The man was monstrously strong,
though, and caught Behr's arm with a viselike grip he
couldn't break. He felt him buck wildly, threatening
to dislodge Behr and flip him.

With a grunt, Behr pulled up and back and thrust
his weight down, dropping an elbow across the man's
brow. He did it again, able to move more freely and
land the elbow more cleanly the second time. And
then once more. His arm finally came free, and Behr
got the pistol out and brought the frame of it down
onto the man's face and skull over and over, feeling
the bones start to give and hearing a liquid sucking
noise. At last there was no more resistance, and the
rag-doll quality to the man's body told Behr it was
done.

Behr fought for breath and forced his way through

the ringing tones and dizziness in his head and balanced on one hand to press himself up to standing. He stumbled forward, clutching for his flashlight, clicking it on left-handed, and with the gore-covered revolver crossed over his wrist, shined it down onto the man's face.

It was the man he knew to be Abler, floating in and out of consciousness, his face battered and torn, strange hairpiece askew and matted with blood, and still more blood spilling out of ripped and broken flesh. The man's mouth moved in dumb gasps. Behr considered the mangled thing at his feet, the garage full of evidence now useless and tainted, and the lost reward. Maybe there was a way to get Abler up, to restrain him and put him back together, and for Breslau to help engineer some legitimate-sounding circumstances for all of it. He pulled Abler to a sitting position by the collar and considered the script he could give him, the threats he could make to force him to follow it. Maybe Behr could claim he was invited in and then attacked. He needed that money for his son.

But then Abler spoke, in what couldn't have been his normal voice, through cracked teeth and a sideways jaw.

'It's you,' he said.

'Yeah.'

'I was coming for you.'

'Here I am.'

'Help me . . .' he said. 'Help me . . .'

Behr wondered how many similar pleas had been made of Abler, and how he must have reveled in it before denying them.

'Kendra Gibbons,' Behr said.

'Who?'

'Up on East Washington, a little over a year and a half ago. A pretty young blond girl.'

'They all are,' the killer said, memories flickering behind his eyes, animating them.

Then Mistretta's words about a man like this in prison flashed through Behr's mind, how he'd luxuriate in his deeds and be treated like a celebrity in safety and relative comfort if he even ended up behind bars at all, and it caused a boiling rage to wash away everything coherent and decent in Behr's being. He stepped down hard on Abler's right shoulder and raised the Mag Pug.

'Don't . . . I . . . want to . . . live,' Abler said.

'You're not going to.'

'Who are you?' he asked.

'I am death,' Behr said, quoting Abler's own words back to him. He felt the valve close inside him. Then he fired two rounds dead center into the man's sternum before he adjusted and put a last one straight into his eye, the left socket disappearing from recognition as it became a punched-in, gore-filled crater.

The rage left Behr along with the final bullet, and he staggered back, murder and failure all over him. Adrenaline shakes hit him hard, along with the pain. He sat down on the floor, away from the pooling blood, hoping it would all subside. The first strike had come out of nowhere. He hadn't heard or sensed Abler was that close. It had cracked some ribs, and Behr felt his breath come now with sharp stabs. He clicked his flashlight on and off twice and then a third time, checking that Abler wasn't rising like some unkillable ghoul. But he was dead, now and forever, his blood running down the channel he'd so carefully designed, and spilling into the well-placed drain that had been used for the blood of so many others.

It was mere luck that found Behr the one sitting where he was and Abler splayed out; luck that the shovel blows to the body hadn't caught him in the liver and incapacitated him, that the strikes to his hard head hadn't knocked him out, as close as they had come, and that he had managed to roll and land that first kick.

Behr waited five, then twenty, then thirty minutes, for someone to respond to the shots, as his pain settled to a dull ache. He spent the time trying to decide what he would say or what he should do. His options ran from fleeing to calling a lawyer, but in the end he did neither. The truth seemed like his only option when they arrived, especially considering what Breslau already knew. Behr would likely be charged with murder. It'd be easy to prove pre-meditation. He'd broken in armed after all. But there was no response. No one came.

He thought back to Abler's arrival. Behr hadn't *heard* it, he'd *felt* it. It was a vibration, an awareness, more than any sound. He got up and shined his flash-light about the garage. That's when he saw the egg crate foam and heavy baffling lining the walls. Abler had soundproofed his personal torture chamber, and he'd done it well. Behr remembered the blacked-out window from his surveillance, and found the light switch and clicked it on. Stark overhead bulbs shined down on the reality of the situation. He'd made a hell of a mess.

He holstered his gun and approached the body. He located the man's wallet and flipped it open to the driver's license. Abler, Reinhard Peter. There was no doubt. Nor was there doubt in Behr's mind at what was going to happen next. He steeled himself for what lay ahead and drew in a breath, then put the wallet in a drawer filled with screws and fuses. He had to be careful now. He couldn't afford any mistakes. There'd be no commemorative photos of what he was about to do. The fact was, he needed to get Abler's body out of the garage, and there was no doing it in one piece.

SEVENTY-FOUR

THE HIGHWAY UNSPOOLED in front of him like a mourner's ribbon. Behr drove through the night, the speedometer pegged at what he hoped was an unticketable sixty-seven miles per hour, his trunk full of the remains of human evil, and the inside of the car heavy with the sense that he'd become the same in order to stop it. He fought white-line fever and visions of himself being found by the staties having fallen asleep at the wheel and crashed into a tree. But mostly he tried to will away the images that kept coming back on him in flashes nonetheless.

—Abler, stripped down, strange skin, pale and waxy. Completely hairless beneath the awkward hair-piece, was he physiologically designed to be more efficient at killing without leaving trace evidence?

—Behr himself stripped down for his work, to just his underwear and shoes.

—The hacksaw and a beef knife.

—The hoisting hooks and the drain.

—The concrete channel running red.

Everything he'd needed was in that garage, from the tools to the heavy rubber gloves, to the construction-grade contractor bags, to the cleaning supplies.

It's just meat, Behr had said to himself as he set about the grimmest task he'd ever faced. *Meat to be handled and processed. Don't think about what it is. Don't think about anything now, just do what needs to be done.*

That was what he'd always told himself in the farmyard as a boy, in the slaughterhouse where he'd worked as a young man, and in the hunting field more recently, and that's what he told himself again. The work was as physical as it was revolting, and he was streaming sweat as he fought back his nausea.

And when it was done, when everything was wrapped in heavy-duty plastic and placed in the stained mason's bags that Behr had found there, and assumed were for that very purpose, and once he'd scrubbed himself off with scouring powder at the slop sink, and had poured bottles of bleach around on the floor, because even though bleach made luminol glow, maybe nobody would think to use it if they didn't *see* any blood, and because it would at least wipe out his own DNA, he paused. There was one more thing he wanted to do.

Behr looked at the refrigerator, and then crossed to it. He took the jar containing the piece of Danielle Crawley's leg and put it in his pocket. He closed the refrigerator door and turned to go when some swatches of color that he'd missed before caught his eye now, with the overhead lights on. They were on top of the refrigerator, in a transparent plastic tub pushed back toward the wall. He saw that inside the tub were a few women's shoes, including a single lavender pump. He reached for it and saw it was size seven, and the brand was Nine West. It was the match to the one found near where Kendra Gibbons had disappeared. The shoe went in his other coat pocket. He'd solved his case, and it did him absolutely no good.

Then it had been time to go. Behr took the entrenching tool, the item that had nearly ended his life, and secured it in the straps of one of the mason's bags and grabbed another small shovel that was leaning against a wall.

He waited, pressing his ear against the door, listening but not hearing a sound outside, until he could wait no more. Gloveless now, he covered the doorknob with a rag and prepared to step out. He considered rigging the garage to burn after he'd left, it wouldn't have been difficult with all the photography chemicals, but he thought better of it. He didn't need the fire department and police responding and looking for Abler right away. The time before any search began would be to his advantage, and later, he knew, be it hours, days, or weeks, someone, perhaps the wife, would enter the garage seeking Abler, and instead discover the trove of horrible evidence. Then either there would be a massive news story with the authorities called in, or there wouldn't be a peep. He wondered at the toll living with a sociopath for all these years had taken on the wife, and if she would tell the world what she had found, or if she had a bit of it in her in the first place, and would keep everything quiet.

Behr shut the lights and let himself out the side door. He half expected to find a ring of police cruisers awaiting him, but there were none. He'd been in the garage close to four hours and it was nearing 10:30. The house was dark, but he stayed close to the garage so as not to make any silhouette. When he'd gotten all the bags outside, he fastened the heavy padlock in place behind him and wiped it down.

The last piece had to do with his car. It was parked around the corner, a long, heavy haul with the bags, especially the thick plastic sack containing the torso, which he'd cinched around his waist. If he was spotted or had gotten a parking ticket, it would be a problem. He would be caught by the very same means by which he'd hoped to catch Abler.

He bent his knees, lacing his fingers through the

handles of the mason's bags, and stood, the dead weight yanking down on the muscles of his back and legs. He made the carry, straining to stand erect, as if not burdened, in case anyone saw him, his arms and legs quivering from the effort, the leather handles cutting into his palms. He turned the corner and reached his car, where he found the windshield blessedly free of tickets. Sweating and panting, he untied the burden around his waist and leaned against the trunk, then opened it with a hand that shook from the exertion. He loaded the bags inside, slammed the trunk lid shut, and drove away.

On his way out of town, before he hit the interstate, but a good five miles away from Abler's house, he stopped at a Citgo station to fill his tank and do what he wished he'd done *before* going to Abler's house: he passcode-locked his phone, wiped it, and hid it behind the toilet in the men's room. He couldn't afford to ping any cell towers where he was going. He paid cash for the gas and the largest cup of coffee and bottle of Gatorade they had and set out, going north and west.

SEVENTY-FIVE

THE ONLY SOUND in the waning moments of the darkness was that of the entrenching tool's blade rasping against frozen ground. Behr had made the Iowa state line in under six hours. He'd gone on and reached his destination, the vast woodlands he'd hunted with Les Dollaway, forty minutes after that, with just under two hours left before sunup in which to work. Behr had seen where the key to the gate that blocked the dirt access road was stashed when Les used it a few months back, and it was still there when he arrived. He drove in slow, without headlights, to a spot not far from where Les had collected his buck. If the landowner spotted him for some crazy reason, Behr would try to sell the story that after hunting the spot with Les the prior season he thought he'd scout game movement for the next year so he didn't face the embarrassment of not filling his tag again.

Behr cut into the cold hardened dirt with the

E-tool, and the vibrations of the handle hurt his hands. He wished he'd had a pickax, but there weren't any at Abler's and he wasn't about to go shopping. He shed his coat and steam came off of him in thick clouds in the cold night air. Once he was below the top crust, the ground was warmer and began to yield more easily, so he could use the shovel, and he picked up speed. He dug until he hit four feet. He didn't have the patience, time, or strength to go any deeper, and the plum-colored sky over the eastern ridge told him the party was almost over.

He dropped the plastic and mason's bags in with no fanfare and even less emotion. The last thing that went into the hole, besides what was left of his conscience, was the entrenching tool, its handle wiped down. Then he used the shovel to fill everything back in and smooth out the topsoil as best he could. He moved some heavy rocks and armfuls of dead leaves and bramble over the dug-up earth, and he felt pretty confident that after a snow or two, and certainly by spring, no one out on the land would notice that the earth had been disturbed.

He was back in the car with the key in the ignition before he realized he'd left his coat behind. He went and retrieved it, trying to shake off the cobwebs and avoid the single mistake that would doom him. The old shovel got jettisoned in a roadside ditch before he was back on the interstate, and he launched the

Mag Pug into the Mississippi River from the I-74 bridge near Bettendorf.

He pushed it as far as he could with what he had left in the tank and was well into Illinois before he had to stop. He paid for another tank of gas with cash, along with a pack of doughnuts and another large cup of coffee.

With the midday sun searing his eyeballs, he considered stopping at every roadside motel he passed, but he forged on, because if he didn't stop at one then there'd be no proof he'd even been by. With an effort that was more physically draining than anything he'd undertaken in his life, including the Chicago Marathon the time he'd run it in weather that had been freakishly hot and humid, he finally wheeled his car up to his place and shut it off. No one from the IMPD was there to meet him. No one was there at all. He walked into his silent house and used his landline to check his cell phone voice mail, but there were no messages. He took a scalding shower, the soap and water stinging his torn and blistered hands. Then he crawled into his bed and collapsed into a black, featureless sleep.

SEVENTY-SIX

BEHR BOLTED UP in his bed, disoriented and racked with pain, a good fourteen hours later. It was the middle of the night again, and he didn't know what continent he was on. Then his actions of the past days seeped back on him like a waking nightmare, and he knew with a bitter certainty in his gut that it would be happening just like this, in varying installments, for a long, long time to come. His body stiff and sore, ribs and neck and head aching, and emotions raw, Behr got up and ate three peanut-butter-and-jelly sandwiches and drank an entire pot of coffee, then he flexed his clawlike hands and realized he had a bit more digging to do.

The Floral Crown Cemetery was empty and quiet at five in the morning, and not nearly as spooky as he expected it to be. Compared to what he'd just gone through, nothing really ever would be again, he imagined. He'd climbed the fence and come in on foot because the gate was locked, but it didn't take long for him to find the plain headstone. He read the inscription by the red glow of his Maglite. DANIELLE CRAWLEY (1989–2014), A GOOD SISTER AND FRIEND. He used a gardening trowel to dig a narrow cylindrical hole two feet into ground that wasn't as tough as that of the Iowa woodlands. In it he buried the jar containing the piece of her leg that made her complete. It wasn't much, but maybe it was something. That summed things up pretty well at the moment.

He was bending down, leaving a padded envelope at the front door of the brick bungalow in Millersville, when it swung open, surprising him. He saw pink sweatpants and fuzzy slippers and looked up to find Kerry Gibbons standing there, an unlit cigarette in her mouth.

'Frank Behr. Thought I heard a car,' she said.

'Sorry to disturb you.'

She waved this away. 'I was up. Didn't think I'd be seeing you again. Figured you'd given it up like the rest. What've you got there?'

Behr handed her the envelope wordlessly. Kerry Gibbons opened it and saw what was inside. Several hues of feeling, from grief to anger to love and finally resolution, played across her face in an instant as she touched her daughter's shoe, and then she looked to him with a knowing squint in her eyes.

'Are you putting in for the reward then?' she asked.

'Well, no one's gonna be standing trial. There won't be any conviction,' Behr said. 'It'd be hard to explain to your donors.'

'I see.'

'A while back you said you just wanted to know what happened . . .' Behr said, his words trailing off.

'I can tell by your face I don't really want to anymore, do I now?'

'No, you don't. In fact, it's best I don't tell you anything.'

She took a deep breath and felt in her sweatpants pockets for a lighter but came up empty.

'You want to come in for coffee?' she asked.

'Thanks all the same,' Behr said, starting to turn away.

That's when she grabbed him and hugged him. He felt her slight body shaking with emotion. Or maybe that was his.

He watched the sun rise over the Citgo and waited a little more than an hour for it to open. The lax cleaning schedule of the facilities worked in his favor, because he found his phone tucked behind the toilet right where he'd left it. Right where he'd temporarily 'lost' it, that is, if anyone had tracked its whereabouts.

SEVENTY-SEVEN

'CAME TO SAY hi and thanks and to get my gun back,' Behr said. 'You're not going to need it anymore.'

'So all is clear for real this time?' Mistretta asked, somehow surprised and not so all at once. Her hunger for the details hid behind the question, but they both knew he couldn't satisfy it.

'Hell, I don't know if *all* is clear, but I think you're gonna be all right for now.'

'You know, we could talk about it,' she offered.

He weighed the offer. He knew he could tell her everything. That she'd lap up the particulars. He imagined the charged sex that would follow, how at first it would seem life affirming. The confession would create a bleak bond between them that could last for a long time, for years, for forever. But underneath that bond would be darkness and death. Maybe it wasn't fair, since it was just her job, but he felt it had leeched into her, and that's what she had become to him. It wasn't what he wanted. Not now. He craved light and life. He wasn't sure he was able to have that, or how to go about deserving it, but it wasn't here for him. He made his decision.

'Probably not a good idea,' he said.

She smiled briefly. Her smile radiated affection and concern but mostly melancholy for what his words meant, and what they weren't going to share together. She disappeared into the house for a moment and returned with the pistol, which he took from her.

'Glad you didn't need it,' he said, 'and to have met you, even though . . .'

'Yeah, despite the circumstances. I get that a lot.'

'Well, I'm sorry,' he said.

'Let's not be, okay, Behr?' she said. 'Let's make this unique for our never being sorry.' He was surprised to see her eyes moisten.

'Good, let's not.' He nodded. They embraced briefly. He felt her body pushing against him, but he pulled back. Then he turned and left.

It was several days later, when the lurid images that were playing in his head, when the quickened breath and the pounding heartbeat he knew to be symptoms of posttraumatic stress, started to relent a bit, that he finally knew it was time.

He got there early, before she'd be leaving for drop-off at day care and then heading on to work. He was so focused on her door, on what would happen after he knocked on it, on what he would say, that he missed the unmarked cruiser.

The plainclothes officer intercepted him when he was halfway across the street.

'Hold up,' the man said.

Behr's heart sank as he pictured jail for the rest of his life, and his growing son's face seen only through glass until he stopped coming to visit altogether. Behr turned to meet the figure, and then he saw it was Gary Breslau.

'Where've you been?' Breslau asked.

'I've been around. Laying low. Resting,' Behr said.

'Uh-huh,' Breslau said.

'How's Quinn doing?' Behr asked.

'They'll fit him for prosthetics soon. That's the easy part. He's still making about as much sense as a bowl of alphabet soup. Docs say there's still some hope for improvement.'

Behr just nodded.

'And the Gibbons case?' Breslau asked.

'I'm done with it. Gotta start making some money.'

'I see,' Breslau said. 'I noticed the billboard came down on 465. Family got tired of renting it?'

Behr shrugged.

'So you didn't end up banking anything on the missing-girl job?' Breslau asked, giving Behr an interrogation-room stare.

'Not a dollar. Would've had to bring you a suspect to arrest for that.'

'Yet I've got this strange feeling I'm not going to have any more young blondes turning up cut to pieces anytime soon. Am I right about that, Frank?'

'Well . . . you know what happens, these guys get caught for other crimes. They get old and get sick and die. There are lots of reasons they stop . . .'

'What the fuck are you telling me?'

'Nothing. The chute got opened, I rode the thing the best I could. It dead-ended.'

'You forget I've got a picture of an unidentified guy that *you* sent me, one that I could go public with. Cops have a professional obligation to follow up on leads. We can't be expected to chase 'em all down, but what if I pursued this one? Someone would come forward and identify him. What would I find if I did that?'

'A dead lead,' Behr said. 'I don't think you'd find much of anything at all.'

Breslau just stared at him for a long moment.

'Listen to me, Behr, one of these days you're gonna get sucked down into this whirlpool of shit you create, and when you do, you're going all the way down.'

405

Breslau grabbed a handful of Behr's shirt. It wasn't a threatening gesture this time, just an attention-getting one, so Behr allowed the hand to remain.

'And I'm not going to be anywhere near it. Steer clear of me from now on. No more favors. Don't ask me for any, don't do any. You roger that?' Breslau said, his voice nearly a snarl.

'Copy,' Behr said. 'Are we done here?'

'Yeah,' Breslau said, releasing his grip. 'You and me are done.' Then the lieutenant stalked off to his car and gunned it away.

Behr stood there alone in the street. He had nothing. No cases, no money, no family, and whatever passed for his soul buried by the shovelful on the edge of an Iowa field. Nothing, save for one thing – Susan was safe. His son was safe. Mistretta was safe. So was the rest of Indianapolis for just this morning or just this moment because he had done the one thing he was able to in the world, which was put monsters in the ground. And he had a door. One door to knock on, and maybe walk through.

She stood there dressed in her work clothes, without any makeup, her blond hair pulled back, looking young and fresh and beautiful. She was everything he wasn't. The baby was playing on the living room floor behind her. Distrust and exasperation came to her eyes when she first saw him, but whatever she read on his face made it go away in an instant. There was only silence between them, the sound of a kid's show on the television in the background.

'Oh, Frank,' she finally said, 'you look like you've been through it.'

'I have,' he said. 'Can I please come in?'

She gave him a sad, kind smile, and with a gesture that proved no act of mercy was a minor one, she opened the door and let him inside.

Don't miss out on Frank Behr's first appearance in

CITY OF THE SUN

Twelve-year-old Jamie Gabriel gets on his bike before dawn to deliver newspapers in his suburban neighborhood. Somewhere en route he vanishes without a trace.

Fourteen months later, still with no sign of Jamie and having lost all faith in the police, his parents make one last desperate plea for help.

Enter Frank Behr – a tough, reclusive ex-cop, abandoned by his former colleagues, separated from his wife and haunted by his own terrible past.

Behr doesn't make it a practice to take on hopeless cases, but the couple's plea for help awakens a personal pain he can't ignore . . .

Here's the first gripping chapter to whet your appetite . . .

ONE

JAMIE GABRIEL WAKES at 5:44, as the clock radio's
volume bursts from the silence. He rolls and
hits the sleep bar, clipping off the words to an
annoying pop song by some boy-band graduate who
wears the same clothes and does the same moves as
his backup dancers. The worst. Kids at school say
they like him. Some do; the rest are just following
along. Jamie listens to Green Day and Linkin Park.
It's three-quarters dark outside. He clicks off the
alarm and puts his feet on the floor. Waking up is
easy.

In the master bedroom sleep Mom and Dad. Carol
and Paul. The carpet is wall-to-wall, light blue. New.
The liver-colored stuff that came with the house
when they bought it is gone. The blue goes better
with the oak bedroom set, Mom says.

It was a good move for the Gabriels, to the split

411

ranch-style on Richards Avenue, Wayne Township. Trees line most all of the blocks here. The houses have yards.

Jamie walks past his school photo, which hangs in the hall on the way to the bathroom. He hates the picture. His wheat-colored hair lay wrong that day. He takes a pee. That's it. He'll brush his teeth when he gets back, after breakfast, before school.

He moves through the kitchen – *Pop-Tart? Nah* – and goes out the utility door into the connected garage. Mom and Dad love it, the garage on the house, the workbench, and space for the white minivan and the blue Buick.

He hoists the garage door halfway up; it sticks on its track. A streak of black fur darts in and hits him low in the legs.

'Where you been, Tater?'

The gray-whiskered Lab's tail thumps against the boy's leg for a moment. After a night of prowling, Tater likes the way the boy ruffles his fur. The boy pushes him aside and crawl-walks under the garage door.

A stack of the morning *Star* waits there, acrid ink smell, still warm from the press. Jamie drags the papers inside and sets to work, folding them into thirds, throwing style.

He loads white canvas sacks and crosses them, one over each shoulder, then straddles his bike. The Mongoose is his. Paid for with six months' delivery money after the move to Richards Avenue. Jamie ducks low and pushes the bike out underneath the garage door, when Tater rubs up against his leg again. The old dog begins to whine. He shimmies and bawls in a way that he never does.

'Whatsa matter?'

Jamie puts his feet on the pedals and cranks off on his route. Tater groans and mewls. Dogs know.

'Should've gone to McDonald's, you fat fuck,' Garth 'Rooster' Mintz said to Tad Ford as he reached across him for a French Toast dipper. Tad's face squeezed in hurt, then relaxed. The smell of gasoline, the fast-food breakfast, and Tad's Old Spice filled the battleship-gray '81 Lincoln.

'You're eating same as me,' Tad said back. 'You're just lucky it doesn't stick to you.'

Rooster said nothing, just started chewing a dipper.

Tad was unsatisfied with the lack of reaction, but that was all he was going to say. Rooster was seventy-five pounds smaller than him, but he was hard. The guy was wiry. Tad could see his sinew. He'd once watched Rooster, piss drunk, tear a guy's nostril open in a bar scrap. The whole left side of the dude's nose was blown out, and just flapped around on his face with each breath after the fight was broken up and Rooster was pulled off.

413

Tad had plenty of targets of opportunity with Rooster – the small man stank much of the time. He didn't shower most days. He left his chin-up, push-up, and sit-up sweat in place, only bothering to wipe down his tattoos. His red-blond hair hung limp and greasy as well. Then there were the scars. Nasty raised red ones that ran up and down his forearms like someone had gone at him with a boning knife. When Tad finally screwed up the nerve to ask where he'd gotten them, Rooster merely replied, 'Around.' Tad left it there.

'You're just lucky it doesn't stick to you,' Tad repeated, chewing on his own French toast.

'Yeah, I'm lucky,' Rooster said, turned, and looked down the street, still dark beneath all the goddamn trees. 'Should've gone to McDonald's.'

Jamie Gabriel, rider, pedals. He flows by silent houses, houses dark on the inside. He tosses papers into yards and onto porches. He works on his arc and velocity with each throw. An automatic sprinkler quietly sweeps one lawn, still blue in the bruised morning light. Jamie slings for the front door of that house so the paper stays dry. He works his pedals. A line of streetlight goes dark with a hiss as morning comes. Dad thinks it's great that they moved to a neighborhood that supports tradition: newspaper routes. Mom's not so sure – her boy needs his rest. Few people know the streets like Jamie does. Dark and empty, they're his streets. Jamie wasn't so sure either, at first, when he was still getting used to the work and slogging through the route on his old Huffy. But then he earned the new bike. He read an old story of a mailman who became an Olympic biker. *Why not him, too?* He has a picture. The black man's thighs bulge and ripple. He looks like he's set to tear his bike apart more than ride it. Jamie checks his watch. His time is looking good.

Rooster glanced at the clock inside the Lincoln. Goddamn Lincoln now smelled of an old fuel leak and Tad's farts over the sickly sweet of the after-shave. But the car was clean. Riggi bought it in a cash deal and dropped it off with fixed-up tags. Rooster hated these goddamned pickups. He flexed his forearm, felt the corded muscle move underneath his wounded and roughly healed skin and light red arm hair. His forearm was thick for his stature. He was ripped. He was disciplined with working out, but he was a lazy bastard, he suspected, when it came to certain parts of the job. Yeah, he hated the fucking snatches. Anybody could do 'em. It wasn't like the house work. *That* was rarefied air, sir.

'Start the car,' Rooster said low, glancing sideways at the clock again. He scanned out the windshield of the Lincoln. The goddamn thing was like the bridge of the starship *Enterprise*.

'Oh, shit,' Tad said, his last bite of hash-brown cake sticking in his gullet. The car turned over, coarse and throaty. They saw movement at the corner.

Jamie puts his head down and digs his pedals. He's got a shot at his record. He's got a shot at the *world* record. He throws and then dips his right shoulder as he makes the corner of Tibbs. The canvas sack on his left has begun to lighten and unbalance him. He straightens the Mongoose and glances up. Car. Dang. Jamie wheels around the corner right into the rusty grille and locks them up.

Tyres bite asphalt and squeal. Smoke and rubber-stink roil. Brakes strain hard and hold. The vehicles come to a stop. Inches separate them.

With a blown-out breath of relief, Jamie shakes his head and starts pushing toward the kerb, bending down to pick up a few papers that have lurched free.

Car doors open. Feet hit the pavement. Jamie looks up at the sound. Two men rise out of the car. They move towards him. He squeezes the hand brake hard as they approach.

Love Harlequin romance?

DISCOVER.

Be the first to find out about promotions, news and exclusive content!

 Facebook.com/HarlequinBooks

 Twitter.com/HarlequinBooks

 Instagram.com/HarlequinBooks

 Pinterest.com/HarlequinBooks

ReaderService.com

EXPLORE.

Sign up for the Harlequin e-newsletter and download a free book from any series at **TryHarlequin.com.**

CONNECT.

Join our Harlequin community to share your thoughts and connect with other romance readers!
Facebook.com/groups/HarlequinConnection

Also by Jennifer Faye

Her Christmas Pregnancy Surprise

Greek Island Brides
Carrying the Greek Tycoon's Baby
Claiming the Drakos Heir
Wearing the Greek Millionaire's Ring

The Bartolini Legacy
The Prince and the Wedding Planner

Also by Allison Leigh

A Weaver Christmas Gift
One Night in Weaver...
The BFF Bride
A Child Under His Tree
Yuletide Baby Bargain
Show Me a Hero
The Rancher's Christmas Promise
A Promise to Keep
Fortune's Homecoming
Wild West Fortune

Discover more at millsandboon.co.uk

and has been nominated for numerous other awards.

Though her name is frequently on bestseller lists, **Allison Leigh**'s high point as a writer is hearing from readers that they laughed, cried or lost sleep while reading her books. She credits her family with great patience for the time she's parked at her computer, and for blessing her with the kind of love she wants her readers to share with the characters living in the pages of her books. Contact her at allisonleigh.com

HIS
LOS ANGELES
Surprise

SHERYL
LISTER

HHARLEQUIN® KIMANI™ ROMANCE

If ... are
th... nd
d... the
p...

Sp... l Lister
... es.

Recycling programs
for this product may
not exist in your area.

ISBN-13: 978-1-335-21691-5

His Los Angeles Surprise

HARLEQUIN®
www.Harlequin.com

Printed in U.S.A.

Sheryl Lister is a former pediatric occupational therapist with over twenty years of experience and has enjoyed reading and writing for as long as she can remember. She's been nominated for an EMMA Award, RT Reviewers' Choice Award, named BRAB's 2015 Best New Author and 2016 Breakout Author, and recently named *Black Pearls Magazine*'s 2017 Author of the Year. When she's not writing, Sheryl can be found on a date with her husband or in the kitchen creating appetizers. Sheryl resides in California and is a wife, mother of three daughters and a son-in-love, and grandmother to two special little boys. Visit her website at www.sheryllister.com.

Books by Sheryl Lister

Harlequin Kimani Romance

Just to Be with You
All of Me
It's Only You
Tender Kisses
Places in My Heart
Unwrapping the Holidays (with Nana Malone)
Giving My All to You
A Touch of Love
Still Loving You

For all those experiencing love the second time around.

Acknowledgments

My Heavenly Father, thank You for my life.
You never cease to amaze me with Your blessings!

To my husband, Lance, you continue to show me
why you'll always be my #1 hero!

To my children, family and friends, thanks for
your continued support. I appreciate and love you!

To my Club NEO sisters, I love you, ladies!

Sherelle Green and Pamela Yaye, you ladies rock!
Thanks for keeping me sane.

A special thank-you to the readers and authors I've met
on this journey. You continue to enrich my life.

Thank you to my editor, Patience Bloom,
for your editorial guidance and support.

A very special thank-you to my agent, Sarah E. Younger.
I can't tell you how much I appreciate having you
in my corner.

Chapter 1

"You've got one nice set of buns!"

Derek Moore whirled around at the sharp pat on his butt and came face-to-face with an elegantly attired woman old enough to be his grandmother. He sighed inwardly. "I, um…"

"Don't let the cane fool you," she said with a wink. "Can you point me in the direction of the table where I can place my bid?"

"It's the one on the far side of the room, in front of the banner." He gestured in that direction. The woman hurried off and Derek shook his head. He had no idea why he'd agreed to attend this function. His mind went back to his father's phone call. *I've been diagnosed with stage 4 prostate cancer and doctors don't think I'm going to make it past the New Year. I'm innocent of the crimes I was convicted of. Before I die, I want to clear my name, and I hope you, my sons, will help me. The Moore legacy is important.*

Moore legacy? Hell, his mother had to fight just to get the name on his birth certificate. He still had his

doubts about the old man's innocence, but he'd promised his brothers, Trey and Max, he would get involved. Pushing down the old anger, he snagged a flute of champagne from a passing waiter. Glancing around the luxurious twelfth-floor penthouse suite in the downtown Los Angeles Fine Arts Building, which housed the LA chapter of Prescott George, aka the Millionaire Moguls, he had to admit the organization had gone all out. This rent-a-bachelor function had been the idea of his older brother, Trey. With the chapter's six-month suspension after their father had been convicted of sabotaging the San Diego chapter, Prescott George needed some quick cash flow for their holiday outreach programs. If the sheer number of women crowding the room—young and old—was any indication, the event would be a huge success. He just hoped he didn't end up having to spend time with someone older than his mother. Derek turned and froze. Or her. He closed his eyes briefly, unnerved that the mere sight of his high school sweetheart stirred something inside of him long forgotten. He promptly dismissed the feeling. He hadn't spoken to Alexis Armstrong in over a decade, though he'd seen the popular supermodel in every media outlet. One thing hadn't changed. She was as beautiful now as she had been at Malibu High, even more so. And still slender, though the strapless navy dress clung enticingly to the curves now filling her tall frame.

"Derek Moore?"

"Yes." Derek didn't recognize the older gentleman standing in front of him. Not surprising, since he'd never been a part of Prescott George until now.

The man stuck out his hand. "Vance Winters. I'm

glad to see you finally taking your rightful place in the Millionaire Moguls. I've heard good things about you from Reginald."

He didn't understand how his father could have said anything about him, since the man knew nothing. As far as Derek taking his "rightful place," that was a long shot. "Is that so?"

Vance smiled. "He's proud of you three boys and your accomplishments."

Before he could reply, someone called out to Vance and he excused himself. "Proud, my ass," Derek mumbled, following his departure. He gulped down the remainder of his drink and placed it on one of the trays that had been set out.

"Well, I must say you clean up nicely."

Why me? Christina North worked as a personal assistant in the LA office and, from the first day he walked in the door, last week, she'd made her attraction to him no secret. "Christina."

Her gaze slowly traveled down his body and back up. "Maybe I should be placing my bid on you." She took a step closer. "One night…no, a week would be fabulous. Don't you agree?"

Derek stepped back. "I don't think so." So far he'd been polite in letting her know he wasn't interested, but she clearly couldn't take no for an answer.

She smiled. "Surely you wouldn't let all my money go to waste."

"In a heartbeat."

Her smile faded. "Derek—"

He held up a hand. "First, I don't think it would look good for you to have the winning bid, seeing as how

you're handling the transactions. Second, as I told you before, I'm not interested in having anything outside of a working relationship with you. Now, if you'll excuse me, I need to find Trey."

Christina muttered something that sounded like "your loss" and stormed off.

Derek scanned the room for Trey and his gaze collided with Alexis's. A slight smile tilted her lips. She saluted him with her glass and gave him an imperceptible nod, then smoothly looked away and continued her conversation. For a brief moment, he toyed with going over to talk to her, but nixed the idea. Some things were better left in the past.

He spotted Trey near the front of the penthouse and started in his direction. Halfway there, he saw several women surround Trey. It took a moment to see why. He had a baby strapped to his chest in one of those carriers. Derek chuckled. He'd talk to him later.

"I didn't think you'd be here." His brother Max materialized out of nowhere.

"I told Trey I'd come and I'm here. I had planned to talk to him, but he's a little preoccupied. Whose baby is that?"

"His sister's. She had to go out of town for a couple of weeks. Does your being here tonight mean you're going to start actively participating in Prescott George?"

"I don't know."

"I know you and Trey don't think so, but I know Dad is innocent."

Derek bit back the acerbic reply poised on the tip of his tongue at the mention of his father's innocence. "That remains to be seen. After all the trouble you and

Trey went through being investigated because of him, you still think he's innocent?" He stopped himself upon seeing the pained expression on Max's face. Max had been the only one of the three who'd grown up having their father in his life, and he loved Reginald. Derek blew out a long breath. "I'm sorry. This is going to take some getting used to."

"I understand. Derek, I know you said earlier that you wouldn't help with the investigation, but I'm hoping you'll change your mind. Trey and I want to meet to talk about it on Sunday."

As much as Derek wanted to walk away and tell Max to forget it, he couldn't. Max had been trying to develop a relationship with Derek and Trey for the longest time and Derek hadn't wanted to be bothered. Now with their father dying, he could see the toll it was taking on Max. "Call me and let me know when."

"Thanks. How long are you going to be here?"

"Probably not much longer."

"Then I'll talk to you on Sunday."

Derek watched him walk away. After being the lone wolf for so long, he'd never cared much about having a relationship with Trey and Max. Maybe it was time he got to know his brothers.

"There's enough eye candy in here to put a woman in a diabetic coma."

Alexis Armstrong chuckled at her best friend, Charlene Rivers. But she did have a point.

"How does this rent-a-bachelor thing work again?"

"You can rent them for a day, week or even an entire month, depending on what the guys have speci-

fied. There are information packets on all the Prescott George members who've agreed to participate on that far table, where assistants are taking the blind bids. For the more tech-savvy crowd, there are also computers with the information and you can place your bid there, as well. Apparently, they need some quick money for their outreach after being on suspension for the past six months."

"What happened?"

Alexis spoke quietly. "One of their high-ranking members was accused of sabotaging the San Diego chapter—break-ins, computer leaks and vandalism. But no charges were brought because they didn't want to incur any bad press. Instead, they just expelled the man behind it and suspended the LA chapter."

"Wow. You'd think with all the money and power, someone wouldn't need to resort to such tactics."

"True, but someone did." Alexis still couldn't believe *who*. "Prescott George does a lot of good." She gestured to the motto on the wall: From Generation to Generation, Lifting Each Other Up.

"That's great to hear. Anyway, back to the reason we're here." Charlene glanced around the room, smiled and sipped her champagne. "Yep. I see a couple of brothers who would be perfect to help end my dating drought, preferably one of those with the open calendar for a month. You should be looking, too. It's about time for you to find someone."

Alexis shook her head. "Don't start. See, this is why I didn't want to invite you," she added with a mock pout.

"Girl, please. You know you're ready to get your groove back. Look at all these *fine* men. Surely one of

them will be happy to help you out. And you know they all have good jobs."

She rolled her eyes, but couldn't stop her smile. "Whatever." She scanned the room. Yes, they all did. Prescott George was an elite organization for African American millionaires started in the 1940s in Florida, as a way to give back to their communities. Now they had chapters all over the world and continued their legacy of outreach. Alexis brought her glass to her lips and froze. *Derek?* What was Derek Moore doing here? She remembered him being adamant about having nothing to do with the organization. It had been close to fourteen years since she'd seen him and she had to admit that time had been good to him.

"Alexis." Charlene waved a hand in her face. "Are you okay?"

Alexis startled. "What? Oh, I'm fine." But she couldn't resist one more peek at Derek.

"So, I see someone *has* caught your eye and I totally understand why. That man is gorgeous. And with his height, it would take a long time to work your way down that sexy body." Charlene fanned herself.

She *had* worked her way down his body and recalled with vivid clarity how it felt to run her hands over all six feet, five inches of his muscled frame. "Yes, he is gorgeous."

Her friend latched on to Alexis's arm. "Let's get one of those information packets. I want to know who he is and what he does."

"I already know who he is and what he does," Alexis confessed.

"I can't believe you've been holding out on me."

Charlene nodded politely to a man passing. "So spill it. How long have you been seeing him?"

"I haven't seen Derek in over a decade."

"Derek?" Her eyes widened. "Are you talking about *Derek Moore*, the guy you dated in high school? The one who—"

"Yes, that's him," Alexis said, cutting her off. She didn't need her business spread across the room. Being a model, much of her life had been played out in the public arena, but some things she liked to keep private. As if sensing her scrutiny, Derek glanced her way. She saluted him with her glass and turned back to Charlene. "He said he'd never step foot in the organization, so I wonder why he's here."

"Something must have changed his mind."

"Mmm-hmm." She wondered if it had to do with his father being expelled from Prescott George. Derek and his father had never been close.

"I think you should rent him."

Alexis almost choked on her drink. "What? Wait, no." She shook her head. "If I know Derek, he's only here to support his half brothers."

"It's the perfect idea. I just saw the look he gave you, and obviously, with the way you've been staring at him, you two have some unfinished business. Think of it this way—you can catch up, and who knows, the spark may still be there. Oh, and it's for a good cause."

"Charlene, I really don't think that's a good idea. Yes, I loved him in high school, but a lot has changed since then. *I've* changed." More importantly, she didn't believe that he had changed. Derek had always been a loner and out to prove that he could make his own mark

on the world. He neither wanted nor needed the money placed in a trust fund for him by his estranged father. "He left me once and I don't want to give him the opportunity to do it again." It surprised Alexis how much his leaving still affected her after all these years.

"Then this is the perfect opportunity to show him what he gave up all those years ago."

Alexis laughed. "You are such a nut."

"Honey, I'm serious. What good is being able to strut down a runway if you're not going to use it for something far more worthwhile? While you're thinking it over, let's go get those packets before they're gone. I don't want to take a chance on missing out on a potential Mr. Right." They made their way across the crowded ballroom and Charlene eased her way between two women to snag a booklet from the table. She held it up triumphantly.

Women of all ages stood lined up in front of the table and computers. "I'm guessing that they're going to raise a lot of money tonight." They moved to an area with less people.

"And I plan to add mine to it," Charlene said, flipping through the pages. She held it up. "I think I found him."

Alexis read the bio. "Sterling Winston. Investments, wealth building... He can definitely give you some good advice for the future."

Charlene grinned. "By the looks of him, he can give me good advice on a lot of things. I'm going to place a bid."

"Knock yourself out. I'll be here waiting when you get back."

"Humph. You need to be getting in line yourself."

She laughed and waved her off. "You'd better hurry so someone else doesn't snatch him up. Didn't I read that the bidding for him lasts only an hour?"

"Be back in a bit." Charlene hurried off.

Still smiling, Alexis turned at the sound of someone calling her name. "Jade." The two women embraced. "I haven't seen you in a while." She and Jade had been paired up on a few modeling assignments early in Alexis's career.

Jade's dark eyes twinkled. "That's because I'm retired. I moved here from New York last year and my new husband is a member of this chapter."

"Congratulations. How long have you two been married?"

"Six months. I'm anxious to start a family, so my days of all-day photo shoots are over. What about you?"

"I've been thinking about dusting off my business degree and doing something else." Being in the business for a decade and a half, Alexis had amassed a closetful of free couture clothing, had her passport stamped with some of the most beautiful locales and had enough money saved and invested that she could live a comfortable life. But she wanted to do more with her life.

"We should keep in touch now that I'm local."

"I'd like that." They exchanged numbers, shared another hug, then Jade floated off to find her husband.

Thinking about Jade's comment regarding starting a family sent a sharp pain through her chest. There were several women ahead of Charlene at the computers, so Alexis decided to step out for a minute to get some much needed air. Halfway to her destination she real-

ized she had to pass Derek. His gaze shifted in her direction as she approached, his expression unreadable. For a second she thought he might ignore her, but he excused himself and stepped into her pathway.

"Hello, Alexis."

"Derek." His voice had deepened to a rich baritone and the goatee framing his mouth gave him an even sexier edge. An awkward silence ensued.

"It's been a long time," she finally said.

"Yes, it has. I would ask what you've been doing, but you're a superstar."

She laughed softly. "I wouldn't say that. I've seen you on a couple of magazine covers, as well." He'd been interviewed as one of the country's top real estate moguls. "It seems as though you got what you wanted."

A rare smile curved his lips, transforming his serious features and making her pulse skip. Then he stared at her intently. "Maybe. Maybe not." Derek placed a soft kiss on her cheek and his hard body brushed against hers. "It's good to see you, Alexis."

"Good to see you, too, Derek."

Giving her another smile, he sauntered off. Alexis watched his fluid gait until he blended with the crowd. She stood there a moment longer before making a decision. She spun around and headed back to the bidding area. *Show him what he missed? Yep.* Charlene met her, smiling broadly. "That smile says you got your bid in before the deadline."

"Yes, I did. And I hope I bid high enough."

"Well, I'm going to take your advice and make a bid of my own."

Charlene rubbed her hands together. "Aw, sookie sookie now!"

Alexis opted for the computers to speed things up, but the one she chose kept giving her an error message. So she went over to the table to ask the woman sitting there about the problem.

The woman took her credit card. "I can help you here. Which Millionaire Mogul are you bidding on?"

"Derek Moore." She wrote down her bid and slid it across the table.

A strange expression crossed the woman's face. "I see."

Alexis's eyebrow lifted a fraction. *What's that all about?*

"It seems there's a problem with your card. The transaction isn't going through."

"Feels like someone doesn't want me to rent Derek," she said with a nervous chuckle. Some of the other women waiting had started to stare. Finally, after five tries, the transaction went through. And just like her friend, Alexis had placed a bid high enough to guarantee a win.

Chapter 2

Saturday morning, instead of checking his emails, voice mail and meeting with the land developer, Derek laced up his tennis shoes and exited the back door of his Malibu beachfront property. After taking a moment to cue up his favorite workout playlist, he stuck his earphones in and started his run down the sandy beach. Though the calendar said mid-September, the temperatures still reflected the warmth of summer. He hoped the run would help clear his mind from all the turmoil that had kept him tossing and turning all night. This mess with his father weighed heavily on his mind. Derek didn't know why he was even considering helping Max and Trey. Reginald had never been there for Derek when he was growing up. He didn't want to carry his name, but his mother insisted and had gone through hell just to prove that Reginald was his father. A court-ordered DNA test finally settled the matter. Now, with his mortality staring him in the face, Reginald Moore had decided to seek amends. His anger rising, Derek increased his pace. After several minutes,

a semblance of calm returned and he slowed a bit. He could deal with this.

Seeing Alexis last night had also occupied his mind. He hadn't expected the surge of memories to overwhelm him as they did. And what had possessed him to kiss her? Granted, it had been only a peck on the cheek, but the sweet scent of her perfume had wafted into his nose and the soft texture of her unblemished skin had thrown him for a loop. Derek dated his fair share of women and had always been up-front with them. He did not do relationships or commitments, and he *never* let his emotions come into play. Initially, he and his dates agreed, and then things changed. When that happened, Derek had no problem walking away without a backward glance. Which made Alexis an anomaly.

He reversed his course and headed back the way he'd come. He assumed by the number of people who'd greeted her that she'd attended several Prescott George events. Another problem. Now that he'd agreed to work with the outreach—reluctantly—he would more than likely run into her again. He was certain that by their next meeting, whatever errant feelings had cropped up would be gone. The longer he thought about it, the more he realized that what he'd experienced amounted to nothing more than some sentimental recollection from her being his first girlfriend.

Derek slowed to a jog and worked on regulating his breathing. By the time he reached his deck, his mind had cleared. He spent another forty-five minutes in his home gym, showered, then loped downstairs to find some food. Deciding on something simple, he scrambled some eggs, made two pieces of toast and poured

a glass of orange juice. While eating, he checked his emails and deleted the junk first. He scrolled back up and clicked on one from Max letting him know that Demetrius Davis would have the information Derek had requested, and he could stop by at his leisure to pick it up. Demetrius was his father's best friend and the man in charge of the LA chapter's fund-raising. Derek had agreed to help with one of the holiday outreach projects for children, but with his busy schedule would most likely not get by there for another week or two.

He saw an email from Christina and let out a deep sigh. How many times did he have to say no for the woman to get it? Derek clicked on the link and sipped his juice. His eyes widened, he choked on the juice going down his throat and he spilled the small amount remaining. *No, no, no!* Trying to recover, he leaned back in the chair and scrubbed a hand down his face, then reread the message, hoping the words would change. Derek, enclosed is the information of the winning bid for your time. His gaze dropped to the name: Alexis Armstrong. Alexis had rented him for a night. Now what the hell was he supposed to do? He took his empty plate and glass to the sink, rinsed them and put them in the dishwasher.

Derek checked the time. He had three properties to show and the meeting with the developer. He jotted down Alexis's address and noted that she lived less than two miles from him. When he finished with the developer, he planned to drive over and tell her he couldn't do it. They had no reason to rehash the past. He'd pay back every dime of her money if he had to.

Hours later, after meeting with the developer, he

drove up to the partially finished building that would house commercial space on the first floor and ten stories of luxury Beverly Hills condominiums. He donned a hard hat and followed the site foreman around, pleased with the progress. A brisk breeze blew as he stood on the top floor in what would become one of three penthouses overlooking the city—the walls of which had yet to be built. Satisfied that everything would be done on schedule, he thanked the man and left. With traffic, it took an hour to get home and it was nearly six when he parked in the circle driveway.

Derek toyed with calling Alexis, but nixed the idea. Something like this needed to be handled face-to-face. After changing out of his suit into a pair of jeans and pullover silk T-shirt, he grabbed his keys and loped back downstairs.

"Might as well get this over with," he muttered as he started the car and drove off.

Derek parked in Alexis's driveway, got out and surveyed the property. He admired the Mediterranean-style two-story home as he walked up the two steps and rang the bell. His head came up when the door opened, and Derek forgot every word he had planned to say. His gaze made a slow tour up Alexis's body from her bare feet, shapely legs, hips covered in a pair of black shorts and a sleeveless button-down blouse tied at the waist that revealed a sliver of her toned stomach. Her face had been scrubbed free of makeup and her hair pulled back into a ponytail. A sharp jolt of lust went straight to his groin.

"Derek! What are you doing here?"

He finally found his voice. "May I come in?"

Alexis smiled and moved aside for him to enter. "Of course. Come on back. I'm in the kitchen."

Derek followed her through the open space with its large columns and wood floor. The kitchen merged into a comfortable living room with a wall of windows that gave a stunning view of the ocean. She had accented the eggshell sofa, love seat and chairs with turquoise pillows, creating a welcoming environment that, unlike his house, felt like a home. And just like his place, her deck had stairs leading to the beach. "You have a beautiful home, Alexis."

"Thanks." She reached into the refrigerator and took out several ingredients, placed them on the counter and folded her arms. "You never said what you're doing here."

"I received an email from the rent-a-bachelor event."

She chuckled. "So you just showed up to collect?"

She'd given him the perfect opportunity to tell her that he didn't plan on collecting at all. Somehow, he couldn't get his mouth to say the words. "Not exactly."

"Well, since you're here…" Alexis let the sentence hang. "I'd planned on something a little more formal, say, like a restaurant, but if you don't mind having dinner here, we can make it work."

Derek crossed the room to where she stood leaning against the counter. "Why?"

"Why what?"

"Why me?"

"It was for a good cause and I already know you." Alexis shrugged. "I thought we could catch up. It's been a very long time," she added softly.

"Yeah." He stuck his hands in his pockets and shifted his gaze back out to the water. "If it's not an imposi-

tion, tonight and here is fine." Besides, the quicker he got this over with the better off he'd be.

Alexis studied Derek standing at the window and couldn't decide which persona she liked better—him in formal wear or casually dressed—and settled on the way he looked tonight. The jeans and silk T made him seem a little less serious. To say he'd surprised her would be an understatement. "I hope you're okay with jambalaya and cornbread." She chopped the sausage and added it to the skillet, mixed the cornbread and slid the pan into the oven.

Derek glanced over his shoulder. "Sounds good. Do you need my help with anything?"

"No, but thanks. Would you like something to drink? I have a bottle of chardonnay I'd planned to have with dinner. I also have some green tea."

He came over. "The wine is fine. If you'll show me where everything is, I'll open it."

She retrieved the bottle from the refrigerator, the opener from a drawer, and handed them to him.

"Would you like a glass?"

"Yes, please," she said, placing two glasses on the bar. Alexis felt as nervous as she had the first time he'd come to her house. She began to think "renting" him may not have been such a good idea. The soft kiss he'd given her last night came back unbidden, and along with it, the memory of the faint notes of his earthy cologne and the heat of his body surrounding her. She immediately shoved the thought away and turned her attention to finishing the meal. Breaking the silence, she asked, "So, where did you go after high school?"

"New York. Finished college and stayed for three years before coming back here." He told her that he'd initially gotten into real estate part-time as a way to make some money while in school. "During a training session, one of the top brokers said, 'If there's anyone in the room doing this as a part-time job, you should leave because you're wasting your time and mine.' I stayed."

"You've done well for yourself. I read about the awards you've received in real estate. Congratulations." Alexis added the rice and stock to the pan and covered it. She picked up her glass and joined him at the bar.

"Thanks. What about you? Are you still enjoying modeling?"

"For the most part. It's been a great way to see the world, for sure."

Derek chuckled. "And for free. Can't beat that. What were your two most favorite places?"

She angled her head thoughtfully. "Africa was absolutely beautiful and the people warm and gracious. My second favorite would have to be anywhere in the Caribbean. Give me a beach, a book and my music and I'm a happy girl."

"Somehow, I thought you'd prefer more lively entertainment."

Alexis took a sip of her wine. "It's okay, but these days I'm finding I enjoy the quiet times." She left to check the food. "It's almost ready. Do you want to eat inside or on the deck?"

"Whichever you want is fine with me."

"Since the weather is nice, we can eat outside." Alexis took advantage of the warm temperatures whenever she could. She enjoyed watching the sun setting

over the water. She added shrimp to the jambalaya and peeked at the cornbread. It would take only about five minutes for the seafood to cook and the bread would be done by then. She got plates, napkins and silverware. It would be easier to serve themselves inside.

She heard a buzzing sound and watched as Derek retrieved his phone. He read for a minute and sighed. He typed something and stuck the cell back into his pocket.

"If you need to take care of some things, I can always take a rain check." Though she found herself enjoying his company.

Derek stood and came around the bar. "It's nothing that can't wait." He gestured to the stove. "Smells good."

She took the cornbread out of the oven. "Hopefully, it will taste the same. Grab a plate. I figured it would be easier to do it this way, rather than carting out all the dishes."

He picked up a plate. "And less dishes to wash."

Alexis burst out laughing. "You still hate washing dishes." It was the one chore he always complained about.

The corner of his mouth kicked up in a slight grin. "Absolutely." He quieted. "I can't believe you remembered that."

"I remember a lot of things," she said softly. He stared at her with an intensity that made her heart race. "Um…you can go first." She handed him a serving spoon, then cut a few pieces of cornbread. The temperature had risen by several degrees and had nothing to do with the heat from the oven.

Alexis placed a generous helping of jambalaya and the corner piece of bread on her plate. She'd just have to work out a little more, because she intended to enjoy

this meal. They carried their food outside. Derek went back in, topped off their glasses and brought them out.

Derek lifted his chardonnay. "To the cook."

Alexis touched her glass to his. "Thank you." For the first several minutes, they ate in companionable silence while listening to the waves crashing against the shore and the birds calling to each other overhead.

"This is really good." He forked up another portion.

"I got the recipe from a woman while in New Orleans two years ago. She said it belonged to her family and it was one they could share." She broke off a piece of cornbread, popped it into her mouth and chewed. "How's your mom?"

Derek paused with the fork midway to his mouth. "She's good."

"You know, I used to love seeing her photos in the magazines. I always thought she was so beautiful, elegant and poised. I wanted to be just like her."

"Seriously? You never told me that."

Alexis shrugged. "You never asked." Back then, he had been so determined to forge his own way that nothing else seemed to matter. They quieted and continued eating. "She did factor in my decision. I thought if she could do it, so could I," she said, picking up where the conversation left off.

"My mom was a pretty successful model, but nowhere near what you've accomplished."

"That's probably because she left the industry so soon."

Derek chuckled. "Yeah. She said she was tired of seeing me grow up through pictures, and wanted to do something else, something to make a difference.

These days, she's enjoying teaching high school English literature."

"I totally understand where she's coming from."

His brow lifted. "Are you thinking of leaving the business?"

A smile curved Alexis's lips. "Yes. Don't get me wrong, I still enjoy what I do. I just want to do more." Now finished eating, she went to stand against the rail. "Maybe it's time to put this business degree to work."

"Any ideas about what you want to do?"

"Actually, yes. I'd like to do something in the area of African American infant mortality. The rates are much higher than any other race and I want our babies to have a fighting chance."

Derek came and stood next to her. "That sounds like a worthwhile project."

She faced him. "I think so, too. But what that looks like, I have no clue right now."

He tucked a loose strand of hair behind her ear. "I have no doubt that whatever you decide will turn out well."

The intimate gesture shook her. "Do you think so?" With him standing so close, she remembered that he towered over her five-foot-ten height by a good seven inches.

"Absolutely. You were the smartest girl in class and I know nothing has changed."

Before she could form a reply, Derek lowered his head and covered her mouth in a sweet, gentle kiss. He slid an arm around her waist and eased her closer. The intensity changed in the blink of an eye, and when it ended, she couldn't tell who was more surprised.

Still holding her, Derek asked, "Should I apologize?"

"Not unless you want to."

His soft laughter floated in the air. "So, is this part of the rental?"

"It could be." Alexis had no idea where those words came from.

Desire blazed in his eyes. "Then I say we should take full advantage and make it worth every penny you invested."

Her pulse skipped. *What have I gotten myself into?* Once again, his mouth moved over hers, stunning her with a passion that stole her breath and turned her knees to jelly. This was *not* some awkwardly cute kiss from a seventeen-year-old boy, but that of a man who had perfected the art of pleasing a woman. He released the band on her hair and groaned as the long tresses spilled over her shoulders. She'd been growing her hair since the age of thirteen, with a vow not to cut it—aside from trims—and it now hung to the middle of her back. It was her turn to moan when his hands roamed up her back and around to massage her breasts. Her head fell back and her eyes closed. Derek transferred his kisses to her exposed throat. She didn't realize that he'd undone the first two buttons on her blouse until she felt the warmth of his tongue skating along her chest.

"Unless you want your neighbors to get an eyeful, I suggest we move this inside," Derek murmured against the shell of her ear, his hands and lips still moving.

Alexis opened her eyes. "Inside where?"

Holding her gaze, he said, "Anywhere you want to take it."

With her body on fire, and since she had declared this a show-him-what-he'd-missed date, there was only one place she wanted to take it.

Chapter 3

Derek didn't stop to analyze what he was doing as he followed Alexis to her bedroom. He paid scant attention to the furnishings, only the woman in front of him. As soon as she lit a lamp, he drew her into his arms again. The way she stared at him with her large, dark eyes and soft smile did something to him, and he tried to push down the sensation. This was nothing more than a case of pure lust. He'd been working nonstop for the past several months and couldn't remember the last time he went on a date. His aroused state let him know it had been way too long.

"Are you certain about this, Alexis? I don't want you to have any regrets."

Alexis looped her arms around his neck. "I'm positive. I can ask you the same question."

He pulled her flush against his straining erection. "Feel what you do to me? I think you know my answer." Derek slanted his mouth over hers and, once again, lost himself in the sweetness of her kiss. Without breaking the seal of their mouths, he slowly stripped away

her blouse. His hands mapped a path over the curve of her hips, her slim waist and up to her breasts. Turning her, he unsnapped her bra and trailed his tongue down her spine.

Alexis moaned.

Derek rotated, sat on the bed and pulled her to stand between his legs. "You are absolutely exquisite. So beautiful." He lowered his head and took one taut nipple in his mouth. She called out his name as he suckled, stroked and teased, first one, then the other. He transferred his kisses to her stomach, dipping his tongue in her belly button. He pulled her shorts and panties off and was instantly engulfed in her womanly scent, arousing him beyond anything he had ever felt. Her legs buckled and he eased her down to the bed.

"Why am I the only one naked?" she asked, leaning up to kiss him.

"An easy fix." Derek reached for the hem of his shirt, but Alexis placed a staying hand on his.

She gave him a sexy smile. "Let me."

He closed his eyes when her hands slid beneath his shirt and touched his bare skin, arousing him further. She slid it up, but didn't remove it.

"Do you need help?" he murmured.

"Not at all. I'm just taking my time." Alexis's hands stilled. "You're not in a hurry, are you?"

Hell, yes! Before he could answer, her warm tongue skated across his chest and stomach and sent a jolt straight to his groin. "Alexis, baby, you're trying to kill me."

She gazed up at him. "No, Derek, I'm trying to give you a night of pleasure you won't forget." She whipped the shirt over his head and pushed him down on the

bed. She kissed her way from his chest to his midsection and ran her tongue across it just above his belt. Derek's breathing increased, his muscles quivered and a low growl erupted from his throat. She continued to torture him with her hands and tongue until he thought he would explode. Unable to take it any longer, he lifted her head and slid his tongue between her parted lips. Pulling her closer, he angled his head and deepened the kiss, teasing, tasting.

Derek captured a chocolate-tipped nipple between his lips. He laved and suckled first one, then the other. He charted a path down the front of her body with his hand and slid two fingers into her slick, wet heat until she was writhing and moaning beneath him. Nearing the end of his control, Derek withdrew his fingers, slid off the bed, undressed. He searched his wallet for condoms and hoped he had at least one. He found three. *Thank goodness.* He tore one off and tossed the others on the nightstand. After rolling it on, he moved over her, grinding his body against hers. They both moaned. He shifted his body over hers and entered her with one smooth thrust, until he was buried to the hilt. He held himself still, savoring the feeling of her tight walls surrounding him. "You feel so good, baby," he whispered against her lips, at the same time he started moving inside her.

"Mmm, and so do you." Alexis wrapped her legs around his waist and pulled his mouth down on hers, their tongues tangling and dancing.

Derek closed his eyes and let the sensations take over as he kept up the relaxed pace. She locked her legs around him and her hands burned a path over his chest

and back. The way her body arched and moved against his made him increase the pace.

"Yes-s-s!"

He lifted her hips as he plunged deeper and faster. Her whimpers and cries of passion excited him in a way he couldn't explain. He gritted his teeth, feeling her nails biting into the skin on his back, but he didn't slow.

"Don't stop," Alexis chanted breathlessly.

No worries there. He couldn't stop even if he wanted to. Not when she felt so good. She arched off the bed and screamed his name. Her body shook and her inner muscles contracted, clamping around him like a vise. Derek groaned loudly and tightened his grip on her hips, driving into her. His orgasm started somewhere around his feet and shot through him with the force of a cannon. Still thrusting, he wrenched his mouth away from hers and yelled out her name.

Their bodies trembled for what seemed like forever as they both gasped for air. She reached up and stroked the sides of his face. He opened his eyes and, when their gazes connected, felt *something*. Derek promptly dismissed it. He slowly withdrew from her and his heart nearly stopped. He muttered a curse.

"What's the matter?" Her concerned gaze roamed over his face.

He cursed under his breath again. He did not need this kind of complication in his life. "The condom broke," he said with a heavy sigh.

Alexis's eyes widened for a split second. "We should be okay. I'm on the pill."

Derek tried to keep the skepticism off his face. The

last woman who'd said that had lied. Obviously, he didn't cover his reaction well enough.

Alexis's face clouded with anger. "You still don't trust anyone, do you? You think everybody is out to get you."

"Don't put words in my mouth, Alexis."

"I didn't have to. I saw the expression on your face." She pushed him off her and stalked across the room to get something out of her purse. She walked back over and slapped the small pink container on the bed.

He sat up "What's this?"

"Open it."

Derek opened it and saw that they were indeed birth control pills.

"And you'll notice I haven't missed one day."

The hurt in her voice didn't sit well with him. He hadn't meant to offend her. He'd learned long ago that he couldn't really count on people—except his mother— and he'd wrapped himself in armor to keep from being hurt. But Alexis didn't deserve this treatment. He was the one who—at the expense of their relationship—had left to pursue his dreams.

"Come here." He gently drew her down onto his lap and wrapped his arms around her. "I believed you when you said it the first time, contrary to what you think. You've never lied to me before."

"And I don't plan to start now."

"I know that," he said, and placed a soft kiss on her temple.

Alexis searched his face, seemingly looking for the truth. Satisfied, she leaned against his chest.

Derek continued to hold her while idly running his

hand up and down her back. A riot of emotions swirled in the pit of his stomach, and not one of them made sense. At length, he said, "I need to clean up."

She lifted her head. "You can use my bathroom."

Somewhere in the back of his mind, warning bells went off and that sage inner voice said he should leave. They'd satisfied their lust and he didn't want her getting any ideas that this might be more than just the one night. Instead, he heard himself ask, "Are you going to join me?"

She leaned away and arched an eyebrow. "Are you sure that's a good idea, with what just happened?"

No, he didn't think it a wise decision, but he'd already tossed common sense aside. He held up the pill pack. "You said we were good." And he wanted to experience one more time just how good it had been.

Alexis chuckled and stood. "Come on." She picked up one of the condoms. "Maybe I should put it on this time so it's done right."

Derek threw his head back and roared with laughter. She sashayed past him with an exaggerated switch of her hips and he felt himself growing hard all over again. He slid off the bed and started to follow her, but turned back to grab the last condom. Just in case.

Alexis awakened hours later and stared down at the man cuddled next to her with the sheets twisted around their lower bodies. Last night, they couldn't get enough of each other. Their first attempt to shower had ended with her hands braced against the wall as he entered her from behind. They never made it to the bed for the last

round. She'd wound up with her legs wrapped around him, where he stood in the middle of her bedroom.

Her gaze lingered over the sculpted planes of his chest and abdomen. He had clearly kept up with his workout regimen. She studied him as he slept and noticed the tired lines etched in his handsome face. Did he ever take time to relax or did he spend all his waking hours working? A smile curved her lips. She reached up and lightly traced his mouth and kissed him. He didn't stir. A quick glance at the clock showed the time to be just after eight in the morning.

She lay back against the pillow and sighed with pleasure. When she'd rented Derek, she never envisioned that they'd end up in bed together. Those old buried emotions she'd had for him had surfaced and almost overwhelmed her. Now she had to wonder where they would go from here.

Alexis carefully left the bed, donned her robe and went to the bathroom. As she opened the door minutes later, she could hear him on the phone. Not wanting to disturb or interrupt him, she decided to wait.

Alexis couldn't help overhearing bits and pieces of the conversation. She heard him say Trey's name and caught enough to know that their father was dying and that he'd asked the three brothers to investigate his expulsion. She shook her head. Her heart hurt for Derek and the torment he must be going through, having to decide whether to help the man, who had never done anything for him.

"Trey, I said I'd be there…against my better judgment," she heard Derek say.

When she reentered the room, Derek was dressing.

"Are you leaving? I thought maybe we could have breakfast before you go."

Derek pulled on his shirt. "That's not necessary." He sat on the side of the bed and put on his tennis shoes.

Alexis leaned against the dresser. "No, it isn't, but I thought after last night, we could spend a little time together this morning, talking."

He paused while tying a shoelace. "Alexis, about last night. I enjoyed being with you, but I'm not looking to start up anything. Having a committed relationship isn't in the cards for me. I'm sorry. I should've been more up-front yesterday."

She should have known this would be the result. He hadn't changed one bit from the closed-off teen who had walked away the first time. "Yeah, you should have." She folded her arms.

Derek finished tying his shoes, braced his hands on his thighs and bowed his head briefly. He rose to his feet and took the few steps to where she stood. He lifted his hand to touch her face and she turned away.

"You don't want to give me the impression you're trying to start anything." Alexis tossed out the words.

He threw up his hands. "What do you want from me? I'm trying to be honest."

"I don't want anything from you, Derek." She had wanted his heart years ago, but he'd had no room in it for love. Apparently, nothing had changed. "I'll walk you out." She pivoted and headed for the front door, leaving him to follow. She held it open and tried to keep her emotions from showing.

"Alexis—"

"You've already stated your position, and it's okay."

Alexis rose up on her toes and kissed his cheek. "Good-bye, Derek."

Derek gave her a bittersweet smile, squeezed her hand and sauntered out to his car.

She closed the door and leaned against it. So much for showing him what he'd missed. All she had managed to do was conjure up long-buried feelings best left in the past.

Chapter 4

Derek stood under the warm shower spray Sunday evening, marveling at how quickly his life had begun to unravel. He had made two decisions that could potentially wreak havoc on his well-being. He bowed his head, let the water run over him and hoped it would wash away all thoughts of being in Alexis's bed. The longer he stood there the more vivid the memories became—of his hands trailing over her smooth skin, her long, toned legs wrapped around his waist as he thrust deeply inside her, her passionate cries as she called his name over and over. His body reacted with lightning speed.

"Dammit!" Derek slammed his hand against the wall. Why hadn't he told her he couldn't do the date, and paid back the money like he'd planned? After two weeks, he still couldn't stop thinking about that night. He adjusted the temperature to cool and tried to think of anything but her, to put out the fire now raging through his veins. By the time he finished, his arousal had calmed somewhat, but now he had another problem. Reginald Moore.

After meeting with Trey and Max, he had reluctantly agreed to take an active part in the investigation.
His brothers had mentioned that Derek might present
a fresh perspective, since he had never been part of the
organization. They had asked him to talk to Reginald's
best friend, Demetrius, who had offered to help with
their inquiry. His brothers had also filled Derek in on
all the details of the case and what they had learned
so far. While Max continued to maintain Reginald's
innocence of the break-ins, computer leaks and vandalism linked to the San Diego chapter, part of Derek
felt the evidence would more than likely lead the trail
right back to their father. For now, he would attend the
Prescott George events, talk to Demetrius and see what
turned up.

The late breakfast from Lou's Diner that Derek had
eaten was long gone and he rummaged in his refrigerator for something quick to fix. Alexis's jambalaya and
cornbread immediately came to mind, and of course,
that only led to more sensuous thoughts. Groaning, he
closed the refrigerator and picked up the phone to place
an order from his favorite Mexican restaurant.

Forty-five minutes later, Derek sat at the kitchen
table eating green chili chicken enchiladas, rice and
black beans, while going over his Monday schedule. He
had worked hard throughout the past decade to reach
his level of success, and went over and beyond to ensure his clients' satisfaction, which accounted for the
many repeat customers and multimillion-dollar deals.
He worked hard and expected those who worked for
him to do the same.

Aside from the typical weekly staff meetings, he

had a training seminar for new recruits tomorrow, and three commercial property showings. He scanned the schedule to see when he could make a quick stop at the Prescott George office. With his late working hours, he'd forgotten to pick up the Dream packet. The building was close to downtown, and barring too much traffic, he could get in and out tomorrow morning, and be across town for his next appointment.

Derek spent a restless night, and when he woke up the next morning, needed a double shot of caffeine to get going. Used to burning the midnight oil, he moved through the day with confidence and efficiency. He arrived at the Fine Arts Building a few minutes later than he had anticipated, parked in a nearby garage and walked back. Derek opened the heavy bronze doors and entered the cathedral-like lobby, where bronze statues of children played in an actual fountain. Upstairs, he found only Christina in the office.

"Hi, Christina. I'm here to pick up some information on the Children's Dream Project. Max said Demetrius left it for me."

"So, you're actually going to start using your membership?" Christina's voice held an edge of sarcasm.

He ignored that and waited.

She searched through the folders on her desk. "I don't have anything here."

"Maybe he left it in his office." When she didn't move, Derek asked, "Are you going to look or should I?"

She gave him an icy glare, slowly rose to her feet and went into Demetrius's office. Derek followed. He scanned the large space with its dark, heavy furniture. Had his father occupied a similar one? *Where did*

that come from? Frowning, he focused his attention on Christina and her search. He came and stood at the side of the desk, and propped a hip on the edge.

Christina continued to look through the various folders on the desk. "Are you sure that's the name of the project?" She rounded the desk and pulled out a drawer containing more files.

"That's what Max said." Derek glanced down as she neared the back of the stack, and something lying in the corner caught his eye. Curious, he reached in, picked it up and went still. *A can of silver spray paint, the exact type and brand found in his father's former office and used in the San Diego incident.* He shook it—half-filled. Derek removed the top and saw paint caked on the nozzle. He turned his questioning gaze to Christina.

"I know what you're thinking, but Demetrius just bought that and dropped it off before leaving an hour ago. It's for one of the holiday projects." She thrust a folder at him. "Here's the information you wanted." She took the spray can, put it in its place and shoved the drawer closed. "Is there anything else? I need to get back to work."

Tapping the folder against his hand, he scanned the office once more and wondered what else could be hidden there. "No."

Christina waited for him to leave, then closed the door, effectively shutting down any chance he had to find anything else.

Derek's senses went on high alert. Christina had been here when everything went down with his father, so he knew she had all the details. Did she actually believe he didn't know the difference between a new and

used can, or was she trying to cover up for her boss? Derek had been convinced that his father was lying, as was his habit, but for the first time, a shred of doubt surfaced.

"Have you talked to Derek since your hot date night?" Charlene asked with a grin.

"No. Not one word." Alexis moved into the extended triangle pose. She'd talked her friend into attending yoga class with her.

"You mean he hasn't called or anything in *three weeks*?" Charlene asked, mimicking the pose.

"I just said that." And it bothered Alexis more than she cared to admit. Granted, he'd said he wasn't interested in a relationship, but she hadn't expected him to treat her like some booty call. With all the history they had, she thought he would at least be friendly. A few minutes later, she glimpsed Charlene trying to do a bridge and chuckled.

"Stop laughing. This body isn't as flexible. What are you going to do about Derek? I figured with all the history between you two, he would at least call you from time to time."

"There's nothing to do but go on. I'm sure our paths will cross more now that he's getting involved in the community projects, but I have no plans to run after him like some lovesick teen."

They finished the set of sequences and Charlene collapsed, breathing hard. "Lexi, I love you like a sister, but I'm never coming here with you again. I need a juicy cheeseburger to offset all this trauma to my body."

Alexis laughed. "The more you do it the easier it'll become."

She groaned and rolled up her mat. "Whatever." Outside, she tossed the mat into the backseat of her car. "I was serious about that cheeseburger, and since you're in my car, you're coming along. You can have salad or whatever healthy food you lovely models eat."

"Fine by me. And for the record, I don't eat salad all the time."

They ended up at a popular grill. Though having a cheeseburger sounded heavenly, Alexis chose grilled chicken and steamed vegetables. Halfway through the meal, she heard her phone buzz. She read the email from her agent stating that *Vogue* wanted Alexis to do a photo shoot in Paris for their magazine. She had been taking fewer assignments, in order to work on the next phase of her life, and wasn't sure she wanted to be gone two to three weeks.

"You're frowning. That's not from Derek, is it?"

"No, my agent. I've been asked to do a photo shoot in Paris."

"Sounds fabulous. Are you going to do it? I know you've been thinking about leaving."

"Yes." Maybe it would be the distraction she needed to get Derek off her mind.

"I wish I could go with you. I had a great time when I went four years ago, and promised myself I'd go back." Charlene ran a nonprofit organization that specialized in finding jobs for disabled adults, and she worked tirelessly to ensure her clients were matched with the best positions for their level of skill and ability.

"Maybe you can sneak in a long weekend." They

shared a smile, finished their meal, and Charlene dropped Alexis off at her house.

"Let me know when you're leaving."

"I will." She threw her a wave and went inside. After kicking off her shoes, she sat out on her deck and re-read the email in its entirety. *I do need to get away.* She dialed her agent. Even though it was after seven on a Friday evening, she knew Rose Buchanan would still be working.

"Hi, Rose. It's Alexis," she said, when her agent answered.

"Hi, Alexis. I assume you're calling about my email."

"Yes. I'll do it."

"Fabulous. I just emailed you the contract."

"Okay." She went inside and booted up her laptop.

"They're scheduled to start shooting on Monday, so I took the liberty of booking you a flight for tomorrow. That way you'll have a day to settle in and rest up from the jet lag."

Alexis clicked on the email. "Just received the contract." They went over every detail and answered all her questions satisfactorily. Rose had been her agent since the beginning and had kept Alexis away from unscrupulous entities that preyed on young girls.

"I'll forward your flight itinerary and the information for the car service picking you up as soon as we get off the phone, and be by in the morning to get your signature on the contract."

"Thanks, Rose. I appreciate you."

"You're welcome. I have to say you've been one of the easiest models I've had the pleasure of working with. Are you still thinking of retiring?"

"Yes. I'm thirty-two, and have had a longer run in the industry than many people, but I know they're always looking for fresh faces."

"True. However, I've known a few women who modeled well into middle age."

Alexis laughed. "Nice try, Rose, but I won't be one of them."

Rose joined her laughter. "You can't blame me for trying. Well, I have a thousand things to do tonight. I'll see you tomorrow."

"Good night." She disconnected. So much for her relaxing evening.

It took four hours for her to do laundry and pack. Alexis reminded herself that the early October temperatures would be at least ten to twenty degrees cooler. She took out the tote bag she always carried on board with her essentials and added her passport. She placed underwear in a Ziploc and stuck it into one of the zippered compartments. Her mother's words rang in her ear: *Make sure to carry a couple pairs of panties in your purse when you travel just in case they lose your luggage. You can wear the same pair of pants, but a woman always needs to be fresh.* Grace Armstrong had told Alexis that the first time she had traveled to a modeling assignment at age seventeen, and she continued the practice to this day.

Alexis remembered she hadn't called Charlene and did so then. They spoke for only a few minutes due to the late hour.

"I'll pick you up from the airport when you get back," Charlene said. "Just send me your itinerary. I

checked my schedule and sneaking in that long week-end is out, but next time, I'm coming with you."

"For sure and will do. Thanks. See you when I get back." She ended the call, checked her bags once more before carrying them downstairs, then got ready for bed.

Rose rang Alexis's doorbell at ten the next morning with the contract and, once she had all the signatures, jetted off to her next stop. Afterward, Alexis cleaned out her refrigerator and set out the trash. By the time she finished, she had half an hour before the car service picked her up for the three-thirty flight. She hated flying out of LAX because of the never-ending construction and traffic, and today was no exception. But she managed to get through the nightmare and relax before boarding. Thankfully, she had a first-class seat on the nonstop flight. No way, with her height, would she survive coach for almost eleven hours.

Alexis arrived in Paris to cool temperatures and a slight drizzle the next morning. She used to be excited every time she had a chance to leave the country on an assignment, and did a mini sightseeing tour as soon as she had dropped her bags off at the hotel. This time she felt nothing but fatigue and the only thing she wanted to do was find some food and a bed. *Maybe I am getting too old for this.* As soon as she made it to the hotel, she ordered room service, showered and changed into her favorite comfortable sweats.

She stood in front of the French doors and stared out at the gray day. Some of her shoots were scheduled to be outside, and if the weather didn't change, she would end up being here longer than planned.

Alexis turned at the sound of a soft knock, then "Room

service" in French-accented English. She opened the door
and a man entered, pushing a cart. She thanked him, gave
him a tip and sat at the small table to eat her vegetable
omelet, fruit and tea. She felt much better when she finished and went back to stand at the French doors. She'd
do this last contract, enjoy her time in Paris and, with
any luck, erase Derek from her mind.

Chapter 5

Though they had chatted briefly by text, it had taken Derek, Trey and Max a week to coordinate their schedules to meet. Trey was already seated near the back of Lou's Diner when Derek arrived. He headed for the table and the two men exchanged a fist bump. "What's up?"

"Busy, as usual," Trey answered. Trey was an Oscar-winning Hollywood screenwriter.

"How's Kiara? Never mind. That goofy grin on your face tells me everything I need to know."

"Hey, what can I say. She's the love of my life. What about you?"

An image of Alexis floated across his mind. "Nothing's changed. The single life suits me just fine."

Trey sighed. "It's time to let go of all that old baggage, Derek. I know—"

Derek was spared more of Trey's big-brother advice when Max slid into a chair.

"Hey." Max divided a glance between Trey and Derek. "What did I miss?"

"Nothing. Just Trey playing big brother again."

Max laughed. "Then I'm glad I was late. How's Kiara?"

Derek smiled. "I just asked him the same thing. The boy is whipped."

"Damn right," Trey said. "And like I told Derek, you should try it, too, Max."

Max waved a hand. "Nah, I'm good. Have you guys ordered yet?"

Both men shook their heads and Trey signaled a passing waiter.

After ordering, Max continued with the conversation. "But Derek here may be next. I saw him cozying up real close with that supermodel. What's her name?" He tapped his finger on the table and angled his head toward Derek as if asking for help in remembering.

Derek remained quiet.

Max brightened. "Alexis! Alexis Armstrong. And guess what, big brother? He even kissed her on the cheek."

Trey chuckled. "So, does that mean…?"

"It doesn't mean a damn thing," Derek said, glowering at them both. "And what, you were stalking me all night?"

"You sure about that? Because I didn't see you kiss any other woman and there were plenty who would've been happy to oblige, judging from the bits of conversation I overheard. And no, I wasn't stalking you," Max added. "I just happened to see that little surprising moment."

He seriously considered punching Max. Was this what he'd missed out on, growing up—having brothers that got on his nerves? Yet a small part of him kind

of liked the bantering. "I've known Alexis a long time and it was just a little good-to-see-you thing. Now, can we move on?"

Still smiling, Trey said to Derek, "You mentioned finding a spray paint can in Demetrius's office."

"Yes. You said that they found the same kind and color of spray paint in Regin—" He cut himself off upon seeing the look on Max's face. "In Dad's office. Christina tried to tell me that Demetrius had just purchased the can, but it was half-empty and had paint caked on the nozzle as if it had been sitting for months."

Max shook his head. "So, with all the other things Trey and I found, this could mean Dad really is innocent."

Trey and Max looked at Derek expectantly. "Okay, I agree this does make me wonder. You said that Demetrius was willing to help us investigate, but after this, I don't know. But you guys know him better, so do you still think it's a good idea?" Over the years, Demetrius had been like a second dad to his brothers, and he had occasionally reached out to Derek.

Trey opened his mouth to answer, but waited until the server placed their food on the table before speaking. "I want to say no, but it might tip him off if we go back on his offer after agreeing."

"Trey has a point. Did you ever get a chance to meet with him about the Children's Dream Project?" Max forked up a portion of eggs.

Derek finished chewing. "Not yet. Haven't had time, with all the new projects I'm dealing with at work."

"Well, see if you can talk to him and feel him out.

He also said Christina would be available to help us, as well."

Derek held up a hand. "No. I don't trust her. Something about her rubs me the wrong way. You two can talk to her if you want." After having Christina come on to him constantly, he didn't want to deal with her unless it was absolutely necessary.

"Are you still coming to the fund-raiser the first Friday in November, to help provide Thanksgiving dinners to families?" Trey asked.

He nodded around a mouthful of waffle.

"And Dad's Thanksgiving dinner?"

Derek groaned inwardly. Their father had invited each of them to his home for Thanksgiving dinner and Derek had yet to agree. "Max, I'm still thinking about it."

Silence fell over the table. Every time Reginald's name came up, it seemed to cause a minor disagreement or tenseness between them. Over the past few weeks, the relationship with his brothers had been growing and Derek didn't want that to change. He, who'd never wanted to be bothered, was now warming up to the idea. Trying to lighten the mood, he said, "Look on the bright side—it's not the 'hell no' I said the first time you asked. Who knows, by then it may be a resounding yes." He pointed his fork at his brothers. "But don't quote me on that."

That broke the tension and they all laughed. Knowing they each had a full schedule, they finished the meal, made plans to meet again soon and said their goodbyes.

Derek spent the entire week and the first part of the

next one working fourteen- to sixteen-hour days, and ended up canceling the meeting he'd set up with Demetrius. He'd been grateful for staying busy, because it kept him from thinking about Alexis all the time. The nights were different. He'd had dreams so erotic he swore he could feel her tight walls clamped around him, and woke up each morning hard and reaching for her. Not good. He never allowed women to dominate the space in his head, but somehow, Alexis was challenging that stance. *Even more reason to stay away from her.*

By Wednesday, he had worked ten days straight, including Sunday, and he wanted to fall out from sheer exhaustion. But he had to pack for a Thursday afternoon flight to Paris. He had been invited to speak at a business mastermind conference over the weekend. Derek had done these types of events before and hoped the organizers had built in some downtime, so he could relax and explore. Early in his career, he'd visited Paris, but back then he had been so focused on making a name for himself that sightseeing and relaxation were nonexistent. He continued to work harder than some people thought he should, but a frank conversation with his mother six months ago had let him know that he needed to learn balance. She had pointedly asked him what good it would be to build all this wealth and be dead at thirty-five, because the last time she checked he couldn't take it with him.

After packing that evening, he sent a text to his brothers to let them know he'd be out of town from Thursday to Monday and would catch up with them when he returned. A few minutes later, his cell buzzed. He read Trey's response and shook his head. "So what,

Paris is supposed to be the city for lovers," he muttered. He hadn't been on a date or talked to a woman since being with Alexis almost a month ago.

Alexis. Derek could still see the hurt on her face when he'd told her he wasn't interested in taking their night further. But if he were being honest with himself, he'd admit that he wanted to see her. More than once, he'd thought about calling her or going by her house, but changed his mind. Doing that would only make the situation worse and give her the wrong impression. He'd moved on and he was sure Alexis had done the same. So why couldn't he stop thinking about her?

Alexis dropped down wearily on the bed and groaned. Her day had started at six this morning and ran well after nine in the evening. Due to the weather, they had done mostly indoor venue or studio shots this week, but the weather was slated to improve next week and she hoped they would be able to finish the shoot. Between someone yanking and tugging at her hair for hours, applying and reapplying makeup, and having her change into a dozen outfits, all she wanted was a hot shower, sleep and some real food. Another reason she felt she needed to do something else careerwise. Years of living on a strict diet had started to take a toll on her physically and mentally. Tonight at dinner with the team from *Vogue*, it had taken all her strength not to wrestle the piece of chocolate cake from Mike, the photographer. She hadn't splurged since having her prized jambalaya and cornbread. To keep herself from eating the rest, she had frozen a small bowlful and given it, along with the leftover cornbread, to Charlene.

Thinking about the dinner brought back memories of her night with Derek. Not like they were ever far from her mind. She closed her eyes and replayed every moment of their time together, from the laughter and conversation to the heated kisses and amazing lovemaking. She sighed. Alexis had only been fooling herself, believing that she could outrun her emotions. No matter how she tried to rationalize them, what she felt for Derek went beyond mere lust. She'd seen glimpses of the serious but fun guy she'd once given her heart to, but as always, he retreated behind the wall he'd built around himself. She understood his need to be successful in his own right, given the circumstances with his father, but Derek had been obsessed with making his own money and not taking one dime from the trust fund his father had set up. However, she didn't understand why he still seemed so closed off. Had he experienced a bad breakup, like hers? Alexis shuddered at the remembrance of her ex-fiancé.

She had met thirty-three-year-old investment banker Julian Douglas on a photo shoot in New York when she was twenty-four. He'd lavished her with flowers, attention and sweet words, and she'd fallen in love within three months. Her mother tried to tell her to slow down, but Alexis had her own place, her own money, and no one could tell her anything. The relationship turned out to be disastrous and she wished she had listened to her mother. Since then, she'd rarely dated. She had no desire to inflict the same kind of pain on herself again.

Alexis halted her trip down memory lane, dragged herself off the bed and went to shower. Saturday would

be another long day. But one way or another, she planned to have at least one butter croissant.

Alexis was up and in the makeup chair at seven the next morning. Today they would start inside one of the museums. Three hours and four wardrobe changes later, she climbed into the car that would take her to the Arc de Triomphe. As they drove, she couldn't help noticing the number of couples strolling hand in hand along the streets or seated outside at the patisseries. Because the sight made her uncharacteristically melancholy, she turned away and took out her phone to check her emails.

Once they arrived, the photographer and his assistant took a few minutes to find the area that would give them the best shots, and then set up their equipment. Tourists milled around, talking and taking pictures, but stopped when Alexis took her place. A small group congregated near the shoot and had their cameras out. After every shot, Mike conferred with his assistant to decide if the picture needed to be redone—not enough light, too much light, shadows. They paused twice to touch up her makeup and hair, and by the time they packed up, four hours had passed. They took a break for dinner, then finished the evening with photos at the Eiffel Tower.

Back at the hotel, Alexis stood in the lobby and talked to Mike about the next week's schedule.

"Monday, we'll start at Jardin du Luxembourg, then go to Place de la Concorde. Tuesday, I want to retake some of the studio shots, and if we have time, the Louvre. If not, we'll do it on Wednesday."

"I guess I need to stock up on my snacks," she teased.

Mike laughed. "Probably. If we need to change some-thing, I'll let you know."

"Thanks, Mike. I'll see you on Monday." With any luck, they'd be done by Thursday and she'd be on her way home. She said good-night and started toward the elevators. Several men stopped and stared, but she was used to the attention and kept walking.

Laughter coming from a hallway drew her atten-tion. She glanced over her shoulder, gasped and almost tripped in her five-inch heels. *What is Derek doing in Paris?* Dressed in a charcoal-gray suit that fit his tall frame to perfection, and with his too-fine face, slim but muscular build and sinfully sexy walk, he looked as if *he* had just left a photo shoot.

And looked good enough to eat. A vision of her trailing her tongue over his magnificent chest floated through her mind and a throbbing began between her thighs. Not wanting him to see her, Alexis increased her pace. She hadn't taken ten steps before she heard Derek call her name. Maybe if she didn't turn around he would think he'd made a mistake and continue with whatever he had been doing. But she should have known better. She felt him before she saw him.

"Alexis?" Derek gently grasped her arm.

Steeling herself, she faced him. "Hey. What are you doing here?"

"I was about to ask you the same thing. I'm a speaker at a business conference." His gaze roamed lazily down her body and up again. "By the way you're dressed, and with that sexy-as-hell strut that had every man in the building salivating when you passed, I'm guessing you're here for work."

Alexis shook her head and couldn't hide her smile. "I'm sure there were a few that didn't even notice."

"Not one."

"Including you?" she asked without thought, and wanted to snatch the words back as soon as they left her mouth.

Derek hesitated a beat. "Including me. Do you want to get some tea or something?" When she didn't answer right away, he said, "I won't keep you long. I just want to talk for a little while."

Say no! "Okay." He led her back to one of the restaurants. "Just great, Alexis. How hard was it to say no?" she muttered under her breath. Even at the late hour, the restaurant was more than half-full.

"See?" he whispered, as the hostess led them to a table.

Her eyebrows knitted as he seated her. "See what?"

"All the men staring your way."

Alexis snorted. "Please." Far more women had followed their progress across the room, and for some reason she wanted to tell them all to stop it.

Derek laughed softly and the deep rumble made her stomach flip. She gave her drink order to the waiter. "So how long have you been here?"

He leaned back in the chair and stretched out his long legs. "A couple of days. You?"

"A week, and I'll most likely be here for another one. So what did you want to talk about?"

Derek shrugged. "Nothing specific. Just wanted to know how you're doing."

She started to tell him he could have called, or driven the two miles to her house, if he was that concerned.

"I'm good. Pretty exhausted from the week, but I plan to sleep in tomorrow."

"That makes one of us. I have to be behind the mic at eight."

The waiter placed tea in front of Alexis and coffee for Derek. "Isn't that going to keep you up all night?"

He added sugar and stirred. "Nah. I'll probably be up for another two or three hours, so it'll be out of my system by then."

They conversed softly while sipping their drinks, and talked about everything from the weather to the sights they'd visited in Paris. Everything except themselves. Alexis finished her tea and stifled a yawn. "Thanks for the tea. I should get going."

"Anytime." Derek signaled a waiter, settled the bill and helped Alexis to her feet.

He placed a hand at the small of her back and guided her to the exit, and she wanted to lean into his touch. They started toward the elevators.

"Would you like to have dinner tomorrow?"

Her steps slowed. "I don't think that's a good idea, Derek. You've already stated your position."

"Alexis—"

"It doesn't matter. You said you didn't want to start anything, but you asked me out for drinks tonight and dinner tomorrow." Alexis pushed the elevator up button. "Usually going out falls under the 'starting something' umbrella. Let's just leave things the way they are."

The mask over his features slipped for a moment and she saw his conflicted emotions. Then, his jaw tight, Derek nodded. He lifted his hand and stroked a finger down her cheek.

"And you don't need to walk me up," she said, when the car arrived. She stepped inside. "Enjoy the rest of your visit."

"You, too," he said.

As the doors closed, her head told her she had made the right decision, but her heart said something entirely different.

Chapter 6

Alexis dropped her bags by the stairs, then collapsed onto the sofa. "I don't think I've ever been this tired after a shoot. Maybe I'm coming down with a cold or something. My head hurts and my appetite has been weird." Instead of finishing that second week, she'd ended up being there until the middle of the third week. She couldn't do this anymore.

Charlene deposited the takeout bag on the bar before sitting on the love seat. She kicked off her shoes and tucked her feet under her. "Neither do I. You looked drained. Was there anything significantly different this time?"

"No, which is why I don't understand this level of fatigue. The one I did six months ago was far more intense and I didn't feel nearly as tired." She took off her shoes, stretched out and groaned. "I think I can sleep for a week."

"Ha, as if you could. Getting up early is in your blood. I, on the other hand, can handle that challenge

quite nicely. At least you don't have to worry about dinner tonight."

"Girl, I appreciate you." Charlene had ordered food from Alexis's favorite Italian restaurant. "I'm going to enjoy every single bite of that seafood Alfredo. I've decided that was my last assignment, Char."

Charlene sat up straight. "You're really going to do it?"

"Yes. The assignments have slowed over the past couple of years and I've lasted far longer than most models. It's time to do something else, something that will make a difference. I'm thinking about going the nonprofit way."

"You know I'll do everything I can to help." She stuck her feet in her shoes.

"Thanks. I'll let you know when I'm ready to start. I want to do a little more research and reach out to some existing agencies that focus on infant mortality first."

"There's a definite need in that area." Charlene checked her watch and stood. "It's almost ten, so I'd better get going. I have an early meeting in the morning."

"Thanks again for picking me up from the airport." Alexis saw her friend to the door and then trudged to the kitchen. She yawned. She knew her internal clock would be messed up for the next couple days because of the nine-hour time difference.

Alexis heated a small portion of the seafood Alfredo and slid onto one of the barstools. For the first several years of her career she'd been on such a restricted diet—she had to maintain a certain weight and look—that it had caused several physical and emotional issues. People tended to think of modeling as a glamorous job, but there were also consequences. With help, she began

to change to healthier eating habits, while still meeting modeling standards. While eating, she scanned the mail, discarding the junk.

Afterward, she stored the rest of the food, rinsed and placed her dishes in the dishwasher and headed for the stairs. She glanced at the luggage sitting at the base of the steps. Too tired to deal with unpacking tonight, she just grabbed her tote. "Tomorrow," she mumbled. Upstairs in her bedroom, she tossed the bag on her bed, stripped and went directly to the bathroom to shower. She would have loved to soak in a warm bubble bath, but as tired as she was, she'd probably fall asleep and drown.

Afterward, she pulled her hair into a ponytail and flopped down on her bed. "*Yes*, my bed." Alexis lay there for several minutes with her eyes closed. The longer she lay there the harder it became to get up. She'd started to doze off when her phone chimed the reminder to take her birth control pill. Groaning, she sat up and dug in her tote for the pack and the water bottle she'd purchased at the airport.

As she pushed out the day's pill from the foil package, it dawned her that her period was late. She mentally counted…*days* late. Once her body had gotten straightened out from the food deprivation, her cycle regulated and she hadn't missed one in almost five years. She swallowed the tablet and washed it down with a sip of water, chalking it up to the stress of traveling for the past three weeks. She placed the bottle on her nightstand, turned the covers back and slid between the crisp, cool sheets.

Alexis sighed with pleasure and closed her eyes. A moment later, she bolted upright in bed, her heart

pounding. *The broken condom.* But she hadn't missed one dose. She tried to relax, but couldn't.

Not able to calm her racing heart, Alexis jumped out of bed, quickly dressed and drove to a drugstore. She had no idea which pregnancy test to buy and ended up purchasing three. The checkout clerk gave her an amused smile, but dropped it after the blazing glare Alexis leveled at him. She crammed them into her purse and strode out.

When she got home, she dumped them out on the bathroom sink and stared. She wrapped an arm around her midsection and sucked in a deep breath. "This can't be happening," she whispered. Alexis debated whether to take the test tonight or wait until morning. Knowing she wouldn't sleep a wink unless she did, she picked up the first one, read and followed the directions. She paced her bedroom for the entire five-minute waiting time. Her heart beating so loudly she could hear it, Alexis picked it up. She nearly passed out when she saw the faint pink plus sign. She braced her hands on the sink to keep from falling.

"Okay, it's barely visible. It could be a fluke or a false positive," Alexis said repeatedly. With all the fatigue from traveling and the stress of deciding on the next phase of her life, her hormones were probably all over the place. It had happened before and that was likely the case now. Relaxing a little, she tossed the dipstick into the trash. By morning, she would be rested and her hormones stabilized enough to get a true reading.

Despite her plans to sleep late, Alexis woke up Friday morning at seven with a start. It had taken her several hours to fall asleep and her anxiety levels had

dropped only marginally. She stared up at the ceiling, wondering what she would do if the results turned out positive. She grabbed her cell, Googled "false positive pregnancy tests" and found several articles that stated it could happen. Armed with that knowledge, she took a second test. Her heart sank when she saw the same faint pink lines.

Alexis dialed her ob-gyn. "Hi, Amy," she said to the receptionist." This is Alexis Armstrong. I was wondering if I could get in to see Dr. Marshall sometime today."

"Hi, Alexis. Your annual isn't for another three months."

"I know. I… My period is a couple of days late."

"Ah. Can you hold on a minute? I need to answer the other line."

"Sure."

Amy came back two minutes later. "Looks like you're in luck. Dr. Marshall's three thirty just canceled, since she had her baby two days ago."

"Great. I'll take it." She didn't know what she would have done if she'd had to wait until Monday.

"We'll see you later."

Alexis could barely concentrate or eat, and by the time she made it to the doctor's office that afternoon, she had butterflies on steroids dancing in her belly. Several women in various stages of pregnancy sat in the crowded waiting area, a few with their significant others. *Please don't let this be me.* She gave her name to the receptionist and took the last empty chair in a corner. She searched through the magazines on a low table, but all were related to pregnancy and babies. Instead of flipping through them, she used her phone to

search for information on infant mortality in the African American community.

"Alexis."

She raised her head and saw the smiling face of the nurse. Alexis stood and followed her back. The woman handed her a sample cup, directed her to the bathroom, and when Alexis came out, escorted her to an examination room.

"The doctor will be with you shortly. There's one patient ahead of you."

"Thank you."

It seemed she'd been waiting for hours when the doctor came in.

Dr. Marshall smiled. "How are you, Alexis?"

"I was hoping you could tell me."

She sat on a rolling stool, opened a file folder and read silently. "Well, congratulations. You're going to be a mother."

Alexis sat back, stunned. She couldn't be pregnant. "No, no, no." She ran a hand through her hair. "I *can't* be pregnant." She jumped up from her seat and paced the confines of the small room.

"Would you like to see the test results?"

"No. How could this happen?"

The doctor chuckled. "There's a chart on the wall behind you that explains."

She shot the woman a glare. "I mean I'm on the pill. I haven't missed one." She held up a finger for emphasis. "I set my alarm so I don't forget. I take it at the same time *every* night, as suggested. This is supposed to be damn near one hundred percent effective. I can not—" Alexis slapped a hand over her mouth.

Dr. Marshall rolled the stool a few feet, retrieved a stainless steel basin and handed it to Alexis.

Alexis emptied the contents of her stomach, then lowered herself into the chair, still feeling queasy.

"Are you done?" The doctor handed her some paper towels. "Alexis," she started gently, "I know this is a shock to you, but no method of birth control is one hundred percent effective. Unless you're practicing abstinence, there's always a chance, and you just happen to fall in that small percentage."

She needed a minute to take all this in. How was she going to tell Derek, and what would he do? Another thought occurred to her. During her engagement to Julian, she'd become pregnant and miscarried. Though still reeling, she knew she couldn't go through that again. "Dr. Marshall, last time…"

"I know what you're thinking, and there's no indication that you won't be able to carry this baby to term. But to set your mind at ease, I'll send you over to imaging to get an ultrasound and check the cervix for any changes that might lead to any complications. I could do it here, but our machine has been giving an error signal intermittently. The technician is due out again next week, but I don't want you to have to cancel if he doesn't get it fixed." Dr. Marshall closed the folder. "Will the father be involved?"

"I don't know."

"Do you plan to tell him?"

"Yes."

"I've known you a long time, Alexis, so I'm going to tell you this off the record. Be completely honest with him about everything—your feelings and the past mis-

carriage. You never know how this will affect him, and believe me, it will cause less problems in the long run."

A small smile crept out on Alexis's face. She'd been seeing Dr. Marshall since age sixteen and the woman had always given her sound advice, particularly during those difficult early modeling years. "Thank you. I will."

The ob-gyn stood. "If you have any questions, let me know." They walked out and down the hall, where the doctor gave Alexis a referral to the imaging center. "I'd like for you to have it done two weeks from now, so make sure you call soon. Amy will schedule your first prenatal appointment, and start taking your prenatal vitamins." She gave Alexis an affectionate pat on the arm and went off to see her next patient.

Ten minutes later, Alexis sat in her parked car, still numb. What now? She grabbed her cell and called the imaging center. Just as Dr. Marshall predicted, the first availability was two weeks away, which was exactly the time frame she needed. If she had to wait any longer, she'd be an emotional mess. She noted the date in her phone's calendar, then called her best friend.

"Hey, Lexi," Charlene said when she answered.

"Hey. Are you still at your office?"

"No, I'm on my way home. Is everything okay?"

"Hardly. I'll meet you at your house."

"Alexis," Charlene started, "what is going on?"

She blew out a long breath. "I'll explain when I get there." She disconnected, started the car and drove out of the lot.

Forty minutes later, Charlene swung the door open before Alexis could knock. "Come on in." Once they

were settled in the sunroom, she said, "Girl, you're scaring me. What the heck is going on, Lexi?"

Alexis tried to think of a diplomatic way to say it, but found none. "I'm pregnant."

Charlene didn't say anything for a full minute. "Um…okay. And the father is Derek."

Alexis nodded.

"When did you guys, you know…?"

"The night he came over for dinner."

"Wow. You didn't mention that part." Charlene frowned. "But aren't you on the pill?"

"Yes, and he used a condom." Alexis explained about the broken condom and Derek's initial reaction. "After I showed him that I hadn't missed taking the pills, he was fine."

"I can't believe it."

"You and me both. And I don't even want to think about what Derek is going to say." That had been her biggest worry.

"After he gets over the shock, I'm sure he'll be fine."

"I don't think so, Char. He made it clear that he doesn't want a relationship or commitment. Having a baby is a huge commitment, a lifelong one." Alexis dropped her head in her hands. "What am I going to do?"

Charlene came and sat next to her. "You're going to tell him. You have to tell him."

"I'd never keep this from him, but whether he chooses to accept it will be his decision. Then there's the miscarriage. What if it happens again?" Charlene had been the only one Alexis had confided in about the loss.

"Did the doctor seem concerned?"

"She said she didn't see any reason why I wouldn't be able to carry to term, but I have an appointment for an ultrasound in two weeks just to make sure everything is okay."

"Good. When are you going to tell Derek?"

"I'll call him when I get home and ask him to stop by. That said, I should go, so I can get this over with."

"Let me know what happens."

"I will." Alexis wasn't looking forward to the conversation.

"Will there be room for convenience businesses, like a small market, bakery and maybe a dry cleaner?" Derek studied the blueprint in front of him. He already knew of a couple of business owners looking for new space.

"Yes. You mentioned that before, so I made sure to include them in the drawings. They'll be on the first floor, along with the other business spaces." The architect pointed out the areas. "The medical center will be located on the second floor. Is there anything else you'd like me to consider?"

He smiled. "Not that I can think of at the moment." He wanted this second luxury condominium project to have every amenity possible. Derek liked to think forward and there had already been inquiries, even though they wouldn't break ground for another month. His cell rang and he fished it out of his pocket. *Alexis?* "Could you excuse me for a moment, Dale? I need to take this."

Derek rose smoothly from his chair and headed out of the office. "Hey, Alexis," he said, stepping into the hallway.

"Hi, Derek. I was wondering if you could stop by sometime tonight. I'd like to talk to you about something."

He knitted his brows in confusion. She had all but told him to get lost when they were in Paris, and now she wanted to talk. He glanced down at his watch. "Sure. I'm in a meeting right now, but it should be wrapping up soon. Is eight okay?"

"Yes. I apologize for interrupting your meeting."

"No problem. I'll see you in a little while." Derek tapped the phone against his hand, pondering what she could possibly want to talk about. He would find out soon enough.

He went back into his meeting and it took another half hour to finalize the details. But Derek felt this would be his best project yet. He'd be using one of the most highly sought after architects and a top-notch developer, and the pairing was already generating buzz.

Once the team departed, he packed up and did the same. He tended to be the last to leave most times, and his assistant would occasionally stay past her normal hours to help him. However, today, she'd left with everyone else at the close of business.

Derek bought a sandwich and some juice from the shop next door to his office building and ate as he drove. He figured if he'd already eaten, it would be easier to turn down any offer Alexis might make, and keep him from staying longer than necessary. He could not afford a repeat of last time.

He arrived a few minutes before eight and rang her bell. Unlike last time, Alexis had on a pair of jeans and a T-shirt.

"Hi." She backed up so he could enter.

"Hey."

"I'm out on the deck."

He followed her there and stood against the rail next to her as she stared out at the water. "What's going on, Alexis? A couple of weeks ago, you told me we should just leave things as they were, and now you're calling out of the blue to talk."

"Two weeks ago, I didn't know I was pregnant," Alexis said softly.

Derek felt like he'd been punched in the gut. "What did you just say?"

She faced him. "I assume that's a rhetorical question."

He scrubbed a hand down his face, paced the length of the deck and came back. "But you said you were on the pill." Okay, the condom broke, but he'd seen the half-filled pack.

"Lucky me. I happen to be in that minuscule percentage where it failed," she said sarcastically.

If this had happened to someone else, he might be congratulating the man on having sperm strong enough to break through a contraception guaranteed to be 99 percent effective. But it wasn't someone else. What the hell was he supposed to do with a kid? He didn't know anything about raising a child. His father had certainly not been a role model. "When did you find out?"

"Today. There are some other things I need to tell you, as well."

There was more? Derek needed a drink, preferably something straight and strong. He lowered himself into one of the chairs, not sure he could take anything else. "What other things?"

"Several years ago, I was engaged. He turned out to be a jerk and I canceled it." At Derek's surprised look, Alexis said, "It was around the time you had just moved back to LA. Anyway, what I didn't know then was that I was six weeks pregnant."

Why hadn't he known she had a baby? Thank goodness he was already sitting.

"I miscarried at eleven weeks and it was the most painful thing I ever had to endure. I couldn't take it if it happened again." Her voice cracked.

"And your ex?"

"He told me the pregnancy was my problem. I didn't bother to tell him about losing the baby."

Despite his own inability to make sense of the situation, he pulled her down onto his lap. Good thing her ex wasn't anywhere near, because Derek wanted to drive to his house and kick his ass for leaving her like that. "I can't begin to understand what you went through. Did the doctor say there might be a problem now?"

She swiped at the tears. "No, but I'm scheduled to have an ultrasound in a couple of weeks to be sure everything is progressing."

Although every part of him screamed that he should run as fast as he could, Derek couldn't let her go through it alone. "I'll go with you. Just let me know the day and time."

Alexis searched his face. "Why?"

"Because you didn't make this baby alone. I'm not going to lie—I'm having a hard time right now. But I plan to do what's right." They didn't speak for several minutes, both seemingly lost in their own thoughts.

"I'm sorry. I forgot to offer you something to drink or eat," she said at length.

"No, thank you. Actually, I need to leave. I'm not walking away, I just need a little time to process all this. I promise to call you tomorrow."

She nodded and stood.

They walked to the door and he had no idea what to say, so he hugged her and tried to communicate *something*. "I'll talk to you tomorrow."

On the way home, Derek stopped at a red light, leaned his head against the steering wheel and sucked in several deep breaths. His world had been tilted on its axis and he had no idea what to do.

He lifted his head and in his peripheral vision saw a large flashing sign hanging in a store window that read Trick or Treat. He definitely felt someone had played a Halloween trick on him, minus the treat. He had always been able to solve his own problems without relying on anyone to help. That way he didn't have to worry about being disappointed. This time, he didn't know how to solve it or even if he could.

At the next corner, Derek executed a U-turn. Tonight he needed to talk to someone.

Chapter 7

"Derek?" Trey's expression mirrored confusion. "Come in."

Derek entered and shoved his hands in his pockets.

"Is everything okay? You never just show up unannounced." He smiled. "Most times we have to drag you out." Trey's smile faded when the look on Derek's face didn't change. "You want to talk about it?"

"Yeah." This would be a first for him and it made him a little uncomfortable. Trey led him back to an expensively decorated family room.

"You mind if I text Max? It shouldn't take him more than fifteen minutes to get here."

Derek shrugged. "Fine."

He sent a text and pocketed the cell. "You look like you could use a drink."

"Preferably something strong."

Trey eyed him. "This must be big." He walked over to a fully stocked bar and held up a bottle. "Scotch on the rocks?"

"That works." He thought about telling Trey to skip

the glass and just bring the bottle, but getting drunk wouldn't solve his problem. He had never been drunk in his life and didn't intend to start now. His brother came back with a glass for each of them. "Thanks. Sorry, I didn't even ask if you were busy."

"I'm never too busy to talk to my brother, Derek. I know this has been hard for all three of us and especially you, but it's about time we start truly acting like the brothers we are. You've never let your guard down or trusted easily, and I get that. You *can* trust me, and the same goes for Max."

Derek took a sip of his drink and didn't want to admit that Trey had described him perfectly. He never did let his guard down, and trust had to be earned. He could count on one hand the number of people he trusted and still have fingers left over. "I'm working on it, Trey. Otherwise, I wouldn't be here."

"Touché." He saluted Derek with his glass. The doorbell rang. "Must be Max. Be right back."

Trey returned a moment later with Max following, and Derek heard him ask how he got there so fast.

"What's up, Derek?" Max said. "I'd just left Westwood, near UCLA, and was only a couple of miles from here." He studied him. "Did you find out more information about Dad?"

"No." Derek took another gulp of his Scotch. "Alexis is pregnant."

Trey choked on his drink and Max's jaw dropped. Derek swirled the contents of the glass. "My thoughts exactly."

Max slowly lowered himself to one of the chairs. "I

thought you said you two hadn't talked. Exactly how did that happen?"

"Max, you have a daughter. You should know how it's done," Trey teased, as he sat on the arm of the sofa.

"Yeah, yeah. You know that's not what I meant."

Both men turned their expectant gazes toward Derek, who set his glass down and placed his head in his hands. "She rented me for an evening. I went over to tell her that I wouldn't be able to do it."

"And?" Max asked, leaning forward with a smile. "Obviously, that didn't work out too well."

Derek glared.

Max waved a hand. "And you can dial down the death glare, big brother. I'm becoming immune."

Trey laughed softly.

Derek forced himself to remain seated and not bolt for the door. He reminded himself of Trey's earlier words, that he could trust them. "I don't know what happened. Maybe it was just that I wanted to catch up because we hadn't seen each other since high school or whatever, but we ended up having the dinner she'd cooked. One minute we were talking and the next we were in her bed."

"Surely, the thought of protection crossed your mind," Trey said incredulously.

"We used protection. The condom broke one of the times, but she's on the pill. And before either of you say something, I believe her. She showed them to me." He would never forget how she strode naked across the room and slapped the pack down in front of him, or her bold statement that she should put the next condom on

to make sure it was done right. She'd done it more than right. He shook off the sensual memories.

A smile spread across Max's face. "Bulletproof sperm."

"Shut up, Max." Derek shook his head.

"How do you feel about Alexis?" Trey asked.

"I don't know. We dated in high school and she was the first girl I fell in love with." *And the only woman.* "But that was a long time ago. I'm not looking for any type of commitments or relationships."

"A little too late for that, since she's having your baby, man."

"Trey's right," Max said. "And remember when we helped Trey out and babysat Matthew? You were a natural." Matthew was Trey's baby nephew.

"That was, like, for an hour, a night. That's not the same as being a father...*forever.*" Just saying the words would have knocked Derek to his knees had he been standing. "And with my past, there's no way in hell I could be a good father. I have no idea what that looks like." Thick tension filled the room. He knew they must have been thinking the same thing, particularly Trey.

"Look, Derek. I know this is a huge shock to you, but you can't let the past dictate your future. Kiara and I won't have children of our own, so we're looking into adoption." Trey paused. "It's up to me, not my upbringing, to decide the kind of father I'll be. I am my own man and so are you. Be *that* man and let go of what you couldn't control."

"I hear you, Trey, and that all sounds good. I just don't know if I can be that man." It would mean opening up and risking his heart to the pain that would surely follow, because nothing lasted forever. Derek

rose swiftly to his feet. "Thanks for listening. I need to go." Without waiting for a reply, he exited, climbed into his car and roared out of the driveway.

Driving down Pacific Coast Highway at night usually filled him with a kind of peace. However, tonight only turmoil reigned. By the time he made it home, Derek still didn't have a clue how to proceed, but he knew he would never be like Reginald Moore. It had been hard growing up and wanting his father's love, and getting only dollars and excuses thrown his way. His father had been absent for every important milestone and showed up at Derek's sporting events with a briefcase full of paperwork, if he came at all. As Derek grew older, he'd stopped caring.

Derek couldn't do that to his own child and planned to be there for his son or daughter every day. As he lay in bed later, the answer came to him. He and Alexis would get married.

Alexis spent the first part of Saturday unpacking, doing laundry and cleaning. She had a service come in once a month to do the thorough detailing, but with her the only person living there, it didn't take much to keep the house picked up.

All that would change once the baby came. She still couldn't believe she'd be having a child. She put away the last of her clothes and rushed to catch her ringing phone.

"Hey, Charlene," Alexis said.

"Hey, girl. I was expecting you to call me last night and tell me how it went with Derek."

"I know, but after the emotional day I'd had, I needed to shut down. He actually took it better than I expected."

"What does that mean?"

"I thought he'd just say 'I'll set up a fund' and leave, but he didn't. Don't get me wrong, he was shocked, and I suspect he didn't like the news one bit, not that I could blame him. I'm still trying to get used to the idea myself." She had been surprised at how calm he'd been, and it gave her hope that they would be able to co-parent amicably.

"It is a lot to take in," Charlene agreed.

"That's why I didn't get upset when he left shortly after. He said he needed time to process and that he'd call me today."

"Well, that's a start. Did you share your concerns about the baby?"

"Yes. Dr. Marshall suggested I be completely honest with him. After I told him everything, he said he'd go with me to the ultrasound." Alexis recalled the way he'd held her and assured her that she wouldn't have to go through any of it again, and it reminded her why she had fallen in love with him all those years ago.

"I'm so glad you don't have to face this alone this time. Derek doesn't impress me as being the same asshole as Julian." Charlene made a sound of disgust. "I don't think it'll be smooth sailing to start, but I do believe Derek won't abandon you."

"I hope you're right."

"Wow, what are the odds that you don't see Derek for over a decade, spend one night together, then don't talk again for six weeks, and bam?"

"Actually, I saw him when I was in Paris," she confessed.

"You didn't mention that when I picked you up."

"Because nothing happened. I saw him in the hotel lobby one night after finishing my day. He said he was there for a business conference, and we had drinks. He invited me to dinner, but I turned him down and told him we should just leave things the way they were."

Charlene laughed. "Guess that's not going to happen now. You two are going to be linked for the rest of your lives. Do you think you'll ever be together for more than just the baby?"

Alexis had wondered the same thing, but his declaration to maintain his noncommitment lifestyle had been said with such conviction, she wouldn't hold out hope. "I honestly don't think so, but as long as we can come to an agreement on co-parenting, I won't worry about the rest."

She frowned at the sound of her doorbell ringing. Lately, solicitors had found out ways to get into the community. She headed to the door. "Charlene, hang on a minute. Someone's at my door." Alexis peered through the peephole and went still upon seeing Derek leaning against the column. "Um…it's Derek. I'll call you back."

"Tonight, Alexis. Don't make me bang on your door at midnight to get the details," she fussed.

"Okay. Gotta go." She took a deep breath and opened the door. "Hi."

"Hi."

"I thought you told me you'd call," she said, waving him in.

"I know, but I figured talking in person would be

best." Derek waited for Alexis to take a seat on the living room sofa, then lowered himself next to her.

She took in his seriously set features and her anxiety level rose a notch. "About the baby?"

He nodded tightly. "By the way, you never sent me the information for the ultrasound."

Alexis rattled off the day and time.

He input the information into his cell and stuck the phone in his pocket. "I believe I have a solution to our dilemma."

"You do?" His use of the word *dilemma* raised her unease another level.

"Yes. We get married," Derek said confidently.

She searched his face for some hint of teasing and realized the man was dead serious. It took her a moment to find her voice. "You're kidding me, right?"

"No, I'm not."

She snorted. "You call that a proposal?"

"I don't know what you mean."

Alexis folded her arms. "If that's supposed to be a proposal, I think you're missing a few things. One, you haven't moved off the sofa and there's no dust on your knees. Two, I don't see a ring. And three, I didn't hear one word about *love*."

Derek's jaw tightened. "It's not that type of proposal. You're pregnant, I'm the father and I plan to do right by you and our child." He grasped her hands. "I want to be there every day and night, a hands-on dad."

His impassioned plea almost made Alexis surrender. She gently pulled out of his grip. "That's great, Derek, but we don't need to be married for you to do all those things."

"I'm not having a baby mama," he tossed out. "*No. I want our baby to have a two-parent home and the same last name.*" The determined set of his features let her know that he truly believed this would be the best course of action.

She got where he was coming from, but she had no intention of changing her mind. Because he'd grown up without a father, he didn't want the same for their child. She understood and applauded his effort, but it wasn't enough.

Alexis cradled his face in her palms. "Derek, I appreciate what you're trying to do, but I can't marry you. How things look to the outside world don't matter. What really counts is the truth, the way things are. If you're saying you love me, then yes, we can talk about marriage. If not, then it can't happen." She dropped her hands. "I will never, *ever* deny your rights to our baby, but I won't live in a loveless marriage."

Alexis had been willing to do that with Julian because of her naïveté and personal insecurities, but when she realized he'd only wanted the access she could give him—a business merger, he'd called it—she'd walked. That young woman had grown up confident and smart, and she refused to settle for less than she deserved. A man who loved her as much as she loved him.

Derek let out an exasperated sigh. "I understand what you're saying, but this isn't about love. It's about doing what's right."

"I wholeheartedly agree. And I'm doing the right thing by turning you down." She would not marry a man who didn't love her. For any reason.

Chapter 8

Derek sat in his father's former office Tuesday evening, finally going over the information for the holiday project. Max would be joining him, but Derek had come in early so he'd be up to speed by then. From what he could tell, the Dream would be about fulfilling children's Christmas wish lists. There were a number of schools taking part and each child would write a personal detailed letter to Santa, which would be forwarded to the chapter's fund-raising committee, headed by Demetrius. Derek guessed that by volunteering, he'd be working with purchasing and matching the gifts.

He thought back on his own Christmas holidays, growing up. Every couple years or so his father would pop in whenever the guilt stacked up high enough, and drop off a pricey present. But Derek's mother made the holiday special each year. Money was never a factor because of her successful modeling career. However, the best gifts he remembered receiving were priceless. He smiled, recalling how excited he'd been when she'd given him tickets to a Lakers basketball game. She'd

said he could take any of his friends, but he chose her because he knew how much she loved the team, too. They'd stuffed their faces with food and cheered so loudly for the home team that both of them lost their voice for a day. That's the kind of father he vowed to be if Alexis would stop being so stubborn.

Derek couldn't believe she'd turned down his proposal. Most women couldn't care less about love and would kill to have a man who not only agreed to provide for their child financially, but also put a ring on her finger. *Alexis isn't like most women. That's what you loved about her in high school.* He dismissed that small voice and tried to focus on the papers in front of him.

Voices coming down the hallway drew his attention.

"Oh, you must be Derek Moore. We were wondering why the office was open. No one's been in here since…" The man trailed off. He cleared his throat and extended his hand. "I'm Howard Jennings. This is Allen Houston. We both sit on the board."

He shook both men's hands. "So you know my father well?"

"Oh, yes," Allen said. "Reginald gave his all to the organization and the members. If someone needed something, he'd find a way to get it done. One time, when my wife was sick, he arranged dinner for an entire week so I wouldn't have to worry about how to balance work and deal with the kids."

Howard laughed. "He had us all taking shifts to have the food delivered. He and Demetrius always kept us going. Then that thing with Ellen—"

Allen gave an almost imperceptible shake of his head. "Demetrius and Ellen were going through a rough

patch last year. Those three were thick as thieves. Reginald even went over to the hotel where she was staying after she and Demetrius split, to convince her to go back. I joined them for lunch and added my two cents. Now that I think about it, I saw Reginald consoling Ellen a couple times."

"Me, too," Howard said. "It was good of Reginald to try to bring Demetrius and Ellen back together."

Derek sat listening. Something didn't add up with the story and the speaking glance between Allen and Howard was not lost on him. An affair maybe? "He and Demetrius are best friends."

Allen nodded. "Demetrius said he didn't know anything about Reginald's involvement in talking to his wife on Demetrius's behalf, but we all knew he just didn't want to admit his marriage was in trouble."

Or Demetrius really didn't know his friend was visiting his wife. "How are Demetrius and Ellen now? Hopefully, very happy."

"I thought they were going to make it, but unfortunately, they ended up divorcing."

"That's too bad," Derek murmured. "When did that happen?"

Howard angled his head as if thinking. "They divorced about a year ago, I believe." He looked for confirmation to Allen, who nodded. "Yes, I remember because it happened right before this mess with the San Diego chapter started."

If his father was such a stand-up guy, why hadn't they fought to clear his name? "Listening to you tells me how much my father loved this organization. He even went so far as to found this chapter. It makes me

wonder why he would be involved in sabotage, knowing he'd be kicked out." Another kernel of suspicion sprouted in Derek's mind.

Allen bowed his head briefly. "We didn't want to believe Reginald was involved with those break-ins and computer leaks, but the evidence pointed directly to him and there was nothing we could do."

Except fight for the man who you say has such a good heart. Derek had believed his father guilty, but there were too many pieces not adding up, especially with regards to Demetrius. He needed to talk to Demetrius sooner rather than later.

Max entered on the tail end of the conversation and, though he tried to hide it, the look on his face mirrored Derek's thoughts. These were men who claimed to be their father's friends, but had turned their backs on him without a second thought, and dragged Max's and Trey's names through the mud in the process. Both brothers had been cleared of any wrongdoing, but had it been Derek, he would have said to hell with them and the organization, regardless of all the good works and giving back.

"Are you two working on the Dream project?" Max asked, after greeting the men.

"No," Howard answered. "We saw the office open. Looks like you two have your hands full, so we'll get out of your way." They beat a hasty retreat.

Derek studied Max. "You okay?"

"Yeah, fine. Still bugs me, though, that they threw Dad under the bus so quickly." Max sat in the chair opposite Derek.

He got up, closed the door and reclaimed his seat.

He spoke quietly. "Do you know anything about Demetrius's ex-wife, Ellen?"

"Just that they divorced last year."

Derek tried to choose his next words carefully. "I don't want you to get upset, but Howard and Allen mentioned that when Demetrius and his wife were going through tough times last year, they saw Dad with her on a few occasions, apparently consoling her. But Howard and Allen had this look that made me wonder if that was actually the case. Could it be possible that they had an affair?"

Max didn't reply immediately. "We all know Dad isn't a choirboy, but I can't believe he would betray his best friend that way. On the other hand, I do remember seeing them together a few times, acting a little suspicious, last year."

"Around the same time as the San Diego fiasco." Derek saw the moment Max understood.

"You think it's possible Demetrius found out about the affair and framed Dad?"

"You know I've had my doubts about the old man's innocence, but this is too much even for me to dismiss."

"Damn." He shook his head. "I'll talk to Trey and see what he says."

"You do know that, at some point, we're going to have to ask Dad about this?"

Max sighed. "Yeah." Obviously not wanting to discuss the subject any longer, he gestured to the papers spread in front of Derek. "You have any questions?"

"Just a few." Since this would be Derek's first project with the organization, he didn't want to overstep

his boundaries. Max answered all the questions and Derek made notes.

"Anything else?"

He glanced down at the sheet and read over what he'd written. "I think I'm good for now."

Max leaned back in the chair and propped an elbow on the desk. "How's it going with Alexis?"

Derek groaned. "It's not. I suggested we get married and she turned me down. I listened to what you and Trey said and I'm trying to do the right thing."

"She had to have a reason."

"She said having a baby didn't mean we should get married and that we could co-parent just fine." He left out the part about her not wanting to accept marriage without love. He still couldn't understand it. They got along reasonably well and he liked her fine, and he could see them building a life based on mutual respect and companionship. Their night together proved that they were more than compatible in the bedroom. What he had with her had topped all his previous encounters with women.

Max shrugged. "Sounds doable, so what's the problem?"

"I don't want my child to grow up without his or her father in the house like I did. You of all people should understand."

"I do, Derek. But you can't make Alexis marry you. You've been apart for a long time and I'm sure you're not the same people you were in high school. You had one night of sex and little else. Have some patience."

Patience had never been one of Derek's strong points. But Max had a point. Derek had certainly changed.

Maybe he and Alexis needed to get to know each other again. It sounded good in theory. But he didn't know how he'd make it work without wanting to strip her naked and reacquaint himself with every inch of her luscious body every time he saw her.

Wednesday afternoon, Alexis listened to Terri Clark describe the Precious Ones program to reduce infant mortality in the African American community. This was the fourth program she had visited this week and the one that interested her the most. The concept of being hands-on with the mothers rather than just passing out information appealed to Alexis on all levels.

"Currently, we have two full-time and two part-time staff members. With all the cuts to organizations like this one, we're operating on a shoestring budget."

"How many women do you serve?"

"It varies from month to month. Most of our clients are low-income and, what with trying to work one or two jobs to make ends meet, find coming here for information or a workshop a low priority."

She hadn't been aware that these babies had a higher rate of mortality than any other demographic until a year ago, when she'd attended a fund-raiser in Atlanta. The group there had been working hard to increase their impact and Alexis knew she'd found her niche. "Ideally, how would you like the program to look?"

Terri laughed. "How much time do you have? I've got an entire notebook filled with my wish list."

Alexis smiled. "How about we start with the first few pages."

"I'd love to find a way to keep these women under

one roof during their pregnancies and until their babies turn two. They would contribute rent on a sliding-fee scale so they're not spending eighty percent of their income on housing, and they'd help with the chores. We'd be able to hold classes on nutrition and exercise, while providing healthy meals and making sure they're going to prenatal appointments. Once the babies are born, I'd also love to bring in an occupational therapist to teach the mothers about play, and collaborate with a couple of preschools to transition the children when they're old enough. Our program director, Della, used to run a preschool and has some contacts."

"Are you talking about renting out a building?"

"Most likely. I want a place large enough to house ten to fifteen women and their children. I know some other programs are doing bigger things, but I want to invest in these women's lives." Terri's passion was clearly evident.

"What if you could find two or three houses on the same block? I think having a home to share would be more intimate than a warehouse-like building." And Alexis knew just the real estate agent to handle such a task.

The woman brought her hands to her mouth. "Oh, my goodness! That's a fabulous idea. The only problem is we don't have the money to rent the houses."

"Would you mind if I checked into some possibilities? I'd really love to work with your program."

"And we'd love to have you."

Alexis stood. "Thank you so much for taking time to meet with me today."

Terri rose to her feet and shook Alexis's hand. "I re-

ally appreciate you taking an interest in our program and look forward to you being part of our Precious Ones family."

"I'll be in touch about the houses." They spoke for another few minutes, then Alexis departed.

Seated in her car, she turned on her cell and saw a text and voice mail from Derek. The text simply asked her to call him. She played the voice mail: "Hey, Alexis. If you're not busy tonight, I was hoping we could have dinner. Give me a call."

She stared at the phone. "Oo-kay." Rather than speculate on his motives, Alexis hit the call button.

"Alexis, hey. Can you hold on for a minute?" Derek said when he answered.

"Sure." She heard muffled voices and traffic in the background.

"I'm back. Are you okay?"

"I'm fine. Why?"

"Just asking. So, do you want to have dinner? Since we're going to be spending a lot of time together, I figured we could work on getting to know each other again."

She didn't reply immediately and stayed silent so long he called her name. "Are you still there?"

"Yes. Just thinking."

"If you're busy tonight, we can do it another time."

"That's not it."

"Then what is it?"

"This isn't some ploy to get me to change my mind about marrying you, is it?"

Derek laughed. "No, Alexis. Although I wish you'd reconsider."

She breathed a sigh of relief. "You already know my answer to that, so I won't bother to repeat it."

"You're hell on a man's ego, baby," he said, still chuckling.

Alexis knew he didn't mean anything by the endearment, but it made her heart skip just the same. "Okay. I'm game. It's almost five now and I probably won't get home for another hour, if I'm lucky."

"Where are you?"

"Inglewood. I had a meeting and I'm just leaving. Actually, I want to talk to you about something, so the timing is great."

"I'm about the same distance out, at a construction site in Beverly Hills. I'll wrap up here and head out. How about seven thirty?"

"That's fine. See you in a little while."

"Be safe."

Alexis didn't know what to make of this change. First the endearment, and now the concern for her safety. He acted almost like he cared about her. She could see herself softening toward him if he kept this up. No, she couldn't afford to get caught up in sentiment. She had to keep her heart out of it. His certainly wouldn't be involved.

Chapter 9

"Sorry I'm late," Derek said, as Alexis opened the door.

"No problem. It took me longer to get here, too. The 405 was a nightmare, as usual."

He nodded in agreement. "Tell me about it."

"You didn't say where we were going, so I wasn't sure how to dress." She had on a lightweight sweater, black slacks and a pair of low-heeled ankle boots. He, on the other hand, had on another tailored suit and she felt underdressed.

He waved a hand. "You're fine. We're eating in."

"I didn't cook anything."

Derek shook his head and smiled. "You weren't supposed to. We're going to my house."

His house? Granted, she'd been curious about what his home looked like, but she thought it best they go out. She remembered what had happened the last time they ate in.

"Problems?"

"No," she lied. "Let me get my jacket."

Alexis jumped slightly when Derek reached to help

her. He escorted her out and held the car door open for her. She hadn't been on a date in so long she'd forgotten how it felt to have a man do those things. The last two times she went out, Alexis had driven herself so she didn't have to deal with the awkward ending to the evening.

Alexis knew Derek lived close by, but he pulled into his stone circular driveway before they could start a conversation. "So, this is it." He pushed an overhead button and the door to one of the three garages opened.

She thought her nearly two-thousand-square-foot, three-bedroom house was big for one person. His house looked to be more than twice that size. But she couldn't deny its beauty. He could have a party for two hundred just in the driveway.

Derek came around to her side and helped her out.

"Your house is stunning," she told him. "I still can't believe we live this close to each other and never knew it. How long have you been here?" As they walked to the front door, she noticed another single garage. To the far left, she had a view of the ocean.

"Thanks. I've lived here going on four years."

"Two years longer than me."

Derek unlocked the door and stepped back so she could enter.

Magnificent immediately came to mind as Alexis followed him through the house. From the gleaming, natural-colored wood floors and wide columns to the elegant furnishings and open floor plan, his home reminded her of one straight out of a magazine. "How many bedrooms do you have?"

He grinned sheepishly. "Six, and five baths."

Alexis chuckled. "What, you get bored with using the same bedroom and bathroom every night?"

"I bring you to my house and the first thing you do is talk about me." Derek folded his arms. "Most women would be impressed. Like I said, you're hell on a man's ego."

She smiled up at him. "Oh, I didn't say I wasn't impressed. I'm just trying to figure out why a man who claims to be an avowed bachelor would need so much room."

"Well, in a few months, I won't be the only one here," he said softly. They quieted. "I'll give you the full tour in a little while. Right now, I'm starving."

Alexis envisioned the laughter of their little one filling the room and felt a pang of sadness. She had grown up with both her parents and they'd loved each other and her. As much as she wanted the same for her child, she had to hold out for love. "Um…are we ordering takeout or are you cooking? Do you cook?"

Derek shook his head with mock exasperation. "Really?"

"What? I don't know whether you can cook or not. All I know is you don't like to do dishes," she said with a smile.

"Which is why I have a couple of rib eye steaks waiting to be cooked on the *grill*."

Throughout the entire time she'd been teasing Derek, he never cracked a smile. If he planned to be that hands-on father, he'd have to loosen up. Babies needed laughter and fun, so she decided that over the next few months she was going to help him shed his dark Lord of Thunder personality. Even Thor smiled and had fun every

now and again. "Whew! You had me worried there for a minute."

Derek's mouth fell open.

Alexis spread her arms wide. "Hey, you said we're supposed to get to know each other again. This is me." She tossed him a bold wink.

He laughed. "Come here." He pulled her into the circle of his arms. "You're something else, you know that?"

Without warning, Derek captured her mouth in a tender kiss. His lips moved over hers unhurriedly, as if he had all the time in the world. Alexis lost herself in each tantalizing stroke of his tongue.

At length, he lifted his head. "Now, can you behave long enough for me to get dinner finished?" He trailed kisses along her jaw. "I didn't hear you, Alexis."

She couldn't answer if her life depended on it. A soft moan escaped her throat and snapped her back to reality. She moved out of his embrace. *See, this is exactly why I didn't want to come to his house!* "So, what else are we having?" she asked, trying to get her breathing under control. She saw the smug look on his face, as if he knew how much the kiss affected her, and wanted to sock him.

Derek smiled knowingly. "I'm going to cut up some honey-gold potatoes, toss them with a little olive oil and fresh herbs and roast them, and we'll have a chopped kale salad. Does that meet with your approval?"

"Absolutely. Do you want me to help?"

"And give you more ammunition? Please. The only thing I need to know is how you like your steak cooked." He tugged his tie loose and removed his suit

coat. "I'm going to change real quick. You can wait in here or out on the screened porch."

"I'll take the porch."

They passed a gourmet kitchen with two islands and a bar. "Would you like something to drink? I have tea, lemonade, juice and water."

"The lemonade sounds good."

He poured her a glass and made sure she was comfortable before going upstairs. "I won't be long."

"Take all the time you need," Alexis mumbled. It would take a miracle for her not to completely fall for him, especially when those long-buried emotions rose higher and higher each time he kissed her.

Upstairs in his bedroom, Derek paced the floor. Why couldn't he keep his hands off Alexis? He hadn't even made it through dinner. Hell, he'd barely made it past the front door. She affected him in ways he could not explain. Rarely—more like never—did he banter with other women. His dates consisted of expensive dinners, theater shows and fund-raisers. Every now and again he'd meet a woman with whom he shared a night of mutual pleasure, but those encounters didn't last past the morning, either at her place or a hotel. True, his and Alexis's predicament made her coming to his house a necessity. Kissing her didn't fall into that category.

He changed into well-worn jeans and a long-sleeved T-shirt, then loped downstairs to the kitchen. Derek went out the sliding glass door to turn on the grill. Back inside, he washed his hands at the sink, preheated the oven and began the preparations for the meal. He stole glances at Alexis as she sat with her feet up on the ot-

toman, sipping her lemonade. He hadn't expected her to be so playful. He searched his mind, trying to recall if she had been that way when they dated, and thought maybe she had. By the end of their senior year, she had already signed a lucrative modeling contract, but he had been filled with anger, determination and a desire to get as far away from his father as possible.

Alexis glanced over her shoulder and smiled. It sent a jolt straight to his groin. She came and leaned against the counter near where he worked, and peered into the bowl where he was adding spices.

"That smells good. Is it for the potatoes?"

"No, the steaks. I like to play around with flavors. Sometimes I keep it simple, with salt and pepper, and other times…" He held up the bowl.

"You didn't say what's in it."

"A little of this and a little of that, but nothing spicy."

Alexis rolled her eyes. "Fine. Keep your secrets. All I know is it better taste good."

"How've you been feeling?"

"Tired, and my appetite has been kind of crazy. I don't have full-on morning sickness, just some occasional nausea."

Derek paused. "Did the doctor say how long it would last?"

"Most women start to feel better around the third month."

He'd heard of the changes women went through during pregnancy, but had never personally been this close to it and didn't know what to do.

"You can get that look off your face. It's a normal part of the process and I'm fine."

He massaged the herbs and spices into the steaks and set the plate off to the side. After another quick wash of his hands, he got the potatoes into the oven, then took the steaks outside. Alexis followed.

"Before I forget, are you busy next Friday evening?" Derek asked. "PG is having a Thanksgiving fund-raiser to provide food to families."

"Let me check." She got her phone out of her purse and, after a moment, said, "I don't have anything. Are we going together?"

"That was the plan, unless you don't want to."

Alexis shrugged. "Okay." She continued to stare at him as if she were trying to read his thoughts.

To distract her, he said, "You said you wanted to talk to me about something."

"Oh, yes. Remember when I told you I wanted to work on infant mortality? I met with a woman from the Precious Ones project and she shared her vision. Right now they don't have a lot in the way of funding, but she had great ideas."

Derek listened while Alexis explained the program's current services and their desire to have increased funding and expand.

"They'd also like to have a residential facility to house up to about fifteen women."

"As in converting a commercial building into housing?"

"Yes. However, I'm thinking more of finding two or three houses on the same block. I feel like the women and their babies would do much better in a real home instead of a facility-type place." She made a face. "That's where I need your help."

At first, Derek didn't know what she meant. Then it dawned on him. "You want me to find the houses."

She gave him a bright smile. "Who better than one of the top real estate moguls in the country? I want the best for Precious Ones and you're the best."

Her confidence captured him, but her smile put it over the top. He'd find the houses she wanted no matter what it took, even if he had to build them himself. "I assume the office is in Inglewood." He turned the steaks with a pair of tongs.

Alexis nodded. "It is, but I'm thinking Torrance or Redondo Beach would give us a better chance of finding something larger."

Off the top of his head, he couldn't think of any property listings in those areas. "I'll see what I can find."

"Thank you!" She grabbed him up in a crushing hug and kissed his cheek, then looked embarrassed. "I'm sorry. I got a little excited."

Derek groaned inwardly at the feel of her soft curves pressed against his body. It took everything in him to keep his hands to himself. He gave her a quick pat on the back. "No need to apologize. I'm going to go check on the potatoes. Be right back."

He needed a few minutes of distance. Inside, after testing the potatoes for doneness, he sucked in a couple deep breaths and grabbed the bagged salad and a bottle of water out of the refrigerator. Derek twisted off the cap and drained the contents of the latter without stopping. "Get it together," he muttered. Dinner, and that's all. No touching, no kissing.

"Potatoes will be done in a few," he said, after re-

turning to the deck. He placed the steaks on a clean plate and turned off the grill.

"Mmm, that smells heavenly," Alexis said, following him back inside.

Five minutes later, they sat out on the screened porch to eat. "Let me know if you get cold. I can turn on the fireplace."

"I'm fine. I can't get over this view! Even at night it's beautiful. I would probably sit here every day for hours."

"You can if you accept my offer."

She eyed him over her glass of lemonade. "I thought you said this was only going to be dinner and not a trick to get me to agree to that crazy proposal."

Derek smiled inwardly. She didn't let up for a minute. "No tricks. You said you enjoyed sitting out here and I was merely trying to suggest a way to make it happen." He shrugged and went back to his meal.

Alexis pointed her potato-filled fork his way. "Mmm-hmm, you're not slick." She popped the food into her mouth and rolled her eyes.

He chuckled.

"Aren't we supposed to be working on this whole getting-to-know-you thing?" she asked.

"We are. I've learned a few things about you already."

"Like what? By the way, this steak is melt-in-your-mouth good. I may have to have you cook for me more often." As if she'd realized what she had said, she held up a hand. "Don't say one word. Just answer the question."

Derek had to admit he was enjoying her company far more than he'd anticipated, and wondered if this was

what being in a relationship would feel like. "I know that when you're passionate about something, you go all out. I also know that you like to tease."

Alexis laughed. "Yeah, well, I've learned a couple of things about you, too. One, you like everything to fall into precise pieces. Two, you're far too serious. You need to relax and enjoy life every now and then."

"With my schedule, I need things to stay organized, and I do enjoy my life."

"Uh-huh. When was the last time you did something for fun and had nothing to do with work or networking? Pure and simple fun."

He thought about it for a long moment and drew a blank.

"I rest my case. Oh, and it's okay to smile a little, too."

Derek couldn't hold back the laughter that spilled from his lips. "I don't seem to have a problem when you're around."

"Then it's a good thing I'm here."

He didn't reply. Whether her presence in his life would be a good thing remained to be seen. One thing was certain: his neatly organized life had started to spiral out of control.

Chapter 10

Derek pushed away from the large conference table and made his way to the exit. Max had asked him to present the update on the Dream project to the board because his brother had to meet with one of his clients. Max managed the careers of some of Hollywood's most famous A-list celebrities and was always on the go.

"Derek. Hold on a moment."

He glanced over his shoulder at the sound of someone calling his name. Demetrius threw up a hand and signaled for him to wait. Derek studied the thin, balding man coming his way. Over the years, Demetrius had made many attempts to be there for Derek and his brothers. Trey and Max had been more receptive, and had a closer relationship with the man.

Demetrius clapped him on the shoulder. "It's good to see you finally taking your rightful place in Prescott George. We can use your expertise in a lot of areas. Let's talk in my office." He pointed to a door on the left.

Derek didn't speak to his comment about taking his *rightful place.* What was it with these people and that

phrase? "Prescott George does great work in the community." He sat in the offered seat.

Demetrius sat in the large leather chair behind his desk. "How's the real estate business? You've made quite a name for yourself. Even though I'm retired now, I still have several friends in the business and your name comes up often."

"It's going well and keeps me busy."

"I have to say that I'm extremely proud of you, Trey and Max, as much as if you were my own sons. I just wish Reginald would have taken a little more time…"

"Thanks. Have you talked to Dad since all this mess began?"

Demetrius shifted uncomfortably and Derek didn't know if it stemmed from the man not backing his best friend or something else.

"Not really. It's been hard on all of us. Your father is like a brother to me and I did everything I could to try and prove he was innocent. But all the evidence kept coming back to him. Trey mentioned that you three were doing your own investigation and I'll do whatever I can to help. I've poked into a few things of late, but have come up empty." He shook his head. "It's been a tough year."

"Very. I didn't know you and Ellen had divorced last year." Derek waited for some kind of reaction, but saw none.

"Well, you know how it is. People change over time and, with the three girls grown and off to New York, you realize that same spark just isn't there anymore."

"I hear you. I'm sorry. It had to be hard going through

all that at the same time as the mess with the San Diego chapter."

"I lost my wife and my best friend," Demetrius said emotionally.

Derek gave him a solemn nod of acknowledgment and stood. "Hopefully, we'll find something to clear Dad's name. Thanks for your help."

Demetrius rounded the desk. "Anytime, son."

Seated in his car in the parking garage, Derek glanced over at the dashboard clock. It was 6:45 p.m. He had no desire to sit in Friday evening rush hour traffic, and decided to find a spot to eat and wait until it died down. He thought back on his conversation with Demetrius and was more confused than ever. Making a decision, he pulled out his cell and sent a text to Trey and Max: Lou's 8:00 p.m. Within five minutes, both had confirmed.

He got to the diner half an hour before the scheduled meet up, found a table in the corner and used the time to search properties in Torrance and Redondo Beach for Alexis. He'd forgotten to ask her about the budget and whether they wanted to rent or buy. He frowned. She'd mentioned the organization having cash flow problems, and he made a mental note to ask her who would be responsible for the down payment and move-in costs. Derek flagged six potential properties that had six bedrooms, and two with seven. He disregarded those with a pool, for safety reasons.

Max slid into the chair to Derek's right. "What's up? Man, you're as bad as Trey with that laptop. New client?"

"Hey. No. It's for Alexis."

"Well, now. Sounds like this relationship is progressing."

Derek slanted Max a glance. "There's no relationship." Not entirely true, but if he kept a firm lid on his emotions, it would save him some grief and heartache down the line. "She's working with an organization on African American infant mortality and they're looking into having a couple of properties to house women and children while they go through the program."

Max nodded. "I like that. Maybe we can get PG involved."

"We'll see." He added the additional listing to the folder he'd created, shut down the laptop and placed it in his bag. While waiting for Trey, Derek brought Max up to speed on the Dream project.

Eventually, he checked his watch. "Do you know if Trey's running late?" On the heels of his question, he spotted his older brother coming in the door, and waved to get his attention.

"Hey," Trey said, pulling up a chair. "Did I miss anything?"

"No. We were about to order." Derek waited until the server had departed before speaking. "I talked to Demetrius today and brought up the subject of Dad and his divorce, but got nowhere."

Trey ran a hand over his head. "I had really hoped we'd have something this time."

"So did I. He came off as this true-blue friend who'd done all he could to help."

"What about the affair?" their younger brother said.

"I didn't outright ask the man if his wife had had an affair, if that's what you mean, Max. I just sort of said

I'd heard about the divorce and how sorry I was that it hadn't worked out. Demetrius told me they divorced, basically, because they'd grown apart." Derek recalled Demetrius's slumped posture. "Even when I mentioned how hard it must have been to lose both Ellen and Reginald at the same time, he didn't flinch. I don't know what to think now."

"I don't, either," Max said. "The affair would be a perfect motive for Demetrius wanting to get back at Dad."

Trey drummed his fingers on the table. "We'll just ask Reginald straight out whether he had the affair. He wants our help, so he's going to have to be honest with us."

Derek's lips settled into a grim line. "I agree." The prostate cancer had already begun to take its toll, and recalling the state of their father's health when they'd questioned him a month ago, Derek wished this was one interrogation he could skip.

The server returned with their meals. His appetite had waned some due to the conversation. He glanced down at the cheeseburger and fries he had planned to enjoy and sighed. Derek added ketchup to both and dug in.

Max pulled out his cell, made a call, then stuck the device back in his pocket. "Dad's expecting us around nine thirty."

Derek stared at his brother incredulously. "What is it with you always having to call and do it right now?"

Trey laughed. "Better late than never."

Derek voted for never.

The three men sat in Reginald's home office, with Trey, in his usual older-brother fashion, directing the

conversation. "You asked us to help you and we're try-ing, but we keep coming up empty, except for Derek finding a can of the same type of spray paint used in the San Diego vandalism. We haven't been able to tie it to anything, though. Did you and Demetrius have a falling out about something prior to the sabotage?"

Reginald sat up straight in his grand office chair. "A falling out? Of course not. We haven't spoken much since then, but there would be no reason for it before."

"Not even if he found out you were having an affair with his wife?" Derek asked mildly. Max shot Derek a glare and Derek shrugged. No use beating around the bush and, since Max had been the one to orchestrate this whole meeting, Derek didn't understand the reason for the hostile look.

"What are you talking about?" Though Reginald might have meant to sound forceful, the disease rav-aging his body had reduced the once tall and robust man to a shell of himself, and the words barely reached across the room.

"Just what I said. Did you or did you not have an af-fair with Ellen Davis?"

"No. Demetrius was my best friend and I'd never betray him that way."

"Dad, if you did, we really need to know," Max said. "I won't think less of you, because we've all done some things in our pasts we're not proud of."

Speak for yourself. The man had cheated on his first wife and devastated his young son, had to be forced into claiming the second son and now possibly had had an affair with his best friend's wife. Derek pinched the bridge of his nose. How much worse could this get?

Reginald sighed. "I did not have an affair with Ellen."

"If you say you didn't, then we believe you," Trey said.

Derek rose to his feet. "It's late and you should get some rest. We'll talk again soon."

At this point, it didn't make sense to bring up what Howard and Allen had mentioned. The three brothers shared a questioning glance. They'd believed they had finally found the reason for the frame up, but Reginald just shot that to hell. Now what?

"Looks like you didn't need my help, after all." Charlene scanned the sheet of paper. "These are some great ideas."

Alexis smiled. "I can't take the credit. Most of these things are from Terri's wish list."

"I really like the idea of the women living in a house. It changes the entire atmosphere."

She agreed and wanted them to have a *home*. "The only thing I didn't see on the list was a way to transition them out of the residential program once the child reaches two. Ideally, six months prior, they'd start the process of looking for their own place."

"Would they be able to afford the rent? It's sky-high everywhere in LA."

"I know." Alexis tapped the pen against her chin. "Having an apartment complex would solve that problem," she said, more to herself. Maybe Derek could point her in the right direction. She'd ask him tomorrow when she accompanied him to the PG fund-raiser. He said he didn't have ulterior motives, but knowing how infrequently he went to any event with a date on his arm, she had to wonder. Refocusing on the task at

hand, she asked, "Do you think we could find a complex willing to rent their apartments or condos at a reduced cost?"

Charlene raised an eyebrow. "In LA? Girl, please. The only way to make that happen is if you own it free and clear."

"Then the rent collected would go to upkeep."

"Alexis, what are you thinking?"

"What you said about owning the complex is brilliant. We just need to find a way to get it done."

"Derek might have some ideas."

"I plan to ask him tomorrow."

"So I guess it's going well between you two now."

"I wouldn't say that." Alexis had enjoyed every moment of dinner with Derek and wished it could always be that way. She saw a totally different person when he relaxed and let go, and that man was dangerous to her heart.

"I thought you told me he wanted to be hands-on."

"Oh, he wants to be hands-on, all right. His solution is for us to get married."

Charlene's jaw dropped. "Okay, wait. Married? But it could be worse. I mean, he's financially stable, fine as fine can get and obviously you guys don't have problems in the bedroom. It could work."

She leveled her friend with a glare.

"I know, I know. I was just saying."

"He doesn't want this baby to grow up like he did—without his father present. I understand where he's coming from, but I can't do it. Not without love."

"I hear you. Yet you gotta give him props for wanting to do what he feels is right."

"True. Don't get me wrong, Derek is a great guy, but I just don't think he'll ever be able to give himself to anyone completely." The thought didn't sit well with Alexis and she refused to analyze why. "Anyway, let's get back to Precious Ones."

They talked more about what resources were necessary to help the women stay connected, and made a list that Alexis would take back to Terri. She also told Charlene about the plans to work with neighboring preschools.

"Would these preschools offer the same sort of fee structure?" Charlene asked.

Alexis pursed her lips. "That's a good question. I'll have to ask Terri." As she made a note on the pad, her cell buzzed. She leaned over to read the display. "Let me answer this and tell Derek I'll call him back."

"Oh, don't get off the phone on my account." Her friend leaned back and folded her arms. "I can wait."

Smiling, Alexis hit the button. "Hey, Derek."

"Hey. Did I catch you at a bad time?"

"Charlene is here and we're discussing Precious Ones."

"I won't hold you long then. I've been researching properties, but I wasn't sure how much they wanted to spend. You mentioned them being strapped for cash, so how are they going to afford the down payment?"

"I'm going to take care of it."

Derek paused. "Is that going to affect you financially?"

"I'll be fine. And I'm hoping you can convince Prescott George to get involved."

"I'll check into it. Are they looking to rent or buy?"

Dear Reader,

Since you are a lover of our books, your opinions are important to us... and so is your time.

That's why we made sure your **"FAST FIVE" READER SURVEY** can be completed in just a few minutes. Your answers to the five questions will help us remain at the forefront of women's fiction.

And, as a thank-you for participating, we'd like to send you **4 FREE THANK-YOU GIFTS!**

Enjoy your gifts with our appreciation,

Pam Powers

To get your
4 FREE THANK-YOU GIFTS:

✳ Quickly complete the "Fast Five" Reader Survey
and return the insert.

▼ DETACH AND MAIL CARD TODAY! ►

"FAST FIVE" READER SURVEY

#	Question		
1	Do you sometimes read a book a second or third time?	○ Yes	○ No
2	Do you often choose reading over other forms of entertainment such as television?	○ Yes	○ No
3	When you were a child, did someone regularly read aloud to you?	○ Yes	○ No
4	Do you sometimes take a book with you when you travel outside the home?	○ Yes	○ No
5	In addition to books, do you regularly read newspapers and magazines?	○ Yes	○ No

YES! I have completed the above Reader Survey. Please send me my 4 FREE GIFTS (gifts worth over $20 retail). I understand that I am under no obligation to buy anything, as explained on the back of this card.

225/326 HDL GM3T

FIRST NAME   LAST NAME

ADDRESS

APT.#   CITY

STATE/PROV.   ZIP/POSTAL CODE

READER SERVICE—Here's how it works:

"In a perfect world I think buying would be a better investment." The organization wouldn't have to constantly worry about the owner deciding to sell.

"I agree. How're you feeling?" he asked softly.

"Pretty good."

"Is the nausea gone?"

"Not completely. It comes and goes and I've changed my eating habits to accommodate it for now." Alexis shifted and met Charlene's smile.

"Let me know if you need something."

"I'll do that. I need to finish up with Charlene."

"See you tomorrow evening."

"Okay."

Charlene squealed when Alexis hung up. "You should have seen your face—all smiling and whatnot—and then heard the way your voice got all soft. You sounded like a teenager talking to her first love."

He had been her first love. But that was then. "Girl, you're getting carried away. He called to ask about this," she said, pointing to the papers spread on the table.

"At first. That last couple of minutes had nothing to do with this stuff and you know it. I think you may be wrong about Derek."

"Maybe." She didn't know if that was a good thing or not.

Chapter 11

Friday evening, Alexis sat admiring Derek's big hands as he drove to the holiday fund-raiser. Those same hands had given her pleasure and comfort. Despite everything between them, she wanted to feel both again.

"What's on your mind?" His voice broke into her musings.

"Nothing." No way would she tell him what she had been thinking. "You typically attend these functions alone, correct?"

"For the most part."

"Why did you ask me to go with you? Is this like a date?"

Derek's eyes left the road briefly to glance her way. "Pretty soon people will know about the baby and I figured they should get used to seeing us together. I don't want anyone to get the impression that—"

"That the father isn't involved," she said, cutting him off. Alexis didn't know whether to be flattered or annoyed. On one hand, she appreciated his loyalty. On the other, she worried that his only concern was to keep up

appearances. "It's nobody's business who the father is, unless I decide to share the information."

"You're not planning to hide the fact that I'm the father, are you?" His voice held a trace of vulnerability.

"No, but I'm not going to wear a Miss America banner across my chest with the words Derek Moore Is the Father, either." Alexis sighed and laid a hand on his arm. His muscles tensed. "Derek, I know you're concerned, and why. Understand this—I *want* and *need* you to be there for our baby, and we'll need to be there for each other in some ways. You won't ever have to worry about that changing." She felt him relax.

Derek reached for her hand and placed a kiss in her palm.

She sat back and watched the passing scenery with a smile. Derek rarely allowed his emotions to surface. For him to do so meant the estrangement between him and his father affected Derek more than he cared to admit. Knowing this, she vowed to be patient and show him that not all relationships were the same.

Parking anywhere downtown was always a hassle, but Prescott George never failed to provide valet parking for their events. Derek escorted her inside the large ballroom and several heads turned their way.

"You're causing quite a stir in that dress," Derek whispered close to her ear. "I can't blame them, though."

Alexis had noticed the looks—some discreet and others outright stares—because of her five-foot-ten-inch height, but she had learned to ignore them over the years. She had chosen a one-shoulder silver gown that molded to her slim curves, one with a thigh-high slit, and four-inch matching heels with rhinestones.

"Then again, they could be staring at you. Not too many men can command a room the way you do." She let her gaze roam lazily up his body. "Especially when you look like you just stepped off the cover of a magazine." Desire leaped into his eyes and Alexis had to look away or succumb right then and there. They walked farther into the room and nodded greetings to those they passed.

Derek stopped abruptly. "Damn," he muttered.

Alexis followed his gaze and gasped softly. She hadn't seen Reginald Moore in a while and the slow-moving, thin man standing several feet away was a direct contrast to the strong, tall man with the booming laugh she remembered. The conversation she'd overheard between Derek and his brothers came back to her and her heart ached for Derek. She reached for his hand and threaded their fingers together. "Your father's not well?"

"No."

The barely audible word told her everything she needed to know. She tightened her grip and was surprised when he reciprocated. Derek seemed torn between whether to go over or not, but someone called out to him, solving the dilemma. They spoke with a few more people before heading over to the tables for the five-course dinner.

"Are you comfortable?" Derek asked.

"Yes. Thank you."

"I'm going to get something from the bar. Do you want me to bring you back some juice or a soft drink?"

"Juice would be great." Alexis followed his fluid gait as he strolled across the room. *Sexy.* In her pe-

ripheral vision she saw his father making his way to a table. She observed a small number of people turning up their noses, but a few gave him welcoming smiles. She wondered if Derek knew the whole story behind his father's expulsion and if the two of them would ever reconcile their differences. Given the look of Reginald, they didn't have much time.

"Excuse me, is this seat taken?"

Alexis glanced up to find a handsome man who looked to be in his mid to late thirties gesturing at the chair to her left. "Not that I'm aware of."

He smiled. "May I?"

"Sure."

He sat and extended his hand. "David Hodges."

"Alexis Armstrong. Nice to meet you."

His smile widened. "The pleasure is all mine. I must say that you're the most beautiful woman in the room tonight."

She stifled an eye roll and smiled politely. "Are you a member of Prescott George?"

"A friend of mine is a member and I always try to support a good cause."

"I agree."

"Here's your juice, baby." Alexis whipped her head around and met Derek's hardened gaze. Her eyebrow lifted. He placed a glass of orange juice in front of her and another glass of unknown contents at his place setting.

Derek stood behind Alexis's chair and stuck out his hand. "Derek Moore."

David divided a glance between Alexis and Derek. His smile faded. He reluctantly shook Derek's hand and

mumbled his name. "If you'll excuse me, I'm going to get a drink."

Derek smoothly slid into his chair and took a sip of his drink.

She shook her head and chuckled. "No need to go all caveman. The man was just making polite conversation."

"Polite conversation, my ass. He's been stalking you since we walked into the room."

"And that would bother you why?"

He remained silent.

Alexis chuckled. "So this is what I have to look forward to for the next few months, huh?" she asked, picking up her glass. His possessiveness touched her in a way that melted her heart. She pushed the feelings aside, knowing she couldn't get caught up in the moment. This was all about business for Derek and she'd do well to remember that fact.

Derek escorted Alexis over to where Trey and Max stood talking. Before he could make introductions, Reginald joined them.

Max immediately moved to Reginald's side. "Hey, Dad. How are you feeling?"

The corner of Reginald's mouth kicked up a bit. "I'm still standing. Trey. Derek." He'd spoken to them, but his gaze remained focused on Alexis.

Trey smiled knowingly. "Good to see you here tonight."

"Yes, it is," Derek said. "Alexis, I don't know if you've met my father, Reginald Moore, and my brothers, Trey and Max." Hearing himself refer to them as his family still felt somewhat strange.

Alexis smiled. "We haven't been formally introduced, but I've seen them at other events. It's nice to meet you all."

Max inclined his head. "It's a pleasure to finally meet you, Alexis."

Trey echoed the sentiment.

Reginald took both of Alexis's hands. "This little lady needs no introduction. You're still as lovely as you were at Malibu High. How are you?"

Alexis's eyes lit with surprise. "I'm fine, thank you. I didn't realize you knew me."

"I wasn't always around like I should have been, but I remember you and Derek taking pictures together after your graduation," he said with a sad smile. "Well, I think I'm going to call it a night."

"Did you drive tonight?"

"No, son." He placed a hand on Max's shoulder. "I called a car service. They should be downstairs waiting now."

"We can walk you down," Trey offered.

Reginald waved him off. "No, no. I'm fine. I'll see you all later."

"I'll see you at Thanksgiving dinner," Derek said.

Max's and Trey's heads whipped in Derek's direction and their mouths fell open.

Reginald's lips tightened with emotion. He nodded, patted Derek on the shoulder and slowly made his way to the exit.

"Hot damn, we got that resounding yes."

Derek shook his head. "That wasn't a resounding yes, Max. It was an I guess I'll go."

Max grinned. "Same thing." He sobered. "It made Dad happy. He's going downhill pretty fast."

He agreed. Though he'd just seen his father a couple days ago, Reginald appeared even more frail. A strange sensation started in the middle of Derek's chest, one he'd never experienced. It startled him to realize that he did actually care about his father. As if sensing his turmoil, Alexis slipped her hand into his and gave it a reassuring squeeze. Just like earlier, her calming touch eased some of his tension.

Trey glanced around the room. "My fiancée, Kiara Woods, is around here somewhere. Hopefully, I'll have a chance to introduce you two later. She owns LA Little Ones Daycare and Preschool."

"Really? I've heard wonderful things about the elite preschool and that there's a yearlong waiting list." Alexis shot a quick glance Derek's way.

Derek interpreted her thoughts: that he must have told his brothers about the baby. He had no doubt she would ask about that on the drive home.

"Well, I'll let you gentlemen catch up. I see a friend of mine I want to speak with." Alexis glanced up at Derek. "Let me know when you're ready."

"Okay." He had a hard time taking his eyes off her as she strutted off to meet her friend. With every step, he was treated to the sight of her bare leg emerging from the slit in her dress, and his body reacted in kind. Dragging his thoughts back to the conversation, he heard Max chuckling. "What?"

"I see why your rent-a-date night went the way it did. She is stunning."

Trey chuckled. "Looks like you've made your deci-

sion about how to handle things with Alexis. Are you two dating?"

"No. Just friends." Derek had already mentioned his proposal to marry Alexis to Max. Evidently, he'd forgotten, and Derek saw no reason to bring it up. "We're going to have to be around each other for the baby, so I figured we'd start now."

"Just friends?" Trey asked skeptically. "Let me know how that works out."

Max laughed. "Yeah, I'm curious, too."

Derek ignored them. "I'm outta here." He pivoted on his heel and strode off, their laughter following. He searched for and spotted Alexis sitting at a table talking to a beautiful dark-skinned woman.

Alexis looked up at his approach. "Are you ready?"

"I can wait, if you're not done."

"It's fine. Jade and I were just catching up. Jade, this is Derek."

"Nice to meet you, Jade."

"Same here," she said with a smile. "It was great talking to you, Alexis."

Alexis stood. "We'll chat again soon."

They made their way out and a valet retrieved his car.

"I should have brought more than this little wrap," she said with a shudder, and settled into the seat.

Derek removed his suit coat and handed it to her. "You can wear this until I get the heat going." Seeing her in his jacket did something to him. They drove in companionable silence for the first few miles, with only the sounds of soft music filling the car's interior.

"You told your brothers about us."

"Yes. Is that a problem?"

"Figured as much when Trey brought up the day care. And no, they're your brothers. I expected you to tell them, just like I told my best friend, Charlene. I didn't realize your father was so sick."

"Stage 4 prostate cancer. The doctors don't think he'll make it past the New Year."

Alexis rolled her head in his direction. "I'm so sorry, Derek. How are you handling it with the two of you at odds?"

"Part of me doesn't want to care because of what he put me and my mother through, but I can't help it. As angry as I still am, I wouldn't want to wish this on anyone. I'm sure you heard about him being kicked out of PG."

"I did."

"He claims he's innocent and wants Trey, Max and me to help clear his name. After having our characters questioned by the organization, I can't believe he had the audacity to ask, especially since he's never been there for Trey or me."

"But you're going to help him, aren't you?"

"Yeah."

"Regardless of how you feel about him, you have to do this for yourself and for him. Maybe then you'll both be able to make peace with the past."

"We'll see." She made it sound so simple. Tonight was the first time he had felt anything other than a strong dislike for the man. Was he finally going to have that peace?

Chapter 12

Tuesday morning, Derek could hardly concentrate on the contract in front of him. He would be accompanying Alexis to her ultrasound appointment in a couple hours and had opted to work from home. He had no idea what to expect and it unnerved him. After another twenty minutes, he gave up and went to stand on his deck. He'd been more than a little shocked to find out she'd been engaged, and even more so about the miscarriage. The fact that her punk-ass ex had left her to deal with the pregnancy incensed him all over again. No, Derek didn't know the first thing about babies or being a father, but he'd learn. He wouldn't turn his back on his responsibility.

He sat out there for another half hour before he changed clothes, then went to pick up Alexis. Her appointment wasn't until eleven thirty, but they had to drive to LA and the traffic didn't care about the time of day.

She met him at the door with a pensive look on her face. "Hey."

"Hey. You worried?"

Alexis gave him a nervous smile. "A little."

Derek gathered her in his embrace and kissed her forehead. "Everything is going to be fine." She buried her face in his shoulder and held him tight. He ran a comforting hand up and down her back. "I'll be right there with you."

"I know." She released him and leaned up to kiss his cheek. "Thank you, Derek."

Her soft smile made his heart leap. "Let's go."

Alexis didn't talk much during the drive and he didn't offer conversation. He could feel her anxiety. Wanting to give her the same kind of assurance she had tried to do with him last Friday, Derek covered her hand with his. He kept it there for the rest of the way.

Inside the imaging center, he found two chairs on the far side of the crowded room and indicated that he would save them while she stood in line to check in.

Alexis joined him a few minutes later, holding a clipboard with several pieces of paper attached. "Good grief. Now I know why they have you come thirty minutes before your actual appointment time. They ask just about everything except the color of your shoes. This would've been so much easier if the ultrasound machine in my doctor's office was working."

Derek chuckled. "I'm glad it's not me."

She rolled her eyes and continued to fill out the sheets. When she finished, she took them back to the desk. They waited another fifteen minutes before the technician called her back. The woman handed Alexis a gown and directed her to an area to change.

"Sir, you can wait right here."

There were only three people waiting in the small area—a couple and a very pregnant woman. He hadn't thought about how Alexis would look in a few months. Would she be moving as slowly as the woman, who eased out of the chair to follow another technician? It turned out to be another waiting game, and by the time they entered the ultrasound room, Derek was damn near hyperventilating. Then he almost passed out when he realized what type of procedure Alexis would be having. He'd assumed it was little more than squirting some gel on her stomach and running the instrument over the top, but no, this particular version—the ultrasound tech called it transvaginal—involved inserting a probe. A sheet was placed over Alexis's waist, and his position near her head spared him from possibly losing his man card.

Derek forgot it all when he saw the small image on the screen. He stared, transfixed, as the woman pointed.

"This is your baby right here. Here's the head and limb buds. In a few weeks, he or she will have all the body parts." She circled her finger around a dark area. "This is the water sac. I'm going to measure your baby." She typed several keys. "Alexis, you're at eight weeks and two days."

"So, my count is right on target."

"Yes, it is. Now, let's see if we can see the heartbeat." She zoomed in on an area and placed her finger there. "Right there. That pulsing is the baby's heartbeat and it's strong at one hundred fifty-five beats per minute." She smiled at them.

Alexis glanced up at him with tears of relief in her eyes and, when their gazes connected, an unnamed

emotion gripped Derek. The realness of the moment penetrated his mind and his heart. He wiped her tears with the pad of his thumb and brushed his lips across hers. "May I take some pictures and record the heart-beat?"

"Sure."

Still amazed, he took out his phone, recorded several seconds and took a few still shots. While waiting for Alexis to change back into her clothes, he replayed the video again and again. A baby. *His* baby. *Their* baby. He had to get Alexis to change her mind about marriage.

Derek stood when she came out. "Are you feeling better now?"

"Much. But I'm hungry. I was too nervous to eat earlier."

He wrapped an arm around her shoulders. "We can stop and get something. You ever been to Lou's Diner?"

"No, but I've heard of it. It's right outside of Holly-wood, right?"

"Yes. You've been missing out on the best breakfast all these years."

Alexis placed her hands on her hips. "You do re-member what I've been doing for the past fifteen years. Big, hearty breakfasts weren't exactly part of my eat-ing plan."

"My bad," Derek said with a grin.

"Yeah, *yo'* bad."

He held the car door open. "Get in, girl."

She laughed and playfully stuck her tongue out at him.

"You're flirting with danger. Do that again."

Still smiling, Alexis slid onto the seat.

He got in on the other side and eyed her.

"Didn't you say we're going to eat? Well, come on."

Derek shook his head and got them underway. The drive took thirty minutes and he had to park a block away. Once they were seated and had menus, he said, "You mentioned hearty breakfasts not being part of your eating plan."

"I had a very strict diet." She looked up from her menu. "For several years, my eating habits were so bad, I had all kinds of physical issues. We had to maintain a certain weight, so I'd find myself barely eating or so starved that I'd devour two or three doughnuts at a time. Those were some hard years," she added.

He knew models had to remain thin, but he had no idea what they went through to accomplish it. "Do you still have problems?"

"Thankfully, no. My mom got me into counseling and I learned to eat healthier and incorporated exercise."

"I'm glad to hear it. You know, I can't get over those pictures."

"Me, either. To see the heart beating and to know he or she is progressing well is a load off my mind."

"Do you know what you want—boy or girl?"

"I hadn't really thought about it. All I want is a healthy baby."

So did he, and preferably with the three of them under one roof. He had his work cut out for him, but Derek was up to the challenge.

Alexis enjoyed being with Derek more and more. "Are you sure you have enough food on your plate?" He

had two huge Belgian waffles covered in warm maple syrup, scrambled eggs, sausage, bacon and potatoes.

"I'm a big guy and I don't eat like this all the time. Although it seems like I've been here more in the past couple of months than I had in three years."

"How do you keep in such good shape? With your long working hours, I know you don't have time to go to the gym."

"I converted one of my bedrooms into a gym and I go running on the beach."

The night they made love, she'd marveled at his well-defined muscles and had been curious about how he kept his body looking that way. "That certainly makes it easier."

"I forgot we never finished the tour when you were at the house. You can see it next time." Derek ate another bite of his waffle.

"Next time?"

"Yep. You should bring a few things to leave, just in case you spend the night. I can do the same at your place."

Alexis paused with her chicken sandwich halfway to her mouth. "Whoa. What? I'm not moving in with you."

"Did you hear me ask you to move in? I'm just saying it would be a good idea if, for some reason, you didn't feel well, wherever we are, you wouldn't have to be alone." He ate a piece of bacon. "Besides, the only woman I'm moving into my house is my wife. Are you saying you changed your mind?" He smiled and tossed her a bold wink.

"You know what." She threw a fry at him.

Derek laughed.

He seemed to be letting his guard down a little and relaxing. She would never forget his expression when they'd seen their baby's heartbeat on the ultrasound. Then the way he'd looked at her, wiped her tears and kissed her made her feel as if they were a real couple. She realized she wanted that with him.

They went back to their meals. Alexis glanced at him across the table a few minutes later. He appeared to be lost in thought. "Are you okay?"

"Yeah. Just thinking about the ultrasound. It's all so surreal and I'm still trying to wrap my head around the fact that we're going to have a baby."

"It's still kind of weird to me, too," she said, dipping a french fry in ketchup and popping it into her mouth.

Derek wiped his hands on a napkin. "I never thought about fatherhood because, honestly, I hadn't planned to have children." He held up a hand. "Before you say anything, I'll admit that the idea scares me to death and that I don't know the first thing about what I'm supposed to do. But I'm going to do my best not to disappoint you or the baby."

I. Can. Not. Fall for this man. Alexis pretended to be engrossed in her food to cover her rising emotions. "You've done fine, so far. I can't tell you how much it meant to have you with me today." Each time her nervousness increased, he'd been right there with a gentle touch of reassurance.

"I'm glad I was there. Did you have anything planned this afternoon?"

"Not really. Why?"

"I found a few houses I want you to take a look at."

"Don't you have to go back to work?"

"I own the company and I will be working. Any more questions?"

"Nope." She mimicked zipping her lips.

A grin stole over Derek's face. "Finish your food, so we can go."

Alexis smiled and did just that.

With Derek using his GPS, they pulled up in front of the first house an hour and a half later. "We won't be able to go inside any of them today, but I wanted you to at least see the style and neighborhood. This one has six bedrooms, four and a half baths, and is about forty-five hundred square feet. I didn't look for properties with a pool, to be on the safe side."

"It's beautiful." The two-story stucco structure had two second-floor balconies and a manicured lawn, and she liked the area.

Derek brought up the property on his laptop and they scrolled through the photos.

"That's a nice-sized backyard and the floor plan is very open. It could work well and, even with so many people living there, wouldn't feel claustrophobic. Can we keep this one on the list?"

He made a notation, pulled up another property and handed her the laptop.

"Okay, where to next?"

"Actually, that house two doors down is for sale, too." He pointed to the screen.

Alexis viewed the photos excitedly. "It's very similar to the other one. Look at that closet. There's enough space to make another full bedroom."

Derek chuckled. "I take it you approve."

"I do. I just need to figure out how to finance them."

Both properties had a selling price of seven figures. "I can handle the down payments, but there's going to have to be some serious fund-raising to get them paid off. Are you still going to talk to someone at Prescott George?"

"Yeah. Probably Max. He does a lot in that area. I have a few other avenues I'm pursuing, as well, and will let you know how they turn out."

"Thanks. I don't want to mention anything to Terri until I know we can do this."

For the next little while they visited other properties, but Alexis was sold on the first two and told him so as they sat parked in front of the last house.

"Okay. I'll get with the owners and see what I can negotiate." He shut down the computer, placed it on the backseat and drove off. "Is there anywhere you want to stop before we head home?"

"Not that I can think of. Oh, there was one other teeny tiny thing."

"Why does that scare me?"

She laughed. "Seriously. In the program, once the babies turn two, the women will need to find other accommodations. What if we could also find a midsize apartment complex?"

Derek scrubbed a hand across his forehead. "So, now you want me to find someone willing to sell an apartment complex?"

"Yes. Or you could always build one. I know for a fact that you've done it before. Those pricey high-rises are selling pretty well."

He slanted her an amused glance. "You don't ask for much, do you?"

Alexis gave him a brilliant smile.

"I'll see what I can do."

She bounced in her seat. "Thank you!"

He leaned over and gave her a quick kiss. "You are something else."

The same could be said about him, she was finding.

Chapter 13

"There are two areas of the market that seem to be in high demand and we need to figure out a way to tap into them," Derek said to his development team. "While much of the focus has been on high-end properties, mid-priced homes that potential buyers can actually afford have been overlooked."

A man raised his hand. "So you're talking maybe urban row homes or tract housing."

He nodded. "As well as starter homes and affordable rental units for young adults just leaving college."

"We would have to figure out how to balance the land costs, price, location and amenities," a woman called out.

"That's why I have you here, Tara."

She smiled. "I guess I walked right into that one." Laughter followed her statement.

Derek chuckled. "True." He liked his staff and had made it a priority to create a relaxed and healthy work environment. As a result, productivity stayed high.

"You mentioned another area."

"Yes, the baby boomers. While some people have retired to senior communities, I've been following some
studies that show a growing number have been affected
by the last recession and will need more affordable so-
lutions. Additionally—" Derek glanced up at his assistant's entrance. Her face registered irritation. Neta
Goodwin was even-tempered and had a way about her
that calmed the most irate buyers and sellers. For her to
have such a look of displeasure gave him pause.

"Just a minute," he said to the team, and walked over
to where Neta still stood near the door. Keeping his
voice low, he asked, "Is there a problem?"

"Yes," Neta said tightly. "There's a woman out here
demanding to see you. I tried to direct her to one of the
other agents, but she insists on seeing only you."

His first thought was Alexis, but she wouldn't do
something like this. He hadn't been involved with a
woman in over eight months, and they had parted amicably after two dates, so he had no clue as to why a
woman would show up at his office. "Who is it?"

"Vera Jenson."

"The one whose husband owns Jenson Pharmaceu-
ticals?"

"The one and only. I tried to explain that you were in a
meeting and do you know what she said? She said go get
him anyway. He won't keep me waiting—no one does."

Derek didn't want or need her kind of drama. The
Jensons might be part of LA's Black elite, but he didn't
disrupt his meetings for anything except an emergency.
This did not fall into that category. "Please tell Mrs.
Jenson that she is welcome to wait until my meeting is

over in about fifteen minutes, or she can schedule an appointment for another day."

"With pleasure."

He walked back over to his seat. "Sorry for the interruption. I was saying that another area for the baby boomers would be helping them sell their larger homes and downsize, or find other living options." Derek wanted to get a jump on these market trends before someone else did.

"Sounds like a potential gold mine if we can figure out a way to create affordable housing for these populations," another staff member pointed out.

"My thoughts exactly." Also, if he couldn't find a suitable apartment complex that fitted Precious Ones' needs, he'd look into building one, as Alexis had pointed out. He hadn't talked to her since her appointment two days ago and decided he'd call her once he had a free moment. Bringing his thoughts back to the meeting, he assigned specific tasks and answered related questions, then got updates on current projects. "Anyone have anything else?" Derek scanned the room. "Okay, then we'll meet again next Thursday at nine."

"Can I talk to you for a moment, Derek?"

"Sure, Enrique."

"My mother is having surgery on Monday and I'd like to take that day and Tuesday off."

"Absolutely. Let me know if you need to be off longer, and I hope all goes well."

"Thanks."

He followed the young man out and went to his office. With any luck, Mrs. Jenson would be gone.

"She's in the small conference office," Neta said be-

fore he could ask. "It was quite comical when I told her what you said. She changed her tune real quick. I already offered her coffee or tea and she declined."

"Thanks." Derek dropped the folder on his desk, picked up a pad and pen and reversed his steps. Taking a deep breath, he opened the door. "Good morning, Mrs. Jenson. Thank you for waiting."

Mrs. Jenson looked at her watch. "Your secretary said fifteen minutes and it's been twenty-two. Are you always this rude in keeping potential clients waiting?"

Derek lowered himself to the chair opposite the woman, mentally counted to ten and reminded himself to remain cordial. "Mrs. Jenson, I wasn't aware that it's considered rude to finish a scheduled meeting and offer someone who does *not* have an appointment the option of waiting or returning at another time. If you feel my staff hasn't met your expectations, you're free to seek services elsewhere."

She glared, but he didn't flinch. He suspected she ran over people daily, but she'd find he wasn't going to become one of her casualties.

After a few tense seconds, she said, "I like you, Mr. Moore. Most people don't have the balls to stand up to me."

"What can I do for you?"

"I need to find a condo near Westwood. My granddaughter is transferring to UCLA in January."

Derek frowned. "I don't typically take on clients of other brokers." He recalled seeing photos in the paper about the man who had sold her multiple properties.

"I've worked with Simon for over ten years and bought properties worth more than thirty million dol-

lars, and now he acts like he doesn't have time to answer my calls," she huffed. "I met with him in September and he still has yet to show me one condo. Time is running short."

"I understand, but I don't operate that way."

"Very well." Mrs. Jenson took her cell out of her purse and dialed a number. "Hello, this is Vera Jenson. Yes, I know Simon is busy. He's been busy for two months. Please let him know his services are no longer needed. Thank you." She disconnected. "I no longer have a broker."

Derek smiled and picked up his pen. "Tell me what you're looking for."

Before she could reply, her cell rang. She fished it out of her purse again, checked the display and rolled her eyes. "Simon. Humph. *Now* he decides to call. Do you mind if I answer?"

He waved a hand. "Please do." He wanted to see how this played out.

"Hello, Simon. Yes, I did just call. And you were about to call me." She whispered to Derek, "As if I believe that lie." She went back to the call. "And you have some properties to show me? Ah, you need a few days. You've had two months. Simon, I'm sorry, I have to go. I'm meeting with my new broker. Mmm-hmm, goodbye." Mrs. Jenson rolled her eyes again. "He must think I'm a fool. I'm sorry. Where were we?"

"You were about to tell me what you're looking for."

"Oh, yes, yes."

Twenty minutes later, with a detailed list, Derek stood. "Either I or one of my senior agents will get back to you no later than Monday." He helped her up.

"Thank you so much."

He walked her out and went back to his office. The woman was a piece of work.

He had enough time before his next meeting to call Alexis, and took a moment to do so.

"Hey, Derek."

"Hey." The sound of her voice instantly made him forget about the last thirty minutes. "How's the appetite today?"

"It's okay. Nowhere near what yours is, though," Alexis said with a laugh.

"I'll have you know that I've only had a smoothie and two boiled eggs today, so far."

"Ah, the day is still young. I'm sure you'll make up for it at lunch and dinner."

"I call to see how you're doing and all I get is this."

"Aw, I'm sorry."

"No, you're not, because I hear you trying to cover your laugh. But that's okay. I like you just the way you are."

"I like you, too."

Her soft declaration made his heart flip. "Can we have dinner tonight?"

"Are you cooking?"

"Not this time. I'd like to take you out."

"As in a real date?"

Derek hesitated a beat. "Yes. Dressy. I'll text you with the time in a few."

"That works."

He hung up, called his favorite restaurant to make a reservation, then texted the information to Alexis. He leaned back in his chair. He wanted to be with Alexis

for more than just the baby. He wanted *her*. And he decided to stop fighting it. He was losing, anyway.

Alexis added the final touches to her makeup. Unlike her modeling days, she opted for a more natural look, wearing only mascara, eyeliner and a tinted lip gloss. She'd chosen a little black dress and slipped into the long-sleeved, body-hugging outfit that stopped just above the knee. She studied herself in the mirror and ran a hand over her still-flat belly. In a couple months, she wouldn't be able to wear anything fitted and would need to shop for a whole new wardrobe. Already there were changes taking place in her body. Her breasts were tender and spilling out of her bras. However, her body wasn't the only thing changing. Her heart had begun to change and open up to Derek.

He checked on her almost daily, always asked how she felt and if she needed anything. Alexis couldn't believe he'd made early dinner reservations. When she questioned him about it, he said he knew she enjoyed watching the sun setting over the water and thought she might like to do it while they ate. On the phone earlier that day, she'd told him she liked him. She more than *liked* him. These new emotions were far stronger than how she'd felt at seventeen and it was becoming harder and harder to keep her guard up.

Derek arrived shortly and drove them to Mastro's Ocean Club on Pacific Coast Highway. The expensive steak house was known for its excellent food, elegant atmosphere and superior service. The hostess led them to a window table.

"Is this table okay?" Derek asked as he seated Alexis.

"It's perfect. Thank you." She had a clear view of the last minutes of the sunset. The sight of the sun resting on the water never failed to take her breath away. "It's so beautiful." When she turned his way, she found him watching her.

"It is, but it doesn't hold a candle to you. I'm finding that there aren't many things that do."

Her heart skipped a beat.

He reached for her hand. "Alexis, I know I said we should start being seen together for the baby's sake, but I don't want that to be the only reason."

"What are you saying?"

"I'm saying that I want to be with you, no business proposals, no bargains. Just a man who has a thing for a beautiful and special woman, who happens to be carrying his child."

Alexis thought she might fall out of her chair. Thankfully, the server came to take their drink order, because she needed a moment to process his words. Once the man left, Derek looked at her expectantly.

He squeezed her hand. "But I have a lot of demons and I don't know if I can—"

"How about we take it slow, one day at a time and see what happens? No commitments." As he'd said, he carried a lot of past hurts. Alexis decided to proceed with caution just in case he couldn't let them go. Otherwise, she'd end up with another broken heart.

She picked up her menu and perused the selections. They started with Caesar salads. Derek chose the rib eye, while she opted for the petit filet, and they shared a one-pound baked potato with the works. While eat-

ing, they talked more about other houses he'd found for her to look at.

"I haven't made any headway on a complex, but I have a couple of my agents working on it. I'll be talking to Trey and Max tomorrow, so I'll see if they have any ideas about that and funding."

"If you email the property listings, I'll look through them and see which ones I like. That way, we don't have to drive by every one."

"Sounds good."

They finished the meal while conversing about Derek's new development projects and the amenities he planned to include in the luxury high-rise complex. "Wow. Have you broken ground already?"

"Yes. The developer and I need to meet with the group who will provide the medical services to make sure we have appropriate wiring for their equipment. I already have a couple of small business owners who've reached out to me about the bakery and coffeehouse. We're expecting it to be open by next summer."

Since Alexis had already imposed on him to find an apartment complex, she refrained from asking him to scrap that first request and, instead, duplicate his luxury condos. The women would definitely benefit from having a mini market, coffeehouse and medical center on-site. Maybe she could reach out to some of her former model associates for help in raising the money.

The server removed their plates and left dessert menus. "See anything you want?" Derek asked after a minute.

Alexis was torn between the signature warm butter cake and chocolate-covered strawberries. "Maybe the

strawberries, but to go, please. Are you going to have something?"

"Not this time."

She smiled. "Still trying to work off those waffles from two days ago, I bet."

Chuckling, he said, "Yeah, something like that." He placed the to-go order, settled the bill and led her out to the car. The drive took less than ten minutes and he walked her to the door.

"You want to come in for a minute?"

"Yeah. For a minute."

Alexis went to the kitchen to put away the berries and Derek followed. She opened the refrigerator and paused.

"What's wrong?"

"Nothing. I'm so full, but I want one of these strawberries." They were huge and the chocolate covered them all the way to the stem. She debated a moment longer, closed the refrigerator and placed the container on the counter. "Do you want one?"

"Nah."

She took one out and bit into it. "Mmm, oh, my goodness. This is *so* good." She turned slightly and noticed Derek staring at her.

"On second thought, maybe I'll have some."

She pushed the container toward him.

Derek ignored it. He took her hand holding the berry and, meeting her gaze, guided it to his mouth and took a bite. "You're right," he murmured. "It's good."

Alexis's breath stacked up in her throat.

"But I know what would taste even better."

He eased the strawberry from her hand and rubbed

it across her lips, then used the tip of his tongue to lick off the juice. She moaned.

"Mmm, better." He picked up another one and fed her a bite, keeping his eyes riveted to her mouth as she chewed. "I think these are the best strawberries I've ever eaten." Derek trailed the strawberry over the tops of her breasts visible above the edge of her dress and followed with his mouth. "Yeah, the best."

Her legs went weak and she gripped the counter behind her to keep from sliding to the floor. He snaked an arm around her waist and pulled her flush against his hard body. Before she could draw her next breath, his mouth came down on hers in a hungry, demanding kiss. The heady combination of the berry, chocolate and his unique flavor made her senses spin.

"Damn, baby. You taste so sweet."

He trailed butterfly kisses down her neck and the valley between her breasts, while his hands skimmed over her thighs, inching her dress higher and higher. He caressed her buttocks and hips, then moved her panties to the side and grazed her core. Alexis cried out. "Derek. Wh-what…" Her protest died on her lips when he slid a finger inside her.

"How does that feel?" he asked, languidly circling the bud. "Do you like that?"

I shouldn't. "Yes." They'd agreed to take things slowly, day by day. Yet the only thing unhurried was the pace of his seduction. Alexis arched against his hand, urging him to give her more. Kissing her again, he added another finger and thrust in and out.

Derek changed the tempo and she gripped his shoulders as his fingers moved faster. She tore her mouth

away from his as a blinding orgasm hit. *"Derek!"* She slumped against him as waves of pleasures consumed her. He withdrew his fingers and she moaned at the loss.

Derek fixed her dress, kissed her deeply and murmured, "Good night." He stroked a finger down her cheek and then he was gone.

Alexis dropped her head on the back of a nearby barstool. Her body still trembled and her breathing came in short gasps. This man did not play fair.

Chapter 14

Derek sat sprawled on the sofa in Max's Santa Monica estate Friday evening, barely listening to what his brothers were saying. Images of Alexis eating that strawberry, him tasting her and her coming apart in his arms last night dominated every corner of his brain. He hadn't been able to concentrate worth a damn all day.

"What do you think, Derek?" Trey's voice interrupted his musings.

"Sorry. What did you ask?"

Trey eyed him. "Are you okay? You've been distracted since you got here."

"I'm fine."

"I asked if you thought we should keep going with the investigation."

"Yes. Something isn't right. I can feel it." As much as he didn't want to admit he might have been wrong about Reginald, too many things weren't adding up.

"I agree. There are way too many inconsistencies and holes," Max said. "And I'm really worried about

Dad. I know this is taking a toll on him and making things worse."

Derek recalled how weak Reginald looked a week ago, and once again his emotions stirred. "Maybe we should keep digging, but spend more time focusing on the old man." Both men turned his way. "What? I won't lie, I still have a lot of anger toward him, but I don't like seeing him like this any more than you two do."

Trey braced his forearms on his thighs. "Have you gone by to see him?"

"No, but I've been thinking about it." Aside from not wanting to have anything to do with Reginald, Derek had no excuse for not visiting. His father lived less than fifteen minutes away in the same city.

"Derek, I hope you and Trey decide to visit. I know you still have issues to resolve, but he'll be happy to see you. And I think you're right. Let's keep searching. Something is bound to show up. I'll continue looking into Demetrius's background."

"Maybe we should add Allen and Howard to the list," Derek said.

Trey's gaze narrowed. "You think they could've had a part in this mess?"

"I can't say, but I had some weird vibes about their story."

"Okay. I'll handle it and let you guys know what I find out."

Derek sat up. "Alexis is working with a nonprofit group called Precious Ones that focuses on African American infant mortality. The group is severely lacking funding and Alexis wanted to know if this is something PG can get behind. Alexis has some big dreams."

He shook his head. "She met with the director and the woman mentioned wanting to have some type of housing facility for the pregnant women to live until their babies turned two."

"I remember you mentioning that when we met at Lou's," Max said. "I'll see what we can do. Is there a specific type of building she's looking to rent?"

"I believe the director had a shelter-type facility in mind. However, Alexis feels they'd thrive better in a home environment. She has me searching for six- and seven-bedroom homes to *buy*, not rent."

Trey chuckled. "Grandiose dreams, but she's got a point. Given the choice, which one of us would opt to stay in a big building with fifteen or twenty other people?"

"Why do you think I agreed? Not only that, she decided that they'd need some type of permanent housing afterward, and also asked me find an apartment complex. I don't think I'm going to be able to locate one in Redondo Beach or Torrance, where we've looked at houses."

"Well, Mr. Real Estate Mogul, you'll just have to build her one," Max drawled. "You don't do anything else with all that money you've got lying around."

Derek let out a short bark of laughter. "Funny, she said the same thing. And how do you know that my money is lying around?"

"Let's see, you live in your office, don't take vacations, haven't bought any substantial purchases outside of your house and two cars, which was, what? Four years ago?" Max ticked off the list on his fingers. "Not

to mention that trust fund Dad set up that you probably have never looked at."

Max was dead-on, but Derek refused to say so. "Whatever. I've already decided to help. Alexis said she'd cover the down payments on the houses."

Trey whistled. "That's some dedication. Speaking of Alexis, how are you two doing?"

He shrugged. "Fine. I keep telling you it's not that kind of relationship." *Then why did you tell her you wanted more?* an annoying inner voice chimed.

Max stroked his chin and smiled. "I totally forgot about that marriage proposal. Has she changed her mind?"

Trey whipped his head in Derek's direction. "Marriage proposal? Hold up. When did that happen?"

Derek sighed.

Max laughed. "You didn't tell Trey? He proposed they have a businesslike marriage for the baby's sake and she turned him down."

Trey shook his head. "Derek, we talked about this. Why would you want to offer her the same type of relationship you've been angry about all your life? It's easy to see that Alexis cares about you, and I know you care about her."

He buried his head in his hands. "Yes, I care about Alexis." If he were being honest, he'd admit that he'd begun to fall for her. But he couldn't do it, could *not* risk his heart.

"Let go, Derek. Kiara is the best thing that ever happened to me and I'm glad I took the risk," his older brother said. "I believe the same about Alexis for you."

"I feel something for her, but I don't know if I can give her what she wants."

"Maybe you should do like we suggested to Trey when he was falling for Kiara," Max stated.

A slow grin made its way across Trey's mouth. "I have to agree with Max. There's nothing like a getaway to put things in perspective. And you can use my jet." Trey had purchased the aircraft when he'd made his first few millions.

Derek thought for a moment. He did have an island hideaway in the Bahamas that would be perfect. He'd gone only twice since having the house built four years ago.

"If you need some options of where to take her—"

"I already have a place on Andros Island in the Bahamas."

Trey grabbed his cell from the table. "What day do you want to leave? I'll let my pilot know."

"I should probably see if Alexis agrees to go first, before you get the jet gassed up."

"You might want to leave soon. Thanksgiving is in a couple weeks."

As was the dinner with Reginald that Derek had consented to attend. "I'll let you know tomorrow, Trey." He owned his company and his senior agents were more than capable of filling in, so leaving wouldn't be a problem. With Alexis deciding to retire from modeling, he hoped it wouldn't be an issue for her, either. And he'd be sure to have some of those chocolate-covered strawberries on hand.

"See, wasn't that easier this time?" Alexis eased the car onto the road Saturday after their yoga class.

Charlene grunted and rolled her eyes. "I don't know

how you people get your bodies in all those crazy positions. *Yoga* is another word for contortionist sport."

Alexis laughed. "You did great and the more you do it, the more flexible you'll become."

"Hey, I wasn't flexible as a kid, so I know this thirty-two-year-old body isn't going to miraculously change." Her friend leaned her head against the back of the seat. "By the way, are you supposed to be doing all this now?"

"Yes, but I'll most likely enroll in one of the prenatal yoga classes." She'd talked to her instructor, who had given her a brochure and suggested she transition soon, as some of the positions weren't suggested for pregnant women.

"Thank goodness. That means I'll be spared from the torture for a while. Although a couple of the positions might work well for a night with a hot guy."

"Speaking of hot guys, how did your date with Sterling go?"

"We went out for dinner and it started off kind of rocky. At first, he came off as some stuffed shirt whose kisses would likely be as stiff as him. I'm happy to say I was wrong on both counts. He has a great sense of humor and is only three years older than me. And his kisses...oh, my *goodness*! The man knows his way around a woman's mouth and it makes me wonder about the rest."

Alexis slanted her an amused glance and refocused on the road. "Does that mean you two are going out again for free?"

"Absolutely," Charlene said, doing a little dance in her seat. "He also said he'd give me some ideas on build-

ing personal wealth and see what he could do to help put the word out about my organization."

She listened to the excitement in her friend's voice and felt a pang of envy. Alexis wished she and Derek could share an open and carefree relationship not hindered by fears and past baggage.

"Is Derek still coming around?"

"We went out to dinner a couple of nights ago."

Charlene sat up and twisted in her seat. "As in like a *date* kind of dinner?"

"Yes, and he said he wants us to be together."

"Ha! I knew he was into you for more than just the baby."

"Maybe, but I told him we should take it slowly, day by day, and see how things go." Though memories of that chocolate strawberry had her wanting to throw caution to the wind. "I'll admit he might have some feelings for me, but I still believe this is all about duty and doing what he thinks is right."

"And you? How do you feel about him?" When Alexis didn't reply, Charlene said, "You're falling for him."

Alexis pulled into her driveway and parked. She turned to face Charlene. "Yeah. In spite of all my resolve *not* to fall, it's not working." From the moment their eyes connected during the ultrasound, she'd been a goner.

"If he's as great a guy as you said, I can understand why."

"Char, you should've seen him when we went for the ultrasound. The look on his face is one I'll never for-

get. He stayed right by me and reassured me at every turn. Since then, he's acted as if we were a real couple."

"Then it's possible he does want you two to be a real couple."

"We'll see." She opened the car door and her cell chimed. She checked the display and smiled.

"Derek?" Charlene stopped at her car, which she'd left in Alexis's driveway before they went to class, and put her bag inside.

"No, an old friend from my modeling days. Give me a minute." Alexis connected as she walked to the front door. "Khalil Gray, I haven't talked to you in ages. How are you?"

Khalil chuckled. "Hey, Alexis. It has been a long time. I'm good, and you?"

"Same. Is this a checking-on-an-old-friend call or something else?"

"How about we call it both. I see you're still in the business."

"Actually, I decided to call it a career. I probably should have done it when you did." She and Khalil had been paired on several modeling assignments and they'd developed a close friendship. It saddened her when he'd quit six years ago, because he was her favorite male model to work with. They had an easy rapport and neither of them liked drama, so shoots always ran smoothly.

"Now that you're a lady of leisure, how busy is your schedule?"

"I just started working with a nonprofit organization, but I have time. What do you need?"

"It's last-minute and I apologize, but next Saturday

I'm hosting a teen modeling summit. Most of the kids are just starting out and I want them to know what to expect—the good, bad and ugly. I was hoping you could talk to the young ladies about maintaining healthy eating habits with the strict industry requirements. The person originally scheduled was called away on an assignment."

Khalil had started a youth modeling foundation a few years ago that offered scholarships to help pay for parental travel, and worked with the teens to find balance, keep up with schoolwork and not fall into drugs and other destructive behaviors.

Alexis placed her bag on a chair in her family room. She mouthed to Charlene to help herself to something to drink. "I'd love to. What time?"

"The summit will run from eight to five, but your session will start at ten and run about an hour and a half."

"All right. Send me all the details. You still have my email address?"

"I do. I can't tell you how much I appreciate this, Alexis. We'll have to catch up and you can meet my wife."

"*Wife?* When did you get married?"

Khalil's laughter came through the line. "A little over a year ago. My baby is a petite fireball and she keeps me in line."

"Wow. Congratulations. I can't wait to meet her." Alexis remembered him saying he'd never marry, so his wife must be a special lady. Alexis had said the same thing after Julian, and now her life was more complicated than ever.

"I won't keep you. Thanks again. If you have any questions, give me a call."

"Okay. Chat with you later." Her smile was still in place when she hung up. Khalil Gray married. She joined Charlene at the bar and shared the details of the phone call.

"You're the perfect person for that session."

"I am. I'll try not to scare them, but I have to be honest." Alexis poured herself a glass of orange juice. "Are you hungry? I need something to snack on."

"Not really, but I will be in about an hour," Charlene said with a little laugh. "Back to Derek. Have you talked to him about the way you're feeling?"

"No, and I don't know if it's a good idea." She decided on half an apple, a handful of grapes, cheese and crackers. She arranged everything on a plate and placed it between herself and Charlene. She was two bites in when her doorbell rang.

"You're pretty popular today."

"Whatever, girl. I'll be right back." She placed a small piece of cheese on a cracker and ate it on the way. She opened the door to find Derek standing on the other side. "Derek. Hey."

"Hey. Can I come in for a minute?"

"Sure."

"I won't keep you long." Derek gestured to Charlene's car. "I see you have a guest."

"Charlene is here. Come on back to the kitchen."

His gaze roamed over her. "Going to work out?"

"Just got back."

Charlene paused in the middle of eating a grape and smiled. "You must be Derek. I'm Charlene," she said,

not waiting for an introduction. She wiped her hands on a napkin and extended the right one.

"Nice to meet you, Charlene. You were with Alexis at the rent-a-bachelor event."

"Yes, I was. I have to say it was one of the most creative fund-raisers I've ever attended." Charlene divided a glance between Derek and Alexis. "I'm sure you two want to talk, so I'll get out of your hair."

"You don't have to leave," Derek said. "I only stopped by for a minute." He faced Alexis. "I just need to ask you something."

"Let's go out on the deck." They started in that direction and Alexis turned back.

Charlene pretended to swoon and gave Alexis the thumbs-up sign.

Alexis rolled her eyes, shook her head and followed Derek outside. He closed the sliding glass door behind him and she immediately became suspicious. "Is something wrong?"

"Not at all." He stood next to her against the railing. "Do you have a busy week coming up?"

"No. I was hoping we could go look at a few more houses one of the days, and I'm going to do a session at a teen modeling summit on Saturday morning."

Derek moved closer, leaving a mere inch between them. "Would you go away with me for a few days?"

"Are you speaking at another conference?"

"No conferences, no meetings. Just you, me and a beautiful island for five days."

She really should tell him no, especially since realizing her feelings ran deeper than she'd originally

thought. Five days alone with him would be so dangerous to her heart. "Where is this island?"

"Andros Island in the Bahamas." He tucked her hair behind her ear, bent and placed a kiss on the spot on her neck he'd bared. "Miles of white sandy beaches, exceptional natural surroundings, a villa so close to the ocean you can taste the salt water, eighty degree temperatures, personal service…" Derek lifted his head. "And me taking care of you, touching you, kissing you and doing whatever else you desire."

Pack your bags, girl! "Yes," she breathed. "When do we leave?"

A sexy grin tilted the corner of his mouth. "Monday morning. It might be easier if we stayed in one house tomorrow night. The drive to LAX is going to be a mess, as always."

She had been to his house only the one time and she was curious about how the rest of it looked. "Yours. You owe me a tour, anyway," she added.

"You're right and I'll make sure you get it." He placed a gentle kiss on her lips. "I'll let you and Charlene get back to your food." Derek opened the door, stepped back inside and closed it behind Alexis. "I'll let you know what time we're leaving after I talk to Trey."

"Are he and Kiara going?"

"No. We're using his jet."

Alexis glanced over in time to see Charlene's mouth drop. "That's nice of him."

Derek nodded. "You don't have to walk me out. I'll see you later, baby."

As soon as Alexis heard the front door close, she turned to Charlene. "Not one word."

"Ooh-wee, a *private jet*? And now you're his *baby*? So much for taking things slow." She popped a grape into her mouth.

Alexis had caved before he finished his pitch. Yeah, so much for that.

Chapter 15

Derek had debated with himself all last night and the first part of Sunday morning about visiting Reginald and had decided to get it over with. He sat parked in Reginald's driveway for a good five minutes before finally getting out and going to the door.

When Reginald opened the door, his face registered surprise and then happiness. "Derek. Come in, son. I was about to have some lunch. Care to join me?"

"No, thanks." He followed his father to a screened-in porch, where a fortysomething-year-old woman stood placing food on a table that seated four.

"This is Mrs. McBride. She helps me out here at the house. Mrs. McBride, this is my son Derek." He pulled out his chair and sat.

She smiled pleasantly. "It's a pleasure to meet you, Derek."

"Same here."

"Would you like me to bring you a plate?"

"No, thank you."

Reginald gestured for Derek to sit. "You've never

visited me before," he said, starting in on a small bowl of soup. His hand shook slightly, but he guided the spoon to his lips without mishap.

"I came by to see how you were doing."

"Some days are pretty good, others not so much. So far, today hasn't been bad. My appetite comes and goes." He continued eating the soup. "But Mrs. McBride's soups tend to be easy on my stomach."

Derek didn't want to be moved by his father's predicament, but found it touched him nonetheless. Because he'd never spent any time with Reginald, Derek searched his mind for a topic of conversation.

"How's business? I saw that you've got two development projects going."

"Both are luxury condos with room for office space on the first floor. They're scheduled to be ready for occupancy next year."

"I sure wish I could be around to see them."

"Maybe you will. The doctors aren't always right."

"Maybe. You and Alexis back together after all these years?"

Derek was caught off guard by the abrupt change in topic. "Sort of...not really. It's complicated." He wanted to jump in with both feet, but a huge part of him was still afraid she'd walk away. "She's pregnant."

Reginald's eyebrows shot up and he set the spoon in the bowl.

"And I plan to be there."

"Unlike I was."

"I didn't say that." Though he definitely thought it.

Reginald sighed. "You didn't have to, Derek. I never did right by your mother or you and I regret it more than

you know. And now I have a grandchild coming that I won't live to see."

Derek reined in his anger. The visit was supposed to be about checking on the old man and then leaving, not rehashing old history. "It's water under the bridge and I didn't come here to discuss that." He peered at his watch. "I'm going out of town tomorrow and I have a few things to take care of."

A look of panic crossed Reginald's face. "Are you still planning to come to Thanksgiving dinner?"

"Yes. I'll only be gone until Friday." Thanksgiving was two weeks away. Although he had some lingering reservations, he'd said he would be there and always kept his word. He waited until Reginald ate the last spoonful before saying, "I need to get going." He stood. Reginald made a move to stand and stumbled. Derek reached out to steady him, again filling with emotions. "Why don't you sit back down? I can find my way out."

He waved Derek off. "I'm okay."

As they walked to the front, Derek kept his steps slow to match his father's pace.

Reginald held the door open. "All is not well between us and I know most of it is my fault, but I really enjoyed this visit." He looked as if he wanted to say more, but didn't.

Derek placed a gentle hand on his shoulder. "Take it easy and I'll see you when I get back." In his car, he inhaled deeply and let the breath out slowly. He had waited his entire life for his father to acknowledge the crappy way he had treated Derek and his mother. He had practiced all the ways he would clap back and yet, when he had the opportunity, couldn't do it. His mother

would have been proud. She'd told him a long time ago that he couldn't control someone else's actions and, by responding negatively, he'd only hurt himself. Derek had enough hurts to last him two lifetimes, and just maybe, by keeping his mouth shut, he wouldn't add another wound.

When Derek got home, he gathered everything he planned to take on his trip and packed. He wanted to be done by the time he picked up Alexis so they would have some uninterrupted time together. An hour later, Derek sent Alexis a text to let her know he'd be there to pick her up at five, and asked her to choose where she wanted to stop for dinner. He figured it would be easier than cooking. He had planned to grocery shop over the weekend before deciding on the trip, so he didn't have much in the way of fresh vegetables and other perishable foods, and all his meat was in the freezer.

He took a few minutes to boot up his laptop, and clicked on the email from Trey detailing where Derek needed to go once they reached the airport. Next, he emailed their arrival time to his housekeeper. She would take care of preparing the meals, but he sent her a short list of snacks, including the strawberries.

Once again that erotic encounter rushed back to him. He grew harder with each lustful vision. He'd wanted to take Alexis upstairs and make love to her until they both were satisfied. Derek vowed to make that fantasy a reality. They had five days and he intended to take full advantage of each one.

Derek placed Alexis's suitcases at the base of the stairs. "We should probably do the tour first."

"Probably," Alexis agreed. The last time they had gotten distracted.

"We'll start down here and work our way up."

She followed him down a short hallway where there were two bedrooms that shared a bathroom. He had converted the larger of the rooms into a state-of-the-art home gym and had as much equipment as the place where she had her yoga class. "Very nice." He flipped on the light switch in the room across the hall, where he'd set up a home office. He had a large mahogany desk, matching bookshelves, comfortable-looking black leather desk chairs and sofa. Alexis scanned the room and noticed a small refrigerator in the corner. "Between the gym and this office, you never have to leave your house."

"I like the convenience of having everything in one place." Derek shrugged. "Anytime you want to work out, you're welcome to use the room. Maybe just for walking on the treadmill, for now," he amended.

Alexis smiled. "I'll let you know. Where to next?"

"Upstairs." Derek stopped to grab her bags and ascended the steps. He placed them in front of double doors.

There were four bedrooms upstairs, three of which sat empty. She glanced up at him questioningly.

"I haven't decided what to put in them, but with the baby coming, we can use the one closest to my bedroom for a nursery."

Nursery? She hadn't even gotten that far in her thought process, yet Derek had already started planning. She surveyed the room. "It's a good size that can grow with him or her."

"I'll let you choose the furnishings and decorations.

If you want to paint the room a different color, we can do that, too."

Currently, the walls were the standard eggshell, but she would like to change it. "I'm thinking something soft, in the green or blue family, will be calming and nurturing."

Derek studied her a long moment. "We can go look at some swatches whenever you're ready." He took her bags into his room and set the larger one on a bench at the foot of the bed and the smaller carry-on on the bed.

Alexis's gaze roamed around the large space. One side held a big bed that looked to be custom sized to fit his height, pairs of dressers and night tables, a flat-screen television mounted on the wall and a sophisticated sound system. Two comfortable loungers with a small table placed between them and a gas fireplace dominated the other side. She spied a balcony through the partially open drapes. "You like a lot of space, don't you?"

He chuckled. "I do. You'll have to sleep in here, since none of the other rooms have beds. Sorry."

"Uh-huh. You're not sorry," she said, trying to hide her smile. "If you were sorry, you would've mentioned that you only had one bed yesterday." She had hoped to sleep somewhere other than with him. However, that the rooms held no furniture negated that choice, and in hindsight, she wished she would have told him they'd stay at her house. Both her spare bedrooms were furnished.

Granted, his tall body might not have fit comfortably in the queen-size beds, but she could have let him have her bed while she slept elsewhere. Not that she thought he'd go for that. Alexis wanted to avoid making love

with him again for as long as she could. Each intimate touch and kiss brought her closer to the edge of falling completely in love with him. She couldn't take having a repeat of her last relationship failure under the exact same circumstances.

A sexy grin spread across his mouth. "What can I say? I've been looking forward to holding you in my arms all night again."

That was exactly what she wanted to prevent. "Are we going to eat? The food is probably getting cold." They had called in an order at a neighborhood Mexican restaurant.

Alexis turned to leave and he gently grasped her hand and gathered her in his embrace. "You don't like it when I hold you, Alexis?" Derek tilted her chin and focused his gaze on her.

I love it. "No…yes." His eyebrow rose. She sighed. "I like it fine, but I don't want that to be all that's between us." The undeniable chemistry they had would make it easy to fall into a physical relationship. Alexis had never been able to separate her emotions.

"Sweetheart, we talked about this at the restaurant and I told you that's not all I wanted, either. We both know there's more going on here than being connected by the baby. Let's do as you suggested and take each day as it comes. I'm not going to lie and say that I won't try to seduce you the first chance I get, but I promise to be sure you're comfortable with whatever direction we decide."

See, that's what I'm talking about. This *is why I can't resist him.* "I know you will, Derek, and I appreciate that."

He caressed her face, brushed his lips across hers and led her out and down to the kitchen. They filled their plates and sat at the kitchen table placed in a nook that overlooked the ocean. "What do you want to drink?"

"I'll have some water, please." Alexis cut into her chicken enchilada with ranchero sauce and brought a bite to her mouth. She hadn't been to the restaurant in such a long time and the food tasted as good as she remembered. "I've missed these enchiladas."

Derek brought her water, a Corona beer for himself, and slid into the chair. "It's my favorite restaurant and I order the same thing every time I go. I tell myself I'm going to try something new and end up with my green chili chicken enchiladas, rice and beans."

"I hear you." She bit into a chip.

After a few minutes, he said, "I've been meaning to ask what you're going to do for Thanksgiving."

"Spending it with my parents in Lakewood. They moved three years ago when my mom's telecommunications corporation transferred their business there." Her mother worked as an electrical engineer. "My dad said if he couldn't find a position at one of the universities close by, he'd just retire, since he's gotten his thirty years in. He said he was too old to commute an hour and a half each way every day."

Derek laughed. "Did he find one?"

"Yep. And he was *not* happy at first. I think he'd already shifted his mind into retirement mode. He's not teaching this semester, though. He and my mother are on one of those sixteen-day cruises to the Caribbean, Panama Canal and Mexico. They're due back on Tuesday."

"They don't know about the baby?"

"Not yet. I guess it's going to be Happy Thanksgiving and You're Going to Be Grandparents all in one greeting. Have you told your mom?"

"Not yet. I may be having the same holiday conversation."

"So, you're spending the holiday with your father and brothers."

His smiled faded. "Yeah. I'll visit with my mom for a while, too."

Just like at the fund-raiser, she could feel his tension. "How do you feel about going?"

He didn't reply immediately. "I'm still not sure. I did it partly to get Max and Trey off my back, and it's not looking good for Reginald."

Alexis fought back tears. Reginald Moore seemed to finally realize that he loved his son and now might not have the opportunity to fully reconcile with him. She remembered the look of relief on his face when Derek had said he'd come to dinner. "I can't begin to imagine what you're going through, but if you need me, I'm here."

"Thanks, but I'm good."

She didn't push because she knew that men didn't often share their pain. He had opened up to her more than she'd expected. "Okay, subject change. This is our favorite food and we should table the heavy conversation until later."

Derek gave her a small smile. "What do you want to talk about?"

Alexis shrugged. "I don't know. What about some music?"

He took his phone out of his pocket, pushed a few buttons and music flowed through hidden speakers. "Anything particular you want to listen to? I have it on an R & B station."

"Oh, no. I'm good with Jill Scott living her life like it's golden," she said, bobbing her head. "Now we can eat." She forked up some rice and winked at Derek.

His smile returned.

They finished the meal while conversing about anything and nothing. "That was much better."

"I agree."

"Ooh! I love this song." Alexis jumped out of her chair, danced around to his side of the table and pulled him up. "Come dance with me." The popular Bruno Mars song was a couple years old, but she still enjoyed dancing to it.

"Alexis. I don't really... I haven't danced in a long time."

"No time like the present to dust off the cobwebs. And it's just you and me here, so if you embarrass yourself no one will know. I won't tease you. Wait." She stopped dancing and tapped her finger against her chin. "Well, maybe not too much."

Derek grabbed her hand. "Just dance, woman."

They laughed and danced to song after song, then the music changed to a soft ballad. He held her close as they swayed to the slow beat.

"I could hold you this way all night," he whispered against her ear.

"And I'd let you." Their eyes met and she lost another part of her heart.

Chapter 16

Derek draped his arm around Alexis's shoulders as the driver took them through the unspoiled lands of Andros Island to his house late Monday afternoon.

"This is fabulous. I can't get over how beautiful and peaceful this place is. How did you find it?"

"The company I worked for when I was starting out sent me and another agent to Nassau to meet with a developer about building a resort here on Andros. After doing some exploring on my own, I asked about building a house. We located what I thought was the perfect spot and got it done."

"How many bedrooms?"

He smiled. "Four. It's a little less square footage than the Malibu house, though."

She shook her head. "But I bet not by much."

He pointed. "See, set back behind the trees?"

Alexis leaned to one side. "*That's* the house?" When he nodded, she said, "I thought you said it was smaller."

"It is." The driver pulled up on the side and Derek got out. The white two-story colonial structure had ve-

randas on both levels. He'd had several trees planted on the property and they served not only as shade, but also as a means of privacy. They offered enough coverage to maintain the personal sanctuary he'd wanted without obstructing the view of the water.

He helped Alexis out while the driver carried their bags to the porch. Derek tipped the man and thanked him, then unlocked the door and moved back so Alexis could enter first.

"I figured we'd have to uncover furniture and air out the place, but it looks as if you've only been gone for a few hours. There isn't a speck of dust and it smells fresh."

"I let my housekeeper know when we were arriving and she took care of everything."

Alexis went from room to room on the first level. "Almost every one has some view of the ocean—the office, kitchen nook."

Derek took quiet joy in the happiness radiating from Alexis's face as she explored the place. "Ready to see upstairs?"

"Absolutely." Once they'd toured the bedrooms on the second level, she stared curiously at the long hallway. "Where does this lead?"

"You'll see." He gestured her forward. At the end sat French doors. "Open them."

She opened the doors and stepped out onto a veranda that ran almost the length of the house. She spun around. "You know you're going to have to pry me out of here with a crowbar. That white sand looks inviting. Can we go for a walk?"

He frowned. "Why don't you rest for a little while, then we'll go."

"I slept on the plane, remember? You have to thank Trey for me. That bed in the back of the jet was perfect."

"I'll tell him. Are you sure you're up to it?" Although the ultrasound showed the baby to be progressing well, Derek had done some reading about miscarriage and didn't want to do anything that might overtax her.

"Women have been birthing babies since forever, some in stressful environments we can't even imagine. A little walk on the beach isn't going to hurt anything."

"But—"

"If I let the anxiety of thinking I might lose this baby consume me, I'd never leave the bed until it was born." Alexis reached up and caressed the side of his face. "Baby, I'm fine."

He went still. She'd never called him "baby" before and the endearment made his chest tighten with emotion. "You win." He would do anything to make her smile. Back downstairs, they took a moment to remove their shoes, then made their way hand in hand toward the water.

"The sky is so clear and blue. How often do you come here?"

"I've only been twice since I had the house built four years ago. You're the only person who knows about this place, other than my mother and brothers."

She stared at him incredulously. "You really need to get out of your office more. That was one of the things I loved most about modeling—getting to visit so many beautiful countries. We didn't always have time to sight-see, but the locales were wonderful."

"Maybe now I'll have more of a reason to come." Derek wouldn't mind walking with her like this every

day. *Where the hell did that thought come from?* Every day meant some kind of permanency and he didn't do forever, or at least that's what he told himself. Lately, his mind and heart were running in opposite directions. His head told him to stick to his guns—*people always leave*—while his heart tried to convince him to let go and take the risk. As a result, he had no clue what to do.

Alexis stopped, lifted her face to the sky and closed her eyes. She inhaled deeply and released the breath slowly, repeating the process several more times. At length, she opened her eyes and smiled up at Derek. "Thank you for bringing me to your special place."

In that moment, Derek felt the scale tip slightly toward his heart. Unable to resist, he lowered his head, covered her mouth in a tender kiss and tried to convey just how much she was coming to mean to him. "We should start back." They had walked a ways from the house and he didn't want to tire her out.

"I'd like to do this again tomorrow."

"We can come every day and as often as you want, baby."

Giving him another radiant smile that made his heart clench, she threaded her fingers through his and they headed back to the house.

"Do I smell food cooking?" Alexis asked, as they reached his place.

He opened the door and waved her in. "Yep. Dinner." She gave him a look and he laughed. "My housekeeper."

"Oh. That's really nice of her. Is this sort of a welcome dinner?"

"No," he answered with a chuckle. "She'll be here all week to cook breakfast, dinner and lunch if we're here."

"Whatever she's cooking smells good."

"I guarantee it'll taste as good."

Alexis grinned. "I can't wait. In the meantime, I want to shower and relax." She started toward the stairs and turned back. "Oh, and like I said before, you're going to have to drag me out of here on Friday." She kissed his cheek. "It's wonderful, and so are you."

The scale tilted further.

Alexis stood under the warm spray and asked herself for the hundredth time why she'd told Derek he was wonderful. Not that he wasn't, but saying those kinds of things revealed too much. She chalked it up to her surroundings—blue skies, crystal clear water, pristine sand. And that sweet kiss near the ocean. Who wouldn't get caught up? She couldn't believe he'd been here only twice. If she had a place like this, she'd come as often as possible.

A wave of fatigue hit her. Alexis finished washing, dried off and donned a long sundress. She unpinned her hair, brushed it and pulled it into a ponytail.

Yawning, she stepped into the master bedroom and froze. Derek lay sprawled across the huge bed— one hand thrown over his head and the other on his stomach—wearing only a pair of basketball shorts, and sound asleep. *Guess I'm not the only one who's exhausted.* Alexis tiptoed toward the bed and studied him. Even in sleep, his features hadn't relaxed and she wanted to smooth the lines away.

She stood there a minute longer, debating whether to join him in here or go to one of the other rooms. Unlike the Malibu house, all the bedrooms here had fur-

niture. She sighed resignedly. "Who am I kidding?" she muttered under her breath, carefully climbing onto the bed so as not to disturb him. She wanted to be right here next to him.

Alexis scooted close to him and inhaled his clean scent. He'd obviously showered in one of the other bathrooms. She made herself comfortable, closed her eyes and drifted off.

A while later, Alexis's eyes fluttered open. It took her a moment to get her bearings and then she realized that, sometime during her nap, she'd shifted and now lay with her head on Derek's chest and her arm across his midsection. She slowly lifted her head and met his dark gaze. "Hey. How long have you been awake?"

"About fifteen minutes. You were sleeping so peacefully and you need the rest. I didn't want to move or wake you."

"That's the same thing I thought about you when I came out of the shower." The clock showed that she had been asleep for almost an hour.

Derek ran a hand over his head. "Yeah, I guess I was tired. But now I'm starving."

"Me, too." Alexis sat up and slid to the edge of the bed. She redid her ponytail, then searched through her luggage for a pair of flat sandals. She waited while Derek pulled on a shirt, and they went downstairs to the kitchen. The fragrant smells wafted into her nose. A petite brown-skinned woman who looked to be in her fifties met them with a smile.

The woman opened her arms. "Welcome home, Derek," she said in accented English. After embracing

him, she wagged a finger his way. "You've been away a long time. You should come more often."

He chuckled and gestured to Alexis. "She said the same thing. Ms. Eliana, this is Alexis."

"It's nice to meet you, Ms. Eliana." Alexis expected a polite nod, but the woman grabbed her up in a crushing hug that belied her small size.

"I'm so happy to meet you, too. Come, dinner is ready."

"It smells heavenly," Alexis said as she followed her to the elegantly set table for two out on the veranda.

Ms. Eliana brought out several dishes. "I hope you enjoy. There's steamed chicken, peas n' rice, coleslaw and johnnycake. Derek, I made sure you have plenty of fried plantains."

Derek smiled. "Thank you." After Ms. Eliana departed, he said to Alexis, "Go ahead and fix your plate first."

"I think I'm going to hurt myself with all this food." She added small portions of everything to her plate as a precaution.

"That's all you're going to eat?" He heaped servings from each dish onto his plate.

"Just making sure it agrees with me, so don't you eat up everything."

Derek laughed. "No promises. I'm going to have to work out like a dog when I get home after eating like this all week."

Alexis propped her elbows on the table, rested her head in her hands. "You wouldn't have to if you took smaller portions."

"I'll make the sacrifice if I can get food this good." He saluted her with his full fork.

"You do have a point." It tasted so good, particularly the johnnycake and plantains, that she ended up taking more of everything and eating every single bite. She groaned. "This was the best food I've had in a while."

"I told you." He rubbed his hand over his stomach. "We can go upstairs and relax on the veranda."

"I can't move. I think I'm going to just sleep here tonight." Alexis leaned her head back and closed her eyes.

"These chairs aren't made for sleeping."

"I don't care," she murmured. Her eyes snapped open when she felt herself being lifted in the air. "What are you doing?"

He didn't stop walking. "You said you couldn't move, so being the gentleman I am, I'm carrying you upstairs. I don't recall you protesting the last time I carried you."

"That was a long time ago, and I can't believe you remembered that." Alexis had twisted her ankle, stepping on a sprinkler head when she'd cut across the grass in the high school quad. Derek had materialized out of nowhere, swooped her up and carried her all the way to the nurse's office.

"You'd be surprised by what I remember." Out on the veranda, he lowered himself into one of the loungers and positioned her between his outstretched legs. He dropped a kiss on her hair and wrapped his arms around her.

She snuggled deeper into his embrace, marveling at the level of contentment she felt. She didn't know how long they sat there before his hands began to roam over her thighs and hips. One hand moved higher until it

reached her belly. He paused and rested it there for several seconds, his gentle caresses stirring her innermost emotions. Alexis angled her face toward his, pulled his head down and kissed him with all he made her feel.

Derek groaned and took over the kiss with a hunger that stunned them both. Without breaking the seal of their mouths, he hiked up her dress and shifted her until she was straddling him. His hands went to the button on the front of her dress and pushed the thin straps off her shoulders. His eyes lit with desire when he discovered she didn't have on a bra. He kissed his way down to her breasts and suckled, first one, then the other. "I can't get enough of touching you and kissing you." He captured her mouth again with hungry urgency.

She couldn't, either. The solid ridge of his erection pressed firmly against her center and she gyrated her hips, trying to get closer. Any notion she had of taking things slow faded with each stroke of his tongue on hers. He palmed her backside and ground his body into hers. Shockwaves of pleasure shot through Alexis. She reached beneath his shirt and ran her hands over the hard planes of his abs and chest.

"Need some help?" He whipped the shirt over his head and tossed it aside.

She gave him a sassy smile and did the same with her dress. "Two can play that game."

"I'm counting on it." Derek fisted his hands in her hair and gently tugged her head back and stared again. He alternately kissed and suckled her neck, shoulders and breasts.

Alexis cried out at the exquisite torture, then treated

him to the same wanton caresses. She reached inside his shorts and wrapped her hand around his thick erection.

Derek jerked upward and muttered a curse. After another few seconds, breathing harshly, he stilled her hand. "Ease up for a minute, baby."

She raised herself slightly and he rid himself of his shorts and underwear, then hooked his thumbs in the waistband of her bikini panties and slid them down and off. Before she could draw her next breath, he lifted her and entered her with one long thrust. They both moaned.

Locking his eyes on her, Derek started with slow, circling movements. He guided her hips as he kept up the measured, insistent rhythm. Alexis shuddered at the feel of him sliding in and out of her at the unhurried pace. She'd never been made love to with such tenderness and the sheer magnitude of her emotions brought tears to her eyes. "Derek," she whispered.

He delved deeper with each rhythmic push, never taking his eyes off her or changing the pace.

Alexis dug her nails into his shoulders as her body trembled. She felt him everywhere, and the sensations were so staggering she thought she might pass out. He tilted her hips and surged upward. Without warning, an orgasm hit. She was seized by a rush of sensation so intense that her breath stalled in her lungs. She screamed his name. Her body shuddered uncontrollably as she gasped for air.

Moments later, Derek went rigid against her, threw his head back and exploded with a shout. Breathing harshly, he closed his eyes and dropped his head back against the lounger, tightening his arms around her.

Alexis collapsed against his shoulders, aftershocks still rocketing her body.

"My sweet Lexi."

He called her name with such reverence, the tears she'd been fighting spilled over. *I love you.*

Chapter 17

Alexis rolled over Saturday morning and saw an empty spot on the bed. After they returned from the Bahamas yesterday, Derek had ended up spending the night. She listened for sounds of him in the bathroom, but heard nothing.

She sat up and searched for him on her balcony and didn't see him. Frowning, she propped herself up on the pillow and saw a piece of paper. She read the note letting her know that he'd gone running, and placed it on the nightstand.

Alexis retrieved the folder with the information on Precious Ones from her tote, and noticed her cell. She'd tossed it in there at the airport at the start of the vacation and forgotten about it. She turned it on and climbed back into bed with the phone and folder. A series of buzzes sounded and she saw several missed calls from her mother, plus three messages, each more frantic than the previous one.

She pushed the button and waited for her mom to pick up.

"Alexis. Thank goodness. I've been calling you all week," her mother said.

"Hi, Mom. Sorry, I forgot to leave you a message letting you know I'd be out of town. How was the trip?"

"Oh, my. Fabulous. I told your father we have to do at least one cruise a year. I ate so much on the ship, I'm going to have to cut down for the next few days so I'll be ready for Thanksgiving."

Alexis laughed. "I'm glad you had a good time."

"You mentioned being out of town. I thought you said Paris would be your last assignment."

"It was. I wasn't working, more like on vacation."

"That's a first. How did it feel, being somewhere just for relaxation, and where did you go?"

"I went to the Bahamas and it was wonderful." So much so that she hadn't wanted to leave.

"Sounds like you enjoyed yourself. You probably would've had more fun if you had someone with you. I know Julian was enough to make a woman want to forget about love forever, but it's been a long time, sweetheart."

"Actually, I didn't go alone."

There was a slight pause. "Really? Was this one of those girl trips?"

"No," she said with a chuckle. "I went with Derek to his vacation house."

"Derek as in Derek Moore, the boy who had you crying for months after he left for college?"

Alexis knew her mother would bring that up. She had been so heartbroken when he told her he couldn't commit to anything because he had something to prove. "Yes, that Derek."

"I didn't know you two had kept in touch."

"We hadn't. Saw him at a fund-raiser in September."
She told her mother about the rent-a-bachelor initiative
and how she'd rented Derek for a night. "It was for a
good cause and I figured we could catch up."

"That's nice. Is he still in real estate?"

"Yes, and he has his own company. He's one of the
top brokers in the country."

Her mother's soft laughter came through the line.
"Well, he was always driven to be successful after that
mess with his father. So you've been dating since the
fund-raiser?"

"Not exactly." Alexis tried to figure out a delicate
way to handle the next piece of information. "We sort
of… I'm pregnant."

"What?" she fairly shouted.

She jerked the phone away from her ear. "I hope you
didn't wake Daddy."

"Honey, it's too early in the morning for this. I guess
you did more than catch up," her mother muttered. "It's
the twenty-first century. Neither of you thought about
protection?"

Alexis rolled her eyes and sighed. "Yes, Mom, we
did. The condom broke and I was on the pill. I just happened to fall in that minuscule percentage of women
that it failed. I'm at ten weeks." Her mother was silent
for so long, Alexis thought she'd hung up. "Mom?"

"I'm here. Just trying to process."

"Welcome to the club."

"And Derek. How did he take it?"

"About the same as you and I," she said with a wry
chuckle. She debated whether to tell her mother about

Derek's initial proposal and decided to do it. She had always been able to talk to her mother and valued her opinion...most times. "After he got over the shock, he came back the next day and said we should get married because it's the right thing to do. He wants the baby to grow up in a two-parent household."

"That's understandable. It makes me happy that he's owning up to his responsibilities. A lot of men would have done the opposite. Derek is also probably thinking about the way his father treated him, and doesn't want the same for his child."

"He said as much. So, do you think I should've agreed?"

"I can't answer that. I take it you turned him down."

"Yes. I told him if I decided to get married, it would be for love and not out of obligation." She still stood by that stance, but as they grew closer, felt some of her resistance draining.

"You love him."

"How did you know?"

"Moms always know," she said with a laugh. "I don't think you ever really stopped from high school. And how does he feel about you?"

"I have no idea."

"You two will find your way. If it's meant to be, it'll happen. Well, I need to get ready for work. We'll talk more next week. No matter what, Alexis, your father and I will be here. Love you, baby."

"I know. Love you, too, Mom." They spoke a moment longer, then ended the call.

Alexis briefly closed her eyes as a rush of emotions filled her. Yes, she loved him and wanted to wake up every morning next to him. After being with him this

week, she knew he felt something for her. But was it love, and if not, would it be enough to build a relationship?

Derek sat out on Alexis's balcony and watched the sunrise. The gray of night gave way to the pinks and oranges that signaled the start of a new day. He enjoyed this time of morning because it helped center his thoughts. Today, however, no matter how hard he tried, he couldn't get his mind off Alexis.

For the past three days and nights, they had behaved as if they were a real couple, and he found himself looking forward to what would come next. He especially enjoyed the nights, with her falling asleep lying on top of him, and the sex was off the charts, particularly the last round they'd had a couple hours ago. But underneath all the lovemaking, intimate dinners, quiet walks and relaxed conversations, the fear of it all going away had a grip on him, and he didn't know how to make it stop. The feelings Derek had for Alexis scared the hell out of him because, outside of his mother, he'd never let anyone get this close.

When he'd gone back inside, his heart swelled at the sight of Alexis curled up on the bed, sound asleep. It had taken all his willpower not to climb back into bed and he thought it best that he leave the room. Derek dressed in the bathroom, got his laptop and went downstairs. He poured himself a glass of juice, sat at the table and checked his emails. He couldn't remember the last time he'd gone more than a day without logging on, and he sighed upon seeing more than three hundred. He sipped the juice while scanning them for anything that might

be important. Derek responded to a few pressing matters at his company, added meeting dates to his calendar and deleted the junk mail. Everything else could wait until Monday.

After finishing his drink, Derek went outside, did a few warm-up stretches and started a slow jog. He'd left a note on the pillow letting Alexis know where he'd gone. The cool morning breeze let him know he wasn't in the Bahamas anymore. The temperatures there hadn't dipped below seventy and he already missed it. He increased his speed, and instead of his mind becoming clearer, the memories and emotions kept pace right alongside him. Derek changed direction. Now that they'd returned, nothing had been settled about their relationship, mainly due to his fears. Part of him had wanted to get off the island as quickly as possible to slow the rush of emotions that told him he was falling in love. But a larger part hadn't wanted to leave their idyllic paradise because it meant going back to the reality that he was still scared. Only he didn't know how he could go back to sleeping alone.

When he entered the sliding door from the deck, he saw Alexis sitting at the bar, eating. "Good morning."

Alexis smiled his way. "Good morning. You're up early."

"Figured I may as well get a jump on working off all the calories I consumed over the week." That was partly the truth. Ms. Eliana had kept them well-fed and left little treats or desserts every day, but his real reason for being up at the crack of dawn had little to do with food or calories. "What time do you want to leave for the teen modeling summit?" Derek hadn't been ready

to end their time together and volunteered to drive her to the event. He also wanted to get a glimpse of her in her element.

"It's seven fifteen now, so how about eight. I'd like to get there an hour before to get whatever details I need and to make sure the room has all the equipment set up. I made breakfast."

"Okay. Let me go clean up and then I'll eat."

After showering and eating, Derek needed to stop for gas, so they left a few minutes earlier than the planned time. They arrived at the hotel in Beverly Hills and followed the directions to the area where the summit was being held. He could hear lively chatter as they approached a large conference room. There had to be at least fifty teens standing around, talking in groups.

A man walked up to the podium. "Everyone take your seats and we'll begin the next session." He waited for everyone to settle, then introduced two people from a modeling agency. Afterward, he headed toward Derek and Alexis with a broad smile. "We can talk in the hallway."

They stepped out and he closed the door, then hugged Alexis. "It's good to see you. You haven't changed one bit. I appreciate you filling in at the last moment."

"No problem. You look good and I like the beard." Alexis touched his face.

He grinned and extended his hand to Derek. "I'm Khalil Gray."

"Derek Moore." Derek wondered if what he felt could be termed jealousy. The way Khalil spoke and touched Alexis made Derek want to punch the man in his face.

He forced himself to remember that the two had been friends for a long time.

"Khalil, this is a great turnout," Alexis said. "I wish we'd had someone to talk to us when we started."

"I hear you." He answered her questions about the room, then said, "I need to check on a few things, but I'll be back before your session starts."

She nodded. After he left she turned to Derek. "No need to give Khalil the death glare. We're only friends and he's married."

"I don't know what you're talking about," he grumbled.

Alexis shook her head and kissed his cheek.

Derek relaxed and a grin stole over his face. She always knew how to make him smile. They slipped inside and sat in the back of the room.

When Khalil introduced Alexis, the first thing she did was have them rearrange the room so that she could sit with the teens. She shared her story, expressed the importance of self-care and maintaining a healthy support system.

Derek was mesmerized by the way she interacted with them, and the fact that she sat in their midst, instead of on the stage, spoke volumes. Her easy rapport with them confirmed what he already knew—she would make a phenomenal mother. Her beautiful laughter floated across the room and he felt the same tug on his heart that he'd been trying to deny. He'd fallen in love with her.

Chapter 18

Derek sat in his home office Thursday afternoon finishing up a couple contracts before going over to Reginald's for Thanksgiving dinner. He'd spent the morning with his mother and, after grilling him for twenty minutes, she had expressed her joy at becoming a grandmother, as well as the fact that Alexis was the mother. He got up and went for a cup of coffee—his third of the day—to keep him awake. He hadn't slept well for the past five nights, ever since he dropped Alexis off on Saturday. Somehow, after less than a week, the solitary life he'd led didn't seem as appealing. Derek thought about calling her, but she had spent last night with her parents and he didn't want to interrupt their time. Alexis had said she would be back early in the evening, so he'd talk to her then. He wanted to know how her parents took the news of her pregnancy. On some level, he felt he should have been there.

He set the cup on his desk and picked up the next contract to review. He was midway through the first

page when his cell rang. "What's up, Trey?" he said, activating the speakerphone.

"Reginald's been rushed to the hospital. It doesn't look good."

Derek's pen stilled. "What happened?"

"I don't know. I was already halfway out to Malibu for dinner when Max called. He didn't have many details, just that Reginald hadn't been feeling well and was complaining of increased pain. I could tell that Max is pretty worried."

"What hospital?" Derek was already on his feet.

Trey rattled off the information. "I'll let you know if something changes before you get here. I should be pulling up in a minute."

"Okay. I'm on my way." He dumped the coffee and jogged up the stairs to grab his wallet. He sped out of the driveway less than a minute later. Fortunately, he didn't have far to go. While driving, Derek rationalized that his urgency had to do more with Max than Reginald, but somewhere over the past couple months getting to know his brothers, Derek had begun to open up to the possibility of having some type of relationship with his father. But it might be too late now, he thought grimly.

Derek parked in the hospital lot and went directly to emergency, assuming that's where Reginald would have been taken. He quickened his steps, rounded the corner and searched the waiting room for Trey or Max. Despite the holiday, several people sat waiting to be seen. He caught Trey's gaze and started toward him. Trey met him halfway. "Any word?"

"I just got a text from Max. He said the fever, chills

and pain might be from an infection because of Reginald's weak immune system."

"I wonder if they're going to keep him." They walked over to where Trey had been sitting.

Trey sank down and leaned his head back against the wall. "I always thought I wouldn't care whether Reginald lived or died, but now that's changed. With him staring death in the face, I'm thinking it's time to make peace with the past."

Derek had been thinking along similar lines. "I hear you, but I don't know how much of that is even possible. I can't just wipe from my mind the fact that the man refused to claim me and put my mother through hell."

The appearance of Max interrupted the conversation. Both men rose and rushed to meet him.

"Is he going to be okay?" Trey asked.

Max dragged a hand down his face and blew out a long breath. "The doctors seem to think so. Based on the test results, he does have an infection and they've already started antibiotics. They're getting ready to transfer him to a room, and you know he's not happy about having to stay after planning this dinner for so long."

Derek placed a hand on Max's shoulder. "How are you holding up?"

"I've been better. It feels like déjà vu. I remember going through the same thing with Mom." Silence stretched between them. "Anyway, they told me it would take about half an hour to get him settled. I'd rather not wait in here."

"We can go to the cafeteria." On the way out, Trey stopped at the desk to ask where they were transferring

Reginald. The receptionist made a call and relayed the information.

"Thanks," all three brothers said.

Once in the cafeteria, Derek asked, "You guys want something to drink?"

"Not unless it's a Scotch on the rocks," Trey said.

Max nodded as they sat at a nearby table. "Amen, my brother."

Derek couldn't agree more. For a few minutes they remained silent, each man lost in his own thoughts.

"Derek, you never said how your trip with Alexis went."

He glanced over at Trey. "We had a good time."

"A good time or a *good* time?" Max asked.

The week replayed in his mind. "The latter." He was still going through withdrawal, and waking up several times a night reaching for Alexis.

Trey scrutinized him a long moment. "Looks like you're ready to make a real proposal."

Derek frowned. "What makes you think that? I don't think spending a few days away qualifies for a life change."

"You were willing to make that life change without having any feelings, so it should be easier now that you've realized you love Alexis." Max shrugged.

He'd never said he loved Alexis, and neither Trey nor Max had been around him enough to figure that out.

"I take it you haven't told her."

"There's nothing to tell, Trey." Not yet, anyway. "We're still taking it slow."

Max cut him a look. "I bet there wasn't one moment of 'taking it slow' during that week."

Derek chuckled. "Actually, there were. We walked on the beach and talked." What stood out in his mind was the first night when they'd made love. That encounter gave new definition to *slow*, and the intense pace went well beyond just sex, connecting them on every level. The orgasm that followed had been unlike anything he'd ever experienced, and rocked him to his soul. Trey and Max laughed. "What?"

Max glanced at his watch and stood. "Those must have been some memories. Do yourself a favor and surrender. We should head up now."

Still chuckling, Trey clapped Derek on the back. "Surrender."

He shrugged off the hand and strode out the door. All playfulness subsided when they walked into Reginald's room. Various machines beeped and hummed, and an IV dripped a clear liquid into a vein through a needle placed in his left hand.

Reginald rolled his head toward the door and his eyes widened. "My boys," he whispered. "I was really looking forward to dinner. We've never—" His voice cracked with emotion.

Derek swallowed the lump in his throat.

Max moved to Reginald's side. "There's always Christmas, Dad. We'll be there."

He turned away and Derek saw him struggling to maintain his composure. He placed a comforting hand on his brother's shoulder. "Max is right. December is right around the corner." Trey came closer and, for the first time, Derek felt the growing strength of their bond as brothers.

"Is there anything you need us to do?" Trey asked.

"No, Trey. Having the three of you here is all I need."

They talked, with intermittent periods of silence. More than once, Reginald brought up the missed dinner. An idea formed in Derek's head. "I'll be right back."

He walked down the hall to a family waiting room, pulled out his cell and called in a favor. He started to pocket the phone, and then changed his mind. He scrolled to Alexis's number and pushed the button. After several rings it went to voice mail. Disappointed, he stuck the phone in his pocket and retraced his steps to the room. Reginald had fallen asleep, and Trey and Max stood in a corner, talking quietly.

A while later, a nurse poked her head in the room. "Is one of you named Derek Moore?"

"Me." Derek followed her out and saw his old buddy. He shook his hand. "Hey, Duke. I appreciate this."

Duke grinned. "Yeah, I bet. I should've figured you'd try to collect on the most inconvenient night of the year." He gestured to two young men carrying heated bags. Duke Mitchell owned a family-style restaurant and Derek had helped him secure the new property when the landlord of the previous building he'd occupied had forced him out by tripling the rent.

"You act like I'm not paying for the food."

"You bet your ass you're paying for it."

He laughed softly. "I assume you brought your square."

Duke smiled and pulled the small device from his pocket. Derek handed over his credit card and added a tip equal to the purchase amount. After signing his name, he turned to the nurse standing there. "Thanksgiving dinner is served."

With Duke's help, they unloaded everything onto the table in his father's room. The nurse brought in an extra rolling tray table.

"What is all this?" Reginald asked, coming awake and struggling into a semi-sitting position.

"Thanksgiving dinner. It's not exactly where you wanted to have it, but we're all here," Derek answered.

Moisture filled Reginald's eyes. "You don't know how much this means to me. Thank you."

"There's enough for the staff, as well."

Max gave Derek a grateful smile. "I'll let them know."

Trey unearthed plates and utensils and dished a small amount of food on a plate for Reginald, per his request.

The nurses drifted in to get food and took it out to the station. Derek was halfway through his meal when his phone buzzed. He smiled when he saw Alexis's name on the display.

"Hey, baby."

"Derek, something is wrong," Alexis cried.

His heart nearly stopped. He placed his plate on the tray table. "What is it?"

"The pa-pain. It's like last time."

Last time? Then it dawned on him—the miscarriage. "I'll be there in ten minutes, okay?"

"Mmm. There's a spare key in the blue box to the left of the door. Code is 4-4-7-2."

"I'm on my way, sweetheart. It's going to be all right." He met his brothers' concerned gazes. "It's Alexis. I have to go. She's in pain."

"Go. We'll take care of all this," Trey said. "Call me."

He nodded and turned to Reginald.

"Go take care of Alexis, son."

Derek ran from the room, all the while praying. He couldn't lose his baby. And he couldn't lose Alexis.

Alexis lay curled up on her bed, willing the pain in her belly to subside. She'd started cramping soon after she got home from her parents' place. She'd thought if she laid down for a while it would go away, but the pain had only gotten stronger and she'd started spotting. Tears ran unchecked down her face. She didn't want to lose this baby, couldn't lose her baby again.

"Alexis!" Derek's voice ricocheted through the house.

She tried to tell him where she was, but managed only a strangled moan. A moment later, he appeared at her bedroom door.

"Alexis." He hunkered down next to her and kissed her forehead. "Is it still hurting?"

"Yes."

Derek whipped out his phone and dialed 9-1-1. He paced the room while waiting and bolted to the door when the ambulance arrived.

While the paramedics tended to her, Alexis's gaze strayed to Derek more than once. He remained in the room, but kept his distance.

The female EMT turned to Derek. "We're going to take her to the hospital."

He immediately stepped forward. "I'm coming, too."

They got her strapped onto a gurney and loaded into the ambulance. Derek climbed in and sat beside her. He held her hand, but she felt something different, saw it in his eyes. As the vehicle started moving, another wave of pain hit and she sucked in a sharp breath. *This is more than I can handle.*

It took less than ten minutes to reach their destination. They wheeled her down the hallway while providing her information to the doctor and nurse striding alongside the gurney. They transferred her to a bed, and after that everything became a blur. They hooked her to machines, wrapped a blood pressure cuff on her arm and stuck a thermometer into her mouth.

Someone rolled an ultrasound machine into the room, and fear gripped Alexis. She glanced over at Derek and saw the apprehension on his face. Unlike the first time she'd had the procedure done, when he'd held her hand, this time he remained in his spot across the room, his eyes fixed on the screen.

At first they heard nothing, and her anxiety mounted. Tears of relief filled her eyes when she heard the sound of the baby's heartbeat. The look on Derek's face mirrored how she felt.

The doctor assured Alexis that the baby was fine, but he wanted to keep her overnight for monitoring. He gave some instructions to the nurse and departed with a smile.

A while later, the hospital staff wheeled her to the room where she would spend the night. Derek came and stood next to the bed. "I'm going to go."

Alexis didn't want him to leave, but she wasn't going to beg him to stay.

"You need to rest. I'll be back in the morning." He didn't move, seemingly trying to decide what course of action to take. Finally, he bent, placed a kiss on her forehead and then walked out.

The ache spreading through her chest hurt as much as the pain in her belly. She was in this alone. Again.

Chapter 19

Derek's heart rate hadn't slowed in twenty-four hours. All night he'd been plagued with images of Alexis writhing in pain, and the moments of panic he'd felt during that small space of time before he heard the baby's heartbeat. This morning had been more of the same. He couldn't take it if something happened to either of them. He wouldn't survive losing Alexis. In order to keep his sanity for the next several months, he had to keep his emotions on lockdown. But he couldn't figure out how to do that without hurting Alexis, and he didn't know how to explain it.

He stepped off the hospital elevator and took slow steps to her room. The closer he got, the harder his heart pounded in his chest. Surely someone would have called if there had been any problems.

Derek poked his head in the door and saw Alexis sitting up in bed. The smile he'd come to look for was absent. "Hey. How are you feeling?"

"Okay."

"And the baby?"

"Fine."

"Did the doctor say how long you'll have to be in the hospital?"

"He said I could go home today."

"Why didn't you call me? I would've come earlier."

Alexis shrugged. "You said you'd be back in the morning." She pushed the button to summon the nurse.

A minute later a petite Asian woman entered. "Ah, I see your ride is here. Since you already have your discharge information, I'll have the wheelchair brought up. Don't forget to follow up with your doctor on Monday."

"I won't."

The nurse turned to Derek. "I'm going to ask you to bring your car around to the entrance. She'll be down as soon as the chair gets here."

"Okay." When the woman left, he asked Alexis, "Do you need me to help you with anything?"

"No." She wouldn't meet his eyes. When she made a move to get up, he crossed the room. "I'm fine. You should go get the car."

Their eyes met. He wanted to hold her, so badly it hurt, but he couldn't do that without surrendering his fears. "See you in a minute."

Derek parked in front of the hospital entrance and leaned against the car to wait. Why couldn't he tell her how afraid he'd been yesterday, or that he loved her? Every time he tried, the words stuck in his throat. He held the passenger door open when the attendant approached with Alexis. Derek thanked the man, closed the door after she got in and went around to the driver's side.

"Do you want to stop anywhere or get some food?" he asked as they headed off.

"No. Thanks."

They made the rest of the drive in complete silence. She still didn't say a word when he walked her inside her house.

Alexis stopped a few feet beyond the door. "Thanks for bringing me home. I'm sure you have some other things to do."

"What's going on here, Alexis?"

"I'm just tired, Derek. Tired of wondering when this is going to become more than duty or doing the right thing for the baby. You hightailed it out of the hospital last night like it was on fire."

"I left because you needed to rest."

She folded her arms and studied him. "Is that really why you left?" She held up a hand. "You don't have to answer that. You left me, Derek."

"What are you talking about? I went with you to the hospital and stayed to make sure you and the baby were okay, and I came back today."

"In all the ways that matter, you weren't there."

He stared at her, confused.

Alexis sighed. "You don't think I felt you retreat five minutes after you got here last night? Yes, you were there, but your heart wasn't. For the past few weeks, you made me feel as if we could possibly have something, and then it was gone in the blink of an eye. I love you, Derek, but I can't do this."

"What?" *She loves me.*

"You heard me. I think we should concentrate on learning to co-parent and leave the rest alone. It'll be better for both of us. Despite everything we've shared,

you still can't move past what your father did and let anyone get close."

"Alexis, that's not…" A churning began in his gut at the thought of losing her for good.

"I can't do this right now." She rubbed her temples and turned to walk away.

"Just listen to me for a minute." Derek had to make her understand that this had nothing to do with his father and everything to do with them. But he didn't want to upset her further and risk a repeat of last night.

"I need to go lie down. Can you lock the door behind you?" Alexis walked off and left him standing there.

He felt like he'd been punched in the gut. He'd lost her.

Alexis picked up her cell, checked the display and let the call go to voice mail, just as she'd done for the past two days.

"You're going to have to talk to him eventually." When Alexis called Charlene to tell her what had happened, her friend had volunteered to come and hang out with Alexis.

"I know. We'll have to make some decisions concerning the baby."

Charlene shook her head. "You know good and well that's not what I'm talking about. You're in love with Derek and that's not going to go away."

"A one-sided relationship will never work and I'm sure these feelings will fade with time." She didn't even blink with that lie. The love she felt for Derek had begun at age sixteen, and though it had been suppressed for years, it had never completely diminished. That love had returned stronger than ever and she was only fool-

ing herself if she believed it would just go away. This baby would tie them together for the rest of their lives, and seeing him so often wouldn't give her the time and space she'd need to get over him.

"Who said it was one-sided? For what it's worth, I think he feels the same."

"I know you aren't taking his side. And he's never said he loved me. No, this is all about the baby for him. I'm starting to wonder if everything he did was to get me to accept that crazy marriage proposal." Alexis wanted to believe he loved her, but he'd never indicated his feelings ran that deep. Even when she told him she loved him, he still didn't say it. That was the final straw for her.

"I'm not taking his side, but you should have at least let him explain."

"He had plenty of time to explain. What hurt the most, though, was the distance. Not once did he hold me and tell me everything would be okay. I needed him and he wasn't there." Tears stung her eyes.

"Hey, don't go getting all upset. Maybe we need to get out of the house for a while." Charlene got her phone. "There should be something good playing at the movies. There always is during the holiday season."

They chose a family comedy drama. Charlene stood. "And since it's early, we can get that Sunday afternoon matinee price."

"It starts in an hour, so we'd better go. I need time to get my popcorn." Alexis laughed, they grabbed their purses and left.

Sitting in the theater later, Alexis realized she'd made a mistake. There were at least three couples in

the movie going through difficulties, but that didn't affect her as much as the one couple whose love she could feel through the screen. The lovemaking scene took her back to that first night in the Bahamas out on the veranda. Her eyes drifted closed as the images came back with vivid clarity, from the tender caresses and heat-filled kisses to the slow slide of his shaft moving in and out of her. *My sweet Lexi.* She could still hear him in her ear and it evoked the same emotional response. Alexis discreetly swiped at her tears, knowing she would never hear those words again.

As they filed out of the theater, Charlene said, "I don't think that was the best choice."

"It was a good movie."

"Yes, but not good for you."

"I'm okay, just feeling a little emotional. Probably hormones." To deflect the coming interrogation, she said, "Since we're out, we should grab an early dinner. My treat, your choice."

"Ooh, I know just where I want to go."

Alexis's heart sank when Charlene parked in the lot of the Mexican restaurant she and Derek had ordered from. Once again, memories of their time together assailed her—the laughter and teasing, Derek opening up about his father, and the dance. He'd said he could hold her all night, and that's exactly what he'd done. She had awakened during the night to the gentle stroke of his hand caressing her back or her hip, but his arm had stayed firmly wrapped around her, making her feel safe and...loved. Alexis pushed down the emotions. She and Derek were done and she needed to move on as best she could.

* * *

The insistent ringing of his doorbell jarred Derek out of his thoughts. Shoving his chair back with a growl, he stalked toward the front door and snatched it open. "What the hell—"

"Happy Sunday to you, too, big brother," Max drawled.

"What are you two doing here?"

Trey brushed past Derek. "We haven't heard from you since that sorry-assed text you sent after dropping Alexis off on Friday, and we wanted to know what happened between you two."

Max closed the door behind him and gestured Derek forward. "Might as well make yourself comfortable because we're not leaving until you tell us." He smiled. "Aren't you glad you have brothers?"

Derek muttered a curse about exactly where he could take that comment. Trey and Max went out to the screened porch and made themselves comfortable.

Trey drilled him with a stare. "So what's going on, Derek? You look terrible."

"Now those are the comforting words I wanted to hear from my big brother," he said sarcastically. He knew how he looked. He hadn't shaved since Friday, needed a haircut, couldn't eat and hadn't slept well since walking out Alexis's door.

"How're Alexis and the baby?"

He wanted to tell Max they were doing well, but he had no idea. "I don't know."

Max glared. "What the hell do you mean, you don't know?"

Derek dropped down on the sofa and leaned his head back. "Just what I said, Max. I took her home on Fri-

day, she told me we should focus on co-parenting and leave the rest alone. She said I'd left her." He could still see the tears standing in her eyes and it caused a searing pain in his heart.

Trey frowned. "I thought you went with her to the hospital."

"I did. She's saying I checked out emotionally. And I did," he confessed. "When I saw her lying on that bed…" He closed his eyes. "I've never been so scared in my life. I don't know what I'd do if I lost her or the baby." For him, it would be easier to lock away his heart so he couldn't experience the pain.

"Basically, you shut her down so you won't get hurt."

Derek jumped up and paced the floor. "You don't understand, Max."

"But I do," Trey said. "You're so afraid, you would rather be alone than risk putting your heart out there. Alexis loves you."

"I know. She told me."

"And you didn't tell her back."

"No." Derek had never said those words to anyone. He'd wanted to, tried to, but didn't know how.

"You need to talk to her, Derek. Let her know you'll be there for her physically *and* emotionally. I did the same with Kiara."

He slowly dropped onto the sofa and let Trey's words sink in.

"Speaking of Kiara, I need to get going. By the way, Reginald is home. We were there before coming here and he asked about you."

"I'll stop by later."

Max clapped Derek on the shoulder. "Don't wait too

long to have that conversation with Alexis. If you need to talk, call."

"Thanks." He saw them out and sighed deeply. They were right. He and Alexis needed to talk, but he still had no idea how to approach the subject, so he opted to get the visit with Reginald out of the way first. He shaved and changed clothes, then headed out.

Mrs. McBride opened the door when he arrived. "Hi, Derek. Come on in."

"How are you, Mrs. McBride?"

"Doing well. Reginald is in his office."

"Thank you." Derek walked to where he knew the room to be and knocked lightly on the open door.

Reginald's head came up and a smile creased his face. He made a move to stand.

"Don't get up." He took one of the chairs across from the desk. "How are you feeling?"

"Not as well as I'd like, but better. How're Alexis and the baby?"

That question again. "Okay."

Reginald studied him for a lengthy minute. "But you're not."

Derek didn't know why, but he found himself telling Reginald what had happened.

His father came around the desk and sat next to him. "Son, I know it's far too late and I'm the last person who should be doling out advice, but if you love Alexis, tell her. It took me a long time to figure out what was important, and by the time I did, I'd messed over two beautiful women who didn't deserve it and alienated my two oldest sons. There's no way to make up for

the past, but don't let that stop you from claiming the woman you love."

Derek eyed his father.

Reginald chuckled. "Oh, I know you love her. That night at the fund-raiser, your eyes gave you away. Tell her you love her. You'll be a great father and an even better husband."

Derek bowed his head. He had to get this straightened out. He was *not* going to lose Alexis.

Chapter 20

Monday morning, Alexis dragged her weary body downstairs to find something to eat. The person delivering her furniture would be arriving shortly. She'd slept like crap and really needed a jolt of caffeine to get her going, but since becoming pregnant, She'd stopped drinking coffee. Not wanting anything heavy, she had toast, a small bowl of melon and a glass of milk. She had decided to turn a portion of her family room into an office space with a desk, chair and organizing shelves. She'd even ordered a partition that she could use to section it off. She hoped the delivery people would move the furniture for her. If they couldn't, at least she wouldn't have to worry about putting anything together. She had made sure to order everything fully assembled. The time it took for her to organize the space would go a long way in keeping her mind occupied.

Once she finished eating, Alexis stood in the area she wanted to transform and tried to imagine how it would look with all the pieces in place. She thought about having the desk face the window, but concluded it might

be counterproductive. She wouldn't get any work done staring out at the water all day.

The doorbell rang and she smiled. Her smile faded when she opened the door and saw Derek standing there. He looked so good she had to keep herself from jumping into his arms. She also noted the tired lines etched in his face. "Hey."

"Hey. May I come in?"

Alexis stepped to the side. When he passed, his body brushed hers and the simple contact sent a shiver through her.

"How are you feeling?"

She folded her arms across her midsection. "Fine."

"No more pain?"

She shook her head.

"Can we sit and talk, baby?"

The soft request, coupled with the endearment, made her cave like a deck of cards. "Sure." He followed her to the family room and she sat on the love seat.

Derek bowed his head briefly and took her hands. "I don't know where to begin. I've been miserable these past five days without you, Alexis." The doorbell rang and he sighed with frustration.

"Sorry. I'm having some furniture delivered. I'll be right back." Alexis went to let the delivery people in and directed them to where she wanted everything placed. When she asked them about helping to move the other furniture, they hesitated.

"Ma'am, we really don't do that, unless it's our product."

Derek stood, his anger at being interrupted plain.

"I'm sure you can make an exception. I'll help, and compensate you for your time."

With Derek's towering height and commanding voice, the men hastily agreed. "Sure, sure. No problem."

Alexis smiled inwardly. It took the three men less than an hour to unload and position the furniture to her satisfaction. Derek took out his wallet to pay the men.

She didn't think it fair for him to pay, since it was her furniture. "Derek, I'll—" His glare stopped her mid-sentence.

Derek paid the men and saw them to the door. He came back. "Are you expecting any more deliveries or guests?"

"No."

"Thank goodness. Can we please talk now?"

"Derek, we agreed to just work on co-parenting."

"No, *we* did not agree to anything. That was your position. I never had a chance to state mine. And my position is hell no, I'm not settling for some friend-type relationship with you."

Her eyes widened.

He took her hands again. "I'm sorry, baby. And you were right. I wasn't there for you in the way I should have been, but not for the reasons you think." He paused, seeming to gather his thoughts. "Alexis, when I saw you lying on the bed in all that pain, the possibility of losing you or the baby was too much for me to handle. I did the thing I do best—retreat."

"You don't have to—"

"I'm not done. It had nothing to do with getting over what my father did to me, though I'm still working on

it. I put a lockdown on my emotions because I could not survive if I lost you."

Alexis's heart started pounding in her chest.

"I know you think I'm doing all this out of duty, as you put it. It may have started that way, but the more time I spent with you, the more I wanted for us. I love you, Alexis. You make me happy with your laughter, your smile and all the loving things you do. When I think about the woman you are—the sweetness of your kiss and warmth of your body lying next to mine—it leaves me breathless. You are the only woman who can make me feel this way."

Tears sprang up in her eyes. "Derek."

"Sweetheart, you don't ever have to wonder how strong and deep my love is for you. I may not always say the words, but listen to what I do. Always remember that's what's in my heart." Derek placed her hand over his heart. "Do you feel that?"

The strong, steady rhythm of his heart beat against her hand. "Yes."

"You, Alexis. You're in my heart…forever."

His last words shattered the wall she'd put up. "I love you."

"How about we take another quick trip this week?"

"To the island?" Alexis asked excitedly.

"Yep."

"Just say when and my bags are packed."

Derek laughed. "I love you, Alexis Armstrong."

"Ditto, Derek Moore. Always have."

He captured her mouth in a slow, sensual kiss filled with healing, restoration and the promise of an ever-lasting love.

* * *

Tuesday, Derek dived into the pile of work that had accumulated with an energy he hadn't felt in years. Trey had been right and so had Reginald, he reluctantly admitted. Opening himself fully to Alexis had released a lifetime of hurts, and now he was free to love her the way they both deserved. After he finished going through the contracts on prospective buyers, he checked his emails. A smile spread across his lips when he clicked on the one he'd been waiting for. He picked up the phone and scheduled appointments for later in the afternoon.

Derek called Alexis next. "Hey, baby," he said when she answered.

"Hey, baby, yourself. What's up?"

The laughter in her voice was back, and filled his heart in every way. "Are you going to be busy this afternoon?"

"I'm meeting with Terri at three."

"Do you think she'll reschedule for an hour later? There are a couple of houses I want to show you and we can look inside. I'll take you by her office afterward."

"I'll call her and let you know. I had really hoped to have at least one home purchased by the end of the year."

Derek smiled. "We have a few weeks."

"Okay. Call you back in a minute."

While waiting, he did a conference call with Trey and Max. "Max, you said you might have a lead on some information that will clear Reginald?"

"Yeah, but it'll take some time to investigate. Even

if this doesn't pan out, I'm confident we'll find something that will."

"It's just a matter of time before we figure out what really happened," Trey said.

"I appreciate you guys helping me look into this, and I'm glad to finally know my brothers," Max stated.

"So am I, Max." He and Trey had proved to Derek that he could count on them for anything and everything.

"Well, well," Max said.

"What?" Derek and Trey chorused.

"I have this Secret Santa who's been leaving some very, shall we say, suggestive gifts for me. I look forward to going to work every day to see what's next."

Trey chuckled. "I say he'll be following us down the path of love soon. What do you think, Derek?"

"Yep. His time is coming. Anyway, I need to get off the phone. I'm waiting for Alexis to call me. Trey, I owe you one for the jet again."

"Hey, you and Max are welcome to it anytime. Enjoy yourselves."

"We plan to."

They said their goodbyes, and as soon as Derek disconnected, Alexis called.

"We're good. Do you want me to meet you at your office?" Alexis asked, after he greeted her.

"No. I'm showing a property out that way in a few and I'll be by to pick you up around one."

"All right. See you then."

Derek rang off and went to meet with his senior staff. He had to put out a couple fires, particularly with Mrs. Jenson. She still wanted to work only with Derek, but

when he let her know he'd be out of town for the rest of the week and she could wait until Monday to sign the papers for the property, she quickly acquiesced. He left to show a beachfront Malibu property to a couple relocating from Florida who wanted something similar to their current home.

He arrived to pick up Alexis on time and she met him at the door with her purse slung on her shoulder. He kissed her. "Are you anxious or something?"

"More like excited, so come on."

The drive took longer than usual due to extra traffic caused by some roadwork. Derek drove up to the first property they'd looked at and got out. "I thought you might like to have a look inside, since this was your favorite. We'll check out the one two doors down, too."

Alexis gave him a brilliant smile. "This is great."

Inside, he watched as she roamed from room to room, taking pictures with her camera and writing down notes.

"I love this house. I hope we can make the finances work. Let's go see the other one."

Derek locked the door and they walked the short distance to the second house. Just as in the previous one, she snapped pictures.

"What do you think?" he finally asked her.

"They're perfect, but I still haven't found much help in the way of donations." She walked back to the front and stared out the big picture window. "Where's the For Sale sign?" A look of panic crossed her face. "Please don't tell me it's off the market."

He pulled her into his arms. "Actually, both properties have been purchased." He released her, took an en-

velope from the inner pocket of his suit coat and handed it to her. Alexis removed the stack of papers and read silently. He knew the moment she figured it out.

"Oh. My. Goodness," she whispered, reading it again. "Does this mean…?"

"Yes. I bought both houses and plan to give them to Precious Ones."

Alexis launched herself at him. "I love you! Thank you, thank you."

"Whoa, sweetheart. Be careful." He placed a gentle hand on her belly. "You're carrying our own precious one."

"Derek, I can't believe you did this. Why?"

"Baby, weren't you listening to what I said? I love you and I will do everything in my power to make you happy."

"I'm more than happy. I'm ecstatic," she shouted.

And that's all that mattered to him.

Epilogue

As soon as they dropped their bags off at the island house, Alexis grabbed Derek's arm and dragged him down to the beach. He laughed. "Slow down, woman. The beach isn't going anywhere."

"I know, but it'll be dark soon." She took his hand and they started a leisurely stroll. "Can we come here a couple of times a year?"

"We can come anytime you want."

Alexis smiled up at him. "If we come whenever I want, we won't be leaving."

"Would you really want to move here?" They stopped and sat on the sand. Derek positioned her between his legs and draped his arms loosely around her waist.

"Probably not. All of our family is back home and I want our baby to grow up knowing their grandparents. Besides, we'll have built-in babysitting services, between your mom and mine."

He smiled. "You're right." He and Alexis had visited her parents and his mother, and now that the shock had worn off, they were excited about being grandpar-

ents. He planned to take Alexis to visit Reginald when they got back.

"Speaking of parents, how's your father doing?"

"He's doing okay. Some days are good, others are not. I want to take you over when we get back."

She snuggled deeper into his arms. "I'd like that. Have you guys found anything else in your investigation?"

"Not yet, but I know we will." Like Trey had said, it was just a matter of time.

They sat in companionable silence, listening to the sounds of nature and the soft waves crashing against the shore. At length, he patted her on the butt. "Okay. Time to head back. Ms. Eliana has dinner waiting."

"You don't have to tell me twice," Alexis said with a huge grin. "If I could smuggle her out of here in my luggage, I would."

Derek laughed. When they returned, he led her upstairs to the veranda.

Alexis brought her hands to her mouth. "Oh, my. It's absolutely *amazing*."

He had asked Ms. Eliana to help him set up a romantic dinner and she had outdone herself. She'd placed lit candles along the railing and scattered red rose petals on the tile floor and on the table. Another candle in a hurricane vase sat in the middle of the table and she'd used his best china and silverware.

"Shall we?" Derek seated Alexis and went around the table to his own place. Ms. Eliana appeared with all Alexis's favorite dishes, and extra plantains. The food had been excellently prepared, but he had a hard time enjoying it because his focus was on the beauti-

ful woman across from him. When the meal came to a close, he stood and extended his hand.

"Thank you for this."

"There's no need to thank me. Alexis, I never apologized for that proposal. I see now that you were right."

"You do?"

"Yes. You shouldn't have to settle for marriage without love." Derek removed the small box from his pocket and lowered himself to one knee. "But I'm hoping you'll settle for one with a man who loves you more than his own life. You're the only woman who stirs my soul. I want to marry you, love you and our baby." He placed a hand on her belly. "I want to spend the rest of my life helping you make all your dreams come true and creating new ones. You'll never have to wonder about my love. Just listen to what I do. Will you marry me?"

"Yes, yes. A thousand times yes!"

He slid the ring on her finger, kissed her passionately and swept her up into his arms. He strode purposely from the veranda to his bedroom.

"What are you doing?" Alexis asked laughingly.

"Getting ready to make love to my future wife. Oh, and we'll be going to Nassau tomorrow to get married. I'm not going to be a baby daddy."

Her laughter filled the room and his heart. She was his high school sweetheart, the mother of his child and the love of his life. Derek had everything he would ever need.

* * * * *

KIMANI
ROMANCE

COMING NEXT MONTH
Available November 20, 2018

#597 BACHELOR UNBOUND
Bachelors in Demand • **by Brenda Jackson**
International jeweler Zion Blackstone felt an instant connection to
Celine Michaels. When she shows up at his house in Rome claiming
kidnappers are after her, he offers the Hollywood producer's daughter his
protection…and passion. But a revelation could upend his chance with
Celine…

#598 A LOS ANGELES RENDEZVOUS
Millionaire Moguls • **by Pamela Yaye**
Jada Allen's Christmas wish list is simple: her gorgeous boss. A-list talent
agent Max Moore counts on Jada to handle his life. Yet workaholic Max never
notices her until a makeover reveals the woman he's taken for granted. Will one
hot night shatter their working relationship or lead to something sweeter?

#599 ANOTHER CHANCE WITH YOU
The DuGrandpres of Charleston • **by Jacquelin Thomas**
Retired Secret Service agent Landon Trent stuns
Jadin DuGrandpre with the announcement that
they're still married. Winning back Jadin's trust
won't be easy—especially when a trial pits the two
Charleston attorneys on opposite sides. But Landon
isn't giving up. Can they recapture what they once
shared?

#600 HER MISTLETOE BACHELOR
Once Upon a Tiara • **by Carolyn Hector**
After a public breakup, CFO Donovan Ravens
plans to spend the holidays alone in a small-town
hotel. But science teacher British Carres has other
ideas for the space the sexy bachelor booked. As
they give in to their chemistry, a threat from the
past could keep them from finding true love…

Her hands were shaking, but she grabbed her purse off the mahogany table and forced a smile, one that concealed the anger simmering inside her. "Max, you know what? You're right," she said, nodding her head. "I'm a lowly administrative assistant. Who am I to tell you what to do? Or advise you about how to parent your daughter? I'm a nobody."

Max tried to interrupt her, to clarify what he'd said seconds earlier, but Jada cut him off.

"*You* asked for my help, but the moment I disagreed with you you decided my opinion was worthless, and now that I know how you *really* feel about me, I can't work for you."

"You're twisting my words. I never said that."

"You didn't have to. I'm quite skilled at reading between the lines..." Her voice wobbled, but she pushed past her emotions and spoke in a self-assured tone. "I'll submit an official letter of resignation first thing Monday, but consider this my two-week notice."

Fear flashed in his eyes. "Jada, you can't quit. I need you. You're the heart and soul of Millennium Talent agency, and I'd be lost without you."

"Nonsense. You're the legendary Max Moore. One of the most revered talent agents in the city. You don't need me, or anyone else. You've got this, remember?"

Her mind made up, she turned and strode through the foyer.

Max slid in front of her, blocking her path. His cologne washed over her, and for a moment Jada forgot why she was mad at him. He licked his lips, and tingles flooded her body.

"You're quitting because I disagreed with you?" he asked, his eyebrows jammed together in a crooked line. "Because we argued about Taylor's outfit for her school dance?"

No, I'm quitting because I love you, and I'm tired of pretending I don't.

"Thanks for everything, Max. It was an honor to work for you. I've learned so much."

"I won't let you quit. We're a team, Jada, and I need you at the agency."

Scared her emotions would get the best of her, and she'd burst into tears if she spoke, Jada stepped past Max and yanked open the front door. He called out to her, but she didn't stop. Ignored his apologies. Increased her pace. Fleeing the million-dollar estate, with the feng shui fountain, the vibrant flower garden and the winding cobblestone driveway, she willed her heart not to fail, and her legs not to buckle.

Jada deactivated the alarm, slipped inside her car and started it. Anxious to leave, she put on her seat belt, then sped through the wrought-iron gates. In her rearview mirror, she spotted Max and his brothers standing on the driveway and wondered if they were discussing her dramatic exit. Jada dismissed the thought, told herself it didn't matter what the Moore brothers were doing. Max was her past, not her future, and she had to stop thinking about him. Gripping the steering wheel, Jada swallowed hard, blinking away the tears in her eyes.

Don't miss A Los Angeles Rendezvous
by Pamela Yaye, available December 2018
wherever Harlequin® Kimani Romance™
books and ebooks are sold.